DI

JENNIFER ASHLEY   ANNA BRADLEY
GRACE BURROWES   KERRIGAN BYRNE
CHRISTI CALDWELL   TANYA ANNE CROSBY

OLIVER
HEBER
BOOKS

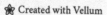

A FIRST-FOOTER FOR LADY JANE

JENNIFER ASHLEY

CHAPTER 1

BERKSHIRE, DECEMBER 31, 1810

*Y*ou know precisely whom I will marry, Grandfather. You tease me to enjoy yourself, but all the games in the world will not change that Major Barnett will someday be my husband."

As she spoke, Lady Jane Randolph regarded her grandfather in half amusement, half exasperation. Grandfather MacDonald sprawled in his chair by the fire in the small drawing room in Jane's father's manor house, his blankets in disarray. Grandfather always occupied the warmest place in a room, in deference to his old bones, but he was not one for sitting still.

His lined face held its usual mirth, his blue eyes twinkling. Grandfather MacDonald liked to hint and joke, pretending a connection to the Scottish witches from Macbeth, who, he said, had given him second sight.

"What I say is true, lass." Grandfather fluttered his hands, broad and blunt, which her grandmother, rest her soul, had claimed could brandish a strong sword and then pick out a tune on the harpsichord with such liveliness one could not help but dance. Indeed, Grandfather often sat of an evening at the pianoforte, coaxing rollicking music from it.

Grandfather had been quite a dancer as well, Grandmother had said, and every young woman had vied for a chance to stand up with the swain. When Hamish MacDonald had first cast his eyes upon her, Grandmother had wanted to swoon, but of course she'd never, ever admitted this to him.

"Mark my words," Grandfather went on. "At Hogmanay, the First-Footer over the threshold will marry the most eligible daughter of the house. Hogmanay begins at midnight, and the most eligible young lady in *this* house is you."

"Perhaps." Jane returned to her embroidery, a task she was not fond of. "But you know I already have an agreement with John. No First-Footer need bother with me. There will be other young ladies—Mama and Papa have invited all their acquaintance."

"But you are not yet engaged." Grandfather's eyes sparkled with a wicked light seventy years hadn't dimmed. "No announcement in the newspapers, no date for the happy event, no ring on your finger."

"There is the small matter of war with France." Jane had marred the pattern in her embroidery, she noticed, an inch back. Sighing in annoyance, she picked out the thread. "Major Barnett is a bit busy on the Peninsula just now. When Bonaparte is defeated, there will be plenty of time for happy events."

Silence met her. Jane looked up from repairing her mistake to find her grandfather glaring at her, his joviality gone.

"Am I hearing ye right?" he demanded. "Ye're discussing your nuptials like ye would decide which field to plant out in the spring. In my day, lassie, we seized the hand of the one who struck our fancy and made sure we hung on to them for life. Didn't matter how

4

many wars we were fighting at the time, and when I was a lad, Highland Scots were being hunted down if we so much as picked up a plaid or spoke our native tongue. Didn't stop Maggie and me running off together, did it?"

Grandfather adored going on about his wild days in the heather, how he and Grandmother never let anything stand in the way of their great passion.

Times had changed, Jane reflected with regret. The war with Napoleon dragged on, the constant worry that France would invade these shores hovering like a distant and evil thunderstorm. She and John must wait until things were resolved—when John came home for good, there would be time enough to make plans for their life together.

The thought that John might never return, that a French artillery shell might end his life, or a bayonet pierce his heart, sent a sudden chill through her.

Jane shuddered and drew a veil over the images. There was no sense in worrying.

She missed another stitch and set the embroidery firmly aside. Grandfather could be most distracting.

"John is in Portugal," she reminded him. "Not likely to be our First-Footer tonight. But someday, perhaps."

"Course he's not likely to be the First-Footer." Grandfather scowled at Jane as though she'd gone simple. "He's a fair-haired man, ain't he? First-Footer needs to be dark. Everyone knows that."

* * *

"YOUR BETROTHED LIVES *HERE*?" Captain Spencer Ingram shook snow from his hat as he climbed from the chaise and gazed at the gabled, rambling, half-timbered monstrosity before him, a holdover from the dark days of knights and bloodthirsty kings.

"Not betrothed," Barnett said quickly. "A childhood understanding. Will lead to an engagement in due time. Probably. Always been that way."

Barnett did not sound as enthusiastic as a man coming home to visit his childhood sweetheart might. Spencer studied his friend, but Barnett's ingenuous face was unconcerned.

Though it was near midnight, every window in the house was lit, and a bonfire leapt high in the night in the fields beyond. Spencer would have preferred wandering to the bonfire, sharing a dram or tankard with villagers no doubt having a dance and a fine time.

The house looked cozy enough, despite its ancient architecture. Lights glowed behind the thick glass windows, welcoming on the frigid evening. The snow was dry and dusty, the night so frozen that no cloud marred the sky. Every star was visible, the carpet of them stretching to infinity. Even better than the bonfire would be a place on the roof and a spyglass through which to gaze at the heavens.

A pair of footmen darted out to seize bags from the compartment in the back of the chaise. Both valises were small, in keeping with soldiers who'd learned to travel with little.

The chaise rattled off toward the stable yard, the driver ready for warmth and a drink. The footmen scurried into the house and disappeared, the front door swinging shut behind them.

Spencer leapt forward to grab the door, but it clanged closed before he reached it.

"What the devil?" Spencer rattled the handle, but the door was now locked. "I call this a poor welcome."

To his surprise, Barnett chuckled. "Lady Jane's family keeps Scots traditions. A visitor arriving after midnight on New Year's—no, we must call it Hogmanay to follow their quaint customs. A visitor arriving after midnight on Hogmanay needs to beg admission, and must bring gifts. I have them here." He held up a canvas sack. "Salt, coal, whisky, shortbread, and black bun."

"Black what?"

"Black bun. A cake of fruit soaked in whisky. It is not bad fare. I obtained the cake from a Scotswoman— the landlord's wife at our accommodations when we first landed."

Spencer had wondered why Barnett insisted on traveling to that inn, well out of the way, the venture taking precious time.

Barnett grinned. "The whole rigmarole is to prove we aren't Norsemen come to pillage the family. 'Tis greatly entertaining, is it not?"

Spencer had other ideas of entertainment. "We stand shivering outside while they decide whether to admit us? There is a good bonfire yonder." He gestured to the fire leaping high in the fields, shadows of revelers around it.

"They'll be waiting just inside. You will see."

Barnett stepped up to the door the footmen had all but slammed in their faces and hammered on it.

"Open, good neighbors. Give us succor." Barnett shot Spencer a merry look. "We must enter into the spirit of the thing."

Spencer heard the bolts rattling, and then the door opened a sliver. "Who is there?" a creaky, elderly man's voice intoned.

"Admit us, good sir." Barnett held the sack aloft. "We bear gifts."

The door opened wider to show a wizened, bent man wrapped in what looked like a long shawl. Spencer sensed several people hovering behind him.

"Then come in, come in. Out of the cold." The man

added something in the Scots language Spencer didn't understand and swung the door open.

Barnett started forward, then stopped himself. "No, indeed. You must lead, Spence. A tall, dark-haired man brings the best luck."

He stepped out of the way and more or less shoved Spencer toward the door. Spencer removed his hat and stepped deferentially into the foyer.

Warmth surrounded him, and light. In the silence, he heard a sharp intake of breath.

Beyond the old Scotsman in his plaid shawl, in the doorway to a room beyond, stood a young woman. She was rather tall, but curved, not willowy. Her hair was so dark it was almost black, her eyes, in contrast, a startling blue, like lapis lazuli. They matched the eyes of the old man, but Spencer could no longer see him.

The vision of beauty, in a silk and net gown of shimmering silver, regarded him in alarm but also in wonder.

"Well met, all 'round," Barnett was saying. "Spence, let me introduce you to Lord and Lady Merrickson—the house you are standing in is theirs. Mr. MacDonald, Lady Merrickson's father, and of course, this angel of perfection is Lady Jane Randolph, Lord Merrickson's only daughter and the correspondent that keeps me at ease during the chaos of army life. Lady Jane, may I present Captain Spencer Ingram, the dearest friend a chap could imagine. He saved my life once, you know."

Lady Jane came forward, gliding like a ghost on the wind. Spencer took her hand. Her eyes never left his as he bowed to her, and her lips remained parted with her initial gasp.

Spencer looked at her, and was lost.

CHAPTER 2

Captain Ingram fixed Jane with eyes as gray as winter and as cool, and she couldn't catch her breath. A spark lay deep within those eyes, gleaming like a sunbeam on a flow of ice.

He was not a cold man, though, she knew at once. He was containing his warmth, his animation, being polite. Of course he was—he'd been dragged here by John, likely expecting an ordinary English family at Christmas, only to be thrust into the midst of eccentric Randolphs and MacDonalds.

Jane forced her limbs into a curtsey. "Good evening, Captain Ingram," she said woodenly.

Captain Ingram jerked his gaze to her hand, which he still held, Jane's fingers swallowed by his large gloved ones. Ingram abruptly released her, a bit rudely, she thought, but Jane was too agitated to be annoyed.

"Greet him properly, Jane," Grandfather said. He pushed his way forward, leaning on his stout ash stick, and gave Captain Ingram a nod. "You know how."

Jane swallowed, her jaw tight, and repeated the words Grandfather had taught her years ago. "Welcome, First-Footer. Please partake of our hospitality."

Why was she so unnerved? Grandfather couldn't

possibly have predicted that John would step back and let his friend enter the house first, in spite of their conversation earlier today. Grandfather didn't truly have second sight—he only pretended.

Captain Ingram's presence meant nothing, absolutely nothing. After the war, John would propose to Jane, as expected, and life would carry on.

Then why had her heart leapt when she'd beheld Captain Ingram's tall form, why had a sense of gladness and even relief flowed over her? For one instant, she'd believed Grandfather's prediction, and she'd been ... *happy?*

A mad streak ran in Jane's mother's family—or so people said. It was why Grandfather MacDonald spouted the odd things he did, why her mother, a genteel but poor Scotswoman, had been able to ensnare the wealthy Earl of Merrickson, a sought-after bachelor in his younger days. Jane's mother had enchanted him, people said, with her dark hair and intense blue eyes of the inhabitants of the Western Isles. So far, her daughter and son had not yet exhibited the madness of the MacDonald side of the family, thankfully.

Only because Jane, for her part, had learned to hide it, she realized. Given the chance, she'd happily race through the heather in a plaid or dance around a bonfire like the ones the villagers had built tonight. And feel strange glee at the thought she might not marry John after all.

John, oblivious to all tension, hefted a cloth sack. "I've brought the things you told me to, Mr. MacDonald."

"Excellent," Grandfather said. "Jane, take the bag and lay out the treasures in the dining room."

Jane's cousins surged to her. They were the carefree Randolph boys, from her father's side of the family. The three lads, ranging from sixteen to twenty-two, fancied themselves men about town and Corinthians, well pleased that Jane's brother, who was spending New Year's with his wife's family, stood between themselves and the responsibility of the earldom. In truth, they were harmless, though mischievous.

"Come, come, come, Cousin Jane," the youngest, Thomas, sang as they led the way to the dining room.

Jane took the bag from John, trying to pay no attention to Captain Ingram, who had not stepped away from her. "How are you, John? How very astonishing to see you."

John winked at her. He had blue eyes and light blond hair, the very picture of an English gentleman. "Amazing to me when we got leave, wasn't it, Spence? Thought I'd surprise you, Janie. Worked, didn't it? You look pole-axed."

Jane clutched the bag to her chest, finding it difficult to form words. "I beg your pardon. I am shocked, is all. Did not expect you."

John sent Captain Ingram a grin. "*I beg your pardon*, she says, all prim and proper. She didn't used to be so. You ought to have seen her running bare-legged through the meadows, screaming like a savage with me, her brother, and her cousins."

Jane went hot. "When I was seven."

"And eight, and nine, and ten … until you were seventeen, I imagine. How old are you now, Janie? I've forgotten."

"Twenty," Jane said with dignity.

"Mind your tongue, Barnett," Captain Ingram broke in with a scowl. "Lady Jane might forgive your ill-mannered question, as our journey was long and arduous, but I would not blame her if she did not. Allow me to carry that for you, my lady."

He reached for the bag, which Jane relinquished, it

being rather heavy, and strode with it into the dining room where the rest of the family had streamed.

"He's gallant that way," John said without rancor. "I knew you'd approve of him. You've grown very pretty, Jane."

"Thank you," Jane said, awkward. "You've grown very frank."

"That's the army for you. You enter a stiff and callow youth and emerge a hot-blooded and crude man. I crave pardon for my jokes. Have I upset you?"

"No, indeed," she said quickly.

In truth, Jane wasn't certain. John was changed—he had been, as he said, stiff and overly polite when he'd come out of university and taken a commission in the army. This grinning buffoon was more like the boy she'd known in her youth.

John offered her his arm. "Shall we?"

Jane acquiesced, and John propelled her into the dining room. The cousins had already emptied the sack and now sifted through its contents with much hilarity.

"A lump of coal—that's for you, Thomas." His oldest brother threw it at him, and Thomas caught it good-naturedly.

"Excellent fielding," John said. "Do you all still play cricket?"

"We do," Thomas said, and the cousins went off on a long aside about cricket games past and present.

Lord Merrickson roared at them to cease, though without rancor. Lady Merrickson greeted John and Captain Ingram with a warm smile. John took on the cross-eyed, smitten look he always wore in front of Jane's mother. Jane did not believe him in love with her mother, exactly, but awed by her. Many gentlemen were.

Captain Ingram, on the other hand, was deferential

and polite to Lady Merrickson, as was her due, but nothing more.

As Ingram moved back to Jane, she noted that his greatcoat was gone—taken by one of the footmen. His uniform beneath, the deep blue of a cavalryman, held the warmth of his body.

He leaned to her. "Do they ever let you insert a word?" he asked quietly.

Jane tried not to shiver at his voice's low rumble. "On occasion," she said. "I play a fine game of cricket myself. Or used to. As John said, I am much too prim and proper now."

"No, she ain't," the middle Randolph cousin, Marcus, proclaimed. "Just this summer she hiked up her petticoats and took up the bat."

"A pity I missed it," John said loudly. "We ought to scare up a team of ladies at camp, Ingram. Officers wives versus …"

Marcus and Thomas burst out laughing, and the oldest cousin, Digby, looked aghast. "I say, old chap. Not in front of Jane."

"Your pardon, Jane." John looked anything but sorry. He was unusually merry tonight. Perhaps he'd imbibed a quantity of brandy to stave off the cold of the journey.

"I am not offended," Jane answered. "But my mother might be."

Lady Merrickson was not at all, Jane knew, but the admonition made John flush. "Er …" he spluttered.

"Whisky!" Digby snatched up the bottle and held it high. "Thank you, John. All is forgiven. Marcus, fetch the glasses. Mr. MacDonald, the black bun is for you, I think."

Grandfather snatched up the cake wrapped in muslin and held it to his nose. "A fine one. Like me old mum used to bake."

13

Grandfather's "old mum" had a cook to do her baking, so Jane had been told. His family had lived well in the Highlands before the '45.

Outside, the piper Grandfather had hired began to drone, the noise of the pipes wrapping around the house.

"What the devil is *that?*" John demanded.

"I believe they are bagpipes," Captain Ingram said. His mild tone made Jane want to laugh. "You have heard them in the Highland regiments."

"Not like that. Phew, what a racket."

Grandfather scowled at him. "Ye wouldn't know good piping from a frog croaking, lad. There are fiddlers and drummers waiting in the ballroom. Off we go."

The cousins, with whisky and glasses, pounded out of the dining room and along the hall to the ballroom in the back of the house. John escorted Jane, hurrying her to the entertainment, while Captain Ingram politely walked with Grandfather. The terrace windows in the ballroom framed the bonfires burning merrily a mile or so away.

Three musicians waited, two with fiddles, one with a drum. They struck up a Scottish tune as the family entered, blending with the piper outside.

Guest who'd been staying at the house and those arriving now that the First-Footer ritual was done swarmed around them. They were neighbors and old friends of the family, and soon laughter and chatter filled the room.

Grandfather spoke a few moments with Captain Ingram, then he threw off his shawl and cane and jigged to the drums and fiddles, cheered on by Jane's cousins and John. Ingram, politely accepting a whisky Digby had thrust at him, watched with interest.

"I am not certain this was the welcome you expected," Jane said when she drifted near him again.

"It will do." Ingram looked down at her, his gray eyes holding fire. "Is every New Year like this for you?"

"I am afraid so," Jane answered. "Grandfather insists."

"He enjoys it, I'd say."

Grandfather kicked up his heels, a move that made him totter, but young Thomas caught him, and the two locked arms and whirled away.

"He does indeed." Some considered Jane's grandfather a foolish old man, but he had more life in him than many insipid young aristocrats she met during the London Season.

The music changed to that of a country dance, and couples formed into lines, ladies facing gentlemen. John immediately went to a young lady who was the daughter of Jane's family's oldest friends and led her out.

"Lady Jane?" Ingram offered his arm. "I am an indifferent dancer, but I will make the attempt."

Jane did not like the way her heart fluttered at the sight of Captain Ingram's hard arm, outlined by the tight sleeve of his coat. Jane was as good as betrothed—she should not have to worry about her heart fluttering again.

Out of nowhere, Jane felt cheated. Grandfather's stories of his courtship with her grandmother, filled with passion and romance, flitted through her mind. The two had been very much in love, had run away together to the dismay of both families, and then defied them all and lived happily ever after. For one intense moment, Jane wanted that.

Such a foolish idea. Better to marry the son of a neighbor everyone approved of. Prudence and wisdom lined the path to true happiness.

Jane gazed at Captain Ingram, inwardly shaking more than she had the first time she'd fallen from a horse. Flying through the air, not knowing where she'd land, had both terrified and exhilarated her.

"I do not wish to dance," she said. Captain Ingram's expression turned to disappointment, but Jane put her hand on his sleeve. "Shall we walk out to the bonfires instead?"

The longing in his eyes was unmistakable. The captain had no wish to be shut up in a hot ballroom with people he didn't know. Jane had no wish to be here either.

Freedom beckoned.

Captain Ingram studied Jane a moment, then he nodded in resolve. "I would enjoy that, yes."

Jane led him from the ballroom, her heart pounding, wondering, as she had that day she'd been flung from her mare's back, if her landing would be rough or splendid.

As much as he wished to, Spencer could not simply rush into the night alone with Lady Jane. Such a thing was not done. Lady Jane bade two footmen, who fetched Jane's and Spencer's wraps, to bundle up and accompany them with lanterns. The lads, eager to be out, set forth, guiding the way into the darkness.

Five people actually tramped to the bonfires, because the youngest of the cousins, Thomas, joined them at the last minute.

"You're saving me," Thomas told Spencer as he fell into step with them. "Aunt Isobel wants me standing up with debutantes, as though I'd propose to one tomorrow. I ain't marrying for a long while, never fear. I want to join the army, like you."

"Army life is harsh, Mr. Randolph," Spencer said. "Unmerciful hours, drilling in all weather, not to mention French soldiers shooting at you."

"Not afraid of the Frenchies," Thomas proclaimed. "Tell him, Janie. I want to be off. I'll volunteer if Uncle won't buy me a commission."

"He does speak of it day and night," Lady Jane said. She walked along briskly but not hurriedly, as though

17

the cold did not trouble her at all. "Do not paint too romantic a picture of army life, please, Captain, or you might find him in your baggage when you go."

"Perhaps Major Barnett should speak to him as a friend of the family," Spencer said, trying to make his tone diffident.

Jane laughed, a sound like music. "It is Major Barnett's fault Thomas wants to be a soldier in the first place. John writes letters full of his bravado. Also of the fine meals he has with his commanding officers, and the balls he attends, which are full of elegant ladies."

Spencer hid his irritation. Lady Jane held a beauty that had struck him to the bone from the moment he'd beheld her—her dark hair and azure eyes more suited to a faery creature floating in the mists of a loch than a young miss dwelling on a country farm in the middle of England.

If Spencer had been fortunate enough to have such a lady waiting for him, he'd write letters describing how he pined for her, not ones about meals with his colonel and wife. As far as Spencer knew, Barnett did not have a mistress, but he did enjoy dancing and chattering with the officers' wives and daughters. Man was an ingrate.

Barnett had mentioned the daughter of his father's closest neighbor on occasion, but not often. Never rejoiced in receiving her letters, never treasured them or read bits out. Nor hinted, with a blush, that he couldn't *possibly* read them out loud.

He'd only spoken the name Lady Jane Randolph that Spencer could remember a few weeks ago, when he'd announced he'd be returning to England for New Year's. He'd obtained leave and had for Spencer as well.

Spencer had been ready to go. Melancholia commanded him much of late, as he saw his future stretching before him, bleak and grim. If he did not end up dead on a battlefield with French bullets inside him, he would continue life as a junior officer without many prospects. Bonaparte was tough to wedge from the Peninsula—he'd already taken over most of the Italian states and much of the Continent, and had his relatives ruling corners of his empire for him. Only England and Portugal held out, and there was nothing to say Portugal would not fall.

Even if Napoleon was defeated, there was noise of coming war in America. Spencer would either continue the slog in the heat and rain of Portugal or be shipped off to the heat and rain of the New World.

Even if Spencer sold his commission in a few years, as he planned, what then? He itched to see the world—not in an army tent or charging his horse across a battlefield, but properly, on the Grand Tour he'd missed because of war. But Bonaparte was everywhere.

More likely, Spencer would go home and learn to run the estate he'd eventually inherit. He didn't like to think of *that* day either, because it would mean his beloved father had died.

John Barnett, rising quickly through the ranks, courtesy of familial influence, had this beautiful woman to return to whenever he chose, one with a large and friendly family in the soft Berkshire countryside.

And the idiot rarely spoke of her, preferring to flirt with the colorless daughters of his colonels and generals.

If Bonaparte's soldiers didn't shoot Barnett, Spencer might.

The village was a mile from the house down a straight road, easy to navigate on a fine night, but Spencer shivered.

"Are you well, Captain Ingram?" Lady Jane asked in concern. "Perhaps we shouldn't have come out. You must be tired from your travels. Holidays are not pleasant when one has a cold."

"I am quite well," Spencer answered, trying to sound cheerful. "I was reflecting how peaceful it all is. Safe." No sharpshooters waiting to take out stragglers, no pockets of French soldiers to capture and torture one. Only starlight, a quiet if icy breeze, a thin blanket of white snow, a lovely woman walking beside him, and warm firelight to beckon them on.

"Yes, it is. Safe." Lady Jane sounded discontented.

"Janie longs for adventure," Thomas confided. "Like me."

"I, on the other hand, believe this a perfect night," Spencer said, his spirits rising. "Companionship, conversation. Beauty."

Thomas snorted with laughter, but Spencer saw Jane's polite smile fade.

At that moment, village children ran to envelope them and drag them to the bonfire.

The footmen eagerly joined friends and family around the blazes. A stoneware jug made its rounds to men and women alike, and voices rose in song.

Jane released Spence's arm, the cold of her absence disheartening. She beamed in true gladness as village women greeted her and pulled her into their circle.

Spencer watched Lady Jane come alive, the primness she'd exhibited in her family home dropping away. Her face blossomed in the firelight, a midnight curl dropped to her shoulder, and her eyes sparkled like starlight—his faery creature in a fur-lined redingote and bonnet.

Barnett has a lot to answer for, he thought in disgust. *She deserves so much more.*

But who was Spencer to interfere with his friend's intentions? Perhaps Barnett loved her dearly and was too bashful to say so.

The devil he was. When Barnett had greeted Jane tonight, he'd betrayed no joy of at last being with her, no need for her presence. He was as obtuse as a brick. Barnett had Jane safely in his sights, and took for granted she'd always be there.

Man needed to be taught a lesson. Spencer decided then and there to be the teacher.

* * *

JANE HAD FORGOTTEN how much she enjoyed the bonfires at New Year's. The villagers had always had a New Year's celebration, and when Grandfather came to live with Jane's family after Grandmother's death, he'd taught them all about Hogmanay. None of the villagers were Scots, and in fact, had ancestors who'd fought Bonnie Prince Charlie, but the lads and lasses of Shefford St. Mary were always keen for a knees-up.

Jane had come to the bonfires every year as a child with her brother and cousins, and tonight, she was welcomed by the village women with smiles, curtseys, and even embraces.

The villagers linked hands to form a ring around one of the fires. Jane found her hand enclosed in Captain Ingram's large, warm one, his grip firm under his glove. Thomas clasped her other hand and nearly dragged Jane off her feet as they began to circle the fire at a rapid pace.

She glanced at Captain Ingram, to find his gray eyes fixed on her, his smile broad and genuine. His reserve evaporated as the circle continued, faster and faster. He'd claimed to be an indifferent dancer, but in wild abandon, he excelled.

Jane found she did too. Before long, she was laughing out loud, kicking up her feet as giddily as Grandfather had, as the villagers snaked back and forth. This was true country dancing, not the orchestrated, rather stiff parading in the ballroom.

The church clocks in this village and the next struck two, the notes shimmering in the cold. Village men seized their sweethearts, their wives, swung them around, and kissed them.

Strong hands landed on Jane's waist. Captain Ingram pulled her in a tight circle, out of the firelight. A warm red glow brushed his face as he dragged Jane impossibly close. Then he kissed her.

The world spun, silence taking the place of laughter, shouting, the crackle of the fire, the dying peal of the bells.

Spencer Ingram's heat washed over Jane, dissolving anything stiff, until she flowed against him, her lips seeking his.

The kiss was tender, a brief moment of longing, of desire simmering below the surface. Jane wanted that moment to stretch forever, through Hogmanay night to welcoming dawn, and for the rest of her life.

Revelers bumped them, and Spencer broke the kiss. Jane hung in his arms, he holding her steady against the crush.

She saw no remorse in his eyes, no shame that he'd kissed another man's intended. Jane felt no remorse either. She was a free woman, not officially betrothed, not yet belonging to John, and she knew this with all her being.

Spencer set her on her feet and gently released her. They continued to study each other, no words between them, only acknowledgment that they had kissed, and that it had meant something.

Thomas came toward them. "We should go back, Janie," he said with regret. "Auntie will be looking for us."

He seemed to have noticed nothing, not the kiss,

not the way Jane and Spencer regarded each other in charged silence.

The moment broke. Jane turned swiftly to Thomas and held out her hand. "Yes, indeed. It is high time we went home."

* * *

"A BONE TO PICK." Spencer closed the door of the large room where Barnett amused himself alone at a billiards table in midmorning sunlight. His eyes were red-rimmed from last night's revelry, but he greeted Spencer with a cheerful nod.

"Only if you procure a cue and join me."

Spencer chose a stout but slender stick from the cabinet and moved to the table as Barnett positioned a red ball on its surface and rolled a white toward Spencer.

Spencer closed his hand over the ball and spun it toward the other end of the table at the same time Barnett did his. Both balls bounced off the cushions and rolled back toward them, Spencer's coming to rest closer to its starting point than Barnett's. Therefore, Spencer's choice as to who went first.

He spread his hands and took a step back. "By all means."

Spencer was not being kind—the second player often had the advantage.

He remained politely silent as Barnett began taking his shots. He was a good player, his white ball kissing the red before the white dropped into a pocket, often clacking against Spencer's white ball as well. Spencer obligingly fished out balls each time so Barnett could continue racking up points.

Only when Barnett fouled out by his white ball

missing the red by a hair and coming to rest in the middle of the table did Spencer speak.

"I must tell you, Barnett, that I find your treatment of Lady Jane appalling."

Barnett blinked and straightened from grimacing at his now-motionless ball. "I beg your pardon? I wasn't aware I'd been appalling to the dear gel."

"You've barely spoken to her at all. I thought this was the lady you wanted to marry."

Barnett nodded. "Suppose I do."

"You *suppose*? She is a beautiful woman, full of fire, with the finest eyes I've ever seen, and you *suppose* you wish to marry her?"

"Well, it's never been settled one way or another. We are of an age, grew up together. Really we are the only two eligible people for miles. We all used to play together—Jane, her brother, her cousins, me." Barnett laughed. "I remember once when we dared her to climb the face of Blackbird Hill, a steep, rough rock, and she did it. And once—"

Spencer cut him off with a sweep of his hand. "A spirited girl, yes. And now a spirited woman fading while she waits for you to say a word. She's halting her life because everyone expects you to propose. It's cruel to her to hesitate. Criminal even."

"Jove, you are in a state." Barnett idly took up chalk and rubbed it on the tip of his cue. He leaned to take a shot, remembered he'd lost his turn, and rose again. "What do you wish me to do? Propose to her, today?" He looked as though this were the last thing on earth he'd wish to do.

"No, I believe you should let her go. If you don't wish to marry her, tell her so. End her uncertainty."

"Hang on. Are you saying Jane is pining for me?" Barnett grinned. "How delicious."

Spencer slammed his cue to the table. "I am saying

you've trapped her. She feels obligated to you because of family expectations, while you go your merry way. Your flirtations at camp border on courtship, and I assumed your intended was a dull wallflower you were avoiding. Now that I've met her ... You're an idiot, Barnett."

"Now, look here, Ingram. *Captain.*"

"You outrank me in the field, *sir*. In civilian life, no. Lady Jane is a fine young woman who does not need to be tied to you. Release her, let her find a suitor in London this Season, let her make her own choice."

Barnett's mouth hung open during Spence's speech, and now he closed it with a snap. "Her own choice—do you mean someone like *you?*"

Spencer scowled at him. "First of all, your tone is insulting. Second, when I say her own choice, I mean it. Cease forcing her to wait for you to come home, to speak. Let her begin her life."

Barnett laid down his cue with exaggerated care. "Very well. I suppose you pulling me away from that Frenchie's bayonet gives you some leave to speak to me so. Happen I might propose to her this very day. Will that gain your approval?"

Not at all. Spencer had hoped to make Barnett realize he didn't care for Lady Jane, never had, not as anything more than a childhood friend.

The man who proposed to Jane should be wildly in love with her, ready to do anything to make her life perfect and happy. She should have no less.

When Spencer had kissed her—

The frivolous, New Year's kiss had instantly changed to one of intense desire. Need had struck Spencer so hard he'd barely been able to remain standing. He'd wanted to hold on to Jane and run with her to Scotland, to jump the broomstick with her before anyone could stop them.

She never would. Spencer already understood that Jane had a deep sense of obligation, which she'd thrown off to dance in the firelight last night, like the wild thing she truly was. But today, she'd be back to responsibility. He hadn't seen her this morning, not at breakfast, which he'd rushed to anxiously, nor moving about the house, and he feared she'd decided to remain in her rooms and avoid him.

Spencer did not know what he'd say to her when she appeared. But he refused to put the kiss behind him, to pretend it never happened.

He didn't want Jane to pretend it hadn't happened either. He'd seen in her eyes the yearnings he felt—for love, for life, for something beyond what each of them had.

Spencer faced Barnett squarely. "Do not propose to her," he said. "Do not force her to plunge further into obligation. She won't refuse you. She'll feel it her duty to accept."

"It is her duty, damn you. What am I to do? Leave her for you?" When Spencer didn't answer, Barnett's eyes widened. "I see. Devil take you, man. I brought you home as a friend."

Spencer held him with a gaze that made Barnett's color rise. "That is true. Are you going to call me out?"

Barnett hesitated, then shook his head. "I'll not sully our friendship by falling out over a woman."

Spencer fought down disgust. "If you loved her, truly loved her, you'd strike me down for even daring to suggest I wanted her, and then you'd leap over my body and rush to her. You don't love her, do you? Not with all your heart."

Barnett shrugged. "Well, I'm fond of the gel, naturally."

"*Fond* is not what I'd feel, deep inside my soul, for the woman I wanted to spend the rest of my life with."

26

Spencer slapped his palm to his chest. "Release her, Barnett. Or love her, madly, passionately. She merits no less than that."

Spencer seized his white ball and spun it across the table. It caromed off one edge, two, three, and then struck the red ball with a crack like a gunshot and plunged into a pocket.

"Add up my points," Spencer said. "If you will not tell Lady Jane what is truly in your heart, *I* will."

He strode from the room, his heart pounding, his blood hot. *The captain is a volatile man,* he'd heard his commanders say of him, *Once he sets his mind on a thing, step out of his way.*

Behind him, Barnett called plaintively, "What about the game? I'll have to consider it a forfeit, you know."

A forfeit, indeed.

Spencer went down the stairs to the main hall and asked the nearest footman to direct him to Lady Jane.

CHAPTER 4

The gardens were covered with snow, the fountains empty and silent, but they suited Jane's mood. She ought to be in the house entertaining guests, or helping her mother, or looking after Grandfather, but she could not behave as though nothing had shaken her life to its foundations.

She should be glad John was home, feel tender happiness as the reward for waiting for his return.

All she could think of was Spencer Ingram's gray eyes sparkling in the firelight after he'd kissed her. Could think only of the heat of his lips on hers, the fiery touch of his tongue. It was as though John Barnett did not exist.

Was she so fickle? So featherheaded that the moment another man crossed her path, she eagerly turned to follow him?

Or was there more than that? John had more or less ignored her since he'd arrived. Instead of resenting his indifference, Jane had been relieved.

Relieved. What was the matter with her?

A pair of statues at the far end of the garden marked the edge of her father's park. Both statues were of Hercules—the one the right battling the Nemean lion; on the left, the hydra. Beyond these guardians lay pasture-land rolling to far hills, today covered with a few inches of snow.

Jane contemplated the uneven land beyond the statues and reluctantly turned to tramp back.

A man in a blue uniform with greatcoat and black boots strode around the fountains and empty flower beds toward her. He was alone, and his trajectory would make him intersect Jane's path. No one else wandered the garden, few bold enough to risk the ice-cold January morning.

Running would look foolish, not to mention Jane had nowhere to go. The fields, cut by a frozen brook, offered hazardous footing. Plus she was cold and ready to return to the house. Why should she flee her own father's garden?

Jane continued resolutely toward Captain Ingram, nodding at him as they neared each other. "Good morning," she said neutrally.

"Good morning," he echoed, halting before her. "Is it good?"

Jane curled her fingers inside her fur muff. "The weather is fair, the sun shining. The guests are enjoying themselves. The New Year's holiday is always pleasant."

Ingram's eyes narrowed. "Pleasant. Enjoying themselves." His voice held a bite of anger. "What about you, Lady Jane? Are you enjoying yourself?"

"Of course. I like to see everyone home. If my brother and his wife could come, that would be even more splendid."

"Liar."

Jane started, her heart beating faster, but she kept her tone light. "I beg your pardon? I truly do long to see my brother."

"You are miserable and cannot wait for the morning Major Barnett and I ride away."

Jane lost her forced smile. "You are rude."

"I am. Many say this of me. But I am a plain speaker and truthful." His gray eyes glinted as he fixed an unrelenting gaze on her. "Tell me why the devil you are tying yourself to Barnett."

Why? There was every reason why—Jane simply had never thought the reasons through. "I have known him a very long time ..."

Spencer stepped closer to her. "If you were madly in love with him, you'd have slapped me silly when I tried to kiss you, last night. Instead you joined me."

Jane rested her muff against her chest, as though it would shield her. "Are you casting my folly up to me? Not very gentlemanly of you."

To her surprise, Spencer smiled, his anger transforming to heat. It was a feral smile, the fierceness in his eyes making her tremble.

"*I* am the fool for kissing you," he said in a hard voice. "I couldn't help myself. I think no less of you for kissing me back. In fact, I have been rejoicing all night and morning that you did. Haven't slept a bloody wink."

Jane swallowed. "Neither have I, as a matter of fact."

"Then you give me hope. Much hope."

He took another step to her, and Jane feared he would kiss her again.

Feared? Or desired it?

She pulled back, but not because he frightened her. She stepped away because she wanted very much to kiss him, properly this time. She'd fling her arms around him and drag him close, enjoying the warmth of him against her.

She touched the muff to her lips, the fur tickling.

Spencer laughed. "You are beautiful, Lady Jane. And enchanting. A wild spirit barely tamed by a respectable dress and winter coat."

"Hardly a wild spirit." Jane moved the muff to speak. "I embroider—not well, I admit—paint watercolors rather better, and help my mother keep house."

"Your grandfather told me stories of himself and your grandmother last night. You are much like her."

Jane wanted to think so. Maggie MacDonald, what Jane remembered of her, had been a laughing, happy woman, given to telling frightening stories of ghosts that haunted the Highlands or playing games with her grandchildren. She also loved to dance. Jane had a memory of her donning a man's kilt and performing a sword dance as gracefully and adeptly as any warrior. Grandfather had watched her with love in his eyes.

"She was a grand woman," Jane said softly. "I can't begin to compare to her."

"She is in your blood." Spencer took another step, pushing the muff downward. "I saw that when we were at the fire. You were free, happy. I will stand here until you admit it."

"I was." Jane could not lie, even to herself. "Last night, I was happy."

"But this morning, you have convinced yourself you must be this other Jane. Dutiful. Tethered. *Un*happy."

Jane ducked from him and started toward the statues at the end of the garden. She had no idea why she did not rush to the house instead—Hercules was far too busy with his own struggles to help her.

Unhappy. Yes, she was. But that was hardly his business.

She heard Spencer's boots on the snow-covered gravel behind her and swung to face him. "Why do you follow me, sir? If I am miserable, perhaps I wish to console myself in solitude."

"Because I want to be with you." Spencer halted a foot from her. "There, I have declared myself. I want to be with you, and no other. I do not care one whit that

31

you and Barnett have an understanding. He is not in love with you—I can see that. Such news might hurt you, but you must know the truth."

It did hurt. Jane had grown complacent about her friendship with John, pleased she could live without worry for her future, thankful she had no need to chase gentlemen during her Season and could simply enjoy London's many entertainments. She assisted other ladies to find husbands instead of considering them rivals.

Spencer's arrival had shattered her complacency, and now its shards lay around her.

She fought to maintain her composure. "Are you suggesting I throw over Major Barnett and declare myself for you?"

"Nothing would make me happier."

Spencer leaned close, and again, Jane thought he'd kiss her. Anything sensible spun out of her head as she anticipated the brush of his lips, the warmth of his touch. He came closer still, his gaze darting to her mouth, his chest rising sharply. Jane's very breath hurt.

When he straightened, disappointment slapped her.

"Nothing would make me happier," Spencer repeated. "But I'm not a blackguard. If you have no regard for me, if you cannot imagine yourself loving me, then I will not press you. I won't press you at all. What I want, my dear lady, is your happiness. I know in my heart it does not lie for you with Major Barnett."

Jane shook her head. "The world is convinced it does."

"Then the world is a fool. I would be the happiest man alive if you chose me. But I won't ask you to, won't coerce you." His dark brows came down. "I want you to be free, Jane. Free to choose. Go to London. Have your Season—laugh, dance, live. If you find a better man than I there, then I'll ... well, I'll sink into despondency for a long while, but that despondency will have a bright note. I'll know you are happy. Find that man, and I will dance at your wedding. I promise."

Her breath came fast. "You amaze me, sir."

"Why?" Again a smile, bright and hot. "I admire you. I hate to see you pressed into a box, your nature stifled, all because of an ass like Major Barnett."

Jane attempted a frown. "Should I throw off my friends the moment they displease me? Is this freedom?" Her voice shook, because in her heart, his words made her sing.

"You know Barnett has been displeasing you for years," Spencer said. "Else you'd have looked happier to see him."

Truth again. Was this man an oracle?

"How dare you?" Jane tried to draw herself up, but her question lacked conviction. Spencer unnerved her, turned her inside out, made her want to laugh and cry. "This is none of your affair, sir."

She ought to threaten to call her father, have Captain Ingram ejected from the house, even arrested for accosting her. Or she could simply slap him, as he'd told her she should have done last night.

Spencer's gaze held her, and Jane could do nothing.

"It is my affair because I care about you," he said. "But *I* do not matter. You do. Please, Jane, be happy."

Blast him. Before he'd arrived, Jane's life had been tranquil. At ease. Now confusion pounded at her, and shame.

Because she knew good and well she hadn't been tranquil at all. She'd been impatient, angry. Stifled, as he said.

Spencer's eyes held anguish, rage, and need. Jane knew somehow that Spencer Ingram would always speak truth to her, whether she liked it or not.

And she knew she wanted to kiss him again.

33

The house was far away, and high yew hedges edged the path on which they stood. No one was about, not even a gardener taking a turn around the empty beds. Most of the servants had been given a holiday.

Jane took the last step toward Spencer. As he regarded her in both trepidation and simmering need, Jane wrapped her arms around his neck and kissed him.

His lips were parted, his breath heating hers an instant before he hauled her against him, his answering kiss hard, savage.

The world melted away. All Jane knew was Spencer's solid, strong body, his hands holding her steady, his mouth on hers.

He pulled her closer, the tall length of him hard against her softness. His lips opened hers, mouth seeking, whiskers scratching her cheek. He filled up everything empty inside her, and Jane learned warmth, joy, longing.

We never let anything stand in the way of us, Grandfather always said about himself and his beloved Maggie.

That was long ago, Jane would reason.

But *this* was now.

Jane abruptly broke the kiss. Spencer gazed at her, desire plain in his eyes. He traced her cheek, and her heart shattered.

Jane drew away from him, and ran. She snatched up the freedom he offered her and sprinted down the main path, her arms open, muff hanging from one hand, and let the cold air come.

* * *

"John, may I have a word?"

Jane was surprised she had breath left after her mad dash through the garden. She'd taken time to shed her outdoor things and compose herself before she sought John.

She found him in the library, book in hand, but he wasn't reading. John gazed rather wistfully out the window to the park in front of the house, the book dangling idly.

When he heard Jane, he rose to his feet and pasted on a polite smile. "Good morning, Jane. Did you have a nice walk?"

Jane halted, her cheeks scalding. Had he seen the kiss? Or been told about it?

John's face, however, held the bland curiosity of a man who had been thinking of everything but Jane, only recalled to her existence by her presence.

"The walk was agreeable," Jane said hastily. She glanced behind her to make certain the few servants who'd agreed to stay and help today did not linger in the hall. She dared not close the door in case a guest insisted that Jane shut into a room with her old friend meant either her ruin or their engagement.

She had no idea how to begin, so she jumped to the point, bypassing politeness.

"John, I would take it kindly if you did not propose to me."

John stared at her as though he didn't understand her words, then his brows climbed, his mouth forming a half smile. "I beg your pardon?"

Jane balled her hands and plunged on. "Please do not propose marriage to me. It will be easier for both of us if I do not have to refuse you."

CHAPTER 5

*O*h." John gaped at her. His features were still very like those he'd had as a child—round cheeks, soft chin, bewildered brown eyes. "Damn and blast—Ingram has got at you, has he? Viper to my bosom."

"Captain Ingram?" Good heavens, had Spencer discussed this with John? "Captain Ingram has nothing to do with this," Jane said heatedly. "Or, if he does, it is that he made me see keeping silent is hurting you as well as myself. We do not care for each other—not in the 'til-death-do-us-part fashion, in any case. Of course I have affection for you as a friend, and always will. We grew up together. But that does not mean we should continue as man and wife, no matter how many members of our family and friends believe so."

John's astonishment grew as Jane rambled, and she trailed off, her face unbearably hot.

John lifted his chin. "I cannot believe you so flighty, Jane, that you could allow a man, who pretends to be a gentleman, change your thoughts so swiftly."

"He did not." Jane shook her head, her heart squeezing. "I've had these thoughts a long time, even if I did not admit them to myself. But I did not want to hurt you, my dear old friend. I believe now that *not* speaking will do even more harm. What happens if, in a year or two, you meet a lady you truly love? One who could be your helpmeet, your friend, the mother of your children? And you were already betrothed or married to me? Let us prevent that tragedy here and now."

John scowled. "Or is it that *you* wish to fall in love with another and not be tied to *me?*"

"Nonsense," Jane said. "I have no intention of marrying anyone."

She flushed even as she spoke. Spencer tempted her, yes, but she barely knew him. She would not fly from an understanding with John to an elopement with Spencer in the space of a day.

Would she?

"I believe you," John said in a hard voice. "Your nose held so high, your frosty demeanor in place. You've grown cold, Jane. If I haven't spoken to you about sharing a stall for life, it is because you are quite disagreeable these days. Your letters to me are so formal, about what calves were born and who danced with whom at the village ball. Enthralling."

Jane's coolness evaporated in a flash. "These in answer to the very few letters you have sent *me*. I've not heard from you since summer, in fact. Do not bother to use the excuse of battles, because your mother has had plenty of letters from you, as has my brother, and I know that the sister of a man in your regiment has heard plenty from *him*—the letters arrive in England on the same ship. But none from you to me."

John reddened. "Hardly seemly, is it, writing to a lady to whom I am not engaged?"

"It did not stop you the first year you were gone, nor has it stopped you scolding me for not writing scintillating letters to you."

John attempted a lofty tone. "You are such a child, Jane."

"No, I am not. I am twenty, as I reminded you last night, older than several ladies of my acquaintance who are already married. Old enough to be on the shelf, as you know. But I will not tie us to a marriage neither of us wants to avoid that fate."

"Ah, so that is why you were always sweet to me, eh, Janie? So you'd never be an ape-leader?" John's mouth pinched. "I'll have you know that I planned to speak to you this week, my dear, but not to propose. To tell you there is the sister of an officer who has caught my eye, and as you have become so cool, and she is quite warm, that we should agree to part."

Jane's heart stung, and she regarded him in remorse. She hadn't wanted to anger John, but how could he not be angry? His stabs at her came from his bafflement and hurt, but Jane sensed that he was more insulted at her refusal than deeply wounded.

John would return to his regiment and happily court the officer's sister, and forget he ever had feelings for Jane. In fact, John had behaved, since his arrival, as though he'd forgotten those feelings already.

Hopefully, in time, John would forgive her, and they'd continue as friends, as they had been all their lives. But friends with no obligation attached.

"Good-bye, John," Jane said, and quietly walked out of the room.

* * *

Spencer did not see Jane the rest of the day. He walked through the gardens, the park, the woods, then took a horse and went on a long ride. It was snowing by the time he returned, and dark.

He did not see Barnett either, which was a mercy.

Spencer then realized he'd seen no one at all as he returned to his chamber. He washed and changed and descended in search of supper, but the residents of the house were elusive. Where had they all gone?

"Hurry up, lad," a voice with a Scottish lilt said to him. "You're the last."

"The last for what, sir?" Spencer asked Lady Jane's grandfather as the elderly man tottered to him.

"The hunt, of course. Here's your list. You're with Thomas and my daughter. Off you go."

Spencer gazed down at a paper with a jumble of items written on it: A flat iron, a locket, a horseshoe, a thimble, and a dozen more bizarre things that did not match.

"What is this?" he asked in bewilderment.

"A scavenger hunt, slow-top. The first team to gather the things wins a prize. Go on with ye."

Spencer hesitated. "Where is Jane? Lady Jane, that is."

"With the older cousins and a friend from down the lane. Why are you still standing here?"

"The thing is, sir, I … I'm not sure who to speak to …"

The old Scotsman waved him away, his plaids swinging. "Aye, I know all about it. Give the lass time to settle, and she'll come 'round. She only gave Major Barnett the elbow a few hours ago."

Spencer's heart leapt. "She did?"

"Yes. Thank the Lord. Now, hurry away. Enjoy yourself while you're still young."

Spencer grinned in sudden hope. "Yes, sir. Of course, sir."

As he dashed away, he heard Grandfather MacDonald muttering behind him. "In my day, I'd have already put the girl over my shoulder and run off with her. Otherwise, she'd not think I was sincere."

* * *

JANE HANDED HER SPOILS—a blue beaded slipper, a quizzing glass, and a small rolling pin—to her cousin Digby, and slipped into the chamber she'd spied her grandfather ducking into. The small anteroom was covered with paintings her father's father had collected. A strange place for Grandfather MacDonald to hide— he believed Van Dyke and Rubens over-praised. Only Scottish painters like Allan Ramsay and Henry Raeburn had ever been any good.

"Grandfather."

Grandfather looked up from a settee, where he'd been nodding off, but his eyes were bright, alert. He came to his feet.

"Yes, my dear? Are you well?"

"No." Jane sank down to a painted silk chair. "Everything is turned upside-down, Grandfather. I need your advice."

"Do you?" Grandfather plopped back onto the settee, smile in place. "Why come to me, lass? Not your mum?"

"Because when things are topsy-turvy, you seem to know what to do."

"True. But so do you."

Jane shivered. "No, I do not. I was perfectly happy with my life as it was. Then John began to change, and Captain Ingram—"

"A fine young man is Ingram," Grandfather said brightly. "My advice is to run off with him. You like kissing him well enough."

Jane's face flamed. "Grandfather!"

"I do not know why you are so ashamed. I saw you kissing him in the garden, and young Thomas says you kissed him at the bonfire." Grandfather shook his head in impatience. "Latch on to him, Janie, and kiss him for life."

Jane's face grew hotter, her mortification complete. "You ought to have made yourself known instead of lurking in the shrubbery."

"Tut, girl. I was out for a walk, a good stride through the yew hedges. Not lurking anywhere. You were standing plain as day by those ridiculous statues. Which is why I don't understand your shame. You did not kick Ingram in the dangles and run away. You embraced him. With enthusiasm."

"Even so." Jane's embarrassment warred with elation as she thought of the kiss. "I cannot disappoint my family and uproot my life on a whim."

"Why not?"

"Because …" Jane waved her hands. "What a fool I'd be. I barely know Captain Ingram. He might be the basest scoundrel on land, ready to abandon me at a moment's notice. The real world is not a fairy tale, Grandfather."

"Thank heavens for that. Fairy tales are horrible—the fae ain't the nice little people painted in books for maiden ladies. Trust me. I'm descended from witches, and I know all about the fae."

"Of course, Grandfather." If not stopped, Grandfather could go on for some time about how Shakespeare based Macbeth's witches on the women in his mother's family. "What I mean is I can't simply change everything because a handsome gentleman kissed me," she said.

"You can, you know. This is why you came to me for advice, young lady, and not your mum. Isobel is my pride and joy, she is, but she's the practical sort. The airiness of your grandmother and the wickedness of my side of the family didn't manifest in her. Isobel's more like me dad, a stolid Scotsman who never put a foot wrong in his life. Didn't stop the Hanoverians taking all he had." Grandfather's gaze held the remote rage of long ago, then he shook his head and refocused on the present.

"Janie, you are unhappy because you believe life should be simple. You long for it to be. You fancied yourself willing to marry Barnett because it was the easy choice. He's familiar to your family, you know what to expect from him, and you'd congratulated yourself for not having to chase down a husband to look after you the rest of your life. But you'd be disappointed in him. He might be the simplest choice for a husband, but you'd end up looking after *him*, and you know it."

"Why is such a thing so bad?" Jane asked, heart heavy. "Grandmother looked after *you*."

Grandfather shook his head. "She and I looked after each other. And we did not have a peaceful life at first—our families were furious with us, and we had to weather that, and find a way to live, *and* raise our children. It weren't no easy matter, my girl, but that is the point. Life is complicated. It's hard, hard work. So many try to find a path around that, but though that path might look clear, it can be full of misery. You sit helplessly while things happen around you instead of grabbing your life by the horns and shaking it about. Happiness is worth the trouble, the difficult choices, the path full of brambles. Do not sit and let things flow by you, Jane. You deserve much more than that. Take your happiness, my love. Do not let this moment pass."

Jane sat silently. She felt limp, drained—had since she'd told John they could never be married. She thought she'd feel freedom once she'd been truthful with John, as Spencer had told her she would, but at present, Jane only wanted to curl up and weep.

"But I could misstep," she said. "I could charge down the difficult path and take a brutal tumble."

"That you could. And then you rise up and try again. Or you could huddle by the wayside and let happiness slip past. If you don't grab joy while you can, you might not have another chance."

Jane's heart began to beat more strongly. "I am a woman. I must be prudent. A man who falls can be helped up by his friends. A woman who falls is ostracized by hers."

Grandfather shook his head. "Only if those friends are scoundrels. I imagine your family would stand by you no matter what happened. I know *I* would." He raised his hands, palms facing her. "But you are worrying because you've been taught to worry. Do you truly believe Ingram is a hardened roué? With a string of broken hearts and ruined women behind him? We'd have heard about such things. Barnett would have told us—you know how much he loves to gossip. And he wouldn't have brought Captain Ingram home to you and your mum and dad if he thought the man a bad 'un, would he?"

Jane had to concede. "I suppose not ..."

"Your dad knows everyone in England, and he's no fool. He'd have heard of Ingram's reputation if the man had a foul one, and he'd have never let him inside. It's harder than you'd think to be a secret rake in this country. *Someone* will know, and feel no remorse spreading the tale."

Jane didn't answer. Everything Grandfather said was reasonable. Still, she'd seen what happened when a woman married badly—she found herself saddled with an insipid, feckless man who did nothing but disgrace his family and distress his friends.

The man John could so easily become ...

"Spencer Ingram seems a fine enough lad to me,"

Grandfather went on. "Family's respectable too, from what I hear. Besides, Ingram is a good Scottish name."

"Of course." Jane gave a shaky laugh. "That is why you like him."

"One of the reasons. There are many others." Grandfather jumped to his feet. "What are you waiting for, Janie? Your happiness walked in the door last night. Go to it—go to *him*."

"I don't regret telling John I will never marry him," Jane said with conviction. "And I suppose you're right. I won't send Captain Ingram away, or push him aside because I'm mortified. He will be visiting a while longer. We can get to know each other, and perhaps …"

Her words faded as Grandfather snorted. "*Get to know each other? Perhaps?* Have you heard nothing I've said?" His eyes flashed. "You are trying to make things comfortable again, which means pushing aside decisions, waiting for things to transpire instead of forcing them to."

He pointed imperiously at the door. "Out you go, Jane. Now. Find Captain Ingram. Tell him you will marry him. No thinking it over, or lying awake pondering choices, or waiting to see what happens. Go to him this instant."

Jane rose, her heart pounding. "I can't tell him I'll marry him, Grandfather. He hasn't asked me."

"Then ask *him*. Your grandmother did me. She tired of me shillyshallying. So she stepped up and told me I either married her, or she walked away and looked for someone else."

Jane covered her fears with a laugh. She could picture Maggie MacDonald doing just that. "But I am not Grandmother."

Grandfather's eyes softened. "Oh, yes, you are. You are so like her, Janie, you don't realize. Her spitting image when she was young, and you have her spirit.

44

She knew it too." Tears beaded on his lashes. "I miss her so."

"Oh, Grandfather." Janie launched herself at him, enfolding him into her arms. Grandfather rested his head on her shoulder, a fragile old man, his bones too light.

After a time, they pushed away from each other, both trying to smile.

"Go to him, Janie," Grandfather said. "For her sake."

Jane kissed his faded cheek and spun for the door. As she turned to close it behind her, she saw Grandfather's tears flow unchecked down his face, he wiping them away with a fold of his plaid.

CHAPTER 6

Spencer observed that Barnett did not seem too morose that Lady Jane had thrown him over. He watched Barnett fling himself into the hunt, crowing over the things he'd found for his group, all the while glancing raptly at the daughter of guests from Kent. His behavior was not so much of a man bereaved as one reprieved.

Spencer knew that if Jane had given *him* the push, he'd be miserable, tearing at his hair and beating his breast like the best operatic hero.

He feared Jane had dismissal in mind when she gazed down from the upper gallery and caught his eye. She gave him a long look before she skimmed down the stairs and disappeared into the library.

Spencer, who'd found none of the items on his list, his heart not in the game, handed his paper to Thomas and told the lad to carry on.

"Jane?" Spencer whispered as he entered the library. It was dark, a few candles burning for the sake of the gamers, the fire half-hearted against the cold. The chill was why no one lingered here—the room was quite empty.

Spencer shut the door. "Jane?"

She turned from the shadows beside the fireplace. Spencer approached her, one reluctant pace at a time.

When he was a few strides away, Jane smiled at him. That smile blazed like sunshine, lighting the room to its darkest corners.

"Captain Ingram," Lady Jane said. "Will you marry me?"

Spencer ceased breathing. He knew his heart continued to beat, because it pounded blood through him in hot washes. But he felt nothing, as though he'd been wound in bandages, like the time a French saber had pierced his shoulder and the surgeon had swaddled his upper body like a babe's.

That shoulder throbbed, the old pain resurfacing, and Spencer's breath rushed back into his lungs.

"Jane ..."

"I am sincere, I assure you," Jane said, as though she supposed he'd argue with her. "I know I am doing this topsy-turvy, but—"

Spencer laid shaking hands on her shoulders, the blue silk of her gown warmed by her body. "Which is the right way 'round for you, my beautiful, beautiful fae."

"Grandfather would faint if he heard you say so," Jane said with merriment. "I believe he's rather afraid of the fae. Even if he married one."

Spencer tightened his clasp on her. He never remembered how Jane ended up in his arms, but in the next instant he was kissing her, deeply, possessively, and she responded with the mad passion he'd seen in her eyes.

That kiss ended, but they scarcely had time to draw a breath before the next kiss began. And the next.

They ended up in the wing chair that reposed before the fire, placed so a reader might keep his or her feet warm. Spencer's large frame took up most of it, but there was room for Jane on his lap.

They kissed again, Spencer cradling her.

How much time sped by, Spencer had no idea, but at last he drew Jane to rest on his shoulder.

"Shall we adjourn to Gretna Green?" he asked in a low voice.

Jane raised her head, her blue eyes bright in the darkened room. "No, indeed. I wish my family and friends to be present. But soon."

"How fortunate that my leave is for a month. Time enough to have the banns read in your parish church. And then what? Follow me and the drum? It can be a hard life."

Jane brushed his cheek. "I do want to go with you. I am willing to face the challenge, to forsake the safer path." She spoke the words forcefully, as though waiting for Spencer to dissuade her.

He had no intention of it. With Jane by his side, camp life would cease to be bleak. "I plan to sell my commission a few years from now, in any case. I do not see myself as a career army man, though I am fond of travel."

"I long to travel."

The words were adamant. With Jane's restlessness and fire, Spencer believed her. "After that, I will have a house waiting for me," he said. "One of my father's minor estates."

Her smile beamed. "Excellent."

"Not really—it needs much work. Again, I am not promising you softness."

"I do not want it." Jane kissed his chin. "I am re-silient. And resourceful. I like to be doing things, and I do not mean embroidery. Come to think of it, my grandmother never did embroidery in her life."

"I know." Spencer nuzzled her hair. "Your grandfather spoke much about her when I met him in London."

Jane stilled. Very slowly, she lifted her head. "You met my grandfather in London?"

Spencer nodded. "Last spring. I was on another leave-taking, much shorter, to visit my family. I spent a night in London, and at the tavern near my lodgings, I met an amusing old Scotsman who was pleased to sit up with me telling stories. I mentioned my friendship with Barnett, and your grandfather was delighted."

"He was, was he?" Jane's tone turned ominous.

"Indeed. But when I arrived last night, he asked me not to speak of our previous meeting to anyone. I have no idea why, but I saw no reason not to indulge him."

He leaned to kiss her again, to enjoy the taste of her fire, but Jane put her hand on his chest.

"Will you excuse me for one moment, Spencer?"

Spencer skimmed his fingertips across her cheek. "When you speak my name, I cannot refuse you, love."

Her eyes softened, but she scrambled from his lap. Spencer rose with her, a steadying hand on her waist. "I won't be long," she promised.

Jane strode from the room, her head high. Spencer watched her go, then chuckled to himself and followed her.

* * *

"GRANDFATHER."

She found he'd moved to a smaller, warmer sitting room, only this time he'd truly nodded off. The old man jumped awake and then to his feet, the whisky flask he'd been holding clanging to the floor.

"What the devil? Janie, what is it?"

Jane pointed an accusing finger at his face. "You met Captain Ingram in London this past spring."

"Did I?" Grandfather frowned, then stroked his jaw in contemplation. "Now that you call it to my mind, I believe I did. My memory ain't what it used to be."

"I cry foul." Jane planted her hands on her hips. "You knew he was John's friend. *You* put the idea into John's head to bring Captain Ingram here for Hogmanay, didn't you? Do not prevaricate with me, please."

"Hmm. I might have mentioned our meeting in a letter to young Barnett."

"And you told John to send Captain Ingram into the house first."

"Well, he is dark-haired. And tall. And what ladies believe is handsome." Grandfather spread his hands. "My prediction came true, you see? You will marry this year's First-Footer. I see by your blush that he has accepted your proposal."

Jane's cheeks indeed were hot. "Prediction, my eye. You planned this from the beginning, you old fraud."

Grandfather drew himself up. "And if I did? And if I met Ingram's family and determined that they were worthy of you? Captain Ingram is a far better match for you than Barnett. My lady ancestors were witches, yes, but they always had contingencies to make certain the spell worked."

Deep, rumbling laughter made Jane spin around. Spencer leaned on the doorframe, gray eyes sparkling in mirth.

"Bless you that you did," he said. He came to Jane and put a strong hand on her arm. "You and your ancestors will always have my gratitude, sir. Jane and I will be married by the end of the month."

Grandfather gave Jane a hopeful look. "All's well, that end's well?"

Jane dashed forward in a burst of love and caught her grandfather in an exuberant embrace. "Yes, Grandfather. Thank you. Thank you. I love you so much."

"Go on with you now." Grandfather struggled away, but the tears in his eyes touched her heart. "The pair of ye, be off. Ye have much more kissing to do. It's Hogmanay still."

Spencer twined his hand through Jane's. "An excellent suggestion."

"And don't either of you worry about Barnett. I've already caught him kissing Miss Pembroke."

Jane blinked. Miss Pembroke was the daughter of her parents' friends from Kent. "He is quick off the mark. The wretch."

"Then he can toast us at our wedding," Spencer said. He pulled Jane firmly to the door. "I believe I'd like to adjourn to the library again, to continue our ... planning."

Jane melted to him, her anger and exasperation dissolving. She needed this man, who'd come to her so unexpectedly to lift her out of her dreary life. "A fine idea."

In the cool of the hall, Spencer bent to Jane and whispered in her ear. "You are beauty and light. I love you, Janie. This I already know."

"I already know I love you too."

They sealed their declaration with a kiss that burned with a wildness Jane had been longing for, the fierce freedom of her youth released once more.

* * *

LEFT ALONE in the sitting room, Hamish MacDonald raised his flask to the painting of a beautiful woman whose flowing hair spilled from under a wide-brimmed hat. She smiled at him over a basket of flowers, her bodice sliding to bare one seductive shoulder. Her eyes were deep blue, her hair black as night.

"I did it, Maggie," he said, his voice scratchy. "I've seen to it that our girl will be happy. Bless you, love."

He toasted the portrait, done by the great Ramsay, and drank deeply of malt whisky.

He swore that Maggie, his beloved wife, heart of his heart, forever in his thoughts, winked at him.

* * *

THANK YOU FOR READING! If you enjoy sweet Regencies, see *Duke in Search of a Duchess*, in which the Duke of Ashford never dreams his children will recruit the busybody young widow next door to help him find a new wife.

Regency Bon Bons

(short, sweet Regencies)

A First-Footer for Lady Jane

Duke in Search of a Duchess

A Kiss for Luck

The Mackenzies Series

The Madness of Lord Ian Mackenzie

Lady Isabella's Scandalous Marriage

The Many Sins of Lord Cameron

The Duke's Perfect Wife

A Mackenzie Family Christmas: The Perfect Gift

The Seduction of Elliot McBride

The Untamed Mackenzie

The Wicked Deeds of Daniel Mackenzie

Scandal and the Duchess

Rules for a Proper Governess

The Stolen Mackenzie Bride

A Mackenzie Clan Gathering

Alec Mackenzie's Art of Seduction

The Devilish Lord Will

A Rogue Meets a Scandalous Lady

A Mackenzie Yuletide

Fiona and the Three Wise Highlanders

Mackenzies II

The Sinful Ways of Jamie Mackenzie

ABOUT THE AUTHOR

New York Times bestselling and award-winning author Jennifer Ashley has written more than 100 published novels and novellas in romance, urban fantasy, mystery, and historical fiction under the names Jennifer Ashley, Allyson James, and Ashley Gardner. Jennifer's books have been translated into more than a dozen languages and have earned starred reviews in *Publisher's Weekly* and *Booklist.* When she isn't writing, Jennifer enjoys playing music (guitar, piano, flute), reading, hiking, and building dollhouse miniatures.

More about Jennifer's books can be found at:
www.jenniferashley.com
To keep up to date on her new releases, join her
newsletter

THEN IN A TWINKLING

ANNA BRADLEY

CHAPTER 1

THE PANDEMONIUM PLAYHOUSE,
LONDON,, NOVEMBER, 1812

"*If* you were half as shrewd as you think you are, Dinah Bishop, you'd have secured Oliver Angel before a lady with a prettier face than yours snatched him up for herself."

Dinah didn't have to glance into the looking glass to see who'd crept up behind her. No matter where she was or what she was about, her entire body prickled with irritation when she heard that sneering voice.

Florentina Fernside, undisputed queen of the Pandemonium Playhouse stage, darling of the drunken rabble in the pit, and tormentor of every actress doomed to tread the boards alongside her.

Dinah resumed stripping the heavy layer of stage powder from her face as if Florentina hadn't spoken. The woman had the attention span of a pot of face paint. If Dinah ignored her, she'd soon grow bored and go away.

"Of course, you're not the first actress here who's made a mess of her opportunities, but I'd taken you for one of the clever ones." Florentina sauntered across the room, skirts twitching, and dropped into the chair beside Dinah's at the dressing table. "Imagine my disappointment at finding you're as dim as all the rest of them."

Dinah tossed aside the damp cloth in her hand with a resigned sigh. Florentina wasn't going to go away on her own, but Dinah was more than willing to chase her off. What a shame she hadn't thought to pick up one of the rotten oranges hurled onto the stage this evening. Witless as she was, even Florentina knew enough to run when spoiled fruit was hurled at her head.

"Or did you think your own face so alluring a man couldn't see past it?" Florentina turned her gaze to her own reflection, her rosy lips curling into a smirk as she tweaked one of her dark ringlets into place.

Dinah met Florentina's narrowed eyes in the mirror. "Is that how you lost Lord Archer? Overestimated the allure of your own pretty face? Pity, but then pride does come before a fall. You should study your Bible more often, Florentina. Book of Proverbs, I believe."

Dinah didn't bother to hide her satisfaction as Florentina's smirk darkened into a scowl. Florentina had lost her wealthy protector to another of the Pandemonium's actresses, Dinah's dearest friend, Penelope Hervey. William Angel, the Earl of Archer had fallen madly in love with Penelope last Christmas, and had made her his countess. Penelope was Lady Archer now, and mistress of Cliff's Edge, a lovely estate situated on the edge of the sea in Essex.

An actress turned countess. Dear me, how shocking! London was still reeling over it, but no one so much as Florentina, who could be relied upon to fall into a fury whenever Penelope's name was mentioned.

"I suppose you thought you'd enjoy a similar happy fate as your friend." Florentina tossed her head. "You should have known better, my dear. Lord Oliver is as constant as a child with a shiny trinket clutched in its fist."

Dinah rolled her eyes. For pity's sake, this again? Everyone in London believed she was Oliver's mistress. It wasn't true, but the truth was far less entertaining than a delicious lie, and no lie was more delicious than a lie about Oliver Angel.

London had suffered a severe blow when they'd lost Lord Archer to Penelope. The ladies might yet be in despair if Archer's younger brother had been anyone less than Oliver Angel. As it was, Lord Oliver's dimpled smile set hearts aflutter all over the city. Dinah's own heart was icier than most, but even hers thawed a degree or two when Oliver grinned at her. There wasn't a lady in London who could resist those deep dimples at the corners of his mouth.

Of course, resistance was a matter of measures. Dinah might admire Oliver's dimples, but more often than not dimples came with a rogue attached, and rogues were too troublesome to bother with. People in general were a great nuisance, but she forgave Oliver his occasional antics because he was entertaining and clever, and truly kind-hearted.

She was fond of him—not *too* fond, because it wasn't wise to be too fond of a man with a smile like Oliver's—but he was one of only a handful of people she considered a friend. "Lord Oliver isn't my protector, Florentina."

Florentina let out a laugh shrill enough to crack the looking glass. "Well no, dear. Not *anymore*. After the spectacle he and Lady Serena made in his box tonight, the entire theatre knows *that*. Why, at one point his tongue nearly fell out of his mouth."

Dinah's hand froze as she reached for her hairbrush. "Lady Serena? Lady Serena Howard? *That* Lady Serena?"

"Who else?" Florentina's fingers flew to her mouth in mock chagrin. "You mean to say you didn't *know* about her? Goodness me. How humiliating for you to find out this way. I do beg your pardon, dear, but then you would have found out soon enough. Every gossip in London will be whispering about it by tomorrow morning."

"Lady Serena was in his box tonight?" Dinah detested having to ask Florentina, but she couldn't see a thing from her own position on the stage aside from the glare from the chandeliers suspended from the ceiling. Oliver might have tumbled from his box into the pit below without her noticing.

"Lord Oliver, Lady Serena, and Lord Erskine. What a trio, to be sure." Florentina rose from her chair and flounced across the room. "You should have predicted his attention would wander, and secured him before it did. Alas, it's too late now."

If the gentleman in question had been anyone other than Oliver Angel, perhaps Dinah would have secured him, just as Florentina suggested. She wouldn't be the first lady to trade the stage for a place in a wealthy gentleman's bed. But for all Oliver's caprices and whims, his quirks and foibles, he deserved better than that.

Better than Lady Serena, as well.

Dinah had recently put some distance between herself and Oliver in hopes he'd overcome a silly little infatuation he'd developed for her, but she hadn't turned him loose so a venomous viper like Lady Serena could snatch him up and devour him.

"Well, my dear, I'm truly sorry for you." Florentina turned to Dinah with a triumphant smile. "Indeed, I am, but it's your own fault, and heaven knows you aren't likely to do any better than Oliver Angel."

With that parting shot, Florentina swept from the room, and Dinah was left alone, staring into the glass at the troubled blue eyes peering back at her.

Lady Serena Howard. Of all the ladies London had

to offer, why would Oliver choose *her*? She was witty and beautiful, yes, and she had a certain lazy elegance the stupider gentlemen seemed to find irresistible, but Oliver was no fool. The woman might be one of London's most sought-after courtesans, but she was notorious for leading her conquests from one disastrous scandal to the next, bleeding them dry of every last guinea, then tossing what was left of them aside before moving onto her next wealthy patron.

Oliver might do as he pleased, of course, but Dinah had thought he had more sense than *that*. Then again, Florentina could be lying, or at the very least exaggerating. The woman lived to stir up mischief. There was no sense in panicking until she'd seen Oliver and Lady Serena together with her own eyes.

She snatched up her things, pulled her cloak around her shoulders and hurried into the corridor outside the dressing room. The performance had ended a half hour ago, but Oliver always waited outside in the mews for her afterwards to take her home in his carriage.

He was there, on the street outside the theater. He hadn't yet forgiven her for her recent standoffishness, and his dimpled smile dimmed a little when he saw her. Dinah pretended not to notice it, or the cool note in his voice when he said, "Here you are at last."

There, it was just as she'd suspected. Florentina had exaggerated entire thing. Oliver was here, just as he always was, and there wasn't a sign of—

"Come along, then, my lord. We've been waiting in this damp alleyway for an age!"

Dinah's gaze jerked to Oliver's carriage, and her eyes narrowed to slits.

There sat Lady Serena, like a queen on her throne. Blast it, why did this have to be the one instance when Florentina was telling the truth?

"Are you ready?" Oliver held out his hand to Dinah.

She didn't take it. It was the first time since she and Oliver became friends a year ago she didn't take his hand when he offered it. She glanced back at the carriage and saw Lady Serena hanging out the window, a generous expanse of her bare, white bosom shoved high against the bodice of her gown.

Dinah's lip curled. That corset was squeezing the life out of her. Either it was two sizes too small, or Lady Serena had another one of her lovers stuffed down her bodice.

Lord Erskine leaned across Lady Serena to peer out the window at Dinah. "Such prudent hesitation! It's unnecessary, I assure you, Miss Bishop. We don't bite."

"No, not unless you ask politely," Lady Serena drawled, her glittering dark eyes roaming possessively over Oliver.

Oliver grinned at her, his dimples winking at the corners of his mouth. "Come now, Lady Serena. We both know you prefer wickedness to manners."

Lady Serena let out a peal of laughter. "I can hardly deny it while I'm sitting in *your* carriage, my lord."

Dinah's eyebrow lifted. Lady Serena may as well have said *bed* as *carriage*, given her suggestive tone, but then subtle courtesans starved, didn't they? If Lady Serena had been casting her lures at anyone but Oliver, Dinah might have even felt a twinge of sympathy for her.

Oliver laughed, then turned back to Dinah with an impatient look. "Shall we go, Miss Bishop?"

"No, I don't need a ride tonight. I told Miss Ward I'd walk home with her. I just came out to tell you." Dinah waved a hand toward his carriage when Oliver hesitated. "Go on, then. I'm more than capable of making my way home myself."

Oliver frowned, then turned without a word and strode into the street and hailed a hack. He reached up to press a few coins into the driver's hand, then opened the carriage door and beckoned to Dinah. "You can drop Miss Ward on your way home."

"Do come along, my lord. The hazard tables await." Lady Serena crooked a black, silk-clad finger at Oliver.

Dinah scowled. Hazard? Surely Oliver wasn't gaming?

He didn't give her a chance to ask. "Good night then, Miss Bishop." He bowed, then bounded over his own carriage and squeezed into the seat next to Lady Serena.

Dinah glared daggers at the carriage as it rattled away.

Oh, no. This wouldn't do. This wouldn't do at all.

Tomorrow, she'd write to Penelope and warn her Lady Serena Howard was angling to get her hooks into Oliver. Lord Archer would know best what should be done. It was possible Oliver was just dallying with her ladyship for an evening, but one didn't like to let such a situation get out of hand.

Someone had to save Oliver from succumbing to his baser instincts.

It may as well be her.

CHAPTER 2

MAYFAIR, LONDON, DECEMBER 26TH

*I*n Dinah's opinion, most of life's problems could be solved with a clever plan, a cool head and a steady hand. Failing that, a lady with precise aim could always resort to a pistol.

The trouble was, Oliver Angel wasn't one of those problems.

She was out of clever plans, and her normally cool head was a bubbling quagmire of frustration. She hadn't tried the pistol, but it was early yet, so she couldn't rule it out. If ever there was a gentleman who could drive a lady to bloodshed, it was Oliver.

She trudged up the steps leading to the closed door of Lord Archer's elegant mansion and paused at the top to peer down Curzon Street. There wasn't a single soul to be seen. No leaping lords or milking maids. No partridges lazing about in pear trees, disturbing the silence with their tedious melody.

They didn't dare. This was Mayfair, after all. Boxing Day would just have to wait for the *ton* to rise and take notice of it, just as everything else in London did.

Dinah no longer had the luxury of time. Since Oliver had taken up with Lady Serena and Lord Erskine a month ago, he'd returned to his wicked ways with a vengeance. The *ton* didn't know whether to be scandalized or delighted by their Tainted Angel, but Lord Archer had run out of patience with his younger brother's antics.

Today, Oliver's debauchery was coming to an end.

Dinah grasped the knocker and let it crash against the wood with a resounding thump. It wasn't as dramatic as a pistol shot, but it would have to do. She winced a little as the thud echoed from the marble floors to the gilded ceiling inside, shattering the silence.

Oliver wasn't expecting her, and he wasn't going to be pleased to see her. It was early enough he'd likely just found his bed an hour or two ago. His bed, or someone else's.

Lady Serena's, for instance.

Dinah grimaced. She didn't fancy the idea of dragging Oliver out of Lady Serena's arms, but he'd promised his family he'd leave London for Essex today. Dinah had come to see to it he kept that promise.

If anyone else had asked Dinah to drag a rake from his bed, she'd have scowled them right out of countenance, but it wasn't anyone else. It was Penelope, and her distress had been plain in every sentence of her last letter.

He listens to you, Dinah. If anyone can get him on his way to Cliff's Edge, it's you.

Dinah wasn't so sure. She and Oliver had hardly spoken this past month. She'd seen him at the Pandemonium a few times, but he seemed always to be taken up with Lady Serena and Lord Erskine. He still sent a hack to collect Dinah after every performance, but he no longer came himself.

Which was just as it should be. No good would come of her expecting him always to be there, waiting for her. Oliver might do as he liked, and in any case, she preferred riding alone. Of course, she did.

Only...

She worried at a loose button on her cloak. He'd only taken up with Lady Serena and resumed his wild antics *after* Dinah had pushed him away. Oliver had been more saint than devil up until then. She'd meant it for his own good, but then he'd fallen right into Lady Serena's arms, and—

Blast it. She'd twisted her button off! Dinah tugged at the frayed thread, then shoved the button into her pocket.

Nonsense. This wasn't *her* fault. No one had forced Oliver to take Lady Serena to his bed. If he chose to drink, wager and keep a poisonous mistress, then he could accept the consequences.

But what if those consequences should prove more dire than he anticipated? Oliver had nearly been killed in a duel last year and judging by the frantic tone of Penelope's last letter, his family was terrified his recent riotous behavior would lead him into another.

If the worst should happen, if Oliver did get into another duel and it turned deadly—

No. It was unthinkable. He must go to Cliff's Edge. With any luck once he was there, he'd remain for a time. Penelope had written that a young lady Oliver admired—a Miss Caroline Spence—had recently returned to the neighborhood. Perhaps her presence would entice Oliver to stay in Essex, far away from Lady Serena's grasping talons.

But first, Dinah had to get him out the door and into the coach. She grasped the knocker again, but before the brass could meet the wood, she heard the muffled sound of footsteps. The door swung open, and Hugo Grimsley's face appeared in the gap.

He blanched when he saw her. "Oh, dear. That is, I beg your pardon, Miss Bishop, but Lord Oliver is, er... indisposed. Will you come back during calling hours?"

Dinah snorted. "Calling hours, Grim? Come, you know better than that."

"Please, Miss Bishop, I beg you—"

"Where is he?" Dinah wedged her foot into space between the door and the frame, pushed past Grim and marched toward the stairs. "Never mind. I'll start with his bedchamber."

Grim scurried after her, wringing his hands. "No! Have mercy, Miss Bishop. Lord Oliver had a trying evening last night."

Trying. Yes, Oliver had had a number of trying evenings this past month. Dinah waved a dismissive hand. "Not to worry, Grim. I'm familiar with the results of Lord Oliver's trying evenings."

"Please, Miss Bishop. You can't go up there," Grim squeaked. "Lord Oliver won't like it."

Dinah sighed. "Oh, very well, but only if you bring him down at once. Lord Archer demands his brother come to Cliff's Edge for the holidays. Lord Oliver is meant to leave today, and I'd rather not drag him from his bed."

Grim paled. "*Drag* his lordship?"

"If I must, yes."

Grim turned without another word and scurried up the stairs.

Dinah wandered down the hallway to the study and fell into the chair behind the desk. Good Lord, she was tired. The pantomime was on at the Pandemonium, and she'd been treading the boards until well past midnight. It was a grueling schedule, but Dinah didn't mind it. If she kept busy, the holidays would fly by.

Why, they'll be over before I know it...

She rested her forehead on her folded arms. Perhaps she'd nap for a few minutes, just long enough to gather her resolve in case Oliver proved difficult. Or worse, charming. If Oliver deployed his dimples, she'd need every bit of strength she had to resist them.

Dinah yawned, and closed her eyes.

* * *

"Go 'way." Oliver reached up a hand to swat aside whatever was tickling his ear, then buried his head under his pillow.

"Forgive me, my lord, but, er...it's rather urgent."

"Grim?" Oliver opened one eye, then closed it with a groan. "For the love of God, man, have some mercy and leave me alone."

"Oh, dear. You do sound cross. I beg your pardon, my lord, but—"

"Is the house on fire, Grim? If not, then I don't want to be disturbed."

"I assure you, my lord, the situation is much graver than a mere conflagration. *Miss Bishop* is here, and she's demanding you come down at once."

"Dinah?" Oliver emerged from under his pillow, tried to peel his eyes open, realized one was swollen shut, and gave up on both. "What the devil is Dinah doing here?"

"She says Lord Archer demands you come to Essex for the Christmas holidays, my lord, and that you're meant to leave for Cliff's Edge this morning. She's quite *insistent*, my lord." Grim gulped. "I doubt she'll leave until you see her. You know how Miss Bishop is."

"Yes, Grim. I do." The first time Oliver laid eyes on Dinah Bishop she'd mistaken him for a highwayman. She'd shot at him with a muff pistol and nearly put a ball in his forehead. He, in turn, had fallen madly in love with her. What man could resist a lady with such enchanting blue eyes who was a crack shot into the bargain?

A strange thing, love. It had transformed him from a notorious Tainted Angel into a respectable gentleman, his current disreputable state aside.

Oliver struggled to a sitting position and opened the one eye that still worked. "What I don't understand, Grim, is how she knows I'm meant to be leaving for Cliff's Edge today."

"I suspect Lady Archer told her, my lord." Grim lowered his voice. "Lady Archer and Miss Bishop being as thick as thieves, my lord."

Oliver groaned again. "I'm doomed, Grim." Once Penelope and Dinah started conspiring, a mere mortal man hadn't a prayer of escaping them.

"Doomed, indeed, my lord. You will you go down and restrain...er, see Miss Bishop, my lord?" Grim's voice wasn't quite steady.

Poor Grim was terrified of Dinah, and for good reason. Oliver was enormously fond of Grim, but one couldn't deny his manservant was no more a match for Dinah Bishop than a baby bird was for a clever, hungry cat. "Yes. Help me to dress, won't you, Grim?"

"Yes, my lord." Grim hurried forward, and after a bit of a struggle they retrieved enough of Oliver's scattered clothing to put him in order.

Well, mostly in order. Dinah wasn't the most patient of ladies, and Oliver didn't linger at the glass. "Will I do, Grim?" He studied his reflection. He'd tugged on a pair of breeches, a shirt, and a crumpled waistcoat. His cravat had given way to his fruitless tugging and was decidedly askew. Neither he nor Grim could find his coat, so Oliver had tossed an embroidered silk banyan over the ensemble.

"Very nice, my lord, but your hair is a bit wild." Grim tried to tame it, to no avail.

Oliver squinted into the glass. "Doesn't it always look like that?"

"Not usually quite so...well, never mind." Grim studied him doubtfully. "I hope your wound doesn't start bleeding again, ladies not being keen on blood, my lord."

"True enough. Fetch me a handkerchief, will you?" Oliver grimaced at the gash in his forehead, but he couldn't do a thing about it, or about his swollen jaw and black eye, either. Erskine was a decent enough bloke, but he could be a trifle unreasonable when he was in his cups, and he hadn't taken kindly to Oliver's dragging him away from the hazard table last night.

"Good man, Grim." Oliver took the handkerchief Grim offered him and made his way down the stairs to the study.

He came to a stop just outside the door. Dinah was slumped in his chair, her body limp with sleep, her face pillowed on her arms and a few strands of her dark hair falling loose.

Tenderness welled inside him, and he stood there drinking her in for a moment before clearing his throat. "You've dragged me out of my bed without so much as a by-your-leave, and now I find you dozing in my study? I don't think so, Miss Bishop. If I'm not to be permitted to sleep, then neither are you."

Dinah opened her eyes and blinked owlishly at him. "Nonsense. I wasn't asleep."

Oliver looked into those blue eyes and his heart gave a wild thump. No matter how often he gazed into them, her eyes rendered him speechless every time. When she looked at him as she was doing now, with all her attention fixed on him, it was as if she could see down to the very depths of his soul.

Did she realize her eyes went soft every time she looked at him, and her pulse fluttered in her throat when he smiled at her? She might deny it to herself—she might banish him from her presence—but Oliver would have wagered his last guinea he'd already won her heart.

The trouble was, Dinah either refused to admit it or didn't know it herself, and her opinion was the only one that mattered.

"Oliver! Oh, *no*. What have you done?"

Oliver jerked his attention back to her. "What do you mean, what have I done? Not a deuced thing that I can recall."

"What's happened to your face, you ridiculous man?" She shot to her feet, hurried across the room to him, and turned his face toward her with a gentle nudge of his chin.

"Don't say it's bleeding *again*." Oliver traced a finger over the jagged cut over his left eye. "Grim did warn me ladies weren't keen on blood. Not quite the thing, is it?"

The cut was deep, but his eye was worse. It was swollen closed, and his jaw was so shadowed with bruises it looked as if someone had slammed a boot into it.

Because someone *had*. Lord Erskine, the devil. "Now, don't look at me like that, if you please. It isn't so bad."

"Bad enough!" Dinah released his chin and took a step back, her gaze sweeping over him from head to toe. "Strip off your banyan, please."

Oliver stifled a sigh. If the circumstances were different, he'd have been delighted to hear those words from her lips. "There's no need, I promise you. Do you suppose I'd be standing here if I'd been shot?"

"You're standing here with a head injury, aren't you? If you're telling the truth, then there's no reason for you not to strip off your banyan."

"You're being absurd." Still, Oliver removed the

banyan and held his arms out. "See? Not a single blood-stain or festering wound."

Dinah studied him with narrowed eyes. "Take off your waistcoat, too."

Oliver huffed impatiently, but he unbuttoned the waistcoat, tossed it aside and turned in a circle before her. "Satisfied?" If he was going to strip off his clothes, *someone* should be.

"You promised your brother there'd be no more brawls." Dinah waved her hand at him. "Put your clothes back on, if you please."

"A brawl? It was a mere disagreement, nothing more. A minor difference of opinion between Lord Erskine and myself." It had been a trifle more than minor, but Dinah didn't need to know that.

She sniffed. "You're fortunate Lord Erskine confined his wrath to your face."

"Of course, he did. He despises my face because it's much prettier than his." Oliver fluttered his eyelashes at her.

Dinah snorted. "You may save your charm for a more susceptible lady, my lord."

"Don't be silly, Miss Bishop. You know you're the only lady I want to charm." Oliver slipped his arms back into his waistcoat and gave her an unrepentant grin.

Dinah ignored his flirtation. "What were you arguing with Lord Erskine about?"

"Nothing of any importance."

"Well, there will be no hiding *that* from Lord Archer." Dinah nodded at his face. "I don't envy you that explanation."

"Explanation?" Oliver asked. "I don't intend to explain a damn thing to Will."

"I don't see you have a choice. He'll demand an explanation when you arrive at Cliff's Edge."

"Cliff's Edge? You must be mad. I'm not going to Cliff's Edge." Oliver ambled across the room toward the fireplace, dropped into a plump leather chair and rested his slippered foot on the grate.

Dinah hurried after him. "Of course, you're going. You've already promised you would."

"That was before Lord Erskine made a mess of my face. I can't turn up at Cliff's Edge looking like this. Penelope and Maddy will fret, Christopher will laugh, and William will be furious." Oliver gave an exaggerated shudder. "I'm much better off staying in London."

"You can't stay in London, Oliver." Dinah's voice cracked as her composure began to desert her. "It's the Christmas holidays, and your family wants you at home. I've promised Penelope I'd see to it you leave today."

"Yes, and why is that, Miss Bishop? Do my brother and sister-in-law suppose I require a nanny, and have appointed you to do the job?" Oliver's voice was harsher than he intended, but it rankled that Will and Penelope thought he needed supervision. He'd given them no reason—

"Perhaps they're not pleased with your new choice of mistress."

Oliver frowned. "Mistress? What mis—"

"Lady Serena, Oliver? One might have hoped you'd choose more wisely."

Oliver stared at her, speechless. For God's sake, did they all think he'd taken Lady Serena as his mistress? How in the world could they ever think he'd choose—

His gaze shot to Dinah, who was looking anywhere but at him.

Ah, now it was starting to make sense. He should have guessed it at once. Dinah had told Penelope he'd made Lady Serena his mistress, Penelope had told Will, and now his entire family was in despair over his imminent ruin.

This rankled as well, but he couldn't really blame them. If they supposed he was bedding Lady Serena, it was no wonder Willian had insisted Oliver return to Cliff's Edge. Lady Serena had ruined the health and fortunes of more than one gentleman, and now she had her claws into Erskine.

"You must go to Cliff's Edge, Oliver. I insist on it. I won't leave here until you promise to go."

Dinah's eyes flashed with temper, and Oliver stared at her, transfixed. Those dark blue eyes of hers... damnation. How could she expect him to do anything other than fall in love with her, with those eyes?

But he didn't say so. He couldn't speak to her about love—not until she agreed to listen to him—and if she had her way, that would be never. She'd done a remarkably good job of avoiding him these past few weeks. How was he meant to win her heart if she refused to ever see him?

Dinah was waiting, her foot tapping anxiously. "I'll have your word on this, Oliver."

He stared at her, an idea taking shape in his mind. It wasn't fair—not at all—but he'd happily tolerate a twinge or two of guilt if it meant winning the hand of his chosen lady. Whoever had said desperate times called for desperate measures had surely been in love.

"Perhaps I *could* see fit to go." Oliver tapped a finger against his lips, as if considering it. "That is, under certain conditions."

Dinah gave him a suspicious look. "What conditions?"

Oliver met her gaze, his heart pounding. "I want you to come with me."

Her eyes went wide. "Go to Cliff's Edge with you? You know I can't, Oliver. I've got the pantomime at the

Playhouse. Why, Silas will go mad if I leave on such short notice!"

"Not if you tell him Lord and Lady Archer have summoned you to Essex." Silas Bragg, the manager of the Pandemonium Playhouse would push Dinah out the door himself if he thought it would gain him Will and Penelope's favor. "Every actress in the theater knows your part. He'll find someone else to take it."

"But I can't possibly...I didn't intend...I'm not pre-pared for the trip." Dinah paced from one end of the room to the other, her brow furrowed.

"It would please Lady Archer if you came. I know she pleaded with you to join us at Cliff's Edge for Christmas. Really, Miss Bishop, I don't know how you can refuse her, given how anxious she is about Baby Angel."

Penelope and Will's first child would arrive early in the new year. Until he or she was born, the child was affectionately referred to by all the family as Baby Angel.

Dinah stopped in the middle of the room, a guilty flush rising in her cheeks.

Oliver nearly gave in when he saw that flush, but this wasn't the time to succumb to a fit of the vapors, for God's sake. He braced himself with a deep breath and plunged ahead. "I see you don't like it. Well, no matter. We'll both remain in London, then. Just as well, really. Travel is such a bother."

I nearly have her...

Oliver clasped his hands behind his head and leaned back in his chair, as if didn't matter one way or the other to him, but underneath his casual manner he was holding his breath. Dinah's next words would seal his lonely fate or ensure his future happiness.

Her happiness, as well. He was certain she loved him, even if she wasn't. Until Dinah dared to trust love,

Oliver would just have to trust in it enough for them both.

He waited, a thousand lifetimes passing by as she made her decision. His hopes soared and then crashed with every fleeting expression on her face, until at last she heaved a deep sigh.

"It never ceases to amaze me how you contrive to get your way every time. Very well, I'll go. It's only a day or two, in any case. What difference can a few days make?"

Far more than you can ever imagine.

Indeed, he was counting on it.

Dinah left soon afterwards. A little while later Grim peered cautiously around the study door and let out a relieved breath when he saw she'd gone. "Will you go to Cliff's Edge after all then, my lord?"

"Listening at the door again?" Oliver laughed when Grim flushed bright red. "Tomorrow morning, and you're coming with us. Tell me, Grim. Do I look like a man about to embark on a courtship?"

"A courtship, my lord?"

"Yes, indeed. As soon as the coach door closes behind us, I intend to begin courting Miss Bishop."

"Courtship in a coach, my lord?" Grim looked doubtful. "That isn't the usual sort of thing, is it?"

Oliver grinned. "No, Grim, it isn't. Not at all."

But Dinah Bishop wasn't the usual sort of lady.

CHAPTER 3

LORD OLIVER'S TRAVELING COACH,
EARLY MORNING, DECEMBER 27TH

*T*hey weren't even an hour into their journey before Dinah realized the depths of her folly in letting Oliver cajole her into this scheme.

She turned from the window to study him. He was lounging on the seat across from her, one booted foot dangling across his knee and his arm thrown over the back of the carriage seat. His dark hair was charmingly disheveled, and his dimple flirted at the corner of his mouth with every twitch of his lips, as if it were playing a game of hide-and-seek.

That blasted dimple. She'd always been wary of its potency, but never more so than now, when she was trapped alone in a coach with him.

Best to avoid looking at him altogether—

"If you don't mind my saying so, Miss Bishop, you look as if you could use a little Christmas escapade." Oliver's dimples flashed in a sly smile, as if he'd read her mind and was determined to make her look at him.

Dinah crossed her arms over her chest, nettled. "I don't like Christmas escapades." She didn't care much for escapades at any time of year, escapades being, in her opinion tedious, bothersome things that led more often to disappointment than pleasure.

In the worst cases, they led to disaster.

Oliver waved this objection away. "Everyone likes a Christmas escapade, and in any case, you couldn't send me off to Cliff's Edge alone in my weakened state."

"How are you weakened? You look perfectly fit to me. Not a single festering wound or pistol ball embedded in you anywhere." Oliver looked better than fit. So much better Dinah was obliged to tear her gaze away from the sight of his lean, muscled form.

"Fit! What about my injuries?" He gestured to the cut above his eye. "It still bleeds now and then, you know. Really, how can you be so hard-hearted?"

Dinah rolled her eyes. She wasn't hard-hearted enough, otherwise she wouldn't be in the coach with him at all. "I'm here, aren't I?"

"You are, indeed, and we'll have a merry enough time together as long as you're prepared to indulge my every whim."

"It's only a day's journey, my lord. I doubt we'll have time to indulge them all."

"May I choose the ones we do indulge?" Oliver asked, his lips quirking in a lazy smile.

Dinah's gaze wandered to those hypnotic dimples again and a resigned sigh left her lips. If she wasn't careful, she might well find herself indulging his every whim.

Very well, then. It was back to not looking at him.

She turned her face to the window and watched as Tottenham gave way to Palmer's Green, and Palmer's Green to Enfield. The sumptuous velvet seats cradled her exhausted limbs, and the monotonous swaying rocked her until her eyelids grew heavy and she leaned her head against the glass.

"Yes, that's it. You'll feel much better after a rest." Oliver's voice was low and soothing. There was a faint rustle, then he tucked something soft and warm around her shoulders. The last thing she remembered before she drifted off to sleep was gentle fingers brushing her hair back from her face.

She woke from a peaceful doze much later, a startled cry on her lips. Her head was fuzzy with sleep, and it was some moments before she realized she'd been thrust into wakefulness with a hard jolt.

She'd had a dream she was falling…

Where was she? Not in her bed. It was far too warm and comfortable. Quiet, too, without the usual shouts and curses from the street below, and not even a hint of the dusty smell of damp and mildew that always assaulted her upon waking.

Instead it smelled divine, like vanilla and cedar with a touch of citrus. Dinah's nose twitched with pleasure as she inhaled the familiar scent. It was J Floris's *Malmaison*—she'd know it anywhere, because it reminded her of—

Oliver.

Yes, of course. She remembered now. She'd gone to Mayfair yesterday morning to fetch Oliver, he'd come down looking as if he'd been trampled by a horse, and the next thing she knew, she'd agreed to go to Cliff's Edge with him. They were in the coach on their way there now.

She wasn't sure how he'd talked her into it, but then Oliver was very, very good at coaxing. He could wheedle the feathers from a bird, the cream from a cat—

"Shall I return you to your seat, or would you prefer to remain where you are?" A husky voice rumbled nearby, and soft breath tickled her ear. "You're quite welcome to stay."

Stay? Yes, perhaps she would. She quite liked it here. Something warm and solid was wrapped around her, and her cheek was resting on a pillow of fresh linen.

She tilted her head back and saw a white cravat tied neatly under a strong, angular jaw shaded with a faint trace of bristly black hair.

Black hair? What—

Dinah's eyes snapped wide open, the last vestiges of sleep evaporating. She wasn't just in the coach with Oliver—she was on his *lap*—and her cheek wasn't resting on a pillow—it was resting on his *chest*.

Dinah leapt free of his arms as if her skirts had caught fire. She shot him a baleful look once she was safely on her side of the carriage, but Oliver only gave her an innocent grin. "I beg your pardon. We had a bit of a jolt. I was obliged to catch you before you tumbled off your seat."

"I see. Were you obliged to wrap your arms around me, too?"

"I thought you might be cold. You were shivering," Oliver replied, looking affronted.

Dinah pinched her lips together. For a gentleman who was so frequently up to mischief, he certainly managed to look incredulous when he was accused of it. "Why have we stopped?"

She peered out her window. It was later than she'd expected—well into the afternoon already, and a light snow was drifting down from the sky.

"The coachman was obliged to stop for a rather stubborn herd of cows who insisted upon taking up the whole of the passable bit of the road."

Dinah frowned. "I don't see any cows."

"Well, no. Not anymore. They've gone on their way, but Rundell & Bridge aren't fond of cows, and they don't care for this coachman. They're refusing to go." Oliver's head coachman had been given leave to visit his family for the holidays, so they had a hired coachman on the box.

82

"Rundell and Bridge? You named your horses after the London jewelers?"

"Yes, because they're as perfect as a matched set of pearls. Now the cows have cleared off, I daresay we'll be on our way as soon as the horses are over their fit of temper."

Dinah glanced out the window again. They should be near Chelmsford by now, but the road didn't look familiar. "Where are we? I don't recognize this road."

"We're in Plumstead." Oliver grinned with delight, as if Plumstead were the only place in the world anyone would care to be on a snowy afternoon in December.

"Plumstead? Cliff's Edge is in *Essex*, Oliver. What are we doing in *Kent*?"

"Alistair Rutherford lives in Kent," Oliver said, as if this explained everything.

Dinah stared at him. "I'm pleased for Alistair Rutherford, but what are *we* doing here?"

Oliver sighed, as if she were being very troublesome. "Rutherford's Scottish, you see—from Bowmore. He fetched a cask of whisky for me last time he was there, and I've come to collect it."

"You couldn't secure a cask of whisky in London?"

"Not Rutherford's whisky, and his is the best. It's a Christmas gift for Christopher. Do you think he'll like it?"

Lord Christopher had a bit of a wild streak, just like his two elder brothers. Lord Christopher with a cask of whisky at his disposal was sure to lead to a debacle. "I think he'll be delighted with it. Whether Lord Archer will think it's as delightful is less certain."

"I've arranged for gifts for everyone." Oliver stretched his long legs out in front of him and leaned back against the squabs with a comfortable grunt, the tips of his boots brushing her hems.

Dinah jerked her skirts back.

Christmas gifts sounded innocent enough. *Too* innocent. "What are you up to, Oliver?"

"Me? Why, not a thing. I just have a stop or two on our way to Cliff's Edge to fetch a few gifts. That doesn't sound too wicked, does it? I even have a gift for you, Miss Bishop."

Dinah stiffened. It had been years since she'd received a gift for Christmas. She never expected any, and it was best to keep it that way. "I don't want any gifts."

"Nonsense. Everyone wants gifts for Christmas. I wouldn't dream of appearing at Cliff's Edge empty-handed." He gave her a reproachful look. "There's no need to look so put-upon. Plumstead isn't so *very* far out of our way."

"It's *south* of London, Oliver. Cliff's Edge is *north*." It was more than an hour out of their way, and another hour to get back on the road toward Chelmsford.

Oliver shrugged, as if two hours was too insignificant to warrant a second thought. "I can't imagine why you're making such a fuss. We'll be back on the road and on our way to Cliff's Edge soon enough."

It couldn't be soon enough for Dinah. For reasons she didn't care to examine, it made her nervous to be alone in the coach with him. He was too...too...enticing, not to mention devious. If she'd known her nap would lead to a detour to Kent, she never would have—

Dinah jerked upright in her seat and fixed Oliver with an accusing glare. "No wonder you were so anxious for me to fall asleep! You lured me into a nap so you could whisk us off to Plumstead without my having a chance to protest!"

Oliver raised an eyebrow. "*Lured*? My, you are suspicious, aren't you? It was nothing so nefarious as that.

You were fatigued, so I encouraged you to rest. That's all."

Dinah subsided against the cushioned seat with a huff. "I suppose I should be grateful you didn't drag me all the way to Scotland to fetch Lord Christopher's whisky."

"Scotland? Don't be ridiculous. We're going south, but only as far as Sittingbourne."

"*Sittingbourne?* That'll take ages!" Dinah hadn't meant to let out quite such a screech, but before she could apologize the horses leapt forward with a start, and just like that they were moving again.

Oliver beamed at her. "Well done, Miss Bishop! I didn't realize you were capable of such a shriek. We'll have to remember that the next time Rundell and Bridge refuse to move."

Next time? Dear God, how often did it happen? Between Oliver and his high-strung horses, a simple journey from London to Essex was turning into a days' long scamper across the English countryside.

She was as foolish as every other lady in London, letting Oliver Angel cajole her into this as if she were a bird-witted debutante. She let out another huff, but the dark emotion swelling in her breast didn't feel like anger.

It felt like fear.

There were times when she thought Oliver could talk her into anything.

* * *

IF OLIVER HAD REALIZED a shriek would get the horses moving again, he would have mentioned Sittingbourne an hour ago. If Rundell and Bridge had gotten over their snit sooner, there might still be a chance they'd reach Cliff's Edge tonight.

As it was, it didn't look promising.

Oliver glanced out the window and a grimace twisted his lips. Darkness would fall soon, and there was the smell of more snow in the air.

A brief stop in Plumstead had seemed safe enough. If an English gentleman wanted fine Scottish whisky, he went to see Alistair Rutherford. It was as simple as that.

But what had seemed simple at the outset was turning more complicated by the moment. Alistair Rutherford was a kindly fellow, the sort who'd insist on their staying the night if the weather proved uncooperative, but Oliver would have to find some way to explain Dinah's presence in his carriage.

He'd be damned if she was mistaken for his mistress. Dinah might not think of herself as a lady, but Oliver did. He wouldn't have her insulted, but an unmarried lady traveling alone in a coach with a man who, despite having given up his profligate ways was still regarded in some circles as a Tainted Angel? No, that wouldn't do. Oliver was going to have to conjure up a chaperone for her, but chaperones, alas, were scarce on the ground in Plumstead.

There was only one thing for it, but it was going to be a tricky bit of business.

When they reached Rutherford Hall, he handed Dinah down from the carriage and motioned to Grim to follow them. He rapped smartly on the door, and after a brief delay Rutherford himself appeared. When he saw Oliver, a smile spread over his face. "Well, Angel! How do you do?"

Rutherford was holding a little girl by the hand. She was six or seven years old, with wide brown eyes fixed curiously on the visitors. One of Rutherford's many grandchildren, no doubt. He'd been married for thirty years to a pink-cheeked, white-haired lady who'd borne him eight children. Those eight children had gone on to give their proud parents twelve grandchildren.

Twelve, and counting.

"Come in, come in. You'll catch a chill standing there." Rutherford waved them inside. A half-dozen laughing imps were running about the entryway, there was a scent of spiced apples in the air, and fresh greenery was piled on every surface. Rutherford Hall was, in short, the essence of holiday cheer.

"Here for Lord Christopher's whisky, are you?" Alistair Rutherford gave Oliver a hearty slap on the back. "Good day," he added, beaming at Dinah and Grim.

Oliver took Dinah's arm and drew her forward. "This is Miss Bishop, my lord, a dear friend of the Countess of Archer's, and of the entire Angel family."

"Is she, then? Well, Miss Bishop, any friend of the Angels is more than welcome at Rutherford Hall. Good lot they are, if a bit riotous, eh?"

Before Dinah could answer, Oliver hauled Grim forward. "This gentleman is Miss Bishop's brother. Mr. Bishop is accompanying us to Cliff's Edge to chaperone his sister. Aren't you, Mr. Bishop?"

Oliver sensed Dinah stiffen in shock at this blatant lie, but he was staring hard at Grim, his eyebrows raised. If there was the least bit of consciousness on Grim's face, their ruse was finished.

Grim had his flaws, but he could think quickly when the situation required it. "I, er...yes, indeed I am. My sister, Mr. Rutherford. Fond of her, you know." He gave Dinah's arm a clumsy pat.

Oliver turned to wink at Dinah. Her cheeks pinkened, and his lips curved. He'd never seen her blush. She looked prettier with that fetching wash of color on her cheeks than he'd ever seen her look before. If he *had* felt just a twinge of guilt at dragging her to Plumstead—and he wasn't saying he *did*—it evaporated like dew after sunrise at the sight of that blush.

"Shall we have some refreshment before we descend to the cellars? It's a cold day, what? Tea will warm you. Do you fancy some tea, Mathilda?" Rutherford smiled down at the little girl still clutching his hand.

Mathilda paused to give this question the gravest consideration. "Will there be cakes?"

"Will there be cakes? Why, my dear child, have you ever known us to have tea without cakes? Run along now and fetch the others, there's a good girl."

Rutherford chuckled as Mathilda scurried off on a pair of chubby little legs. "I hope you don't mind an informal tea," he said to them as he led them through the entryway into a spacious drawing room. "We gave that up after the twelfth grandchild learned to walk."

Informal wasn't the word Oliver would use to describe tea at Rutherford Hall.

It was bloody chaos.

They hadn't yet raised their teacups to their lips before they were set upon by a swarm of children of various ages, all of them demanding cakes. Dozens of pattering feet ran from one end of the room to the other, and a quartet of tiny black kittens gamboled about, pouncing on the cake crumbs that fell in the children's wake.

The noise was unholy, with everyone shouting at once. Oliver had never enjoyed himself more, but he cast a few anxious glances at Dinah, who sat amidst the tumult, her brow furrowed, as if she'd found herself in a foreign country and didn't know what to make of it. Not surprising, since taking tea with a family like the Rutherfords would be no more familiar to her than taking tea with the queen.

"Let's see to your whisky, shall we, Angel?" Rutherford said, rising to his feet when tea gave way to a haphazard game of charades. "I've set aside a cask for Lord Christopher, but I thought you and Mr. Bishop might like to have a wander through the cellars."

"I'd enjoy that. Is that agreeable, Bishop?"

Grim seemed to think this was an occasion that called for a formal bow and bent awkwardly at the waist. "I can't imagine anything more delightful."

Oliver hid his grin. "Very good, Mr. Bishop. Miss Bishop? Do you fancy a wander through the cellars, or will you—"

He stopped short, one eyebrow inching up.

Rutherford's granddaughter Mathilda had grasped a fold of Dinah's skirt, and Dinah was staring down at the child as if she were trying to work out what sort of creature Mathilda might be.

"Oh, no. She must come with me and play with the kittens. You will come, won't you?" Mathilda clung to Dinah's skirts and gazed up at her with pleading brown eyes.

"I...well, I...yes, I suppose I will." Dinah darted a quick glance at Oliver, but she let the child led her by the hand toward the parlor.

Oliver, Rutherford and Grim descended to the cellars. Rutherford was proud of his collection, and they spent quite some time ambling about, pausing now and again as Lord Rutherford pointed out some of his rarer bottles, and held forth on the topics of fermentation and malted mash.

When they returned to the parlor, they found Mathilda chattering away to Dinah in that way young children do when they've found a favorite. Oliver couldn't hear everything Mathilda said, but she seemed to be talking of the black kittens and listing off their names to Dinah.

Dinah said very little, but she sat calmly on the floor

beside Mathilda, one of the kittens curled up in her lap, listening quietly as the child prattled on.

"We've finished in the cellars, Miss Bishop." Oliver offered Dinah his hand.

Dinah scooped up the kitten in her lap and placed it gently in Mathilda's hands. "Thank you for sharing your kittens with me, Mathilda." She nestled her fingertips in Oliver's palm. He drew her to her feet, his hand tingling from the slide of her skin against his.

Rutherford led them to the entryway, a servant following behind with the cask of whisky, but when they opened the door, they were nearly knocked off their feet by a blast of cold air. The temperature had dropped considerably while they were inside, and just as Oliver had feared, plump white flakes of snow were falling from the sky.

"Well now, we can't send you and your friends out in this weather, Angel." Rutherford shook his head at the gray clouds. "It's nearly dark, and there's no telling how much snow we'll have."

"Oh, but we can't stay! We told Lady Archer we'd arrive tonight." Dinah glanced up at the sky, her teeth worrying her lower lip.

"Better to arrive late than not at all, my dear." Rutherford gave Dinah's hand a reassuring pat. "You're very welcome to stay here tonight."

Grim cleared his throat loftily. "Indeed, sister, we must stay. Our dear mother will never forgive me if I risk your safety."

There wasn't much Dinah could say to that, but she turned a look on Grim that made him flinch. "Since you insist on it, *brother*, of course we'll stay, and hope for a better day tomorrow."

CHAPTER 4

PLUMSTEAD, ENGLAND, DECEMBER
28TH

"*W*hat do you think, Grim? When Miss Bishop asks, should I say we...Grim? For God's sakes, man. What ails you?" Oliver paused beside the coach and frowned up at his manservant.

Poor Grim was looking a trifle green.

Grim cast a wary look over his shoulder before shifting his attention to Oliver. "I beg your pardon, my lord. I thought you were Miss Bishop."

"No. Miss Bishop is a good deal smaller than me, and she's generally wearing skirts rather than breeches, what with her being female. I can certainly understand how you'd confuse us, however."

Oliver grinned to show he was teasing, but Grim was preoccupied with scrutinizing his surroundings from his vantage point on the box, and didn't notice. "Yes, my lord. It's just that Miss Bishop is cross with me, and I don't like to be caught unawares, Miss Bishop being a mite...*unpredictable* when she's cross."

"Oh, I shouldn't worry if I were you, Grim. She isn't likely to harm her only brother, is she?"

This didn't seem to comfort Grim. He remained vigilant, as if he expected Dinah to leap out from the shadows at any moment and shove him from the box.

"Your attention please, Grim, if you'd be so kind. Now, when Miss Bishop asks, should I refer to our journey today as an adventure, a caper, or a frolic?" Oliver wasn't usually so unsure of himself, but courtships were a delicate matter, and this one more than most.

"Didn't you settle on escapade, my lord? I'm sure I heard Miss Bishop grumbling about an escapade."

"I did, but Miss Bishop has informed she doesn't care for escapades. I suppose that leaves adventure out too, doesn't it? A lady who doesn't care for escapades isn't like to approve of adventures, either. A Christmas revel? A romp, an exploit?" No, exploit wouldn't do. It had a touch of the hedonistic about it.

"A lark, my lord?" Grim asked. "I can't speak for Miss Bishop, but I'm fond of a good lark, myself."

"A lark." Oliver rolled the word around in his mouth, then nodded in approval. "A lark, yes. It's an innocent, childlike word, isn't it? You're brilliant, Grim."

Grim flushed with pleasure. "Yes, my lord. Thank you, my lord."

Dinah hadn't been pleased to discover Oliver wished to go so far south, and he expected she'd demand an explanation from him this morning, but when Dinah emerged from Rutherford Hall, she didn't spare Grim a glance, and she gave Oliver only a distracted nod.

It was early still, but the hour and the bite in the air hadn't prevented Rutherford and a half-dozen of his grandchildren from bustling into the drive to see them off. Dinah hurried to scramble into the carriage, but Mathilda ran after her, caught Dinah's skirts in her chubby fist and refused to let go until Dinah accepted a kiss.

As soon as the coach door closed behind them Oliver opened his mouth to defend the journey south, but Dinah never asked. She didn't say a single word. He might have been riding in the coach alone for all the attention she paid him.

Well, this wouldn't do. He'd rather deal with her anger than this distant silence. "You're preoccupied this morning, Miss Bishop. What's made you so pensive?" he asked, hoping to pry open the floodgates of her wrath.

It didn't work. "Am I pensive?" she asked in surprise.

Oliver frowned. She wasn't acting like herself. "Yes. Is it Grim? Are you still cross with him?"

She gave him a blank look. "No. Why should I be cross with Grim?"

"Well, he did pretend to be your brother, and he was a trifle high-handed, as brothers go."

"Oh, *that*. No, no. That was your doing, not his. If I should be cross with anyone, it's you."

"Are you cross with me?" If so, he'd just as soon she admitted it and took him to task so they could get past it.

"Not really, no." She looked taken aback, then shrugged. "Curious, isn't it?"

"What is it, then? You don't need to worry about the horses taking a fit again." After hearing about the debacle with the cows the day before, Rutherford had ordered his own coachman, Ferris, to drive them to Sittingbourne, and then back to Plumstead.

"It was kind of Mr. Rutherford to offer his coachman, wasn't it?"

"Yes, yes, very kind." Oliver shifted impatiently against the seat. He didn't care for this calm, reasonable version of Dinah. "You can't have any complaint about our host. Rutherford's a lively, merry soul, just the sort of fellow one likes to visit during the holidays. I've never seen a more cheerful, obliging family."

"Not a single complaint. They're lovely, and their home is..." Dinah hesitated, then blurted, "It's like a Christmas painting come to life."

A Christmas painting come to life? That was a whimsical description, especially for Dinah, who wasn't one to indulge in whimsy. There'd been a yearning note in her voice, as well. She'd sounded almost...wistful. Oliver studied her with a frown. There was something off about her, some expression on her face he couldn't decipher—

He froze as it dawned on him what it was.

Sadness. She looked *sad*.

The day before, when they'd taken tea, she'd seemed bewildered, as if she didn't know what to make of the joyful tumult around her. Then afterwards, when Mathilda had taken her hand, she'd looked almost frightened, as if those little fingers would somehow drag her down into an abyss.

Oliver couldn't think of a better place on earth for her to experience the wonder and childlike happiness of Christmas than Rutherford Hall, but mightn't Dinah have seen it differently? Perhaps it didn't seem like a blessing to her so much as a false promise, a fragile glass bubble destined to shatter.

She never talked about her family, but Oliver knew her Christmases hadn't been filled with warmth and laughter, with sugar plums and kissing balls. He wanted those things for her—not just for a single, fleeting moment, but for a lifetime. If Dinah would let him, he'd share his joy with her. If only she could find the courage to reach out her hands and grasp it, it would be hers.

But how did one grasp a thing they didn't know they wanted? A thing they'd never had, and no longer even hoped to have? Oliver had always regarded hope as a glorious thing, but his hopes hadn't been crushed again and again. How many times could one be disappointed before hope became a sharp, jagged thing? How long before it became so painful to hope one simply gave it up forever?

He glanced across to the seat where Dinah was sitting, her cheek pressed to the window and her eyes closed. "What's troubling you, Miss Bishop? You'll feel better if we get to the heart of it."

Dinah must have heard something in his voice—some compassion or tenderness, because her entire body stiffened. Her eyes flew open and she offered him a blank stare. "I don't know what you mean. Nothing's troubling me."

"Miss Bishop—"

"I'm fatigued, that's all."

Ah, so that was how it was going to be, was it? If the only way forward was to open a crack in her façade and let whatever was inside ooze out, so be it. He'd rather it oozed all over the damn coach and spoiled the lovely velvet upholstery than fester inside Dinah like poison.

As luck would have it, he was quite good at teasing a person into a temper. He had two brothers, after all. "I'll help you, shall I? Is it the fine wine we drank at dinner last night? The evening spent round the pianoforte, singing Christmas carols? Or was it the dozens of laughing children that upset you?"

Dinah's only answer was resounding silence.

He tutted when she didn't reply. "Perhaps it was all that irritatingly fresh greenery scattered everywhere. I loathe the scent of fresh pine, don't you?"

Dinah pressed her lips together as if to bite back a sharp retort.

Ah, yes. This was working nicely.

"Was it the black kittens that offended you so grievously? Nasty things, what with the soft fur and the warmth and the purring—"

"Stop it, my lord. You're being ridiculous," Dinah gritted out through clenched teeth.

"I know!" Oliver snapped his fingers, as if he'd figured it out. "It was Mathilda Rutherford, wasn't it?"

Dinah glared at him. "Hush, will you? It's nothing to do with her."

"Children are tedious, and particularly one so unpleasant as that!" Oliver went on, as if she hadn't spoken. "A *kiss*, of all ridiculous things. For God's sake, the child hardly knows you! What does the girl mean, going about kissing strangers? Why do her parents allow it? No good can come from such rash friendliness."

Dinah's throat worked, and an irritated flush spread over her cheeks.

Nearly there...

"Those wide brown eyes, and that gap-toothed smile!" Oliver added with an exaggerated shudder. "I wonder you didn't refuse to present your cheek."

"I don't care for children, that's all," she snapped.

Oliver was quiet for a moment, then he murmured, "I saw your face, Miss Bishop. When Mathilda Rutherford asked you for a kiss, I saw your face."

"What of it? I told you, I don't care for—"

"I saw your face," Oliver repeated softly. "It didn't look to me as if you didn't care for her. Just the opposite. Lie to me if you must, but don't lie to yourself."

"You didn't see anything." Dinah's voice rose. "You got a vivid imagination, that's all."

"No." He shook his head. "No one's imagination is that vivid. Why do you say things you don't mean?"

She stared at him, her face as pale as death. For the first time Oliver could remember, she looked frightened. "I don't...I can't—"

"Yes, you can." Oliver reached out and took her hand. "One thing, Miss Bishop. Tell me one true thing. That's enough for now."

He waited with his breath held. Just one small crack was all he needed—one tiny fracture in that shell she hid behind where he could creep in and open a space for himself in her heart.

"I did sleep well last night." Dinah's voice was small, but her gaze met his. "Mathilda gave me one of the kittens to take to bed with me, but it was crying, and I thought it must be cold, so I picked it up and put it on my chest. It burrowed under my chin, curled up against my neck and fell asleep. I don't think it...*she*, that is... was cold, after all. I think she just wanted to feel my pulse beating, so she knew she wasn't alone."

Alone. Her face, when she said that word...

A lump rose in Oliver's throat and lodged there, choking off his breath. "Did you have kittens when you were a little girl?"

"There were kittens at one point, I think. I was very young at the time—so young I don't know how I even remember it. There was a gray tabby cat, quite wild, and she gave birth to four black kittens in our barn. They were lovely little things." Dinah's fingers flexed, as if she were recalling the warmth of their soft fur, the vibration of their purr against her fingertips.

He squeezed her hand. "What became of them?"

"I'm not sure. I brought them bits of food until they got old enough to hunt, and I suppose they became barn cats." She frowned as she tried to remember. "I don't recall, really. My father left soon after that, and we lost the farm. Those kittens were the closest thing I ever had to a pet."

"Perhaps you'll have another someday. Until then, I think you'll enjoy the Christmas gift I chose for Will."

Some of the pain drained from her face, and she offered him a weak smile. "Don't say you've gotten him a passel of kittens for Christmas."

Oliver smiled back at her. "No, a hunting dog. Well, he's a pup now, but someday he'll be a hunting dog."

Her tentative smile blossomed into such a delighted grin if Oliver had had the pup in his hands just then, he would have given it to her, his brother be damned.

"What sort of dog is he?"

"You'll see for yourself soon enough." Oliver nodded toward the window. "We're neatly in Dartford."

CHAPTER 5

DARTFORD, ENGLAND

*L*ord Archer's new hunting dog was a springer spaniel with soft, floppy ears and a brown and white spotted nose. He gazed at Dinah with sorrowful blue eyes, his chin balanced on Oliver's knee.

He was smaller than she'd thought he'd be—larger than a teapot, but much smaller than a sack of flour. Dinah eyed him from her corner of the coach. She didn't know much about puppies, but this one seemed remarkably composed.

"He has blue eyes. I've never seen a springer spaniel with blue eyes." They were a most unusual color—velvety lapis centers surrounded by a ring of cerulean. They were the prettiest blue eyes Dinah had ever seen.

"All springer pups have blue eyes. They'll change as he gets older, much like a baby's eyes do. He's a fine pup, isn't he?" Oliver chuckled as the puppy nipped at his fingers. "He'll make a fit hunting dog for an earl."

"He's, ah…well, he's quite small, isn't he?" Dinah frowned at the pup. He stared back at her with a mournful expression, as if he were very put-upon, indeed. She couldn't imagine why he should look so desolate, enthroned on Oliver's lap as he was, with Oliver's big, gentle hands stroking his head. "What's his name?"

"He doesn't have one yet. I thought I'd let my brother name him. I hope William approves of him." Oliver had been looking down at the pup, crooning nonsense to it, but now he glanced up at Dinah, his own blue eyes bright with excitement.

Dinah swallowed. Perhaps the puppy's eyes weren't *quite* the prettiest blue eyes she'd ever seen. She watched the rhythmic movement of Oliver's hands, the slow glide of his long fingers over the pup's silky fur.

She might have watched for hours, mesmerized, if Oliver hadn't startled her back to herself with his low chuckle. "He's a little bit of a thing now, but he'll grow, and make a capital bird dog. Will's been going on about wanting a hunting dog for ages."

"Don't they have hunting dogs in London?" As soon as she said it Dinah frowned, annoyed with herself. Why was she was making such a fuss over Oliver's fetching a few Christmas gifts for his family? It wasn't as if he'd taken them that far out of their way. Dartford was only eight miles south of Plumstead.

"Not like this one. Lord Dunton's gamekeeper, John Massie is known throughout England for his springers. His dogs are the best. Every gentleman in London wants one, but Dunton is notoriously possessive of them. He won't part with his dogs for a king's ransom."

"If he's so stingy, how did you get this one?"

Oliver's eyes twinkled. "Won a king's ransom from Dunton at whist one night at White's. I offered to return his vowels in exchange for a pup. William's going to be so pleased. Even in his fondest imaginings he wouldn't dream he'd ever get one of Massie's pups."

Dinah tried not to let herself melt, but with those two pairs of lovely blue eyes gazing at her and the sweet smile on Oliver's face, even her flinty heart shuddered on its foundations.

She'd resisted dozens of engaging smiles since she

came to London four years ago. She'd sent a number of handsome, charming rogues on their way without a twinge of regret, but there was far more to Oliver Angel than a handsome face and a charming manner.

London might gossip all they liked about him. They might gasp over his antics and shake their heads over his sins. They might whisper behind their hands about his brawls and wagering, but when Dinah looked at Oliver, she didn't see a Tainted Angel. She saw how truly kind he was, how deeply he loved.

That was the trouble, wasn't it? That was why she kept fussing over the delays on their way to Cliff's Edge. It was easy enough to avoid Oliver in London, but they'd been alone together in this coach for little more than a day, and already her heart was fraying at the edges. The longer the journey took, the worse it would become. She was in danger of forgetting he was her friend only—a man she was fond of, but not *too* fond.

Lie to me if you must, but don't lie to yourself.

"Miss Bishop? Are you ill? You've the strangest expression on your face."

Oliver's voice was unexpectedly gentle. To Dinah's horror, tears pricked behind her eyes, and she rushed into speech to stop them from falling. "You've gone to some trouble arranging gifts for your family. Gifts you clearly intended to retrieve on your way from London to Cliff's Edge. You never intended to remain in London for the holidays, did you, Oliver?"

He continued to stroke the puppy's head, but his gaze held Dinah's. "No. I would have delayed the journey for several days to give my injuries time to heal, but I would have gone to Cliff's Edge sooner or later."

Dinah let out a deep sigh. A part of her had hoped

he'd lie about it so she could scold him. It was safer when she scolded. "You lied to me, then."

"Yes." Something flickered in his eyes. Not regret, but something else.

"Why?" Dinah tried to be outraged, but the familiar anger she'd grown to depend on refused to respond to her prodding.

He was quiet for so long she gave up on getting an answer, but then he muttered, "You wouldn't have come with me otherwise."

Yes, I would.

If Oliver had asked it of her, she would have come. A part of her wanted to say so, to blurt out the truth and feel relief overwhelm the tightness in her chest, but once she told it, there would be no taking it back. "We'll never know now, will we?"

A slight smile drifted across Oliver's lips, but he didn't look happy when he murmured, "Is it really so awful to have to spend a few days with me, Dinah?"

His hushed voice, his use of her Christian name, the way his eyes darkened to a deep, midnight blue as he studied her caused a strange, fluttery sensation deep inside Dinah's chest.

No. It isn't awful. That's the trouble.

But again, she wouldn't say so. Instead she pasted a smile on her face and asked brightly, "This Christmas escapade of yours, Oliver. Where will it take us next?"

Dinah half-expected him to balk at the change in topic, but Oliver's lips quirked in a grin. "Yes, about that. I prefer we call it a lark from now on, if you don't mind."

"A lark?" Dinah laughed. "Very well, if you wish, but I don't see what the difference is."

"You told me you don't care for escapades, but there's nothing you can object to in a lark. They're playful, harmless bits of fun."

"Very well, then. Where will this Christmas lark take us next?"

Oliver glanced down at the pup, who'd curled up in his lap and fallen asleep. "To Southfleet, to fetch Maddy's gift."

* * *

HE'D NEARLY TOLD her the truth.

Oliver had vowed to wait until she was ready to hear it. He'd opened his mouth a dozen times since they left London to tell her everything, then closed it again without a word. For all his careful plans and promises to himself, it hadn't taken more than her fleeting look of panic before he'd nearly told Dinah the truth.

He'd nearly said he loved her. That he'd loved her since her pistol ball had come within half an inch of striking his forehead. That it must have struck his heart instead, because he'd lost it to her that day. That when they'd returned to London, he'd followed his heart straight to the Pandemonium Playhouse, and never looked back. That he was full of love he wanted to give her, and he wanted her love in return. That by the time Twelfth Night had passed and the new year was upon them, he wanted her by his side, as his wife.

He might call it a lark, but there was nothing harmless about this courtship. There was every chance his heart would be in tatters by the time they reached Cliff's Edge, and that was to say nothing of their friendship. If Dinah rejected his suit, she'd refuse to see him once they returned to London. If she felt as much for him as he suspected, they'd both be hurt by that.

This courtship would decide nothing less than their future happiness.

If he made of mess of it, he wouldn't get another

chance. He couldn't tip his hand. Not yet. Not until Dinah was ready to hear him—

"This is lovely, Oliver. Maddy will be delighted with it."

Oliver was still shaking at how close he'd come to blurting out the truth, but he jerked his attention back to Mr. Thurman, the jeweler, who'd laid Maddy's locket out on a square of black velvet for Oliver's inspection.

Dinah was bent over it, murmuring with appreciation. "Such dainty etching!" She traced a finger over the delicate vines and flowers carved into the face of the oval locket, sighing at the scattering of seed pearls embedded in the gold. "It's not a new piece, is it?"

"No. It belonged to my grandmother. William and Penelope have been sorting through her jewelry. Penelope has set most of it aside for Maddy. I saw this piece, and thought I'd have it restored as a Christmas gift for her."

Dinah arched a brow, but a smile hovered on her lips. "Naturally you couldn't have turned it over to a London jeweler."

"Certainly not, Miss Bishop. My grandfather commissioned this piece from Mr. Thurman's father, you see, so naturally I couldn't turn it over to anyone but him." Oliver fumbled at the hinge and opened the locket to show Dinah the inside, where the same elegant scrollwork and seed pearls framed the tiny sheets of crystal. "The crystals slide out, so she might put a portrait or a lock of hair inside."

"It's perfect for Maddy." Dinah didn't touch it again, only gazed at it with a rapt expression before turning her attention to the glass cases lining the walls of the shop. She ambled down the row, pausing now and then to admire the jewels inside.

Oliver watched her, an ache in his chest. Sapphires

would suit Dinah. Sapphires set in diamonds, to match her eyes—

"Will the locket do, my lord?"

"What? Oh, yes. As the lady said, it's perfect for my sister. I'd be grateful if you'd wrap it for me, Mr. Thurman." Oliver waved a distracted hand at the jeweler, then turned his attention back to Dinah. She'd stopped beside one of the cases. "What have you there?"

"What? Oh, it's nothing."

Dinah turned away from the case, but Oliver strode toward her and took her arm before she could scurry away. As soon as he glanced into the case, he knew which piece had caught her eye. "The sapphire necklace?"

"Yes. The blue is pretty." Dinah gazed down at it for a moment longer before wandering off, but Oliver lingered, staring down at the necklace. It was simple but stunning, two perfect midnight blue stones set into a delicate gold filigree setting, surrounded by tiny diamonds. There were ear bobs, hair pins and a brooch to match it.

It might have been made for Dinah, with her fine, pale skin and dark blue eyes, but she'd never allow him to make a gift of it to her. Then again, if she did agree to become his wife, he might give it to her on the day of their betrothal.

It was better to be hopeful, surely?

If Mr. Thurman hadn't reappeared just then, Oliver might not have done what he did. If he'd stopped for even a moment to consider the thing rationally, he might have hesitated, but gentlemen in love being what they were—rash, reckless creatures—he didn't.

He waited until Dinah was on the other side of the shop, then he beckoned Mr. Thurman over, pointed silently to the sapphire parure, and nodded. Mr. Thurman, who knew the value of discretion opened the case, whisked out the jewels and disappeared into the back of the shop before Dinah turned around.

Ten minutes later Oliver escorted Dinah back to the carriage, Maddy's locket and Dinah's sapphires tucked safely into his greatcoat pocket. "All right, Grim? Ferris?" He handed Dinah into the carriage, tucked a few rugs around her to ward off the cold, then retrieved the pup from Grim.

"He's a proper little gentleman, this one." Grim held the pup up high to admire him, then handed him down to Oliver.

Ferris nodded his agreement. "Did his business, then snuggled up to Mr. Grimsley here and dropped off to sleep like a wee angel, he did. It's his fancy breeding what makes him so agreeable, I reckon. Good bloodlines, like."

"He'll make a proper hunter for Lord Archer." Oliver climbed into the coach, settled the pup on his chest and wrapped them both up in his greatcoat for warmth. When the pup fell asleep again at once, Oliver was inclined to agree with Ferris's reflections on superior canine breeding.

That is, until he was awakened from a nap by the sound of cloth tearing and discovered even a puppy with excellent bloodlines could cause quite a bit of damage when he was left unsupervised. "What the devil? What are you about?"

The pup had taken a sudden and intense interest in the lining of Oliver's greatcoat, which shouldn't have been terribly surprising, since Oliver had tucked a few of the savories Massie had given him into his pocket. Canine boredom and the tantalizing scent of treats had led to naughty behavior utterly unworthy of a pup with such elevated breeding.

"Why, you little imp." Oliver tugged the wriggling, squirming devil from the folds of his coat. "What have you got there?" he demanded, snatching at a corner of soggy cloth the pup had clamped between his teeth. "My pocket!" The pup had torn his greatcoat pocket clean off and was now attempting to eat it.

"No! Bad dog." Oliver tried to wrestle the bit of silk away from him, afraid he'd swallow it, but the puppy, a hunter down to his superior bloodlines held on, thrashing his head from side to side and letting loose with small, puppy-like growls that would have been adorable under any other circumstances.

"What in the world?" Dinah struggled upright on her seat, rubbing her eyes. "What are you doing to that puppy, Oliver?"

"Me? He's destroyed my greatcoat. It's lucky I woke, or he would have bitten a hole right through me!"

Dinah made a sound suspiciously like a choked laugh and reached down to pick up something from the floor. "Here, you've nearly lost Maddy's locket. What's this? Did you buy something else?"

Oh, no. Oliver abruptly abandoned the battle over his pocket. "I...it wasn't...I didn't..."

But he *had*, and the truth was about to erupt in all its messy, inconvenient, and inevitably destructive glory.

Dinah's face drained of color when she lifted the lid off the case and saw the glittering sapphires laying in their bed of pale gray velvet. "Oliver?"

"I...they're for you." Oliver swallowed. "I knew you wouldn't like...I didn't think you'd accept...I want you to have them."

"You can't have bought them for me." Dinah closed the lid of the case with a snap. "You can't think I'd ever accept jewels from you, unless..." She jerked her head up, her stricken gaze meeting his. "Unless you think to make me your—"

"Wife," Oliver blurted.

"Mistress," Dinah said at the same time.

They stared at each other in disbelief.

"Not my mistress, Dinah," Oliver whispered, when the silence between them grew unbearable. "I want you to be my wife."

CHAPTER 6

SOMEWHERE BETWEEN SOUTHFLEET
AND ROCHESTER, LORD OLIVER'S COACH

"*Y*our *wife!*" Dinah's piercing cry echoed throughout the coach.

Oliver grabbed the strap as the horses' startled lurch nearly bounced him off his seat. "You really must stop doing that. If we had a hired coachman at the reins instead of Ferris, we'd be in the ditch by now."

Dinah knew she should be mortified at shrieking like a madwoman, but she was so overwhelmed with shock there was no room left for mortification. His *wife*. Dear God. "Fashionable aristocratic gentlemen don't take actresses for their wives, Oliver."

He gave her an incredulous look. "You do recall my brother's an earl, don't you? An earl who plucked an actress straight from the Pandemonium Playhouse's stage, married her, and made her mistress of Cliff's Edge?"

"I...well, yes, but..." Dinah fumbled for a reply, but what could she say? She'd never seen a married couple more devoted to each other than Lord Archer and Penelope. Indeed, they seemed to have been made for each other.

But Dinah wasn't like Penelope. It had been inevitable Dinah would end up on the London stage, or worse, the London streets. That had never been true for Penelope, who was nothing like the jaded women who earned their bread on the stage, or on their backs. Penelope was lovely and gracious and refined. Her father had been a vicar, and at heart Penelope had always been a clergyman's daughter. The stage hadn't changed her, yet Penelope's marriage to Lord Archer had still been a scandal, despite her claims to gentility. A tragedy, even, according to the *ton*.

Fashionable London would swoon with horror if Oliver followed in his brother's appalling footsteps. There'd be no end to the scandal and gossip when the *ton* discovered Dinah's own father had been a wastrel who'd abandoned his wife and daughter, and her mother...well, the less said about her mother, the better.

She didn't care for what the *ton* thought of her, but Oliver would become a laughingstock if she became his wife. His aristocratic friends would ridicule and then abandon him, and he'd come to regret marrying her.

Oh, but this was terrible. She'd known for weeks Oliver was nursing a mild *tendre* for her, but it had never occurred to her he wanted to make her his *wife*. His mistress, yes, but then he'd taken up with Lady Serena, and Dinah had thought—

Lady Serena. Dinah seized on her like a lifeline. "You can't marry me. You have a mistress." It was an absurd argument, of course. One couldn't stir a step in London without stumbling over some married aristocrat's mistress.

Oliver raised a skeptical eyebrow at this, as well he might. "Is that your only objection? Because Lady Serena *isn't* my mistress, despite every wagging tongue in London insisting she is."

Dinah stared at him. "Not your mistress? But she's—"

"I'm surprised at you, Dinah. You should know better than to listen to the actresses at the Pandemonium. They're the worst gossips in London. If you recall, they also claimed *you* were my mistress, and we both know that to be false."

Dinah couldn't deny the London gossips were about as reliable as a pack of chattering monkeys, but if Lady Serena wasn't Oliver's mistress, what was she to him? "You've been seen all over London with her these past weeks. If she's not your mistress, then what—"

"Lady Serena is Lord Erskine's mistress. I've been seen all over London with the two of them because I've been trying to pry him from her clutches before she ruins him."

Dinah stared at him, speechless.

Oliver gestured to his eye. The swelling had gone down enough he could open it now, but it was still a dozen different shades of black, blue and yellow. "How else do you suppose I ended up with this? I tried to drag Erskine from the hazard tables before Lady Serena wagered away his fortune and got his fists in my face for my trouble."

"It wasn't a brawl, then?" Dinah was rather ashamed at having given Oliver so little credit, and she couldn't quite meet his eyes.

"Oh, it was a brawl, and rather an ugly one, but not nearly as ugly as Erskine's mother and four sisters being tossed onto the streets because their brother wagered away every penny of his fortune."

Dinah opened her mouth, then closed it again.

"Do you have any other objections to a marriage between us?" he asked politely, as if he were enquiring about the weather. "If so, let's have them out now, shall we?"

Dinah *did* have further objections. Dozens of them, the principal one being he'd be far happier with a sweet, proper young lady as his wife, someone respectable he'd be proud to introduce to his friends. Someone like—

"Miss Spence!" Dinah blurted. "You can't marry me because you're going to marry Miss Spence. Indeed, the sooner we arrive at Cliff's Edge the sooner you can get on with the business of falling in love with her and marrying her."

Oliver's jaw dropped open. "Miss Spence? Who the *devil* is Miss Spence?"

Dinah bit her lip. She and Penelope had agreed it would be best if Dinah didn't mention Miss Spence to Oliver, it being preferable for the thing to come about naturally. She hadn't had much choice, given the circumstances, but perhaps she shouldn't have announced it quite so clumsily.

When she didn't reply Oliver leaned forward in his seat, his eyes narrowed. "Well, Dinah? Who is she, and why am I meant to be marrying a lady I've never met?"

"You have met her. Caroline Spence. From what I understand, she was at the house party last year at Cliff's Edge. Penelope said she's fair-haired with brown eyes, and that you admired her. Miss Spence is a respectable, proper young lady, and so Penelope thought—"

"She thought I'd *marry* her?" Oliver laughed. "I don't like to disappoint my sister-in-law, but I'm afraid that's out of the question. Whatever admiration I may once have felt for Caroline Spence must have been fleeting, because I don't even remember her."

"But if you only met her again, you'd—"

"No. I'm sure she's a lovely young lady, but my affections lay elsewhere, and I won't marry a lady I don't love."

Love.

That last word fell between them with a thud. Dinah stared at him, her heart crowding into her throat. No, it couldn't be. Surely, he wasn't saying he loved...*her*?

But the look on his face as gazed at her, the softness in his blue eyes said more than his words ever could. Denials rushed to Dinah's lips—argument and pleas—but she didn't speak them. She could only sit there, dread raising a chill on her skin.

Oliver knew just what *he* wanted to say, however. It was as if he'd imagined this moment many times in his head. "This is a courtship, Dinah." He waved a hand around to indicate the coach.

Dinah stared blankly at him. "W-what is?"

"Our journey together from London to Cliff's Edge. I realize it's a bit unconventional as courtships go, but you've refused to see me these four weeks and more. I had no other choice than to take drastic measures."

"Why should you want to court me?" Dinah asked, then winced at the stupidity of the question. She *knew* why. But understanding a thing in her head was not the same thing as believing it in her heart.

Oliver gave her a crooked smile. "For the same reason most gentlemen wish to court a lady. Because I want to marry you, Dinah."

Dinah shook her head. Perhaps he thought he did *now*, but it wouldn't last. "You don't want to marry me, Oliver."

"I do. I've wanted to marry you since you fired a pistol at me." Oliver took her hand. "I'm in love with you, Dinah. I've been in love with you since the first moment I saw you, and I believe you're in love with me."

Dinah gaped at him. How could he imagine *she*, with her icy cold heart—*she*, who didn't love anything or anyone—could be in love with him? "You're wrong. I don't love you. That is, I do care for you, but as my friend, not my..."

What? Her husband, or her lover?

No, no, no. She was not saying the word *lover* to Oliver Angel. Even speaking the word aloud acknowledged it to be a possibility, and that was dangerous. She snatched her hand free of Oliver's grip. "I'm sorry, Oliver, but I can't marry you."

"I know you're afraid, but you don't need to be." Oliver reached for her hand again and pressed it to his chest, over his heart. "You don't have to say you love me back. Not until you're ready, and if you never are, well, that's all right, too. I have enough love for both of us."

Dinah snatched her hand away, but not before she felt his heartbeat against her palm, swift and strong, pounding with love wasted on a lady who could never return it—a lady who could never love anyone.

Not him, and not herself.

Pain sliced through her, so terrible she lost her breath, and the anger buried underneath the hurt swelled against her ribs. Why was he putting them through this? Why was he making her refuse him so cruelly? "I'm not afraid of anything. I don't love you, and I never can."

"If you'd just give me a chance, I—"

"No. I know my own mind, Oliver. I don't...I can't ever think of you that way. You'll only ever be my friend, nothing more." Dinah sank her teeth into her lower lip until she tasted blood on her tongue. If it felt like a lie—as if she were lying to him and to herself—it would pass soon enough. All that mattered was the thing was done, and there was no reason for them to ever speak of love or marriage again.

"I don't believe you."

Dinah's gaze shot to Oliver's face. "You what? What do you mean, you don't believe me?"

"Just what I said. I don't believe you see me as only your friend." Oliver regarded her with cool blue eyes. "There's no shame in being afraid, Dinah, but don't be a coward."

"I'm not a coward!" Dinah stamped her foot on the floor of the carriage and the puppy jump aside with a startled yelp. "I'm not...I don't desire you, Oliver. Is that so difficult for you to believe?"

Oliver leaned forward and pinned her with stormy blue eyes. "Yes, because I've seen the way you look at me. I've seen the way your eyes darken when I take your hand to assist you from the carriage. I've felt the pulse in your wrist flutter madly against my thumb when I touch you, and I've heard your breath catch when I smile at you."

Dinah stared into his eyes, and for a long, terrifying moment she wondered if she'd ever find the strength to tear her gaze away. "You're seeing what you want to see, that's all."

He sighed, as if he were disappointed in her. "You're such a dreadful liar."

She raised a hand to her throat, but then snatched it back again when she felt the frenzied flutter of her pulse, the swift rise and fall of her chest. "I'm not lying."

"Oh?" Oliver leaned threw a casual arm across the back of his seat, but his blue eyes were glittering with frustration. "Prove it."

Dinah sucked in a breath. "That's absurd! How am I meant to prove it?"

But she knew, even before he opened his mouth, she knew...

A dimple flashed at the corner of Oliver's lips, but his smile was grim. "Kiss me."

* * *

OLIVER'S GAZE roamed slowly over her, noting the flush of color on her cheeks and throat, her parted lips and hectic breaths, the way her pupils swallowed the blue of her eyes.

He might be a fool in love, but he wasn't blind.

She could reject his proposals. She could deny she loved him and try and persuade them both she never could. She could refuse to marry him and banish him from her presence forever.

But nothing—*nothing* she said would ever convince him she didn't desire him.

He'd never been in love before, and God knew he'd made a mess of it thus far. But Oliver knew desire when he saw it, and he'd had quite enough of this nonsense. "Well, Dinah? What are you waiting for? Prove to me you don't want me, and I'll never speak of it again."

Dinah crossed her arms over her chest. "Your...this is ridiculous."

Oliver raised an eyebrow. "Is that a refusal?"

"I don't have to prove anything to you," Dinah muttered, her lips turned down.

"Of course not," Oliver agreed. "But it would be an ideal way to silence me on this subject."

She glanced at him then looked quickly away, her cheeks coloring. Oliver waited, his heart pounding in his chest as indecision wrestled with stubborn pride on her face.

He'd just about given up hope when she held out her hand.

Oliver took it. He could feel her slender body trembling like a reed in the wind as he urged her gently down into the seat beside him. They turned toward each other, the promise of the moment swelling between them, but Dinah's head was down, her gaze on her lap.

"Look at me, Dinah," Oliver murmured huskily, tilting her head up with a touch of his thumb to her chin.

She swallowed, her long, graceful throat moving as her dark blue eyes met his.

Oliver ached to gather her into his arms and take her lips with his, but he didn't do either of those things. He'd bared his heart to her. He'd offered her his love, his devotion, his life, and she'd rejected him.

This time, Dinah would have to come to him.

She rested a hand on his chest. Her eyes lowered again, the dark, lush fan of her lashes brushing her cheeks. Oliver tensed, his entire body straining toward her as she leaned closer. He felt the drift of her warm breath against his skin, the press of her fingers against his chest, and then...

She let out a soft sigh and touched her lips to his cheek.

Her lips were soft, her hands warm, and her kiss...

Oliver felt it everywhere, echoing in recurring vibrations through every part of him, like a tuning fork finding the perfect pitch. He'd shared kisses with other ladies—open-mouthed, passionate kisses, but he'd never experienced anything more erotic in his life than the quick, shy press of her lips against his cheek.

"Thank you," he whispered. He stroked his knuckles over the delicate arch of her cheekbone and traced his thumb over her jaw before easing slightly away from her.

He expected her to leave him then, to pull away, retreat to her side of the carriage and never spare him another glance the rest of the way to Cliff's Edge.

But that wasn't what she did.

A shuddering sigh left her lips, and her fingers

curled into the edge of his waistcoat. She opened her devastating blue eyes and gazed up at him for a heartbeat before her eyelids fluttered closed again.

And then...

Then she leaned forward and touched her lips to his.

As desperate as Oliver was for her mouth, he never would have taken such a liberty, never would had stolen from a kiss from lips she hadn't offered him, but as soon as her mouth touched his it was as if a flame had been set to dry kindling. "Dinah." He gathered her against him with a groan and opened his lips under hers.

Dear God, her mouth...it was so soft, so sweet. He'd imagined kissing her a hundred times, but he could never imagine the desire, the tenderness and love that crashed over him like a tidal wave.

This is what it feels like to kiss the woman you love.

He was lost to her, lost *in* her, hers in every way a man could belong to a woman. He could never kiss another, not after her. "Dinah, I...please, sweetheart." Oliver didn't know what he was begging her for, unless it was *more.* More of her mouth, more of her lips, more of her touch.

Dinah's only answer was a soft whimper, but she twined her arms around his neck and sank her fingers into his hair, pulling him closer.

"Open your mouth for me, love." Oliver's restless hands moved up and down her spine, molding and coaxing her body into his until they fit together like two puzzle pieces. His mouth grew more demanding, even as some distant part of him warned him if she was going to deny him—if she was going to tear herself from his arms—it would be *now.*

But she didn't. She let out a soft, breathy sigh, and opened her mouth against his.

It was an invitation. A hoarse groan tore from Oliver's throat as he seized it, his tongue invading every corner of her mouth, caressing and teasing and urging her to match his eager thrusts with her own.

He nipped at her bottom lip, then slicked his tongue over the tender pink flesh. "Every corner of your mouth is sweeter than the next."

She bit his bottom lip in return, her lips curving against his mouth when he gasped, and his body jerked against hers. She pressed closer, close enough so her plump breasts were crushed against his chest.

Oliver was losing himself in the taste of her, her touch, the supple curves of her body pressed against his. "I'll never get enough of you, Dinah. Never." He tangled his hands in her hair, groaning as a few loose locks brushed against the skin of his hands. "You're *mine*, sweetheart. You'll always be mine."

He didn't realize he'd said the wrong thing until she stiffened against him, and by then it was too late. She was drawing away, leaving a cold, empty space in his arms where her body had been. "No. Dinah, wait—"

She tore her mouth from his, breaking the kiss, and before he could draw a breath she was across the carriage, staring at him with dazed eyes as she raised a shaking hand to her swollen lips.

Oliver wanted to weep at the loss of her. "Dinah, it's all right." He held out his hand to her. "Come here, sweetheart. Let me take care of you."

"No. I shouldn't have...we shouldn't have..." Her chin shot up. "This doesn't change anything."

Oliver's heart shuddered at her words, at the confusion in her eyes, and fear made his voice harsher than he meant it to be. "Yes, it does. It changes everything."

She wouldn't meet his eyes. "No. It changes nothing, Oliver."

"You want me," he insisted hoarsely.

Her throat worked, but she shook her head. "Desire isn't love."

Dinah was as good a shot with words as she was with a pistol, and she'd aimed well. Oliver felt as if his heart was exploding inside his chest. Pain and anger pressed against his throat, tried to spill from his lips, but he wouldn't chastise her. Couldn't, not when she was gazing at him with wide, frightened eyes.

"When we get to Rochester, I'll hire a hack to take me back to London." Dinah's voice was quiet, but it seemed loud in the silence.

Oliver stiffened at her words. "Running away, Dinah?"

She didn't answer, but it didn't matter. They both knew she was.

He shook his head. "I won't permit you to ride all the way back to London alone. It's not safe."

"Grim can accompany—"

"*No.* If you insist on returning to London, I'll go with you."

Her face paled. "You can't do that, Oliver. You're meant to be spending the holidays at Cliff's Edge. Your family is expecting you."

Oliver laughed, but the taste of it was bitter on his tongue. "And spend the next few weeks fending off Miss Spence? No. I'll send my apologies to my family. They'll understand."

"I don't think—"

"I said no. Either we both return to London, or we both go from Rochester to Sittingbourne, and from there north to Cliff's Edge. Those are your choices, Miss Bishop. We'll arrive in Rochester in the next half hour. You have until then to make up your mind."

CHAPTER 7

ROCHESTER, ENGLAND

*A*fter Dinah put an end to Oliver's courtship, neither of them knew what to say to the other. With every silent mile that passed, the dark, tangled thing inside her chest pulled tighter and tighter.

She was no stranger to awkward situations. They were common enough when one was an actress on London's most notorious stage. But she'd never encountered a situation quite so awkward as traveling with a gentleman whose proposals she'd just rejected.

Right before she'd kissed him, that is, and before he'd kissed her back—a kiss so sweetly devastating it had been all she could do not to climb into his lap.

But there was nothing for it. She couldn't return to London—not if Oliver insisted on accompanying her. No, all she could do now was get through the rest of the journey and then flee Cliff's Edge as soon as they arrived, just like the coward Oliver had accused her of being.

Without Dinah there to distract him, Oliver might take a fancy to Miss Spence, after all. He could be smitten with her by Twelfth Night, madly in love with her soon thereafter, and married to her by the spring thaw. It was just what Dinah hoped would happen—of course, it was. And if there was a hollow, frozen space inside her chest where her heart should be, well, it would save her a lot of bother, wouldn't it?

It wasn't as if she had any use for her heart.

Given her morose outlook, she was certain she'd find Rochester a dismal, gloomy place, but as if determined to make a mockery of her feelings the town was light, bright and absurdly picturesque.

Dinah's spirits gave a sluggish twitch at her first glimpse of Rochester Cathedral. The rows of arched, stained glass windows glittered gold, red and green in the sun, and the central spire soared high into the sky, piercing the endless blue and catching the edge of the white clouds on its tip.

She pressed her face to the glass as the coach made its way down High Street. Once they'd reached the far end Oliver signaled to Ferris to stop the carriage, then he turned to Dinah. "Would you care for a walk? You might enjoy the shop."

Dinah tried not to notice the frigid politeness with which Oliver addressed her, but another shard of ice penetrated her useless heart. Still, she pasted a smile on her lips and held out her hand to him. "Yes, of course."

He helped her from the carriage and led her to a tiny shop on the corner—a bright, cheerful little place called Claridge's. Dinah peeked through the large window that looked out onto the street and gasped with pleasure at the riot of color and movement she glimpsed inside.

And then there was the music.

One tinkling note chased another through the closed door of the shop onto the sidewalk beyond, where they hung for a quivering instant before they were swept up into the cold air. There was no pattern or rhyme to it, just dozens of notes drifting about like snowflakes, but what should have been a confusing cacophony somehow melted together into a glorious symphony of sound.

"Shall we, Miss Bishop?" Oliver opened the door of the shop and ushered her inside.

As lovely as the shop was from the outside, inside it was a wonderland of twirling, spinning, glittery things —a child's dream come true. Dinah paused a few steps from the threshold, her mouth falling open. Her gaze found one wonderful music box after another, and the heaviness in her heart gave way to pure delight.

"Lord Oliver Angel?" A plump lady hurried from behind the counter and approached them with a smile. "Well, it must be you, mustn't it? I don't expect any other customers today, what with it being Christmastime."

"Mrs. Claridge. How do you do?" Oliver strode across the shop to greet her. "It's kind of you to meet me this morning. This lady is Miss Bishop."

Dinah nodded, her lips curving in an involuntary smile. Mrs. Claridge, with her sweet face and silvery gray hair reminded her a bit of a much beloved, now deceased grandmother. "What a lovely shop you have, Mrs. Claridge."

"Thank you, dear." Mrs. Claridge beamed. "I have your music box ready, my lord. I'll just go fetch it for you, shall I?"

"Thank you, Mrs. Claridge."

Mrs. Claridge disappeared through a door that led to the back of shop. Dinah wandered around the store, gawking at the bevy of mechanical wonders. There were large boxes and small, and polished wooden music boxes with enameled lids. There were music boxes where one could peek through a small glass window and watch the cylinders inside churn out the tune. There were painted porcelain boxes, gilt and silver boxes, and boxes shaped like all manner of different things. There were birds and dancers, and even one shaped like a harp, and another like a tiny pianoforte.

"Charming, aren't they?" Oliver murmured, but he wasn't looking at the music boxes.

He was looking at *her*.

The shop, the lovely boxes and the tinkling notes all fell away for an endless moment as their gazes held. A thousand unspoken words passed between them until Dinah's cheeks heated, and she tore her gaze away. "They truly are."

"Every child born into the Angel family receives the gift of a music box on the day of their birth. William and Penelope asked me to choose one for Baby Angel."

Dinah couldn't say whether she was more astonished to find such lovely things existed, or that there were children fortunate enough to have one for themselves. She reached out to trace a spray of vibrant blue cornflowers on the lid of a small, ivory-colored porcelain box which had been put to one side on the display counter. "I can't imagine anyone not liking one of these." She opened the lid and gasped when a familiar strain met her ears. "My grandmother used to sing me this song before she died. I was very young at the time, but I've always remembered it."

Oliver leaned closer to listen, then murmured, "*Voi Che Sapete*, from Mozart's *Marriage of Figaro*."

He lay his fingers on her wrist. Startled, Dinah turned to him, but he didn't speak. He simply looked down at her with the oddest expression on his face. He seemed to be struggling for words. When they emerged at last, his voice was hoarse. "Dinah, will you let me—"

"Here we are, my lord!" Mrs. Claridge bustled back into the shop, a small box in her hands. "May I show it to you?"

Oliver's gaze roamed over Dinah's face before he turned to Mrs. Claridge. "Yes, of course."

"Suitable for a boy or a girl, just as you asked."

Mrs. Claridge placed the rectangular box carefully on the glass counter, and Dinah and Oliver leaned over to inspect it. "Oh, it's perfect," Dinah breathed, clasping her hands.

It truly was.

It wasn't as ornate as some of the other boxes in the shop—just a simple dark wood polished to a high gloss, set on four miniature brass feet. One might easily overlook it in favor of its more flamboyant neighbors, unless they paused long enough to study the painting on the lid. It depicted two children, a boy and a girl standing in a garden, surrounded by birds and flowers. The brushwork was exquisite, the flower petals and birds' plumage accentuated by glimmering pieces of mother-of-pearl.

Oliver carefully raised the lid. On the inside in neat script were the words, *From your loving uncle Oliver Angel. Christmas, 1812.* "Just as I asked. I couldn't be more pleased, Mrs. Claridge."

Mrs. Claridge flushed with pleasure. "I don't mind saying it's one of my favorites, my lord. So simple and elegant!"

"Tell me about this box here, Mrs. Claridge. It's very pretty." Oliver nodded at the round porcelain box with the cornflowers. "I notice you have it set to one side. Has it already been purchased?"

"Yes…well, no. You see, I made that box for my first grandchild, but I've no use for it now." Mrs. Claridge noticed Dinah's stricken expression and hastened to clarify. "Oh, no, Miss Bishop. It's nothing like that. It's only I was so certain the child would be a girl, but my Sarah gave birth to a healthy, strapping boy." Mrs. Claridge's face glowed with pride. "This dainty little box won't do for a boy, so I'll find him another."

Dinah frowned as a shadow passed over Mrs. Claridge's face. "How old is your grandson, Mrs. Claridge?"

The older woman's shoulders drooped. "Just five days old. I thought I'd be with my daughter's family this Christmas, but poor Mr. Edwards—that's my son-in-law—was taken with the gout in his foot, and he isn't fit to come and fetch me. So, I'm obliged to spend my Christmas here in Rochester."

Alone.

Mrs. Claridge didn't say it, but it was clear enough from her desolate expression.

"Can't you take the stagecoach?" Oliver asked.

"Oh heavens, no. I'm too old for that nonsense, my lord. The stagecoach isn't safe for such a one as me, what with the way they crowd the people in these days. Why, some poor older gentleman was thrown off and trampled to death just last week!" Mrs. Claridge shook her head. "I don't mind telling you I'm heartbroken to miss my grandson's first Christmas, but I'd just as soon live to see him grow up, you understand."

"Where does your daughter live, Mrs. Claridge?" Dinah's stomach was fluttering. Perhaps her luck was turning at last.

"A few miles west of Canvey Island. Too far for an old lady like me to travel alone."

"Canvey Island? That's north of here, somewhere between Grays and Southend-on-Sea, I think?"

"Yes, just off the coast."

Dinah's breath left her lungs in a rush. "Why, what a happy coincidence! Lord Oliver and Gr—that is, my brother, Mr. Bishop and I are headed north as well, to Brightlingsea. We'd be pleased to take you to Canvey Island in our carriage. Wouldn't we, my lord?"

Oliver quirked an eyebrow at her. "We'd agreed on a

southern route, I believe, Miss Bishop, toward Sittingbourne."

"*Did* we agree? The way I remember it, I reminded you we promised Lady Archer we'd arrive at Cliff's Edge this evening, and you said your errand in Sittingbourne could wait for another day."

Oliver shook his head, but one corner of his lip was twitching. "Is that how you remember it? How curious."

Dinah ignored this and turned a bright smile on Mrs. Claridge. "Really, you must allow us to take you. I can't bear to think of you here in Rochester alone when your daughter must yearn to have you with her. Why, I can't think of anything more heartbreaking. Can you, my lord?"

Oliver glanced from Dinah to Mrs. Claridge, who's hands were clasped against her chest, her eyes shining with hope. "Certainly not. It would be our pleasure to take you to Canvey Island, Mrs. Claridge."

"That's wonderful, my lord!" Dinah gushed, offering him her brightest smile. Oh, she was a wicked, sneaky thing to take such shameless advantage of Oliver's good nature, but it was better this way. There was no sense in prolonging a doomed courtship.

Oliver snorted out a laugh. "Wonderful, yes. How *clever* you are, Miss Bishop. I don't know why I didn't think of it myself."

* * *

BY THE TIME they rejoined Grim and Ferris the horses had been seen to and the puppy had exhausted his mischievous tendencies with a romp in the snow. Dinah was well pleased with her triumph, and Mrs. Claridge was nearly bursting with joy.

Oliver, who cared only for seeing a smile on Dinah's face was reconciled to their change of plans and as cheerful as he could be, given his heart was as battered as his face.

Battered, but not broken, and not despairing.

He hadn't enjoyed hearing words of rejection from Dinah any more than any gentleman would from the lips of the lady he loved, but he hadn't expected he'd have her for the asking.

He was, however, still hopeful she'd be his in the end. He'd seen the glimmer of raw emotion in her face when he told her he loved her, the anguish in her blue eyes when she'd refused his suit. He'd felt the desire shivering through her when he kissed her, the tenderness of her fingers stroking his cheek.

Dinah was far from indifferent to him.

So, Oliver was as easy as a man wildly in love could be as they set out for Canvey Island. He settled himself comfortably in his seat and stroked the pup's head, listening with half an ear to Dinah and Mrs. Claridge's chatter.

Dinah was *his*. She simply hadn't realized it yet.

* * *

"YE'D BEST KEEP yer wits about ye when you get near Canvey Island, Mr. Grimsley. Why, I'd just as soon be dead as go anywhere near that place."

Dead? Grim gulped.

"I go wherever Lord Oliver bids me to go," Grim declared, mustering every bit of bravado he could, but a tremor rolled through him at Ferris's forbidding tone.

Ferris sniffed. "Well, he shouldn't tell ye to go *there*. The place is haunted, right enough. Can't stir a step in Canvey Island without stumbling over some ghost or other."

"Haunted?" A feeble whimper escaped from Grim's throat. "Ghost? What sort of ghost?"

"The haunted sort, and not just one of them, nei-ther. Canvey Island's filthy with poor, undead souls, and anyone who knows a thing about ghosts knows it."

"Mayhap they'll keep to themselves, it being nearly Twelfth Night?" They were thirty miles or more from Canvey Island, but Grim wasn't keen on disembodied spirits, and his teeth were already chattering.

"I doubt it," Ferris replied unhelpfully. "Can't see what use ghosts have for Twelfth Night. I don't mind saying I'll be right relieved to part ways with ye at Plumstead."

Grim made another noise—a squeak or a sniffle, perhaps—and it dawned on Mr. Ferris his companion was frightened out of his wits. "Not but what I wish ye the best, Mr. Grimsley. I'll say a prayer for ye, if it makes ye feel better."

"I—I th-thank you for that, Mr. Ferris. You're very kind," Grim managed, his voice faint. "You won't forget the prayer?"

"No, not a bit of it. Cheer up, lad. I'm sure all will be well." This short speech might have reassured Grim if Ferris hadn't added, "Still, ye'll want to stay clear of the Viking ghost. He's a big one, with a bushy beard. Wears a horned helmet, he does, and carries a sword. It's said he drowned, and he's none too happy about it, neither."

Grim wasn't terribly happy about it himself.

He spent the rest of the journey from Rochester to Plumstead conjuring up increasingly ghastly pictures of a shaggy-haired, sword-wielding, infuriated Viking ghost lurking in the shadows, waiting for a chance to wreak his sinister revenge on every hapless traveler who crossed his path.

CHAPTER 8

CANVEY ISLAND, ENGLAND

*G*hosts, of all bloody things. Not just any ghost, either, but a *Viking* ghost.

"Don't try and speak, Grim. You've put quite a dent in your skull, I'm afraid." Oliver prodded as gently as he could at the knot at the back of Grim's head, then ripped off his cravat and tucked it against the wound when his fingers came away sticky with blood.

Damn it. He should have known something like this would happen. Grim had been looking a bit peaked since they'd returned Ferris to Rutherford in Plumstead, but they'd made it through Purfleet and then east through Stanford-le-Hope and Benfleet without incident. Oliver, Dinah and Hester Claridge had whiled away the time in pleasant chat, and even Will's naughty pup had kept himself busy chewing on the scraps of silk he'd torn from Oliver's greatcoat.

If Grim hadn't been quite his usual cheerful self, Oliver had put it down to Rundell and Bridge reacting to the change in driver with a sudden surge of high spirits. Grim didn't care for equine feistiness, but the coachman Oliver had hired in Plumstead had held them steady.

But just as Oliver was reflecting on the ease of the journey, disaster had struck. It came out of nowhere and landed on them in spectacular fashion.

"Miss Bishop, and the other lady…"

Grim tried to struggle upright, but Oliver braced his hands on Grim's forearms to keep him still. He didn't dare touch Grim's shoulders, as one of them looked to be broken, or at the very least dislocated. "We're all perfectly fine. Not a single scratch on any of us."

Remarkable, really, give the wrench they'd taken when the horses bolted. Oliver had had horrific visions of splintered wood, shattered glass and broken limbs, but by some miracle the coach had remained upright when it careened into the ditch.

They'd been knocked from their seats, and the pup had slid from one side of the coach to the other, his little paws scrabbling for purchase, but none of them had been injured. Even Rundell and Bridge had escaped unharmed. They now stood patiently, apparently well satisfied with the mischief they'd caused.

Poor Grim hadn't been so lucky. He'd been thrown off the box into the muddy field on the other side of the ditch. Grim was conscious when Oliver reached him, but he'd been muttering something about Vikings and ghosts. Oliver had feared his wits were addled by the blow to his head, but as it happened, the injury hadn't a thing to do with it.

No, Grim's wits were addled by a vivid imagination.

"The horses startled, my lord, and I thought we were done for, what with it getting dark and that ghost running loose, but it happens it was just a pair of rabbits darting across the road."

Oliver blinked. "*Ghost?* What ghost?"

"Mr. Ferris told me Canvey Island's overrun with ghosts, and the Viking ghost the worst of the lot." Grim paled at the mere mention of him. "He has a wicked sword, and he cuts off the heads of his victims, on account of being angry at being drowned."

Oliver pinched the bridge of his nose. "There aren't any ghosts, Grim."

"No, my lord," Grim replied miserably. "But I saw those rabbits, and I thought it was the ghost, and I... well, I may have screamed. Just a little bit, to warn the coachman, not wanting the ghost to cut off all our heads, you understand, but the horses took exception to it and went into the ditch."

"If you were afraid of a Viking ghost, Grim, why didn't you just ride inside the coach?"

"What, with Miss Bishop?" Grim looked horrified. "I'd rather face the Viking ghost, my lord."

"Well, I don't see him about anywhere, Grim, so I daresay we've escaped with our heads intact." Oliver sighed, but he didn't have the heart to scold Grim. The ghost might be a figment of his imagination, but his injuries were all too real. "Now, just be still until Mrs. Claridge's son-in-law brings his wagon, won't you?"

Fortunately for them all, Grim had waited to succumb to his macabre fancies until they were less than a mile from the Edwards' farm, which was just on the other side of the field. The coachman had gone off to fetch Mr. Edwards.

So, here they sat in a field of half-frozen mud, Grim breathless with pain, and Oliver, who felt as though he should have realized something was amiss, overcome with guilt. The only one of the three of them who was pleased was William's pup, who frolicked about happily, digging his nose into the mud and chasing rabbits.

* * *

PERHAPS THE DETOUR to Canvey Island hadn't been such a clever idea.

A shiver wracked Dinah's body, and she tucked the carriage rug tighter around her legs. It had grown colder since they'd left the Edwards' house, so cold she could no longer feel her toes.

The horses were agitated after the ditch fiasco, so instead of hiring another coachman, Oliver had taken the reins himself. The pup, after he'd made it clear with an expressive waggling of his eyebrows that Dinah was a distant second choice, reluctantly curled up on her lap. She wrapped another rug around him and tugged him tight against her chest.

She couldn't regret delivering Mrs. Claridge into her daughter's arms for the Christmas holidays. No one who'd seen the joy on her face when Mrs. Edwards lay her newborn son in his grandmother's arm *could* regret it.

But God in heaven, poor Grim!

She'd always rather liked Grim. That is, she hadn't *wanted* to like him. She'd done her best to find him as tiresome as she did most people, but it hadn't worked. It was a great nuisance, really, but disliking Grim was rather like disliking iced teacakes, or puppies, or roaring fires on a frigid winter's night.

It just wasn't done.

When she saw Grim lying motionless on the ground, she'd feared the worst, but the doctor didn't expect him to suffer any lasting effects from his injuries. Still, Grim was obliged to remain in bed while he healed, and so Dinah and Oliver had left him under the sympathetic eye of Mrs. Claridge and Sarah Edwards. He'd follow them to Cliff's Edge in a few days, when he was able to travel.

Dinah might scoff at the idea of ghosts in general, and Viking ghosts in particular, but when they'd come upon Grim half buried in the mud, clutching his shoulder with his face twisted in pain, even her stoicism had deserted her.

She sighed, her head falling back against the squabs. A dislocated shoulder and a mild concussion, the doctor had said. Poor Grim was facing a Christmas spent in an unfamiliar bed, surrounded by people he didn't know. The Edwards were very kind, but they were still strangers.

She wriggled her feet inside her boots to thaw her frozen toes. If she was as cold as this, what must Oliver be feeling right now?

He'd seen Dinah safely settled inside the carriage with half a dozen rugs to warm her, then he'd climbed onto the box without a word of complaint and pointed the horses' heads toward Southend-on-Sea.

And that, seemingly, was that. They'd arrive at Cliff's Edge in the early morning hours, and Dinah would have fulfilled her promise to Penelope. She was pleased about it, of course. Very pleased, indeed. It was what she'd wanted all along, only…

It was so dreadfully cold outside, and it seemed to be growing more so by the mile. The icy rain would likely turn to snow soon enough, making a mess of the roads, and God knew the horses were fussy enough as it was.

Well, it couldn't be helped. Dinah held onto that thought as she stretched out on the seat, trying to find a comfortable position. Perhaps if she lay all the way down…ah, yes, that was much better. She balanced the pup on her chest and closed her eyes, determined to fall asleep.

Less than ten seconds later her eyes popped open again. Had the wind just picked up? It seemed to be blowing with unusual force now, and what was that dreadful cracking sound? Had a rock or tree limb hit the carriage? Had it hurt Oliver? He was already injured, his face battered and bruised. Could he even see out of that black eye? Or was he struggling through the darkness half-blind?

She threw her limbs this way and that, squirming and cursing the carriage springs—springs that had been perfectly comfortable until this moment—and the pup tumbled off her chest and onto the floor with a protesting yelp.

"You needn't look so judgmental," Dinah scolded, frowning down into the puppy's reproachful blue eyes. "It wasn't *me* who injured Grim. It was the Viking ghost."

The pup didn't appear to be impressed with this argument. He stared up at her, his eyes growing more mournful by the second.

"I know what you're thinking. I was the one who suggested we come to Canvey Island." Dinah scooped up the pup and laid him on his back across her knees. "If you insist on looking at it that way, you *could* argue I'm at fault for everything that followed."

The pup wriggled and squirmed and kicked his furry legs.

Dinah tucked the pup into the curve of her shoulder with a sigh. "There's some merit to your argument, I suppose."

Oliver hadn't said so, but given the injuries on his face it stood to reason he was bruised and aching all over, and now he was doomed to spend the darkest hours of the night alone on the box with freezing rain dripping down his neck. If he caught his death of a cold and expired from fever, it would be all Dinah's fault.

At least, according to the puppy's logic, it would be.

Well, that decided it, then. She refused to have Oliver's death on her conscience.

Dinah patted and crooned to the pup until he grew drowsy, then she settled him on the seat, made a nest of carriage rugs around him, and banged her fist against the roof.

The carriage slowed at once, then stopped and sagged to the side as Oliver jumped down from the box. A moment later his face appeared at the open door. "What's the trouble, Miss Bishop? Are you unwell?"

His cheeks were reddened with wind and cold and his hat and coat looked to be soaked through. Some troubling emotion burned through Dinah—regret, perhaps, or worse, tenderness. "No trouble. I'm perfectly well. I signaled you to stop because I'm joining you on the box."

Oliver's eyebrows shot so high they disappeared under the brim of his hat. "Have you lost your wits?"

It was a fair question. Dinah was half-convinced she *had* lost them, but her mind, such as it was, was made up. She slid across the seat to the carriage door and gestured for Oliver to move aside. "I beg your pardon, my lord."

He didn't stir a step. "You're not riding on the box. It's wet and miserable. You'll freeze."

"If you can tolerate it, then so can I."

Dinah waved him aside again, but Oliver braced his feet and crossed his arms over his chest. She tried to dart past him, but he blocked her, and a push against his shoulder proved equally ineffectual. She may as well try to push the carriage over as move a man Oliver's size.

He smirked. "Are you quite finished? Because we've miles ahead of us still, and you're wasting our—"

Dinah was across the seat and out the other door before Oliver could finish his sentence. She just had time to scramble onto the box before he rounded the side of the carriage. "If you want me down, you'll have to drag me off."

"Do you suppose I won't?" Oliver's shoulders were

rigid and his jaw tight with anger. He looked more than capable of dragging her off the box and tossing her into the carriage.

Dinah gripped the rails and braced herself for a battle, but he only stood there, his arms at his sides, his hands clenching and unclenching. They stared at each other without speaking as the wind and rain swirled around them, until Oliver shook his head. "What's this about, Dinah?"

"I just...I can't...I don't want you to be left out here alone."

She slapped a hand over her mouth, but it was too late. Dear God, how had *that* slipped out? She waited in an agony of embarrassment for Oliver to laugh at her, but he didn't. He simply stood beside the carriage gazing up at her, and despite the dark she saw his blue eyes soften, and the tension ease from his jaw.

He didn't say another word, but went around the carriage, ascended the box and took up the reins. The horses started forward. Dinah and Oliver sat side by side, neither of them speaking as Rundell and Bridge picked their way over the rutted road. A half dozen miles had passed beneath the carriage wheels before Oliver asked, "Are you cold?"

She pulled her cloak tighter around her throat. "Yes."

There was no sense lying about it. Any person of flesh and blood would be cold, given the circumstances. What Dinah didn't say, however, was despite the rugs and the luxurious velvet seats, she was far more comfortable beside him on the box than she'd been in the carriage.

Oliver only nodded, and another long silence passed as Dinah wracked her brains for something to say. He'd begun, and it was only fair she should do her part. "The music box for the baby..." she began, then fell silent again.

She wasn't sure how to say she thought it was the loveliest gift she'd ever seen.

From your loving uncle...

"Yes?"

"It...I...you asked me if I thought the child would like it, and I never answered you. I think... I think your niece or nephew will treasure it."

Oliver turned to her in surprise. "Thank you."

After another mile of trying to keep silent, Dinah gave up the struggle. "What sort of gift did you mean to give Penelope? That is, you haven't known her long, and I just wondered..."

I wondered if you take such exquisite care of all the people you love.

"Exotic pineapples," Oliver said, without taking his attention off the road.

Pineapples? Dinah's brows drew together. She'd never tasted a pineapple herself, but she knew they were meant to be sweet and delicious. As far as she knew, Penelope wasn't particularly fond of the fruit, but ladies did sometimes experience the strangest cravings when they were with child. "Has she developed a taste for pineapples?"

Oliver lips curved in a brief smile. "This one isn't for eating. Well, not at once, anyway. It's for planting."

Ah, that made more sense. Penelope had a passion for plants and flowers. For as long as Dinah had known her, Penelope had spoken wistfully about how lovely it would be to have a garden. Cliff's Edge had extensive grounds, and sometimes Dinah teased Penelope she'd married Lord Archer for his gardens alone.

"You can't grow proper pineapples in England," Oliver was saying. "It's too wet and cold, but there's an earl in Sittingbourne, a Lord Horace, who grows his own in his greenhouses. Penelope can grow them herself if she has a pineapple to start. You simply cut the top off the fruit, soak it in water for a time, then plant it."

"But where will she plant it? You just said England is too cold to grow pineapples."

"It is, but I happen to know Will's Christmas gift to Penelope is a greenhouse. It's ridiculously large—a monstrosity, really—but you know how Will is." Oliver chuckled. "Nothing is too good for his wife. You mustn't tell Penelope, though. It's a surprise."

"No, I won't. How did you come to find out about Lord Horace's pineapples?" Dinah's voice was faint, because she was speaking around a lump in her throat. She'd known Penelope for much longer than Oliver had, but even she couldn't think of anything her friend would love more than Oliver's gift. He just seemed to know, instinctively, how to bring joy to those he loved.

Oliver shrugged. "I asked around a bit, and soon enough someone pointed me to Lord Horace. You can find anything in England if you're willing to search it out. Indeed, it was much easier to get Lord Horace's name than it was to secure an appointment with him. It took weeks to get him to agree to meet with me."

Penelope swallowed. "Oh?"

"Yes. He's a bit of a recluse, and protective of his plants. I sent him half a dozen letters before he agreed to see me, and even then, I had to promise Penelope would take exquisite care of his pineapples."

Weeks of planning, a half-dozen letters…this wasn't simply a whim of Oliver's. He'd put a great deal of thought into Penelope's gift, and in the space of one day, Dinah had spoiled it for him. "If you miss your appointment with Lord Horace, he's isn't likely to grant you another, is he?"

If Oliver had been waiting to take her to task for

upsetting his plans, this would be the moment to do so, but not a word of recrimination passed his lips. He only shrugged. "No."

Dinah said nothing, but she was busily adding up miles and hours in her head. Sittingbourne was south of Rochester, nearly a fifty miles ride from Canvey Island. It would take them all night too get there, but what was a single night when weighed against exotic pineapples?

"Let's go." Dinah lay her hand on Oliver's arm. "To Sittingbourne. Let's go and fetch Penelope's pineapples."

Oliver stared at her for a moment, then his lips curved in a wide, breath-stealing, heart-stopping smile. "Are you sure?"

Dinah paused to take in his distracting dimples before she raised her gaze to his warm blue eyes. "I'm sure."

And she was. She'd never been surer of anything in her life.

CHAPTER 9

SITTINGBOURNE, ENGLAND, DECEMBER
29TH

*I*t was a pity Shakespeare wasn't still alive to
pen the tale of Oliver's courtship, because it
would have made a wonderful play. It had been a
comedy of errors from the start, and now it looked as if
the final act would be as farcical as the first two.

Without the joyous wedding, that is.

Their journey to Cliff's Edge was nearly over, and
all he had to show for this courtship so far was a pock-
etful of dark blue sapphires to match the eyes of the
lady who'd refused to become his wife.

Perhaps it wasn't a comedy, after all. Perhaps it had
been destined to be a tragedy from the start, and the
only one who hadn't realized it was him.

"Is this Lord Horace's property?" Dinah asked,
trying to hide the chattering of her teeth.

"Yes, since the turn half a mile back." Despite Oliver's entreaties, Dinah had remained beside him on the
box for the entire journey, even when it dragged on
into the early morning hours. Bad roads, uncertain
weather, and the occasional equine rebellion had complicated the drive.

There wasn't enough time for Oliver to take Dinah
to an inn. Lord Horace's estate, while it *was* in Sitting-

bourne was so remote as to be an hour's drive from the town proper, and Lord Horace, who wasn't a gentleman who troubled himself much about fashionable calling hours had set an early morning appointment.

So, Oliver had a half-frozen, bedraggled lady on his hands, and not the faintest idea what to do with her.

He should have put her back inside the coach hours ago, despite her protests. Her cloak was damp through, and she was shivering in her wet boots. A more generous man—a gentleman—would have taken better care of her, but Oliver hadn't been able to bring himself to part with her. He was greedy when it came to Dinah Bishop—greedy for her conversation, her smile, her laugh—even her scowls and scolds.

Weren't all gentlemen in love the same?

"I don't suppose we can arrive at Lord Horace's door looking like this." Dinah waved a hand at her crumpled skirts, then turned to take in Oliver's appearance. "I believe your hat is ruined, my lord."

"My hat, my coat, my breeches, and very likely my boots," Oliver agreed. "William's pup is the only one of the three of us who's presentable. I'd send him in to fetch Penelope's pineapple if I wasn't certain he'd chew it to bits."

Dinah tried to tuck a few straggling dark locks of her hair under her hat, but soon gave it up with a sigh. "Perhaps I'll wait in the coach."

Oliver raised an eyebrow at that. He didn't fancy the idea of greeting Lord Horace looking like a half-drowned street urchin any more than she did, but Dinah couldn't remain in the coach. She needed a comfortable seat beside a roaring fire and a nip or two of brandy, followed by a pot of hot tea. "No, I can't allow you to…"

His voice trailed off as he caught a glimpse of a building through the thick rows of trees lining the drive. He slowed the coach as they drew closer. The building was long and narrow, with a peaked roof and tall, arched windows arranged neatly across the south facing wall. The few beams of moonlight peeking through the clouds gleamed dully on pale, gray stone.

They were some distance from the main estate, and it was too big to be a folly. It looked like...*yes*, it was.

One of Lord Horace's famed greenhouses.

William had made Oliver look at dozens of different plans for Penelope's greenhouse—so many Oliver could build one himself by now. This one was in a slightly older style and lacked the fashionable glass roof, but if Lord Horace was wintering his exotic plants and fruits here, the building must be heated by a system of stoves beneath the floor.

They might tidy and warm themselves inside, and perhaps snatch a few moments of rest before they met with Lord Horace. It would be dreadful indeed if they were caught out, but it was early yet, and none of Lord Horace's gardeners seemed to be about. Oliver glanced at Dinah, and the blue tinge to her lips made up his mind.

She turned to him in surprise when he pointed the horses' heads toward the building. "Where are we going? Don't say you mean to break into Lord Horace's greenhouse."

"I mean to get inside, yes, but I'm hoping we don't have to break anything." Oliver brought the coach to a halt and jumped down off the box, wincing a bit as the blood rushed back into his stiff legs. Dinah offered him her hand to help her alight, but he ignored it and grasped her around the waist.

"Oliver! What are you—"

"Making certain you don't fall." He swung her down from the coach. "Your limbs will be numb by now." He waited until he was certain she was steady on her feet, then he reluctantly released her and retrieved the puppy and the carriage rugs from the coach. He led Dinah toward the greenhouse door, and offered her an extravagant bow. "After you, Miss Bishop."

Dinah hesitated. "Perhaps this isn't a good idea. I daresay the door is locked, in any case."

"It's a perfectly wonderful idea, by virtue of it's being our *only* idea. As for the door, there's one way to know whether or not it's locked." Oliver grasped the latch and let out a sigh of relief as it turned easily in his hand. "See, Miss Bishop? It's as good as an invitation."

He pressed a hand to the small of her back to usher her inside. It wasn't as warm as Oliver had hoped it would be, but it was certainly warmer than it was outside, and with a pleasing scent of soil and green, growing things.

Oliver set down the pup, who immediately went off to explore, tail wagging. He turned his back to give Dinah privacy, then tossed his hat aside, tore off the damp cravat that had been driving him mad for the past few hours, and removed his coat and waistcoat, hoping the damp linen shirt he wore underneath would dry before he was obliged to meet with Lord Horace.

Dinah removed her hat and cloak and shook out her limp skirts while Oliver gathered up the pile of carriage rugs and arranged them on the floor. "There. Your makeshift bed awaits. I doubt it will be terribly comfortable, but given the..." He turned to face Dinah, and immediately forgot what he'd been about to say. "Your hair."

She let out a self-conscious laugh and reached a hand to her head. "Oh, yes. It will dry more quickly if it's loose."

"It's..." Oliver began, but none of the words that rushed to his tongue could begin to do justice to the sight before him. Fragments of extravagantly romantic poetry floated through his head—odes to ribbons of dark silk, effusions on dusky, magical locks and water-falls of sable curls— but no poem could capture the pure, raw beauty of Dinah standing before him with her hair tumbling down her back.

An ache pierced his chest, joy and paid at once, be-cause she was so truly herself like this, so perfect in her vulnerability, so much the woman he'd dreamed of making his, and he may never have the privilege of seeing her this way again.

"W-Will you lie down? That is, not *lie down*. I didn't mean..." Oliver stammered, trying to gather his wits. "What I mean is, if you'd like to rest, I've made a place for you here."

Dinah glanced uncertainly at the nest of rugs spread on onto the floor, then back to Oliver's face. "Yes, I... thank you, I will."

Oliver waited until Dinah had settled herself among the rugs, then he seated himself on the floor and leaned his back against the wall. For a while the only sound was the faint hiss of steam from the pipes. Oliver was certain Dinah must have drifted off, but then she stirred.

"Can't you sleep?" he asked.

She sighed. "No. I'm too agitated, I suppose."

Oliver remembered something then, something he hadn't yet shown to her. "I'll be back in a moment." He darted out the door, rummaged about inside the coach until he found what he was looking for, then went back inside, closing the greenhouse door behind him.

"Oliver?" Dinah was sitting up.

"I know you said you won't accept a gift from me, but it's just a small thing, and I want you to have it." Oliver knelt next to her, the ivory music box with the blue cornflowers cradled in his palms. He turned the silver knob on the bottom, then set the box carefully on the floor beside her. "Maybe this will help you sleep."

Dinah sucked in a breath as the first tinkling notes of *Voi Che Sapete* drifted through the air. "The music box."

Her soft voice, the wonderment on her face as she gazed up at him...it took every bit of control he had not to touch her, stroke his fingertips down her cheek. "Yes. You said your grandmother used to sing this song to you at bedtime."

They were both quiet as they listened to the music, then Oliver started to rise.

Dinah stayed him with a hand on his arm. "Wait, Oliver."

Oliver caught his breath at the softness in her dark blue eyes. "Yes?"

She lay back down, then shifted the rugs aside to make a space for him. "Don't go. Stay with me."

* * *

DINAH DIDN'T WAIT for Oliver to gather her against him, and she didn't wait for him to kiss her. Instead, without a word she opened her arms to him and brushed her lips over his.

She'd regret it later, perhaps, but she wouldn't think of that now—not with his lips on hers, his soft exhalations drifting over her face and his breathless murmurs in her ear. Not when he told her with his every word and touch how much she meant to him.

How much he loved her.

And he did. For now, he did.

As for later, well...some things were only meant to be for instant, suspended and breathless and out of time. Once, when Dinah was very young, she'd held a butterfly in her palm. Its wings had stilled for only a heartbeat before it fluttered away, and even as young as she'd been, she'd understood the moment was more precious for having been fleeting.

This time with Oliver was the same—precious, but fleeting.

But that didn't matter now, not when he was kissing her, his lips trailing over her cheek, the shell of her ear, her throat. He found every inch of her bare skin and caressed her until her body grew restless under his.

"Oliver, please."

Dinah wasn't sure what she was asking—a plea for his hands, for his mouth—but she didn't need to beg for him, because she'd hardly breathed the words before his lips found hers. He kissed her and kissed her—deep, drugging kisses that left her breathless and dazed. He teased his tongue over the seam of her lips again and again, soft groans tearing from his chest when she opened her mouth under his.

"Arms over your head, sweetheart." He didn't wait for her to obey but wrapped his fingers around her wrists and raised her arms over her head, then held them there as he scraped his teeth lightly over the curves of her neck. "I've dreamed of tasting you," he murmured, his breath hot against her ear. "If I had you forever, I'd still never have enough of you."

Dinah arched her neck, a silent plea for his kiss. His mouth was hot, his tongue curling around hers until she was gasping for breath, then he moved lower to bite gently at the hollow of her throat before closing his lips around her nipple.

"*Oliver.*" Dinah arched against him, breathing hard as he teased at the straining peak. She struggled under him as he nipped at her, trying to get closer as he tormented her, his eager mouth wetting the fabric.

"No," he rumbled against her ear when she tried to lower her arms. He shifted to take both her wrists in one hand, then reached down to caress her other nipple with lazy strokes of his thumb. "I want you like this, spread out for me."

Dinah shivered at the command in his voice, the sensual promise. She let her arms go lax over her head, and stretched her body under his, offering herself without reserve. Oliver sensed her surrender and let out a purely masculine growl of satisfaction. "Yes, love, just like that. I want to touch you everywhere, sweetheart."

And he did.

He touched her lips, her neck, her breasts, and between her legs, stroking the tender, swollen flesh until she was incoherent with need, helpless whimpers and pleas vibrating in her throat. In those breathless, unguarded moments, where there was no place for fear, Dinah could no longer deny to herself Oliver was everything she'd ever wanted, and everything she hadn't believed existed.

Not just the playful rogue who made her smile, but a gentleman, and a man of honor. A passionate man, and a demanding lover, but also a true friend who protected and cherished her. A man with such a deep well of love inside him a lifetime of sharing it could never bleed it dry, never diminish it.

And he wanted to share it with *her*.

A sound tore from her chest—a sob of passion, pain, gratitude and love. She might have wept forever, but Oliver was there in an instant, soothing the hurt she'd long ago buried in the deepest part of her heart, and kissing the cries from her lips. "You're safe here, Dinah," he whispered, "You're safe with me. Let go for me, sweetheart."

Oh, she wanted to, wanted it more than she'd ever wanted anything, and he was helping her, easing her closer to faith and trust and joy. Every caress of his fingers, every stroke of his tongue, every whispered word nudged her toward the edge of a dream where there were no questions, and no regrets. No thought at all, only *him*, his warm body wrapped around her, his tongue curling against hers until Dinah was gasping for breath, utterly lost to him.

But Oliver wasn't lost. He knew just how to touch her, just how to coax the reaction he wanted from her quivering body. His lips and fingers seemed to be everywhere at once, petting and circling, drawing her body tighter and tighter until at last the knot inside her unfurled in waves of bliss so intense she was panting and moaning with it.

"Yes," he whispered, his lips tracing her skin. "Take your pleasure, sweetheart."

His blue eyes blazed as he gazed down at her, and she could feel him, his hard length pressed against her hip. He moved against her, but his thrusts were slow, lazy, as if her pleasure was enough for him, and he was content to simply hold her, and ride the fine edge between desire and satisfaction.

Dinah cradled his face in her hands and brought his mouth down to hers. He groaned when she slicked her tongue over his bottom lip and took it into her mouth to suck on it, but he didn't raise her skirts, or make any other move to take her. He only placed a sweet kiss on the end of her nose, then began to draw away.

Dinah twined her arms around his neck, stilling him. "You didn't...you're still—"

Another helpless groan tore from Oliver's lips when she arched against him, her legs parting slightly as her hips pressed into his, but he only pressed a quick, tender kiss to her lips, then shifted his body away from hers.

"No. Don't go." Dinah clutched at him, panic unlike

any she'd ever felt before overwhelming her. She couldn't let him leave her, couldn't lose him—

"Shhh." Oliver brushed his lips over her forehead. "I have to, sweetheart. I meant it when I said I don't want you as my mistress, Dinah. I want you to be my wife. You'll never be truly mine otherwise, and I'm not a man who takes what isn't mine."

There was no rancor in his tone, no accusation.

Nothing for her to say in reply.

She was afraid he'd leave her then, but he didn't. He pulled the carriage rugs around them, then wrapped her in his arms and eased her head down to his chest with a gentle hand on her neck. "Sleep, sweetheart," he murmured, resting his cheek on the top of her head. "Sleep."

CHAPTER 10

ABBERTON, ENGLAND, DECEMBER 30TH

*I*t had taken four days, but fate had finally caught up with her.

Dinah couldn't pinpoint the precise moment it occurred or the specific event that provoked it, but somehow between casks of Scottish whiskey and black kittens, sapphires and music boxes, Viking ghosts and greenhouses and breathtaking blue eyes, the inevitable had happened.

Dinah had lost her wits.

Looking back, she was surprised it hadn't happened sooner. She's been flirting with madness since they'd left London. Now, twenty miles from Cliff's Edge, there could be no doubt she'd succumbed at last.

Madness was the only reasonable explanation for why she should be perched on the edge of the seat in Oliver's coach, a sleeping puppy sprawled on his back across her knees and a pineapple clutched to her chest. The spiked ends were poking into her chin, but Dinah didn't dare set it aside. Lord Horace, for all his rambling about proper soil composition, root rot and predatory insects had made one point perfectly plain.

The pineapple mustn't freeze.

If it did, it wouldn't bear fruit. If it didn't bear fruit,

Oliver's gift would be spoiled, and they'd have nothing to show for their trip to Sittingbourne but a dead pineapple. Penelope would be dreadfully disappointed, and everything would be ruined.

Dinah was doing all she could to keep it warm, but the temperature had dropped since they'd left Lord Horace's estate. She wrapped her hands around the pineapple's rough sides and hugged it closer, drawing the edge of her cloak around it, but it felt hopeless, as if the best she could do would never be enough to save it.

It was going to freeze, despite her best efforts. Already it felt cold and hard against her fingers, and they were only as far as Abberton. It would be another three hours before they reached Cliff's Edge. By then the pineapple would be nothing but a prickly block of ice—fit for nothing, and useful to no one.

Foolishness, to imagine *she* could take care of something so rare, so precious. She should have refused to let Oliver relinquish it to her. She should have made him understand he couldn't trust her with it, that she couldn't keep it safe.

Pineapples were delicate, fragile things. They needed warmth and light and gentle nurturing—all things Dinah couldn't give. How could she? No one had ever shown her those things, or taught her how to offer them to…to…

To a pineapple.

All that sweet, tender golden flesh, ruined by her ignorance.

A beautiful, loving heart, one filled with laughter and light, broken by her coldness…

Dinah's vision blurred and she squeezed her eyes closed.

Those hours she'd spent with Oliver in London—all those nights he'd come to the Pandemonium to watch her perform, then waited out in the mews afterwards to take her home. All that time, he'd been looking out for her. He'd been teaching her what it meant to take care of someone, to love them.

All the times he'd made her smile, made her laugh, given her joy...

He'd been showing her how much he loved her, and what had she done for him in return? She'd taken everything he offered in her greedy hands without understanding what it was, or having the vaguest idea how to give it back to him.

How many times had she looked into his eyes and disregarded his love and ignored how much sweeter her life had become since she'd found him, all while telling herself *she* was the one taking care of *him*?

She was in love with him. Perhaps she had been all along, ever since that dark night a year ago when she'd fired a pistol at him and he'd dragged her from her carriage to prevent her from taking another shot.

Oliver believed love could overcome any obstacle, turn coldness into warmth and darkness into light, but Dinah knew better. She'd freeze his warmth, swallow his light. He couldn't see that yet, but years from now, when Oliver had a family like Alistair Rutherford's—a family he could be proud of—he'd look back on this mad journey from London to Essex and be grateful it had come to nothing.

Dinah tucked the pineapple into the crook of her elbow and let her mind drift, as it had time and again today, to the delirious kisses she'd shared with Oliver in the greenhouse this morning. The touch of his lips to hers, the gentle, almost reverent glide of his fingertips over her skin, his soft words in her ears...

You're safe here, Dinah. Safe with me.

She was. She'd always been safe with Oliver.

The trouble was, Oliver wasn't safe with her.

The puppy whined as she squirmed against the

cushion. She cupped one hand around his warm, round belly, her other arm still wrapped around the pineapple. "Hush, now. It's all right."

She didn't intend to fall asleep, but she did, and dreamed of Oliver's lips against hers, his husky whisper in her ear.

I love you, and I believe you love me, Dinah—

"Dinah!"

The shout penetrated the haze of sleep, and Dinah startled awake. The pup was racing in excited circles at her feet, it's stubby tail waving madly, having abandoned her lap for a much more amusing pursuit.

"Oh, no." She'd dropped the pineapple in her sleep, and now it was rolling about on the floor of the coach, with the puppy leaping gamely after it. She reached down and snatched it up, but the spikey green leaves were covered with the puppy's teeth marks, and it was heavier than it had been, now more ice than fruit.

"Dinah!" The coach door flew open.

Dinah blinked at the light. They were in the circular drive at Cliff's Edge, and Penelope was peering into the coach, a blinding smile on her face. "How I've missed you!"

"Miss Bishop. We're so glad you decided to join us for Christmas. Lady Archer has hardly been able to contain her excitement." Lord Archer stepped forward and reached for Dinah's hand, but before he could take it the puppy darted toward the open door and tumbled onto the drive at Penelope's feet.

Lord Archer reached down and plucked him up. "Who's this handsome fellow? Fine pup, Oliver. Where did you get him?"

"Lord Dunton." Oliver stepped forward, took Dinah's cold hand in his warm one and helped her from the coach. "He's one of Massie's."

Lord Archer's eyes widened. "How did you manage

that? Wait, never mind," he added with a chuckle, before Oliver could answer. "It's probably best if I don't know. Fine animal, or he will be, once he grows a little. He'll be a capital hunter. All of Massie's dogs are." Lord Archer stroked the puppy's head, his tone wistful.

Oliver was gazing at Dinah, his brow creased in an anxious from, but he offered his brother a distracted smile. "I'm glad you approve, Will, because he's yours."

Lord Archer's mouth fell open. "Mine?"

"He's your Christmas gift. You did say you wanted a hunter, didn't you?"

"I did. I *do*. I never dreamed I'd get one of Massie's dogs, though." Lord Archer grinned, delighted. "He's perfect. Thank you, Oliver."

Oliver didn't seem to hear his brother. "Are you quite all right, Din—that is, Miss Bishop? You look pale."

"Never mind Miss Bishop, Oliver." Penelope rose to her tiptoes to kiss Oliver's cheek, then made a shooing gesture. "You may leave her to me. I'll take good care of her."

Oliver didn't move, his gaze still locked on Dinah's face. Penelope shot her husband a look, and Lord Archer slapped Oliver on the back. "Come on, then. Let's see if the pup will chase a stick."

"Better make it a twig," Oliver grumbled. He cast one last anxious look at Dinah, but allowed himself to be led away.

"Thank goodness they're gone. You look as if you could use some tea. Here, let me take that." Penelope nodded at Dinah's hands.

Dinah blinked down at herself. She hadn't realized she was still clutching the pineapple. Penelope drew it away from her, then slid her arm through Dinah's and led her to the house. When they reached the drawing room, she placed the pineapple carefully on the tea table, and led Dinah to a seat beside the fire.

Dinah allowed herself to be seated, but she only nodded in response to Penelope's cheerful chatter. She was afraid if she spoke, she'd burst into tears.

Penelope didn't seem to notice. "Christopher and Maddy are out riding, but they're both anxious to see you. Maddy has a suitor—did I tell you? I thought Christopher might have settled on Miss Everard, but he's such a dreadful flirt it's difficult to tell. There's to be a supper tomorrow evening with dancing afterward, so you'll have to help me determine if—"

"I won't be here tomorrow evening. I'm returning to London in the morning."

Penelope returned the teapot to the tray with exaggerated precision. "Oh? May I ask why?"

"I, er...I need to get back to the Pandemonium. You know how Silas is. He'll have a fit if I'm not back on stage soon." It wasn't the real reason, of course, but it was plausible enough.

Penelope lifted her tea cup to her lips and took a dainty sip. "Silas isn't the reason you want to leave. Try again."

"He's...I...I don't know what you want me to...will Miss Spence be at the supper tomorrow evening?" Dinah snapped her mouth closed, horrified. Why, why, *why* had she brought up Miss Spence? If she could have snatched the words out of the air, she would have.

Penelope was no fool. She'd realize at once Oliver was the reason Dinah was fleeing Cliff's Edge, and she'd never cease teasing until she had the whole story.

But Penelope's next words shocked her. "No. There isn't any Miss Spence. I invented her."

Dinah stared. "*Invented* her?" No, that couldn't be true. She must have misheard—

"Invented her, yes. Right out of thin air, just like

that." Penelope snapped her fingers. "You see, I knew if you thought there was a Miss Spence, you'd make certain Oliver came to Cliff's Edge so you might deliver him into a respectable young lady's arms and save him from marrying a wicked actress."

Dinah's mouth dropped open. "Penelope! How could you do such a—"

"You're the wicked actress in this scenario, in case that's not clear," Penelope interrupted, stirring another lump of sugar into her tea.

"But that's...you—"

"I knew Oliver—being wildly in love with you—would make the most of his time alone with you in the coach. Am I correct?"

"You seem to know a great deal more about this than I do," Dinah hissed, frazzled to the last degree. "Why don't you tell me?"

Penelope shrugged. "Certainly, if you like. I believe it's something like this. Oliver is madly, wildly in love with you, has been since the moment he saw you and has, in his own odd way, been courting you for a year now."

"Not precisely courting—"

"You've made up your mind you can't have him," Penelope went on. "Despite having realized during your journey from London you're as madly, wildly in love with him as he is with you. Is that correct?"

"It's not...it's more complicated than that." Wasn't it? Dinah thought it must be, but her thoughts were all muddled, and she couldn't make sense of any of this.

"No, it isn't. The only trouble here is you've decided it won't do for Oliver to marry you, because you're certain he'll be made unhappy by it, despite ample evidence the Angel brothers marry for love, and make exceptionally devoted husbands." Penelope patted her swollen belly. "Now then, let's try this again, shall we?

Why do you insist on leaving tomorrow morning, Dinah?"

Dinah threw her hands up in the air. "To get out of Oliver's way, so he can get on with the business of falling in love with Miss Spence—"

"Who doesn't exist," Penelope reminded her.

"...and save him from years of regret—"

"Save him from a lifetime of happiness, you mean."

"...and to keep him from making a dreadful mistake!"

Penelope snorted. "The dreadful mistake of marrying the lady he loves? Dear me, that *is* a good plan. I wonder I didn't think of it myself."

Dinah stared at Penelope, unable to say a word. All at once, all she wanted in the world was to lay her head on her friend's shoulder and let her tears fall.

Penelope's face softened. "Do you love him, Dinah?"

Dinah pressed her hand to her stomach, nausea rising in her throat. "A marriage between us would be a farce. No, worse than that. It would be a blasphemy. It will lead to a lifetime of regret for Oliver, and a lifetime of guilt and shame for me."

Penelope regarded Dinah with steady brown eyes. "That's not what I asked, Dinah. Do you love him?"

Dinah let her face fall into her hands. She'd lied to Oliver, lied to herself, and now she was about to lie to Penelope, her dearest friend, and she just...she simply couldn't do it anymore. "Oh, Penelope, of course, I do! How could I not? I've never known anyone like him. He has the purest, most loving heart. If I didn't know him to be flesh and blood, I'd never believe a man with a heart like his could exist."

"Ah, now we're getting somewhere. Have you told him you love him?"

"No! He can't ever know. If he finds out, he'll never let me go until I promise to marry him." That sharp blue gaze of his would pry under her hard surface to the tender, raw skin beneath, and he'd see everything.

"You're right, he won't. What does that tell you, Dinah? What does it tell you when a man with a heart as fine and pure as Oliver's refuses to give you up?"

Dinah didn't have an answer to that, so she remained silent, her gaze on her hands. Penelope was also silent, waiting, and they might have sat there all afternoon if they hadn't been interrupted by the sound of a man clearing his throat.

They both turned to find Oliver standing in the doorway. "William sent me to fetch you, Penelope," he said, but he was looking at Dinah, his face tight with worry.

"Yes, of course." Penelope arched a meaningful eyebrow at Dinah before she leapt to her feet and disappeared through the door.

"Are you all right?" Oliver asked quietly, stepping further into the room. "You look...unlike yourself."

"Yes, I'm..." Dinah began, but she couldn't lie to him, not when he was gazing at her with those worried blue eyes. She whirled around, turning her back to Oliver just as the tears burning in her eyes began running down her cheeks.

"Don't turn away from me, Dinah." Oliver strode across the room, took her shoulders in his hands and turned her toward him. As soon as he saw her face he froze, horrified. "What's the matter, love? Why are you crying?"

Because I love you and I can't have you.

Words were bruising her ribs, burning her throat, shoving against her lips, and she couldn't stop them, couldn't hold them back. They were gushing from her mouth, bursting forth—

"I...I killed the pineapple!" Dinah blurted, then

buried her face in her hands as hot tears slid down her cheeks.

"The pineapple?" Oliver took her wrists and gently lowered her hands from her face. "Dinah, the pineapple doesn't matter."

"Look at it!" Dinah pointed a dramatic finger at the pineapple, which was still sitting on the tea table, looking particularly forlorn. "I tried to take care of it, but it was so cold, and I could tell it was freezing, and then I fell asleep and dropped it and the puppy chewed on its...its...spikes, and now it's dead, and it won't bear fruit, and I've spoiled your gift for Penelope!"

"Sweetheart, I don't care about the pineapple." Oliver cupped her face in his hands. "Look at me. I only care about *you*."

"But don't you see, Oliver?" Dinah gulped in a few shuddering breaths. "I can't be trusted with anything p-p-precious. I don't know how t-to care for things."

"Things? Do you mean...no, Dinah, don't look away from me." Oliver tipped her chin up. "Are we talking about pineapples, or something else?"

"Everything," she whispered. "Pineapples, and animals, and people."

"That isn't true, Dinah. What about the kittens?"

Dinah raised her tear-stained face to his. "Mathilda's kittens?"

Oliver brushed damp strands of hair back from her cheeks. "Well, yes, those kittens, but I was thinking of the kittens you had as a child. The barn cats. You took care of them, didn't you?"

"Yes, but that was just—"

"Then there's Penelope. You've been taking care of her since she came to the Pandemonium, haven't you? And Maddy. You've always taken care of her as if she were your own sister."

"Yes, but anyone would—"

"The puppy, too. You've been taking care of him since we left Dartford, though God knows he's naughty enough to put anyone out of temper."

Dinah sniffled. "Well, he doesn't like me much."

A hint of a smile crossed Oliver's lips. "I don't know about that. He didn't chew *your* pocket to bits."

"Well, no."

"No. Tell me then, sweetheart. What are these 'other things' you can't be trusted to take care of?"

Dinah bit her lip. Once she said it, he'd know the truth, and there'd be no taking it back, but maybe... maybe she'd come too far for that, and maybe she no longer wanted to take it back.

"A heart," she whispered at last. "Such a precious heart. I'm afraid if it's trusted to me, I'll make mistakes, and I'll...I'll break it."

Oliver brushed his thumbs over her cheeks, but he was quiet for a long time before he asked, "Whose heart, Dinah?"

She tried to look down at her hands, but Oliver wouldn't allow it. "No, look at me. Whose heart is so precious to you, you're afraid to trust yourself with it?"

Dinah drew in a long, shaky breath, then she lay a trembling hand on his chest. Under her palm his heart was thundering, the beat strong and steady and true. "Yours."

There was a brief, fraught silence, and then Oliver was gathering her against him, pressing his lips into her hair. "Oh, sweetheart. Don't you see? My heart isn't mine anymore. It's *yours*. Nothing will ever change that. The only way you could break it is by leaving me, and even then, it would still be yours."

Dinah gripped his coat and let her forehead rest against his chest.

He held her, nuzzling her temple and scattering sweet, tender kisses over her cheeks, her eyelids and the tip of her nose. When her breathing calmed and her tears slowed, he eased her away from him so he could gaze down into her eyes. "Your heart is pounding." He touched a fingertip to the hollow of her throat where her pulse was beating wildly.

"Yes." She took his hand and pressed his palm flat against her chest, over her heart. "Perhaps it's not frozen, after all."

"It never was, Dinah." He gazed down at her, his blue eyes bright with fear and love and hope. "It was just...waiting until it was safe."

Dinah reached up and traced his lips with a hesitant finger. "It was waiting for *you*. I-I love you, Oliver."

Oliver closed his eyes, as if he'd waited a lifetime to hear her say those words, and needed a quiet moment to treasure them. When he opened them again, they were glowing with joy and love. "I love you so much, sweetheart. You'll marry me, Dinah? You'll be my wife?"

Dinah hesitated, but for only a moment. She was still afraid, but this was no time to turn coward. When a man like Oliver Angel offered you his heart you took it, and spent a lifetime cherishing it.

"Yes. I'll marry you. How could I not, after such a courtship?" She wrapped her arms around his neck and smiled up at him. "Or did we decide it was an escapade? A Christmas courtship caper?"

"It was a lark. A playful, harmless bit of fun, and the first in a lifetime of adventures together." He smiled down at her, his dimples flashing.

Dinah's breath caught. She'd seen Oliver smile thousands of times, but never before had she seen him smile like *this*. It burst across his face like a sunrise, the warmth of its rays melting in an instant the last tiny shard of ice buried deep inside her heart.

EPILOGUE

CLIFF'S EDGE, ESSEX, ENGLAND, LATE APRIL, 1813

*M*arriage had made Dinah shamefully lazy.

Or perhaps it wasn't marriage itself. Perhaps it was just a blissful marriage to a man she adored, but a lady did tend to spend a great deal more time lounging in bed when she was safely snuggled in her husband's arms, her cheek pillowed on his bare chest and his hands stroking her hair.

Oh my, yes. She was every inch the languid, indolent lady these days. A contented smile curved her lips as she reached across the bed for Oliver. But instead of the smooth, warm skin and wild, rumpled hair that made her fingertips tingle with delight, her hand found only cool sheets.

"Oliver?" She sat up, frowning. The scent of *Malmaison* lingered in the folds of the sheets but it was faint, just an echo of vanilla and cedar. She glanced toward the window. A sliver of pale, dappled moonlight peeked between the drapes.

Where on earth was Oliver? She didn't fancy a midnight game of hide and seek, but there wasn't a chance she'd fall asleep again without him by her side.

She indulged in one last long, languid stretch, her arms over her head and her toes curling, but before she could throw the coverlet aside and commence a search for her wayward husband she was interrupted by a low, husky drawl from the doorway.

"Ah, now there's a tantalizing vision."

Dinah turned her head on the pillow. Oliver had one hip propped against the doorframe, his glittering blue eyes taking her in from head to toe.

"There you are." Dinah rose onto her elbow and rested her head on her hand. "Where have you been?" Her gaze lingered on the bare expanse of skin revealed by the open neck of his shirt. "I missed you." She held out a hand to him. "Come back to bed."

Oliver's eyes darkened and a flush rose in his cheeks, but he shook his head. "Soon. I want to show you something first. Come with me, sweetheart."

"Can't it wait?" She crooked a finger at him, an inviting smile curving her lips.

Oliver's lips parted on a soft groan, but he kept a stubborn distance between himself and the bed. "No. You'll like it, I promise you."

She threw the covers aside with a sigh and rose from the bed. "Oh, very well. Do I have to get dressed, or...Oliver? What's the matter?"

He looked pained, his hands clenching and un-clenching at his sides. "The moonlight, behind you. I can see every inch of you through your night rail. You're so beautiful, love."

Dinah looked down at herself, her cheeks heating. She'd never been the sort of lady who blushed, but Oliver's hungry gaze seared her.

He strode across the room and snatched her into his arms. His hands moved restlessly over her curves as he nuzzled into her neck, inhaling deeply. "Dear God, you smell good. How do you always manage to smell so good?"

Dinah tangled her fingers in his hair. "I smell like *you*."

"Hmmm. I smell lovely, then." He bit gently at her throat, letting out a low growl. "Perhaps we should return to bed, after all."

"Certainly not, my lord," Dinah said with mock sternness. "I'm up now."

"Yes, well, so am I." He nudged his thigh between her legs. "Just let me…"

He trailed off with a groan as Dinah sank her teeth into his earlobe. She teased the tender flesh between her lips until Oliver was panting, but then she set him gently away from her. "If I let you do anything, we'll never leave this bedchamber, and I'm curious to see what got you out of it in the first place."

"A thing so magical I left my lovely wife alone in our bed, which was no easy feat. Here, you'll need this." Oliver took up the thick woolen shawl draped across the foot of the bed and draped it over her shoulders, then grabbed her hand and led her from the bedchamber and down the stairs to the ground floor.

"My goodness, Oliver. Where are you taking me?"

"Shhh." Oliver pressed a brief kiss to her lips. They crept down the darkened hallway and into William's study, then slipped through the glass doors onto the terrace. They dashed across the west lawn, the dew dampening the toes of Dinah's slippers, then stopped at the door to Penelope's greenhouse.

"Good Lord, what a monstrosity." Oliver eyed the octagonal building. "It's a wonder there's any glazing or cast-iron left in England."

Dinah laughed. William had gone a bit too far with the greenhouse, but Penelope was delighted with it, and spent many happy hours inside, fussing over her plants. "Oh, come now. It's lovely."

"I will admit I find greenhouses a great deal more intriguing since our visit to Lord Horace."

Oliver waggled his eyebrows, making Dinah laugh again. "I hope you haven't brought me out here to debauch me in Penelope's greenhouse."

"Not tonight, but you can be sure I'll keep it in mind for another time. For now, I believe I'll settle for a pineapple."

"Another pineapple?" Dinah groaned. She hadn't had much luck with pineapples.

Oliver gave her an enigmatic smile. "Not *another* pineapple, but Lord Horace's pineapple." He led her by the hand to the back of the greenhouse, where Penelope kept a row of citrus trees in pots against the southern wall.

That was when Dinah saw it.

There, amid the orange trees with their cluster of white blossoms was Lord Horace's lone pineapple, and it was…

She gasped softly. "It isn't dead."

"No, sweetheart, it isn't." Oliver squeezed her shoulders. "See that bit of green, just at the base there? It's a new leaf. The plant won't flower for some time yet, but it's not dead."

Dinah leaned closer, staring in wonder at the tiny green bud. "I-I told Penelope it was dead. I wonder she took the time to plant it at all."

Oliver dropped a kiss on the back of her neck. "I asked her to plant it as a favor to me."

"*You* did?" Dinah turned to face him, her heart rushing into her throat. "Why, Oliver?"

He was quiet for a while before murmuring, "Sometimes a thing can appear hopeless when really it's just—"

"Waiting," Dinah whispered.

"Yes." He smiled down at her, his eyes warm.

"Until it feels safe." She caressed the dimple in Oliver's cheek.

"Until it feels safe." Oliver opened his arms to her then, and Dinah rushed into his embrace. She pressed her cheek against his chest, listened to his heart beating, and marveled over Christmas larks, joyful blue eyes, and the astounding resilience of hearts, and pineapples.

ABOUT THE AUTHOR

Anna Bradley writes steamy, sexy Regency historical romance—think garters, fops and riding crops! Readers can get in touch with Anna via her webpage at www.annabradley.net. Anna lives with her husband and two children in Portland, OR, where people are delightfully weird and love to read.

THE MARQUESS OF MISTLETOE

GRACE BURROWES

"*T*his is no way to court a lady or to celebrate the holidays." Raphael Jones put world of reproach into his observation, a version of which, he'd been offering for the past five snowy miles.

"Hush, you," Leopold, Marques of Cadeau retorted. "Choosing a bride is a pragmatic undertaking for a man newly saddled with a title,. You will please cease your sentimental maunderings on a topic about which you know little."

Leopold had left military life behind months ago when a second cousin's title had been dumped in his lap, as unappealing and demanding as a squalling infant.

Raphael Jones, Leo's former batman, had marched with him across Spain, through France, and at Waterloo. When Leo had acquired the title, Rafe had appointed himself valet, general factotum, and conscience to the new marquess. Nothing Leo promised, threatened, or demanded dislodged Rafe from his post.

Perhaps Leo's new marchioness would know what to do with an old soldier who refused to follow orders.

"It's Christmas Day, your worship," Rafe said, as if corner glee clubs tipsy with wassail, shouted holiday greetings, and the very calendar had escaped Leo's notice. "To be looking over a lady during the holidays as if she's a mare on offer at Tatts is a sacrilege."

The cold had numbed everything Leo owned—from his toes to the tip of his nose to his saddle-weary fundament—but it hadn't quite driven out his doubts. Rafe had a point: What sort of man ignored Yuletide family gatherings to interview a prospective wife?

A man who wanted the whole business concluded, that's what sort. Leo had endured months in Vienna as a marquess with means, and didn't care to repeat that ordeal in London. Forced marches were one thing, German princesses popping out of powder rooms—and their bodices—were quite another.

Though what sort of woman spent Boxing Day looking over a prospective husband?

"Your cork-brained notion of courting will be the death of us both," Rafe went on. "Can't imagine you've asked a lady to travel in this weather. And at Christmas."

Cold alone wasn't that much of a challenge. Between stout wool, a sound horse, and common sense, Leo could deal with cold. But the wind...

The bitter weather came straight at them, as if Nature herself was determined that Leo not reach his objective. Leo couldn't say if snow was falling, but it was certainly blowing in his face, a million grains of frigid misery, telling him to seek shelter and rethink the contract he was considering signing.

"You will please recall," Leo said, above the soughing of the wind, "the lady has asked me to travel at the holidays, and she'll be looking me over too. I'm to be her Boxing Day gift, or my wealth and title are."

"Can't take wealth and a title to bed, your royal pig-headedness. Can't make babies cuddling up to wealth and a title, can't—bedamned stinking excuse for a spavined mule, watch where you're going!"

Rafe's horse had slipped, likely from fatigue, for the snow wasn't that deep.

"Spend more effort guiding that creature, and less haranguing me, and you won't risk his hide."

"I'm trying to guide your perishing self," Rafe said, patting his horse. "Thankless, hopeless job though it is, and this being Christmas too."

The Yuletide season was an ironic time for Leo to become engaged. He'd once dreamed of children and a future with a woman who'd have made a wonderful mother and a devoted wife. Marielle Redford had been his best friend, his dearest delight, and then she'd become his deepest regret.

Now she would be nothing but a memory, which was for the best. She'd married another, Leo had gone for a soldier—not in that order—and life had moved on, one bitter, bleak mile at a time.

"See what you've gone and done," Rafe said, half a mile later. "You've lamed my poor, wee Wellington with your mad scheme."

Wellington stood eighteen hands in his bare feet, could pull a laden canal barge without breaking a sweat, and—unlike his owner—was the soul of uncomplaining calm. He'd been a gift from Leo to Rafe years ago, and the pair took excellent care of each other.

"He's not lame," Leo said, assessing the horse's gait. "He's tired of listening to you whine and prattle, as am I, as is Beowulf."

Leo's horse shook his reins, suggesting at least one creature in all of creation still had some respect for his employer.

"I tell you, the old boy's going off, just like he did north of Toulouse."

Which, thankfully, had been more than two years

ago. "He wasn't lame, he was simply tired and you were drunk."

Leo obliged Rafe with further argument for the next two miles, mostly so they'd both stay awake. The wind howled, the horses plodded onward, and London came inevitably nearer. Leo was riding toward his future, toward marriage to a woman of suitable rank to marry a marquess.

Somehow, years ago, Marielle Redford had managed to walk up the church aisle and put youthful dreams behind her. How had she done it, and had she spared a thought for the young man who'd once loved her more than life itself?

"We're stopping at the next inn," Rafe declared. "A man who's served the crown loyally for years deserves to use a chamber pot in a nice cozy parlor rather than freeze his pizzle off in the inn yard. I could also use a toddy, should some kind soul be interested in preserving me from a cruel death on the road. A plate of cheese toast wouldn't go amiss either."

They'd reached a hamlet west of Chelsea. Leo hadn't been here for years, hadn't let himself acknowledge that his travels would take him past this monument to his dashed hopes.

"Looks like a right, snug establishment with a proper respect for the joyous season," Rafe observed.

The Ox and Ass was festooned with pine roping, wreaths hung in the windows, and red ribbons had been twined about the porch pillars. Evening was an hour away, but the lamps in the yard were already lit, and two noisy boys were pelting each other with snowballs.

"We'll stop long enough to rest the horses and get warm," Leo said. "Then we push on to Chelsea, because I must be punctual for my appointment tomorrow morning. A gentleman does not keep a lady waiting, no matter the weather."

Or the holiday.

"A gentleman," Rafe said, "does not marry a lady he's never met, nor undertake his courting in the office of a bedamned, useless, sniveling solicitor on Boxing Day."

Next Rafe would visit the topic of the head injury Leo had supposedly sustained at Badajoz, or the daft notions of the Quality, for if nothing else, acquiring a title had promoted Leo from gentry to Quality.

"My solicitors don't snivel," Leo retorted. They fawned though, and they sent along bills for services at a great rate.

"Methinks you need a toddy," Rafe said. "The cold has gone to your brain."

"For once, I agree with you. A toddy is in order, and we can drink to the health of my bride." Leo's potential bride. Nobody had signed any settlements, nobody had agreed to anything, but Leo was prepared to be generous.

"He's gone barmy," Rafe informed his horse. "Poor sod left the better part of himself on the battlefields, and this damned title has about finished off his common sense. What has the world come to, when a man whose bravery was noted by Old Hooky himself, an officer whose men marched through hell for him without complaint..."

Rafe's litany continued as they rode into the inn yard, ceasing only when the ordeal of dismounting had to be faced. Leo swung down carefully, and his frozen feet accepted his weight with a predictable agony of protest.

Nothing for it, but to solider on. Leo hoped the woman he was to court was more sanguine about their union than he could be. Fate had landed him at the last place he'd kissed Marielle, and the least he could do was raise a warm glass of spirits to feckless dreams and the woman who'd inspired them.

* * *

THE DREARIEST EXCUSE for a Christmas Day blew snow squalls about beneath a bleak sky beyond the window of Marielle's sitting room.

"I was an idiot for choosing to spend the night here." A sentimental idiot.

"Yes, milady," Petunia muttered as she poured Marielle another cup of tea.

"You aren't supposed to agree with me that easily," Marielle countered, returning to her seat near the fire. The room was chilly, except for the small area near the hearth circled with fire screens. Even there, the carpeted floor was drafty.

"Yes, milady. I mean, no milady." Petunia passed Marielle a teacup that did not match its saucer. "Shall I ask the innkeeper's wife for a tisane, milady?"

Milady, milady, milady. Marielle had been born a plain miss, and then she'd become Lady Drew Semple, wife to the third son of a marquess. Nearly a decade after speaking her vows, she still wasn't comfortable being addressed as my lady.

Which she'd just have to get over.

"I do not need a tisane. Traveling at the holidays ought not to agree with anybody."

Petunia's face was carefully expressionless, suggesting she'd heard the talk about Marielle's ancient history. A competent companion walked a slippery path between status as a family member—Petunia was a cousin-in-law at some remove on the Semple side— and the upper servants. She was unfailingly polite, but never quite warm.

As Marielle's feet hadn't been warm for days. "I have

good memories of this inn," Marielle said, rubbing one slippered foot over the other.

She also had sad memories.

Petunia wrapped a linen towel about the tea pot. "I had the maid put your sheets on the beds, and we've a private dining room reserved for supper."

A Christmas feast, the innkeeper had said, though from what Marielle had seen, nobody else had been demented enough to travel on Christmas Day, braving weather that would freeze Lucifer's ears off.

"You might as well eat the shortbread, Petunia. I don't care for it." Leopold had loved shortbread, and so Marielle had made it for him at Yuletide, batch after batch. When adolescence had begun adding inches to his height at a great rate, he'd gone so far as to put both butter and jam on his shortbread.

"I do care for it," Petunia said, "especially with a dash of cinnamon to mark the holidays. I have never met a proper Englishwoman who takes as little interest in the Yuletide season as you do, milady."

The tea was tepid and weak, which did not stop Petunia from dunking her shortbread into it.

"Do you imply I'm not a proper Englishwoman, Petunia?"

"Of course not, milady. I suspect the holidays make you sad."

The holidays made Marielle angry. She'd taken years to figure that out. "I have both fond and difficult memories of this time of year. I'm going out."

The shortbread didn't make it to Petunia's mouth. "But the weather!"

"Is simply weather. I won't be gone long."

Petunia didn't offer to accompany Marielle, which was fortunate. Marielle wanted to be alone when she revisited the place where she'd last kissed Leopold Drake, the same place she'd waited for him until the bitter weather had given her a lung fever from which she'd nearly died.

* * *

"GO INSIDE and secure us rooms under your name," Leo said, taking Wellington's reins from Rafe. "And order us a double round of toddies while you're about it. Mind you don't mention the title, or we'll be charged a king's ransom for a night's lodging."

"At once, your highness," Rafe said, saluting. "On the double, despite the fact that my old bones are nigh frozen to death. I live to serve, and—"

The entire point of the exercise was to get Rafe's old bones indoors before lung fever stalked him. "I can no longer court martial you, Raphael, but I can sack you."

"And put coal in my stocking too, sir. A dire fate for such a loyal—"

Leo took Rafe by the shoulders and gave him a small shove in the direction of the inn, for Rafe would hover over both Leo and the horses like an anxious guardian angel.

"Two plates of cheese toast," Leo said. "And some victuals for our next leg of the journey."

Rafe was as solid as a barn door, but couldn't be moved half so easily. Leo had rank, two inches of height, and some muscle on the older man, all of which he applied as gently as he could.

"There will be no next leg of the journey for me," Rafe said. "Not today. Here I shall bide, for it's Christmas—"

"March, Raphael."

Rafe trudged off, pausing long enough to pitch a snowball at one of the dodging, shrieking boys. The children were happy—today *was* Christmas—and once, long ago, Leo had been such a boy, grateful for a holiday and a playmate.

"Come along," Leo said to the horses. "There's a warm stall, hay, and a rest for you both. I'll ask the grooms to take the chill off your water, and they'll think I'm daft, but a soldier learns things. Can't charge into battle on a colicky mount."

Can't make babies cuddling up to wealth and a title. Rafe's warning followed Leo into the relative warmth of the stable. A stable lad swaddled in mittens, scarf, and gloves greeted them at the door, though Leo would see to his own horses. A marquess probably wouldn't be allowed that courtesy in Merry Olde England, but a soldier would.

A former soldier.

Leo waved the groom away, and sent Welly into the first empty loose box. Beowulf got the one beside it because comrades should be billeted together when possible.

"Another guest of the inn is in the saddle room," the groom said. "I'm up the steps with the coachmen, if you need anything, sir." He tugged his cap and went scampering up wooden steps that lead to the hayloft, and apparently, to winter quarters for the stable help.

Within minutes, Wulf and Welly were dispatching their hay with the steady munching of hungry equines. Leo stacked his saddle over Rafe's and carried both down the barn aisle to the saddle room. He couldn't unlatch the door to the saddle room with arms full of gear, so he set the saddles on a rack and pushed the door open.

The guest in the saddle room was *female*. She sat on a trunk, her back to the door. Beneath a lovely red velvet cloak, her shoulders were hunched with what could only be dejection. Leo considered turning tail and retreating, but a thought stopped him: The lady was quietly weeping, and she was alone.

A gentleman, be he a soldier or a marquess, would not leave a damsel in distress without offering his aid—especially not on Christmas.

* * *

THE MEMORIES ASSAILED Marielle like so many blows to her dignity. Waiting and waiting in this same small, tidy space, the scents of horse and leather twining with her hopes as the minutes, then the hours crawled by.

Leo had left her here alone in a deepening winter chill to face his abandonment and to face her future.

Before that, on many occasions Leo had kissed her here and promised her the world. They'd done more than kiss—a lot more—and only Leo's honor had prevented them from anticipating vows that had never been uttered.

As a girl of seventeen, Marielle had spoken those vows in her heart. Whether Leo had left her a maid out of good sense, honor, or an unstated plan to leave her for an officer's life, she didn't know. She'd bitterly regretted never having made love with him—he might have at least shared that much with her— but now, for the first time, she could thank him.

She'd gone to her husband a chaste, if unenthusiastic bride, and Drew had been a good husband.

Marielle had convinced herself that the friendship she and Drew had developed was a far more trustworthy basis for a relationship than the passion Leo had inspired, but a decade later, her tears were hot and heartfelt.

She and Leo had been so young and so in love, and the whole world had thought them daft—the whole world being their parents—but such a love had deserved a chance. Leo had bought his colors instead, and Marielle still kept him in her prayers. He'd never been named among the dead or the missing in battle, and she took comfort from that.

"Madam," said a masculine voice. "You will please cease this lachrymosity."

A widow in tears exercised a right no other woman in the realm had—to order men about. "Go away," she said, keeping her back to the intruder. Her nose was likely red, and her eyes were puffy, and she was entitled to privacy with her regrets. "I mourn for a soldier lost to me years ago. You will leave me in peace if you've any charity—"

Bootsteps sounded on the plank floor, and the scent of damp wool blended with the other scents of the saddle room. A hint of vetiver joined the barnyard bouquet. Leo had worn vetiver...

"It's Christmas," the man said, coming around to stand before Marielle's perch on the trunk. "Surely your tears can wait for some other day?"

He was tall, and his great coat swirled about him with the drape of fine tailoring. Other impressions—broad shoulders, dark hair, riding boots damp from the snow—registered beneath the timbre of his voice.

That voice.

"Leo?" Marielle said. "Leopold Drake?" His features had matured from adolescent beauty into a man's rugged countenance. The years of soldiering were marked in the lines beside his eyes and mouth, and in blue eyes that had once been merry. Those eyes were chilly now, and guarded.

Marielle fell silent. Her body was both hot and shivery, as memory and reality collided in the man she beheld.

"Miss Redford." He bowed correctly, which was

ridiculous given the setting, then produced a wrinkled handkerchief.

Marielle took it and dabbed at her cheeks. "What are you doing here, Leo, and is this a flag of truce?" How calm she sounded, though the hand clutching his handkerchief shook.

One corner of his mouth quirked up. "Happy Christmas to you, too, ma'am. You are looking well."

"I look a fright. You look to be thriving." Her splotchy cheeks and puffy eyes were his fault, for which she was grateful. The sight of him—the simple sight of him—well, whole, and healthy, threatened to turn her weepy again.

"I am well, if a bit chilled. How is your husband?"

Must he sound so damnably calm? Must he look so damnably attractive?

Though Leo did not look *friendly*. His question was clearly meant to establish some sort of picket lines, and that would not do. Leo's abandonment had hurt, but Marielle refused to make an enemy of him—tempted though she might be.

"He's dead, Leo. Gone three years, from a wasting disease. I'm a comfortably well off widow." Without children, and Drew's dying regret had been that they'd never had offspring. Marielle hadn't understood the intensity of Drew's sadness over that lack until she'd been wearing her weeds, listening to the bishop drone on about God's will and faith and other platitudes.

Children were somebody to love, and without somebody to love, meaning in life was hard to come by. Remarriage loomed as a solution to the problem of the childless widow in society's eyes, and lately, in Marielle's too.

"My condolences on the loss of your spouse," Leo said. "What of your father?"

Leo's voice had deepened, and acquired an implied

hint of command. He expected his questions to be answered.

"Papa died shortly after I married. He'd apparently been unwell for some time." Drew had thought Marielle was mourning her papa, and she had been, but she'd also been mourning her first love.

Leo took a scowling visual inventory of the saddle room, as if rearranging his own view of the past.

"It's cold enough to freeze Lucifer's ears off in here," he said. "May I escort you to the inn?"

That was Marielle's turn of phrase, borrowed from a long-ago nanny. Leo had kept that much of her with him. Had he carried other memories of her into battle, and exactly what had prompted him to choose the constant threat of death over her hand in marriage?

"We're shall talk, Leo Drake," Marielle said, rising and dusting off her backside. "For Christmas, you will give me the answers I deserved ten years ago."

He peered down at her—he'd not been this tall as a lad of seventeen—his expression unreadable. Ten years ago, Marielle had been able to accurately translate his sighs, the angle of his shoulders, his stride, his word choices, even his silences.

Now, he was a stranger inhabiting the person of her dearest, lost love—a handsome stranger—and one who had not kept close track of her. But then again, how exactly did a soldier at war keep track of anybody back home?

"Perhaps you'll favor me with a few answers too, madam."

Marielle was tempted to ask if Leo had married, but she'd moved on with her life, made other plans. His present marital status was no concern of hers. Perhaps it was for the best that she and Leo had encountered each other like this. She could close the door to her

past before stepping through the door to her future, all
tidy and calm.

She preceded Leo into the barn aisle, waited while
he stowed his gear—a half-pay officer wouldn't expect
the stable lads to wait on him hand and foot—and then
permitted him to escort her across the frigid, snowy
inn yard.

She was Lady Drew Semple now, widowed, and of
means and consequence.

So why was her heart pounding if she were a seven-
teen-year-old girl on the eve of an elopement?

188

CHAPTER 2

*O*f all the ambushes in all the villages in all the hinterlands, coming upon Marielle Redford at the same hostelry where Leo had last heard her declarations of undying devotion was the most diabolical.

Surely, only a very, very naughty fellow deserved that blow on Christmas Day, though this year past year especially, Leo had been nearly a monk where the ladies were concerned.

Marielle was prettier than ever—another blow—but she'd lost an ebullience that had come through even when she'd sat quietly and read. Marielle as a very young woman had been like the sun, bringing light no matter how cold the day, and a determined optimism Leo had missed brutally as he'd marched through years of war.

Her chestnut hair was pulled back in a tidy chignon, and her brown eyes bore a woman's sense of self-confidence. She'd become altogether more impressive for acquiring a faint air of restraint, but he missed his impetuous Marielle.

As much as Leo wanted to resent the lady before him, he could not. A woman made her way in the world as best she could, and clearly, Marielle's way now was adequately smoothed with coin. She was in good health, in good looks, and expensively attired. Her cloak was velvet, doubtless lined with satin, and cut in the latest style.

"I've ordered toddies and toast," Leo said as he escorted her across the inn yard. "Will you join me?"

Marielle paused outside the main door. They were sheltered from the wind, and all around them, holiday decorations conveyed yuletide good cheer. And yet, the bleakness that assailed Leo was bone deep and colder than a winter night.

He had lost her. He'd accepted a commission, convinced she'd spurned him. The girl he'd known had been impetuous, passionate, and not always sensible—who was at seventeen?—but she'd been unfailingly kind. Perhaps Marielle had thought sending him off to the glamor of an officer's life was a kindness, though the romance of soldiering and the reality had been only distantly related.

She gazed across the innyard, at the stately oak that had sheltered so many of their encounters. Her expression suggested some sorrow deeper than regret, some grief that echoed the bleakness in Leo's heart.

"Marielle, I'm sorry." The young man in Leo was also furious with her—joining a war when he'd planned to attend his own wedding had been a horrible coming of age—but his regrets were genuine too. "I'd like to know why you did what you did, but mostly, I'm sorry we couldn't be together."

She had grown formidable with the passing years. Widowhood could do that. Marielle had tossed Leo aside to marry some aristocrat, and she had to have loved her husband fiercely.

Maybe more fiercely than she'd loved Leo, though in all humility, he hadn't thought such a thing possible.

"*You* want answers from *me?*" she replied, looking

him up and down as if he'd arrived to a fancy dress ball in muddy boots. "That's rich, Leopold, when you were the one who preferred war to wedded bliss. A gentleman holds a door for a lady."

Marielle had always had a temper, but the passing years had taught how to wield that temper with cool precision.

Leo bowed her through the door. "A gentleman also doesn't argue with a lady, but clearly, I'm about to have a rousing disagreement with you. A private parlor is in order, don't you agree? I've known you since you gave up sucking your thumb. We can share a plate of toast without offending the dictates of propriety."

As a younger woman, she might have dressed him down sorely, and he'd have caught her in his arms and jollied her out of her temper.

In the inn's foyer, she turned her back to him, as the lady of the manor turns her back in expectation of the butler removing her wrap. Leo obliged, and folded her cloak over his arm. The scent of Christmas spices wafted from her garment—cinnamon, cloves, a touch of mace. An expensive and unusual perfume.

"I will oblige you with the disagreement you seek," she said, taking her cloak from him. "We were friends once, so I'll not kill you without a fair hearing."

She stalked off into the common and had the maid scurrying forth from the kitchen and disappearing up the steps with the cloak.

Well. If Marielle wanted a battle, Leo would show her exactly what a soldier knew about winning a war, even a war of words. For ten years, he'd been held hostage to her memory, and clearing the air before he took a bride only made sense.

So why was he looking forward to this disagreement with a past love far more than he was to tomorrow's introduction to his potential fiancée?

* * *

Unfair, unfair, unfair... Marielle sent that protest heavenward, to whatever unlucky angels presided over the fate of thwarted lovers.

Leo was no longer a boy. In every way, he'd matured into the promise Marielle had seen in him as a young man. He was handsome, self-possessed, and apparently had found financial success. When he hung his caped great coat on a hook by the common's front windows, he revealed riding attire that was bang up to the nines. His cravat was tied in some fancy knot and sported a gold pin adorned with a tastefully discreet sapphire. His left little finger bore a signet ring, and his posture was militarily impressive.

He *had* to be married. No man with that much to recommend him would have gone unclaimed. Leo's family had been gentry—*mere* gentry, according to Papa—but their fortunes must have prospered over the past ten years, or perhaps plundering Spain had left Leo well to do.

Papa had said Leo would never amount to anything.

Marielle was delighted to see Papa had been wrong.

Marielle was happy for Leo, but she was also *quite* sad, for she had been right about Leo, and she'd let him go with barely a whimper.

Leo crossed the common to one of the private parlors and again held the door for her. A fire crackled in the grate, and a table had been set immediately before it. The room also held a settee, and there Marielle did take a seat.

"You'll let out the heat if you don't close the door," she said. "I'm widowed, and need not shiver for the sake of my chastity ever again."

"You're also angry with me," Leo said, poking some

air into the fire. "I have a few questions for you too, but ladies first, Ellie."

Only Leo had called her that. Had he used her nickname as a weapon or an olive branch?

"I am furious with you, which makes no sense. We were young and foolish, and the past has no bearing on the present."

He propped an elbow on the mantel, looking twelve kinds of too delicious. "Humor me. We were friends once."

They'd grown up together, their papas owning neighboring estates. When Leo had gone off to public school, Marielle had cried for weeks, and sneaked splotchy letters into the post, knowing he could not reply. He'd brought her a journal at the holiday break, full of the sentiments he'd not been able to send her.

She still had the journal, though she'd not read it since the night before her wedding. "We were playmates."

He pushed away from the mantel. "And then we were lovers, or the next thing to it. I proposed to you."

Oh, he had. On bended knee, her hand in his, and it had been perfect. The memory distressed Marielle now, because it was both precious and false. While she grappled with that incongruity, Leo opened the door and said something to a maid, then closed the door.

"You proposed," Marielle said, "and I accepted your proposal."

"Then you married another."

She had, months after Leo had gone haring off on his adventures. Marielle rose and stalked over to him.

"You left me, waiting like the most gullible dupe ever to plight her troth. Left me waiting in that cold, dingy saddle room, for hours. I cried for you, Leopold, and when Papa found me, I swore I would never cry for you again. The humiliation faded, but not the sense of betrayal. If you were so mad to buy your colors, why not ask me to follow the drum? Why not marry me before you went chasing glory on the battlefield? I would have waited... Oh, damn you."

They stood close enough to embrace, while Marielle fisted her hand around the handkerchief in her pocket —his handkerchief. She'd learned not to cry, but indulging in tears earlier had weakened her defenses.

"You waited for me?" Leo's question was cautious, as if he repeated a phrase he couldn't quite translate from a foreign tongue.

"For hours," Marielle said, pity for her younger self swamping her. "Until I was so cold, I couldn't feel anything except the shame of falling in love with a coward. How could you face Boney's guns, *but not face me?* I would have been hurt that you'd changed your mind, Leo, but I loved you. I would have let you go. I would have tried to understand."

Leo dropped to the sofa and held out his hand. Marielle didn't at first grasp that he wanted her to sit beside him.

"I'm still trying to understand," he said. "You waited in the saddle room."

Marielle took the place beside him. "I waited so long that I caught a serious lung fever," she said. "I don't know how many times I was bled, but I suspect the problem was a broken heart rather than an ailment of the body. You were in Spain by then, and Papa had no idea which regiment you'd signed up with."

"A simple inquiry at Horse Guards would have told him that much." Leo stared into the fire as if fairies danced in its depths. "But Marielle, he had no need to ask for me at Horse Guards, because he bought my commission with his own coin."

If Leo had kicked Marielle in the ribs, he could not

have delivered a more stunning blow. "*My father* sent you to war?"

"With a handsome rank, a new uniform, and hearty best wishes. He also assured me I'd get over your rejection in time, though I was to step aside graciously, for you were intent on making a more suitable match. Eight months later, I read in a three-week-old newspaper that you had made your choice. I stayed drunk for a week."

"You abhor inebriation."

"Right now," Leo said, "I abhor your father even more."

Marielle sat beside her first love, her heart and mind reeling. "*My father* sent you to war, and then he arranged a perfectly safe, dull match for me. He told me young men were legendarily faithless, and I must not hold your decision too much against you."

Leo continued staring at the fire until a knock sounded on the door. Marielle rose to answer it, and admitted a maid carrying a large tray. The girl set the tray on the table, bobbed a curtsey and withdrew, closing the door behind her.

The tray was laden with a pot of chocolate, slices of Christmas stollen, a teapot, a plate of short bread, butter, and a little pot of raspberry jam.

Raspberry was Leo's favorite, and he apparently still put butter and jam on his shortbread. Marielle lifted the lid of the teapot, intent on checking the strength of the brew. Warm, tea-scented steam wafted up, and then the lid went clattering back to the tray.

"Marielle?" Leo was beside her. "Ellie?"

He put the lid back on the tea pot and took her in his arms. His embrace was both familiar and new, comforting and harrowing.

"He s-sent you to war," she managed. "My own father, sent you to war. He told you I'd played you false. I never played you false, Leo. N-Never."

"I believe you."

And then she began to sob.

* * *

To hold Marielle again, simply to hold her...

Leo had marched halfway across Spain, convinced that any day, he'd receive a letter from Marielle, apologizing and begging him to come back to her. He'd gone to bed at night—or to whatever patch of ground he was bivouacking on—praying for Marielle's wellbeing, and grateful he'd at least not put her at risk for bearing a child.

Then he'd read not of her betrothal per se, but a sly piece of gossip about the Viscount H., much respected denizen of Whitbyshire, contracting for the creation of a full trousseau for his daughter, the lovely Miss M.R. The wedding was rumored to be scheduled immediately after her come out and first Season, but no groom had been named.

Leo would have died from overconsuming rum, except Rafe had found him passed out in his tent, and deposited him in the nearest creek. Leo's headache had lasted for weeks, following him into battle and fueling a reckless bravery the senior officers had noted favorably in their dispatches. Promotions had followed, and eventually, the business of war had replaced the heartache of Marielle's betrayal.

"Ellie, don't cry," Leo murmured, for this was not ladylike weeping. Marielle's tears were noisy and heartrending.

Leo scooped her up and settled on the settee with her in his lap. She subsided to shuddering and muttered curses, while Leo held her.

To hold her again... Perhaps this was a Christmas gift from on high, to hold Marielle again. A chance to make peace with the past, to forgive and be forgiven.

"I should have written to you," Leo said. "Your father warned me not to humiliate myself with letters that you'd only return unopened. I could not have borne that, but I should have written to you."

She was clutching his cravat with one hand, and held his handkerchief with the other. He'd always loved her hands, loved the grace and competence of them.

"I should have made inquiries at Horse Guards," she said. "It never occurred to me. They would have told me where you were. I could have written, once I was well."

Another shudder went through her. She was warm in Leo's arms, and still his Ellie, but also not. Her dress was a rich burgundy velvet no young girl would be permitted to wear, and her fragrance was not the uncomplicated lavender water young women favored. Instead her fragrance whispered of spices—expensive, exotic spices.

My Ellie, and not my Ellie.

"Tell me about your husband," Leo said. The lucky sod had better have treated Marielle well, or Leo might have to get drunk for another week.

"He made me laugh. That's why I noticed him. He didn't ask prying questions, he took me out walking when I wanted only to grow old in my sick room. My husband was a decent man. He neither sought nor offered me great passion, but we were cordial, and eventually we had a comfortable match."

Was Leo to hate the man more or hate him less for having offered Marielle only a decent, comfortable, *cordial* match?

"I learned to appreciate a soldier's life," Leo said, stroking his hand over Marielle's hair. She'd once professed to hate her hair for being merely a coppery brown. "I wasn't so highborn that the men disrespected me on sight, nor so much a commoner that the other officers resented me. I had a knack for settling disputes, and doing what needed doing. Those qualities were appreciated. I also had enough Hessians in my unit that I learned German to go with my French, and thus I ended up in Vienna."

"So far away," Marielle murmured. "What made you come back?"

German princesses intent on becoming his marchioness. "I was homesick, and I have responsibilities here. My father has been gone five years, and Mama and the girls expect me to look after things."

Then there were the holdings of the marquessate. Leo had acquired no less than five estates, four of which he'd yet to even lay eyes on.

Fortunately, Marielle turned the conversation to the topic of Leo's three sisters and their various husbands and offspring. Leo eventually parted with the pleasure of holding Marielle on his lap, and as darkness fell, they did justice to the servings on the tray.

Leo was still hungry when he put the empty tray outside the door, but he was also at peace in a way he hadn't been for years.

Marielle hadn't abandoned him, hadn't accepted his proposal then turned her back on him. She had remained his friend all along. As Leo watched her straightening the pillows on the settee—liked things tidy, did his Ellie—he had the uncomfortable suspicion she might also still be the love of his life.

That would rather put a crimp in his plans to marry the lovely, titled widow in the New Year, wouldn't it?

* * *

Leopold Drake still made Marielle's pulse flutter, and her heart sing, and all those other stupid, fatuous—*accurate*—metaphors. In one sense, she was relieved—she might be a widow of mature years, but she could still be inspired to passion.

Provided Leopold Drake was in the vicinity.

In another sense, she bitterly resented Leo's timing. Why must he turn up, so charming, handsome, and blameless, *now*? She'd been determined to get on with her life, to put fanciful thoughts behind her once and for all...

"Do you not care for the wine?" Leo asked. He'd invited her to join him for supper, and the meal had been superb.

"The wine is lovely, and your compliments were rightly sent to the cook," Marielle replied. "I don't know when I've had better."

Leo had acquired *savoir faire*—he knew how to conduct himself. His dismissal of the inn's serving maid had conveyed both authority and appreciation for her efforts. He poured the wine with that practiced motion of the wrist that prevented stray droplets from marring the linen. He told anecdotes from his time on the Continent that amused without offending.

While Marielle was ready to dump her delicious pear compote over his head. He prattled on and on, while she was aware that they were wasting precious hours, after having wasted precious years.

"Soldiering taught me to appreciate pleasures in the moment," he said, "rather than save them up for some other day. A good meal deserves to be consumed with relish, and fine music should be listened to, not ignored in favor of gathering up the week's gossip."

"I could not agree more," Marielle said, "which is why I hope you'll share my bed tonight." Marielle spent the entire meal coming to that decision and trying to put it into words, and Leo—who'd spent years in conversation with her—had no reply.

He toyed with his pears, which had been served with a brandied cream, and sprinkled with cinnamon.

"You heard me aright," Marielle said. "I'm a widow, and I can find comfort where I please, provided I'm discreet. Ten years ago, you were taken from me, and I've always wished…"

It's Christmas, and I've been so good for so long and all that lonely propriety has nearly smothered me. If I'm not careful, I'll spend another ten years being equally well-behaved in the same sort of sweet, cordial, boring company my first husband afforded me…

She would not justify her request though. If Leo didn't share her longing to explore what might have been, to take advantage of the single night fate had handed them, then so be it.

He laid his hand over hers. "I've wished too, Marielle. Across Spain, into France, at Waterloo, and then on to Vienna. I wished that even once, we might have anticipated our vows. I told myself that if I'd shared such intimacy with you, you would not have cast me aside. But those were a young man's thoughts, and my desire for you is that of a grown man for a woman who knows her own mind."

Desire. An accurate term, but not quite adequate. "My longing is not exclusively of the body, Leo. You were my first love."

And despite marrying a good man, an honorable man, Marielle hadn't met Leo's like since they'd parted. He *listened* to her, he thought for himself. His humility was as genuine as his self-respect. The longer they'd talked, the more the past had merged with the present into one, bottomless ache.

Party joy, part sorrow, all longing.

"And you were my first love," Leo replied, "but I am

not entirely free to accept the offer you make, much as I'd like to."

Well, damn and blast. "You're married," Marielle said, rising. "I envy your wife, Leo, and will thank you not to share specifics of this encounter with her."

He was on his feet before Marielle had left the table. "I am not married."

A small, selfish consolation. "And yet, you're reluctant. I understand. We'd both put the past behind us, and now I throw myself at you, the epitome of the pathetic widow, and you're no longer interested in what I have—"

Leo put a finger to her lips. "I'm glad to see you haven't lost all of your impetuosity. I am not married, I am interested in spending the night with you, but I am also about to embark on marriage negotiations with a suitable *parti*. We've agreed in principle to negotiate, nothing more."

That was how the whole business began, as Marielle well knew. "You've incurred no obligation to this woman. I have no obligations to a prospective husband either."

Though she'd been considering a suitable *parti* herself, as Leo had. A titled fellow of an age to settle down and see to the succession. Marielle was considering his suit only half-seriously, and mostly out of boredom and loneliness.

Leo took her hand in both of his, his grasp warm. The fire in the hearth had burned down, and the candles would soon gutter. The shadows showed her both the youth he'd been, and the man he'd become. Handsome would gradually yield to distinguished, and she would always, always find him attractive.

"What is it you want from me, Ellie?"

She wanted the past ten years restored to them, and yet, that wasn't reasonable. Leo had apparently prospered during their years apart, and Marielle's life would be the envy of many.

"I want to share this night with you, Leo. Let's start there."

He kissed her knuckles. "I want to share this night with you too, and will do so joyfully, but in the morning, I must see to some business."

Was he limiting their encounter to a single night, or sharing his calendar with her? "I have an appointment scheduled for tomorrow as well."

Though Marielle already knew she'd be canceling her Boxing Day meeting. After the night she planned to spend with Leo, she'd need her rest.

And if he truly meant to pursue those negotiations with that dratted suitable woman, Marielle would need time to recover from the blow of losing him all over again.

* * *

LEO HADN'T INDULGED in many assignations. Trysting was a lot of bother, women sometimes got the wrong ideas, and in the back of his mind, always, was the thought: *She's not Marielle.*

He knew enough though, to part from Marielle at her door, spend twenty minutes tending to his ablutions while ignoring Rafe's snores, then steal down the corridor and tap softly on Marielle's door.

She opened it instantly and hauled him into her sitting room by the sleeve of his dressing gown.

"Petunia is asleep across the hall," she said. "She hears better than a hound, and sometimes has trouble sleeping."

Marielle was in a blue velvet robe that swathed her from neck to ankles, and her sitting room was chilly.

The door to the bedroom was ajar, and the covers had already been turned down on the bed.

Sometimes, impetuosity was lovely. "Petunia is your companion?"

"My companion, my conscience, my worst fear. I'm afraid I'll look in the mirror one day and see I've become the older relation nobody truly wants to invite for a visit, but they do so out of pity."

She locked the door, then paced to the window, where she twitched at curtains already closed.

"That fate will never befall you," Leo said. "Are you nervous, Marielle?"

"Yes, and no. People do this—have liaisons."

She hadn't done this. Leo concluded as much from the way she eyed the open bedroom door, as if unsure she wanted to cross the threshold.

"It's only me, Ellie. If you've changed your mind, I'll understand." And Leo would die a little too. To have his heart's desire restored to him, then snatched away by doubts...

If nothing else, this encounter with Marielle had clarified one important point: He'd acquired a marquess's title and wealth, but to acquire a marchioness through the calculation and cold-heartedness of a typical aristocrat was beyond him. The lovely widow probably *was* lovely, but what sort of woman chose her husband based on his title and his bank balance?

He'd keep tomorrow's appointment, and make his apologies to all parties, as honor demanded.

"You've been to the Continent," Marielle muttered, as if the fleshpots of Egypt had somehow been on his itinerary. "You've probably waltzed with Italian contessas and German princesses."

"A few." None of whom Leo could recall even by title.

"Leo... I was married to one fairly unimaginative

man, who never sought passion from me, and hadn't—I'm making a hash of this."

Leo took her in his arms, loving the feel of her. "On Tuesdays, when you would often leave a letter for me in the oak tree, I'd pace and pace and pace, waiting for the sun to go down, waiting for my family to seek their beds. Waiting for the moon to rise. Minutes were like years to me then, and yet, when the time finally came to climb out my window—"

"You hesitated," Marielle said, wrapping her arms around his waist. "Because what if there wasn't a letter waiting? How would you stand the disappointment, and endure until we might steal a few minutes in the churchyard on Sunday?"

His letters to her had been carefully placed in the crook of the tree trunk on Fridays, wrapped in oilskin in case the gods of weather were so disobliging as to send rain.

"There's a letter in the tree for both of us tonight, Marielle. It says, 'Don't fret away this one, lovely opportunity. Trust your heart, and be brave.'" He kissed her, because once Marielle started fretting, she became fixed on her worries.

"I hate being brave," she said, kissing him back. "I'm glad you're here, Leo. Glad you didn't come to harm during all those years of soldiering."

"So am I." Leo was also a little bit sorry for her late spouse, because the man had died without realizing what a lovely, passionate, special woman he'd been married to.

As a young man, Leo had been able to kiss endlessly, despite rampant desire clamoring for greater intimacies. Finally, finally, he need not exercise such heroic restraint with Marielle, nor she with him.

"Please take me to bed, Leo, or I'll have my way with you here on this drafty floor."

He scooped her up in his arms, carried her to the bed, and placed her on the mattress. "Door open or closed?"

The room would grow that much colder with the door closed.

"Closed. Petunia might barge in here at an ungodly hour, and the last thing—Leo, I want to see you."

The cold became his ally, as he draped his dressing gown over the chest at the foot of the bed. His silk trousers went next, while Marielle sat up on the bed and watched him as a cat watches an oblivious sparrow.

"You were wounded," she said, as Leo drew his shirt over his head. "More than once. Come here." She traced a finger over the scar on his arm, then laid her palm over the mark the bullet had left on his shoulder. "I hate that you were injured."

"I suffered far less than many others. Raphael would allow only competent surgeons to tend me, and he made sure I healed properly."

"He's that great beast of a man I saw in the common?"

"One and the same. Have you looked your fill?"

She frankly studied his erection. "One suspected you would not be overly burdened with modesty."

"Are you pleased to have your conjectures confirmed?"

Marielle smiled, reminding him of the adventurous, determined girl she'd been. "Several of my conjectures about you have proved happily accurate. I'm trying to savor the moment."

She was also delaying the removal of her own clothing. Leo made a circuit of the room, blowing out candles, banking the fire, and considering strategy.

"I'd make a request of you," he said, when Marielle

had passed him her night robe. Her nightgown could have served as a horse blanket, it was so voluminous.

"Now, you want to negotiate?"

"Negotiation is for mercantile endeavors, Marielle. I'm asking for your trust, as a man honestly communicates with his lover."

"This sounds serious," she said, rubbing her arms.

"If this is to be the only night I share with you, then I'd ask you to keep your impetuosity in check. Give me time, Marielle, to become reacquainted with you. You have been precious to me for most of my life. I don't want to make love to your memory, I want to make love with *you*."

"You were always like this," she said, holding up the covers for him. "You could turn up serious and sweet at the most unpredictable times. I adored you for it."

Past tense. Leo spooned himself around her, gathered her close, and set about turning the past tense into the present. He'd never been naked with Marielle before, never held her with only a thin silk nightgown between them.

For Christmas, he'd been given a chance to revisit a dream, and he intended to make the most of it, even if it broke his heart to let her go in the morning.

* * *

WHY HAD Marielle asked Leo for this? A woman married for years knew exactly what transpired between the sheets. Her husband—or lover, if she was adventurous, which Marielle was not—spent a few minutes kissing her and fondling the parts he'd never touch under any other circumstances. Then he climbed over her, heaved and poked about for a bit, and came to a shuddering conclusion.

He'd finish by lying atop her, panting like an overtaxed hound while she stroked his hair and hoped the sheets wouldn't become untidy, though they often did, which one would never mention.

Some of it was nice enough—the closeness and cuddling, if the man didn't fall immediately asleep. Within two months of becoming a wife, though, Marielle had concluded that what fascinated most men, the forbidden ecstasy of intimate congress, was in truth rather tedious and none too dignified for the lady.

With Leo, she'd never worried about her dignity, never been bored by kissing and fondling. She'd loved every moment shared with him. The shared meal in the cozy private parlor had confirmed that they still had the gift of conversation with each other.

Even while she'd mentally castigated Leo for abandoning her, she'd always wondered if his lovemaking would have been more exciting than her marital experiences.

"You were my guilty secret," she said, as Leo's arms came around her in the bed. He was a good cuddler, damn him. Always had been. "I've wondered if I didn't choose an unremarkable man for my husband, so I wouldn't try to measure him against you."

"Was he unremarkable?"

Marielle hadn't given her marriage much thought, once the shock and sadness of burying a spouse too young had faded, and the mourning period observed.

"My father objected to you because you were merely gentry, but I see that you were attractive to me in part because your family did not come from great wealth and a lofty title."

"Your feet would freeze the Thames. I'd forgotten that about you. You don't care for titles now?"

"I don't care for an indolent life, Leo. My husband got up in the morning and went for a hack in the park if the weather was fine. Then he joined me for breakfast and read the paper, then he went off to his club to read another paper, and smoke, or gossip about politics. His afternoons were spent at the tailor's, Jackson's, Tatts, browsing Hatchards… what was the point? This was the much-vaunted life of a gentleman, and what was the point of all that indolence?"

"You were bored."

"Within an inch of my sanity. Your father was always busy, Leo. He knew every acre of his holdings, knew his mares by name, and consulted with every tenant regularly. You were frequently at his side, and shared his sense of responsibility. Would you mind rubbing my shoulders?"

"You promise not to fall asleep?"

"With you prodding me in the backside, I'm not likely to fall asleep."

Leo was aroused, gloriously so, and yet, he didn't seem compelled to do anything about it… yet. He'd asked Marielle not to rush him, and dashing through this encounter as if it were some silly tryst was the last thing she wanted.

He kneaded her shoulders slowly and firmly, as he had on many occasions, and tension flowed out of her. Leo was a toucher, affectionate by nature, and given to using his hands. He'd often whiled away an afternoon whittling beside her on a blanket while she'd read or embroidered.

"I've missed this," he said, some moments later. "Missed being with you, touching you, hearing you argue against enslavement and war and manufactories."

She'd been so young, with opinions about everything.

"I lost a baby." The words were a surprise to Marielle even as she spoke them, but of course, she could tell Leo anything.

He wrapped her in a hug and kissed her shoulder. "Ellie, I'm sorry."

"I wasn't far along, not even showing, but I knew, Leo. I was different. It was spring, and I couldn't stand the smell of flowers. I'd always loved flowers."

"And now you wear the fragrance of spices."

Well, yes. She hadn't connected the miscarriage and discarding the perfumes she'd preferred as a debutante. Leo was good at that too—at putting puzzle pieces together.

God, she'd missed him. Marielle sat up and pulled her nightgown over her head. "Does this count as being impetuous?"

"It counts as being lovely and brave."

She lay on her back, took Leo's hand, and settled it over her breast. He'd loved her breasts, and thus she'd been pleased with them as well.

"Do you still like this?" he asked, leaning over and putting his mouth to her nipple.

She'd forgotten the sensations he could provoke— hot, needy, and lovely. Her reply was to arch into his touch, to pull his hair and sigh and wiggle, knowing he enjoyed her responses. She didn't have to worry about what behavior suited a proper wife...

"Leo?"

"Hmm?"

"I know I'm not to rush you, but might I *encourage* you?"

"Ellie, if I were any more encouraged I'd risk making a mess of the sheets."

So one did mention it. With Leo. "Bother the sheets, Leo Drake. It's not as if I'll send you back to your own bed at the first opportunity."

He bit her, gently, delightfully. "But back to my own bed, I will go. Your reputation matters to me, Ellie."

"My sanity matters to me, and if you don't bestir yourself—"

He rose over her, and situated himself between her legs. "Did it ever occur to you, that when you scold me, that *bestirs* me in the most intimate sense?"

She'd scolded him frequently, long ago. For not combing his hair, for forgetting to scrape the mud off his boots, for bringing her flowers from his mama's garden, for winking at her in church.

"You provoked me on purpose," she said, wrapping her legs about his flanks. The feel of him was perfect, all male, all over. Warm, strong, healthy, and hers.

For now.

"We provoked each other," he said, bracing himself on his forearms. "Kiss me, Ellie."

He was a fiend, orchestrating a kiss that counter-pointed slow, careful thrusts, a deft caress to her breasts, and an embrace of infinite tenderness. Marielle rubbed her breasts against his chest, sank her finger-nails into his backside, and mourned for the years they'd lost.

This was not a polite marital accommodation, a duty, a vaguely bothersome if infrequent imposition.

This was lovemaking, and it was different. Marielle couldn't maintain any perspective, any distance be-tween the sensations swamping her and the emotions cresting higher moment by moment. She had missed Leo in every corner of her mind and every cranny of her soul, and all she wanted was to be close to him, and then closer still.

Leo had diabolical self-restraint, while Marielle was coming unraveled. She surrendered to a joy so wide, deep, and profound, that for an eternal moment, she was joined with him, one soul, one transcendently—shockingly—well pleasured soul.

When she could muster the will to move, she turned

her head and kissed his chin. "Happy Christmas, Leo Drake." Though the hour was probably late enough that Christmas had passed, and Boxing Day begun.

"Happy Christmas, Ellie my love."

The old endearment made her heart ache. "Leo, my lover."

He gave her sweet kisses, and then more pleasure, until Marielle lay beneath him, a dazed heap of satisfied, happy female. He withdrew and spent on her belly, and—her joy was complete—tidied up without leaving evidence of their passion on the sheets.

"Don't go yet," she murmured, cuddling up to his side.

He wrapped his arm around her, and swept her hair back in a slow, easy caress that turned her thoughts to moonbeams. She'd missed him more than she knew, and he'd been everything she'd longed for in a lover. Now her past, present, and future were all a hazy confusion, and she couldn't keep her eyes open.

Marielle promised herself she'd sort it all out in the morning over a hearty breakfast shared with the man she loved.

Except in the morning, she rose to find that Leo had departed from the inn, without leaving her so much as a note.

CHAPTER 3

"*W*hat do you mean, the colonel has departed?" Marielle fired that question at the innkeeper's wife, a stolid, round-faced lady with an incongruous sprig of mistletoe affixed to her lace cap.

"Not an hour past, milady," the woman replied. "Perhaps he had Boxing Day errands?"

Boxing Day errands? *Boxing Day errands?* He'd said he had an appointment, not that he meant to disappear without a word.

"Did he leave a note, a letter, anything?" Marielle had dashed off a note to her solicitors before she'd even rung for a breakfast tray.

The innkeeper's wife shot Petunia a look that suggested Marielle should have asked Father Christmas to deliver some common sense. Petunia busied herself poking at the sitting room's fire, which had done little to take the chill off Marielle's quarters.

"Colonel Drake didn't leave any notes, milady. He paid his fare, then he and his manservant saddled their own horses, and went on their way." Her tone suggested that notes passed between a lady and a single gentleman would not do at a proper establishment.

Marielle sank to the chair nearest the fire. Last night had been the best Christmas gift two people could share, and now Leo had hared off. He wouldn't do that to her. As a young woman, she'd been cozened by her father's machinations, but she knew better now.

Or did she? Leo had made her no promises and been at pains to inform her he'd caught the interest of another woman.

Could a man intent on marriage to another make love *like that*?

Both the proprietress and Petunia were sending Marielle nervous glances, and well they should.

"We're leaving, Petunia. Mrs. Somerset, you will please prepare my bill. Your hospitality has been excellent, and I wish you Happy Christmas."

The woman withdrew on a curtsey so hasty, the mistletoe on her cap flapped against her forehead.

"Are we off to Chelsea then?" Petunia asked, taking the last triangle of toast from the breakfast tray.

Chelsea, where Marielle had thought to begin the next phase of her life, with the cool logic of a woman who expected little from marriage, but still desperately longed for children.

"We're going back to London, and from there, possibly onto the Continent."

"Of course, milady."

Something about the way Petunia munched her toast—loudly—suggested she had more to say.

"The colonel apparently wasn't interested in anything permanent, Petunia. He was clear on that point." *Somewhat* clear. Marielle had been too intent on sharing Christmas night with Leo to grasp any subtleties he'd been trying to convey. He'd mentioned attending to business, but his business might have been in the Hebrides for all the details he'd given her.

Petunia took the opposite chair and poured herself

another cup of tea. "I gather the colonel was an old acquaintance?"

He'd been Marielle's best friend in childhood, her first and only romantic passion, her greatest loss, and her fondest memories.

"We were infatuated, before my come out. We'd grown up together, spent all of our holidays and summers racketing about, and then friendship turned to foolishness. I fancied myself in love with him."

"Have some tea," Petunia said. "It's not cold yet."

But it would be tepid. Marielle was done with tepid comforts. "No, thank you, but I'll have that shortbread, please."

Petunia passed the plate. "Was your head turned by all the wonders of Town, milady? Was that why you and his lordship parted ways all those years ago?"

Marielle and Leo had pieced together the details of their separation over supper. "My father intercepted a note from me wherein I'd agreed to elope with Leo, and to meet him here at the Ox and Ass at a specified time and date. Papa copied the note, but moved the time up by several hours, and met Leo here in my stead."

"Papas can be vexatiously interfering." Petunia rapped her spoon against her tea cup with particular vigor.

For a moment, Marielle's woes subsided beneath surprise. "Petunia, my dear, you have a past."

"I had a beau," she said, glowering at her tea. "A lovely lad by the name Charlie Dale, though Papa didn't care for him. Charlie would have waited for me forever, then one of his second cousins was caught misbehaving with some earl's son, and Charlie was told to offer for her. Kept the money in the family, my mother said, but mostly, it kept my Charlie and me apart. Mr. Jones put me in mind of Charlie."

Were all papas so bent on ruining their daughters' happiness? "Petunia, I had no idea. I'm sorry." Though who on earth was Mr. Jones?

"I made up my mind, if I couldn't have my Charlie, then nobody would have me. Papa ought not to have meddled."

"Meddling is too kind a word for it. My father told Leo I'd had a change of heart, that I wanted my London Season and a chance to marry a man of suitable rank. He convinced Leo that the better part of gentlemanly honor was to accept a commission and leave me to the future I'd chosen."

"So you ended up with Lord Drew. His cousins called him Dreary Drew, growing up, because he was such a bookish little fellow."

"He was a good man." But dreary wasn't much of a stretch, God rest him.

"Mr. Jones says his lordship is a wonderful man," Petunia said, swirling her tea. "They've been together for years and years."

Ah, Mr. Jones was the loyal Raphael. "When did you talk to Mr. Jones?"

"We shared a toddy or two while you and his lordship were getting re-acquainted. One shouldn't celebrate the holidays alone, I always say. Mr. Jones sang his lordship's praises, said he'd never met a better man."

Marielle dabbed butter and jam on her shortbread. "Why do you refer to the colonel as his lordship?"

"I thought you and he were old friends."

"We are." And more than that, Marielle had hoped. "But I know only that he rose to the rank of colonel. His father was Whitbyshire gentry, and comfortable, but certainly not titled."

"My lady, your fellow is a blooming marquess now, the Marquess of Cadeau. He inherited from some distant cousin and has come back from the Continent to find himself a proper English wife. Mr. Jones said his lordship was on his way to finalize the settlements." Petunia glanced around, as if she feared the parlor's plain furnishings might carry tales. "I'm sorry, milady. I'm so very sorry. Mr. Jones vowed his lordship was the most honorable of gentlemen."

Leo was honorable, so honorable he'd even told Marielle about being on the hunt for a wife, but this revelation turned everything on its head.

Leo was the *Marquess of Cadeau*, the wealthy nobleman who'd been "traveling on the Continent" for years and was ready to settle down.

Merciful Cupid. What an absolute muddle.

Was Leo so honorable, he'd terminate marriage discussions with the lady in person before embarking on a courtship with Marielle? Didn't he know to whom she'd been married? Or had he known exactly with whom he disported, and decamped at first light rather than keep his appointment in Chelsea?

"We'll depart for London," Marielle said, rising. "If his lordship is interested in pursuing his acquaintance with me, he can find me through my solicitors."

Except solicitors were always going on about privacy and discretion. Even Leo might not be given specifics, and Marielle lived quietly rather than as a society widow.

"He seemed like such a nice man," Petunia said, draining the last of her tea.

"His lordship?"

"Mr. Jones. Put me very much in mind of my dear, departed Charlie. He assured me his lordship was in every way a worthy fellow. too."

Doubting Leo had cost Marielle ten years with him, ten years when Leo had risked his neck daily in battle after battle, and Marielle had gone slowly daft stitching endless samplers.

"I need to borrow your lap desk again," Marielle said, "and somewhere in this inn, I must find an oilskin. Then we're for London."

And if Leo didn't present himself on her doorstep by the New Year, well then, Lisbon was warm even in winter, and it was time Marielle saw something of the world.

* * *

"THE ROADS ARE A TRIFLE DIFFICULT," Mr. Hollyburn said, for the third time. "I'm sure her ladyship will be here shortly, my lord."

Leo had refused tea three times, assured Hollyburn of Mama's good health twice, and paced a hole in the solicitor's carpet waiting for the widowed Lady Drew Semple to keep her appointment.

"Women aren't as punctual as we gentlemen," Mr. Inverivy said. "They get distracted easily, poor dears."

Marielle didn't get distracted. She fixed on an objective and flew at it, and Leo had been certain his future was her target. "Her ladyship is your client, Mr. Inverivy," Leo said. "Do you imply she can't tell time?"

The solicitors exchanged a look that Leo had seen enlisted men toss among themselves when a newly commissioned captain gave some daft order.

"Perhaps," Hollyburn said, "Mr. Inverivy meant that her ladyship didn't account for Boxing Day traffic in Town, or how her progress would be hampered by the weather. We are getting a bit of snow, my lord."

The snow started had after Leo had left the Ox and Ass, and had the steady, relentless quality of a substantial winter storm.

"No wife of mine would fail to grasp something as obvious as winter weather or holiday traffic," Leo said, which was ridiculous as he hadn't ever had a wife. "In any case, I'm here to inform you both that I'll not be pursuing negotiations with Lady Drew. I'm sure she's a lovely woman, and I'd be lucky to have her for my marchioness, but I'll not be making an offer."

A beat of silence went by, and then both solicitors babbled at once.

"But my lord, her ladyship is in every way appropriate to one in your unusual circumstances!"

"You can't mean that, sir. I spent hours and hours coming up with a list, and you'll not do better."

Not do better, Inverivy implied, because Leo's people had been little more than wealthy farmers. Marielle hadn't cared about that, and Leo hoped she was still indifferent to rank and title.

A knock interrupted the solicitors' exhortations.

A skinny boy in a worn coat tugged off his cap. "A note, Mr. Hollyburn, for his lordship."

Leo took the note from the boy before Hollyburn could snatch it, and tossed the lad a coin. "Happy Christmas."

"Thank you, milord!" The boy scampered off, while Leo eyed the sealed note. Lady Semple had put pen to paper, her hand remarkably like Marielle's. Perhaps all English school girls developed the same graceful, looping script while they waited for English schoolboys to mature into worthy articles. Leo slit the seal with some foreboding.

MY LORD,

I am exercising a lady's prerogative and changing my mind. You are without doubt a fine man, and I wish you a happy future, but I can assure you from experience, marriage to a relative stranger would be a tepid undertaking at best. I deserve better, and so, I daresay, do you. Please accept my apologies for causing you needless travel on a day cold enough to freeze Lucifer's ears off.

Lady Drew Semple

"THE LADY and I are in agreement," Leo informed the solicitors. "We've both thought better than to proceed with a negotiated courtship. She won't be joining us, nor will she become my marchioness."

Her ladyship's decision solved a considerable problem, and Leo was grateful to her for her honesty. The irony wasn't lost on him though—but for this errand in Chelsea, he'd not have spent the most wonderful night of his life with Marielle.

Who was doubtless waiting for word from him back at the Ox and Ass. He jammed the note into his pocket, departed on the moment, and was soon enduring Rafe's grumblings as they waited for their horses at the livery stable.

"We'll return to the inn," Leo said. "We should get there before noon, if the wind stays at our backs."

"We're going right back the way we came?"

"Right back to where I ought to have stayed, ten years ago, until I'd had a chance to discuss matters with the lady herself. Marielle deserved that much from me, but I was too willing to believe her father's lies."

Lady Drew's note crackled in Leo's pocket as he swung into a frigid saddle. She sounded like a practical soul, and kind, but determined on her objectives. Leo wished her well, and would hoist a holiday toast to her, just as soon as he and Marielle were reunited.

"The wind is apparently no respecter of daft marquesses," Rafe said as they trotted onto the main road and took the brunt of a winter breeze right in the face. "But don't mind me. Nothing I'd rather do on Boxing Day than freeze my jewels off, traipsing back and forth along the same misbegotten stretch of miserable English road. I'll learn the names of all the highwaymen and their horses. The holidays are supposed to be a friendly time of year, after all."

"Raphael, if you're getting too old to accompany me on my travels, I'll buy you a cottage in Dorset and write to you twice a year."

Though Rafe again had a point: The temperature was dropping, and if Leo hadn't been traveling back to Marielle's side, he'd have waited out the weather for at least another day.

"I don't fancy Dorset," Rafe said. "Too many sheep, not enough taverns. God's hairy arse, it wasn't this cold in Austria."

"Cold enough to freeze Lucifer's…."

"Bum," Rafe went on. "Though as best I recall, it's hot where Old Scratch bides. My sainted granny was convinced of it, and she knew everything, including all the places I hid my papa's brandy."

Cold enough to freeze Lucifer's ears off. Across a dozen countries and a dozen years, Leo had encountered only one woman who used that comparison.

"I might like to settle down," Rafe mused, "now that you mention my centuries of loyal service. I'd forgotten the pleasure of time spent with a good Englishwoman on a chilly afternoon. The dark-eyed lasses on the Continent have their charms, but there's nothing like a pair of kind blue eyes to warm a man's heart."

Cold enough to freeze Lucifer's ears off. Leo pulled Wulf to a halt, extracted the note from his pocket, and read it again. He hadn't seen Marielle's penmanship in more than ten years, but this could well be her writing. A tickle of heat up Leo's spine more than suggested that fate was playing a vast, seasonal joke on him.

Or maybe Marielle was? Had she intentionally spent the night with a man she was about to reject?

"Have you lost your everlovin' marbles, my lord colonel? It's bloody awful cold, the wind is howling, and the snow is getting deeper by the moment. I could be sitting in the snug with Miss Petunia, sharing another round of toddies, and here you are, impersonating a statue on the king's highway."

"Miss Petunia is Marielle's companion," Leo said, stashing the note away. "How did you meet her?"

"Had to share my toddies with somebody when you went off with her ladyship, didn't I? Not even your daft lordship would let good hot toddies go to waste."

"Who is her ladyship?"

Rafe gazed up at the snowy heavens, then speared Leo with a patient look. "Miss Petunia Semple is companion to Lady Drew Semple, in whose bedroom—if I am not mistaken—you passed Christmas night. I considered you was having a last lark before sticking your neck in the noose of aristocratic stupidity. Using solicitors to find a wife, God save us. The Quality is daft, and the nobs are barking mad."

Rafe nudged his horse into a trot, while Leo remained unmoving on Wulf.

Marielle was Lady Drew Semple. The facts all fit, and yet, what had her motivation been? Had she known she was bedding the Marquess of Cadeau?

Wulf shook his reins and stomped his hoof, clearly unhappy about being separated from the retreating Welly.

"I owe my lady a fair hearing," Leo said. "I owe her a chance to explain. I owe her... to hell with that. I want to give her my name, and children, God willing, and every Christmas night for the rest of my life."

He tapped his heel against Wulf 's sides, cantered past Welly, and didn't stop until the Ox and Ass had once more come into view.

Rafe lead the horses in to the stable, while Leo

tromped up the snowy steps and bellowed for the innkeeper.

"Beggin' your pardon," Mrs. Somerset said, bustling out of the kitchen. "Himself is bringing in extra coal on account of the storm. Will you be bidin' here with us again tonight, sir?"

"I will, and you please inform Lady Drew that I've returned."

Mrs. Somerset wore a ridiculous sprig of mistletoe, the white berries dangling from her cap. "I'm afraid I can't do that, Colonel. Lady Drew was off this morning, shortly after breakfast. Coachy said she was on her way to back Town, hoping to beat the storm."

What in the hell was Marielle up to? "She's not here?"

"I hope she's safe and snug back in Town, sir. Will you be needing a room?"

Rafe stomped through the door, shaking snow from his greatcoat, scarf and mittens.

"A room," Leo said, "and a good meal for Mr. Jones and myself. We'll be off at first light, though, unless the weather prevents it."

"The weather will prevent it," Rafe said. "And so will my frozen jewels."

To Leo's great frustration, the weather proved Rafe absolutely correct: No sane man would venture forth into a storm that showed no signs of letting up.

* * *

MARIELLE WATCHED the steady dripping from the icicles hanging beyond her parlor window, each drop landing on her last nerve. Christmas had been five days ago, and she'd not had a word from Leo.

"We should leave for Paris, Petunia, before the spring crowds."

The seat of Leo's marquessate was far to the north—Petunia had recalled that much about the Cadeau title—and Leo might well have gone directly there after receiving Marielle's note at the solicitors.

"His lordship might not have received the note you left him, milady," Petunia replied, threading her needle with green silk. "The weather did turn up powerful bad."

Leo might have been caught in the storm while journeying north. "I find Leo after all these years, only to lose him."

Marielle had been hoping he'd return to the Ox and Ass, for that was the logical place to rest his horses on the way to his family's Whitbyshire holding.

And it was there he and she had lost each other, and found each other again, and there where he'd know exactly where to find a confidential note from her.

"The roads will soon be passable again, milady. Perhaps we ought to travel out to that inn and see if his lordship left word for you."

Marielle was tempted to do just that. "I'm the daughter-in-law of a marquess. Leo can find me easily enough by making inquiries among his peers."

Except that Leo had had the title for less than year, and hadn't taken his seat in the House of Lords. He wouldn't know the Semple family, or any other titled aristocrats unless the connection was through the military.

Maybe Leo would never find her. "Drew wasn't acquainted with many officers."

Petunia readjusted the portion of fabric in her embroidery hoop. "Beg your pardon, milady?"

"Nothing of any moment. I've become fretful. I can't stand doing nothing, Petunia."

Patient blue eyes looked up at Marielle. "You have become increasingly impetuous since Lord Drew died, but Paris isn't going anywhere, and a winter crossing is seldom easy. If you are determined to leave for Paris, then I will arrange to spend time with my sister in Dorset."

Good heavens, rebellion in the ranks. "I'm being impossible," Marielle said, taking the place beside Petunia on the settee. "I'm sorry. Seeing Leo upset me and all my fancies have turned to fears."

Seeing Leo had given her hope, and reconnected her with the young woman who'd loved passionately. To lose Leo now…

"I would love to see Paris," Petunia said, drawing the needle through the fabric, "but I also like that Mr. Jones. You can afford to wait a bit for the roads to clear, can't you, milady?"

Petunia was embroidering a figure of green, white, and gold mistletoe onto a white linen handkerchief.

"Is that for Mr. Jones?" Marielle asked. "It's gorgeous, Petunia."

"Let's just say it's for my trousseau, should ever I need one."

Petunia was not a young woman, though she wasn't ancient either. She'd waited decades for a man who could pry her loyalty from her dear, departed Charles, while Marielle was railing against a few days of silence from Leo.

"We'll wait," Marielle said. "We'll wait until after the new year, and then reassess our situation."

The new year wasn't even a week off. Surely even Marielle could wait that long?

* * *

"STOP FUSSING AT ME," Leo snapped. "I'm calling on an old friend, not making my bow before the sovereign."

That farce had been tended to within a week of Leo's return to England.

"You're calling on an old friend," Rafe said, stepping to the left to avoid the snowmelt dripping onto Marielle's front porch, "and you've a special license in your pocket."

"Which fact, you will not mention to anyone." Leo wasn't certain he'd have an opportunity to use the license, but after being thwarted by bad weather, Welly's loose shoe, and nearly a foot and a half of snow, he wasn't about to take chances.

The door opened, and a liveried footman admitted them. Leo handed over his card and asked to see Lady Drew. Rafe, who'd donned rare finery, asked if Miss Petunia was at home. Miss Petunia herself came down the front steps a moment later, and the joy in her eyes as Rafe greeted her with a kiss to the cheek surely qualified as a holiday miracle.

"May I show you the conservatory, gentlemen?" she asked. "We've decorated for the holidays, the same as we do every year, and it's really quite lovely."

"I'll wait here for Mari—for Lady Drew," Leo said.

Miss Petunia linked arms with Rafe, and all but marched him—quite unresisting—down the corridor.

Leaving Leo to inspect Marielle's home. Her residence was on a fashionable square, and commodious without being cavernous. The main foyer was festooned with ropes of pine, wrapping about the banister, twining around the chandelier chain, and decorating the curtain rods. The resulting scent was lovely, particularly with cloved oranges adding a spicy note.

These accommodations were far better than Leo could have given Marielle for much of the past ten years. He said a silent thank-you to Lord Drew Semple, because Marielle deserved the elegance and comfort

Leo saw on every hand. Polished marble floors, a newel post carved in the shape of a cat sitting on its haunches, and red velvet ribbons dangling from the sheaf of mistletoe beneath the chandelier.

A door softly clicked shut, and Marielle stood across the main foyer, a vision in aubergine. Gold trim accented her cuffs and hems, and Leo had a sudden vision of her as an older woman. Her hair might become snowy, her gait might slow, but she would always have a sheer presence that drew him.

"Leopold, welcome."

"I found your note." Thank God he'd thought to look in the crook of the old oak, though nearly a foot of snow had obscured the oilskin tucked between the branches. "I found your note, *Lady Drew*."

For moment, the only sound was the eaves dripping, a sign of moderating weather, then Marielle's steps clattered across the foyer. She threw herself into Leo's arms, holding him tight even as laughter shook her.

"Leo, what were we thinking? Using solicitors to find a spouse? I must have been barmy, but Petunia said some ladies will advertise for a husband, and I started thinking about growing old without children, pitied, lonely, and—"

"—without my best friend," Leo concluded. "Without the one person who always encouraged my dreams, never laughed at my fears. When I got back to the inn and you weren't there…. I died inside Marielle, as surely as if some Frenchman had taken me captive."

She unwound herself from him enough to tuck an arm around his waist, but that was as far as Leo was willing to let her go.

"I woke up, and you were gone," she said, leading him across the foyer. "I knew you had business to tend to, but what was I to make of your absence, Leo? I was left to think the worst, again."

Self-recrimination washed through him, for the thousandth time in five days. "I'm sorry, Ellie. I owed Lady Drew Semple my personal apology, and was certain I could return to the inn and to you free of any encumbrances. I owed her that much. Then the weather interfered, among other things, and your solicitors would not give me your direction."

Marielle paused with him in the middle of the foyer. "So I nearly lost you because you owed her ladyship a personal rejection?"

"No, Marielle, you did not nearly lose me. I would have found you, come what may. This time, nothing— not distance, familial obligation, worldly means, or misunderstandings—would have kept me from finding you again." He dropped to one knee, and took her hand in his, as he had once before years ago.

"Marielle, Lady Drew, Ellie—will you marry me? Will you share with me every Christmas and all the seasons of the year for the rest of our lives?"

She peered down at him. "Leo, are you being impetuous? I rather like it on you."

He sprang to his feet. "I am being romantic. Ten years is long enough to wait for the woman I love to look with favor on my suit."

She patted his lapel. "Yes, I will marry you. The sooner the better."

Thank God. Thank God, Marielle, fate, and the kindly angels. The relief of being claimed by her, clearly and truly, inspired Leo to kiss his intended, right there in full view of the front door.

Marielle kissed him back, passionately, and even when somebody cleared his throat, Leo was reluctant to let her go.

"Beggin' your lordship's pardon," Rafe said, Miss Petunia standing beside him. "And your ladyship's."

Marielle recovered first, though Leo kept her hand in his.

"Petunia, some sustenance for our guests is in order. The marquess and I will join you in the blue parlor in a moment."

"Yes, milady." Petunia led a happily-dazed looking Rafe across the foyer.

"I think they'll suit," Leo said. "I think they'll suit wonderfully."

"Not as wonderfully as we will," Marielle replied. "When did you acquire this impetuous streak, Leopold? Kissing me without warning where any might see?"

Leo was happy to improve on his capacity for impetuosity, but he pointed upward to a sheaf of greenery bound with a red ribbon. "Not impetuosity, Ellie my love. Seasonal good cheer."

"Very well," she said. "I will simply tell our children I married the Marquess of Mistletoe."

"And you shall be my marchioness," Leo replied, kissing her all over again.

Rafe and Petunia had enjoyed a full pot of tea before Leo and Marielle joined them, and Marielle's endearment became a family legend—Leopold came to expect seasonal revivals of his title as Marquess of Mistletoe, and with the aid of his devoted marchioness, lived up to her expectations every single time they found themselves beneath a bundle of holiday greenery.

AFTERWORD

To my dear readers,

I do love a holiday happily ever after, complete with snow storms, wassail, and guardian angels—and mistletoe too, of course!

If you're in the mood for another serving of yuletide romance, I've written a longer holiday novella, *A Rogue in Winter*, to go with my **Rogues to Riches** series. This is the tale of Vicar Pietr Sorenson, who has been a very good fellow for a very long time, and Miss Joy Danforth, a lady preparing to make an advantageous match to salvage the family finances.

Joy is determined to do her duty. Pietr has accepted a new post at some dreary cathedral, and it's going to take some very special mistletoe to get these two sorted out. Wheeee! Excerpt below.

And in January, I'll be releasing my third **Mischief in Mayfair** title, **Miss Dignified**. Captain Dylan Powell meets his match, and her weapons of choice are a feather duster and some lovely kisses. The captain surrenders, but not without a fight. (And Lydia Lovelace surrenders too!) Order your copy **here**.

In addition to wishing you lots of love, good health,

and prosperity, I hope the holidays and the new year bring you tons of wonderful reading!

Grace Burrowes

Read on for an excerpt from *A Rogue in Winter*!

PREVIEW: A ROGUE IN WINTER

A ROGUES TO RICHES NOVELLA

Vicar Pietr Sorenson has just seen his housekeeper off to visit family for the holidays, when Ned Wentworth comes to call. Pietr expects to spend his Yuletide season—as usual—enjoying much needed solitude at the darkest time of year. The best laid plans....

"Come in for a cup of tea, Mr. Wentworth. Give the shops an hour to get their parlor stoves roaring. Mrs. Baker has left me to make shift, but she always fills the larder with holiday treats before she departs."

Wentworth looked skeptical. "I truly do have errands to run, Vicar. I suspect the ladies wanted me out from underfoot while the decorating got under way at Lynley Vale. Lord Nathaniel is trying to help, and Stephen is making suggestions, while the footmen have all developed bad hearing. I was one dunderheaded male too many."

That was a falsehood, and right now, watching the Wentworth ducal coach trot out of the village, Pietr was inclined to name it as such.

"You are not a Wentworth by blood, so you banished yourself from what you regarded as a family undertaking. Forget the tea, let's have a tot to ward off the chill. Frequent doses of wassail are how we get through our winters here."

"Wassail?"

"Wassail, toddies, a nip from the flask. Everybody thinks Yorkshiremen are tough. We're more determined than tough, and we've learned to make our peace with the elements. Inside with you, Mr. Wentworth, and we will see what Mrs. Baker has left in the way of sweets."

"Jane said I shouldn't underestimate you."

Jane being Her Grace of Walden, a formidable woman who made duchessing look much easier than it was. But then, Jane was married to Quinton, Duke of Walden, and compared to being that fellow's wife, wearing a tiara was doubtless a Sunday stroll.

"You need not estimate me at all," Pietr said, leading the way up the vicarage's steps. "I'm a humble country parson living a placid existence in the bucolic splendor of rural nowhere." He'd meant that observation as a jest, but it had come out sounding a bit... forlorn?

Whiny?

"Pour me a bracer," Mr. Wentworth said, "and you can be my new best friend. I really am not accustomed to this cold."

"Has anybody given you the sermon for southerners yet?" Pietr asked, taking his guest's hat, coat, and gloves. "If leaving home, always dress as if you'll be outside all day, for you might be. Layers of wool are best, and that means two pairs of stockings if possible. Three if you can manage it. Forget vanity. Winter here will kill you if you give it a chance. If you are caught out in bad weather, try to keep moving at a slow, steady pace, provided you can see where you are going. If you sit for a moment to rest, next thing you will close your eyes, and Saint Peter will be offering you a pair of wings."

Mr. Wentworth glanced around the vicarage, which

Mrs. Baker kept spotless. The place was less than a hundred years old—thus it was the new vicarage—and detached from the church, unlike the prior manse, which was now used for Sunday school, meetings, and fellowship meals.

Like every other durable structure in Yorkshire, the vicarage was a stone edifice. The interior was lightened by whitewashed plaster walls, mullioned windows, and polished oak floors covered with sturdy braided rugs. Darkness in the form of exposed beams, wainscoting, and fieldstone hearths did battle with light, and on an overcast winter morning, the gloom was winning.

"The Lynley Vale butler says we're in for more foul weather," Mr. Wentworth observed, following Pietr into his study. "I have never seen snow like you have up here. Acres of snow, waist-deep, and the sky looks like nothing so much as more snow preparing to further bury a landscape we won't see again until July."

"The first winter is something of an adventure," Pietr said, going to the decanters on the sideboard. "Brandy?"

"If you will join me."

Pietr poured two generous servings and passed one to his guest. "The second winter, you realize about halfway through that it's not an adventure, it's a penance. You endure the third winter on the strength of grim resignation, and the fourth winter, you resolve to move south come spring."

Wentworth sipped his drink. "How long have you been here?"

"More than four winters is simply referred to as 'too long' to one not born in these surrounds, but the other seasons are glorious. Would you care for a hand of cribbage? Chess, perhaps?"

Men could not simply sit and talk with one another. Learning that had taken Pietr several years. Women, perhaps because their work was so unrelenting, had the knack of purely spending time in one another's company. Men were more difficult to put at ease.

"It's damned snowing again." Mr. Wentworth's tone was indignant as he took his drink to the window. "Pardon my language, but it snowed yesterday and the day before."

"I would not want to be the bearer of bad news,"— vicars were frequently exactly that—"but it's likely to snow again tomorrow and the next day." Pietr considered his drink, though really, consuming spirits this early in the day, and so shortly after Mrs. Baker's departure, was ill-advised. "To an early spring."

Mr. Wentworth drank to that. "I dread the hike back to Lynley Vale, and I consider myself as stouthearted as the next man."

"You consort with Wentworths. You are more stouthearted than most. What brings you to the village?"

Mr. Wentworth, whose daily business put him at the throbbing heart of international commerce and whose nearest associations were one step short of royalty, made a face as if he'd been served cold mashed turnips.

"Holiday shopping."

"Ah." Pietr joined Wentworth at the window, and indeed, fat, white snowflakes were drifting down from a pewter sky. Nothing to be alarmed about—yet. Mrs. Baker would reach York safely, though if the coachman was wise, he'd spend the night in town before asking the team to make the return journey.

"What am I supposed to give people who can buy entire counties if they so desire?" Mr. Wentworth asked.

Pietr handed out the same advice he gave to yeomen and gentry alike. "For the ladies, something small, unique, and pretty. For the gents, something comfortable and comforting. Avoid the useful and the necessary, which should be provided outside the context of holiday tokens. If you can make your gifts with your own hands, so much the better."

"I make deals," Mr. Wentworth said. "I make business transactions. I make coldly rational decisions."

This was the recitation of a man who'd never been in love. Of course Christmas would baffle him.

"We have a talented wood-carver in the person of Dody Wiles, who can usually be found holding forth in the inn's snug on a winter afternoon. For a price, he will make you birds, kittens, flowers... He can fashion them into coasters, or use a heavy wood such as mahogany to make a paperweight. His pipes are works of art, though he does require time to finish his creations."

"A wood-carver?"

"He was a drover who nearly lost a foot to frostbite. He needed a sedentary occupation, and the herds' loss is our gain. What on earth is that fellow thinking?"

A coach and four was rocketing along the far side of the village green, matched blacks in the traces.

"Fancy carriage," Mr. Wentworth muttered. "Fine horseflesh. What is a conveyance like that doing in a place like this?"

The vehicle rocked to a stop outside the coaching inn. A man climbed out. Youngish, based on the way he moved, dark-haired. He wore neither hat nor scarf nor gloves, though his greatcoat sported three capes.

He had no sooner put his booted foot to the snowy ground than he went careening onto his face into the nearest drift.

"Is this what passes for entertainment in a Yorkshire village?" Mr. Wentworth asked.

A lady climbed out of the coach. Her age was impossible to tell because she did wear a bonnet and scarf. She was spry, though, and she alit without benefit of a male hand to hold. She marched to her fallen comrade and stood over him, hands on hips.

He remained in the snow, facedown, unmoving.

"This is not entertainment," Pietr said, setting his drink aside. "This is a problem, and one I must deal with. The lady's coachy appears to be a madman and her escort three sheets to the wind. You are welcome to bide here, Mr. Wentworth, but I must pour oil on troubled waters and speak peace unto the heathen."

"You can't leave it to the innkeeper?"

"The hostlers aren't changing out the team, and our humble inn is full to the gills with holiday travelers. Yesterday's clouds promise that at some point today, the snow will mean business, and that woman will be stranded on the Dales with a drunk for an escort and an imbecile at the reins. Nobody will intervene now because she's not their problem, but I am a vicar and thus have a license to meddle."

Mr. Wentworth finished his drink and set the glass on the sideboard. "I have a propensity for meddling myself. Walden pays me to meddle, in fact. I didn't know there was a profession for it."

"Neither did I. You figure that part out after it's too late." Pietr did not bother with a hat, though he did tarry long enough to whip a scarf about his neck and pull on fleece-lined gloves. He stalked directly across the green, snow crunching beneath his boots, Mr. Wentworth tromping along at his side.

By the time they reached the coach, so had the innkeeper, his wife, two aldermen, the blacksmith, Mrs. Peabody, and any number of guests from the inn.

"Mr. Sorenson, it's as well you've troubled yourself to join us." Mrs. Peabody managed to convey that Pietr had dawdled half the day away. As head of the pastoral committee, she took seriously her duty to ensure that her vicar walked *humbly* with his God. "Somebody is sorely in need of last rites."

"Looks to me," Mr. Wentworth said, "as if somebody needs a bit of hair of the dog."

Mrs. Peabody drew in a breath, like a seventy-four gunner unfurling her sails. "Sir, I don't know who you are, or why you feel—"

"Excuse me," Pietr said, bending over the prostrate man. "This fellow needs help. Mr. Wentworth, if you'd assist me to get him to his feet." Many a Yorkshire wayfarer had frozen to death while sleeping off the effects of drink in the cozy embrace of a fluffy snowdrift.

Pietr took one of the fellow's arms, Wentworth got the other, and they eased the man to his feet. He was flushed and bore the scent of spirits.

"What do you think you're doing with my brother?" The traveling companion's voice cracked like river ice giving way under a winter sun. What she lacked in stature she made up for in ire.

Jolly delightful. The situation needed only jugglers, a dancing bear, and a learned pig. Alas, Pietr would have to manage as best he could without those reinforcements.

As usual.

Order your copy of *A Rogue in Winter*!
Learn more about **Miss Dignified**

ABOUT THE AUTHOR

I started writing as an antidote to empty nest and soon found it an antidote to life in general. I am the sixth out of seven children, and was raised in the rural surrounds of central Pennsylvania. Early in life I spent a lot of time reading romance novels and practicing the piano. My first career was as a technical writer and editor in the Washington, DC, area, a busy profession that nonetheless left enough time to read a lot of romance novels.

It also left enough time to grab a law degree through an evening program, produce Beloved Offspring (only one, but she is a lion), and eventually move to the lovely Maryland countryside.

While reading yet still more romance novels (there is a trend here) I opened a law practice, acquired a master's degree in Conflict Transformation (I had a teenage daughter by then) and started thinking about writing.... romance novels. This aim was realized when Beloved Offspring struck out into the Big World. ("Mom, why doesn't anybody tell you being a grown-up is hard?")

I eventually got up the courage to start pitching manuscripts to agents and editors. The query letter that resulted in "the call" started out: "I am the buffoon in the bar at the writer's retreat who could not keep her heroines straight, could not look you in the eye, and could not stop blushing--and if that doesn't narrow down the possibilities, your job is even harder than I thought." (The dear lady bought the book anyway.)

You can contact me though email at graceburrowes@yahoo.com or through my website at graceburrowes.com

MAKING MERRY

KERRIGAN BYRNE

CHAPTER 1

CALVINE VILLAGE, HIGHLANDS, SCOTLAND – 1891, WINTER SOLSTICE

*F*ate had been Vanessa Latimer's foe since she could remember.

She was the most unlucky, ungainly person of her acquaintance, and had resigned herself to an early death. However, she always imagined said death would be glorious, as well.

Or at least memorable.

Something like tripping and accidentally sacrificing herself to a volcano in the Pacific Islands. Or perhaps becoming the unfortunate snack of a Nile crocodile or a tiger in Calcutta.

Meeting her end as a human icicle in the Scottish Highlands had never made it on the list.

Not until the angry blizzard turned the road to Inverness treacherous, and something had spooked the horse, sending the carriage careening into a boulder the size of a small cottage.

The driver informed her that the wheel was irreparably damaged, and that she must stay in the carriage while he went for help.

That had been hours ago.

When the dark of the storm became the dark of the

late afternoon on this, the shortest day of the year, the temperatures plummeted alarmingly. Even though Vanessa had been left with furs and blankets, she worried she wouldn't survive the night, and set off along the road with a lantern and the most important of her luggage.

Now, huddled on the landing beneath the creaking shingle of Balthazar's Inn, she clutched her increasingly heavy case to her chest, shielding the precious contents with her body.

The surly innkeeper's impossibly thick eyebrows came together in a scowl as he wedged his bulk into the crack of the open door to effectively block any attempt at entry. Even the gale forces didn't save her nostrils from being singed by his flammable scotch-soaked breath. "As ye can see, lass, ye're not the only traveler stranded in this bollocks storm, and I let our last remaining room to the other rank idiot not clever enough to seek shelter before the storm fell upon us. So, nay. Ye'll have to try elsewhere."

"Was that rank idiot a shifty-eyed man in his fifties named McMurray?" she asked, forcing the words out of her lungs like a stubborn bellows to be heard over the din. The wind buffeted her skirts this way and that, plastering them to her trembling legs.

"Aye," he said with a self-satisfied smirk as he also managed to leer. "But doona think to be offering to share his bed; we're a reputable establishment."

"Never! I wouldn't—that isn't—what—" Vanessa gaped and shuddered for a reason that had nothing to do with the cold. Her driver had left her out there to freeze to death while *he'd* purchased a room with her fare? She should have listened when her instincts had warned her off hiring him.

Her case, growing heavier by the moment, threatened to slide out of the circle of her arms and down her body, so she bucked it higher with her hips and redoubled her efforts to hold it aloft with fingers she could no longer feel. "Is there somewhere nearby that might take me in?" she called, coughing as a particularly icy gust stole her breath.

"Aye." He jerked his chin in a vaguely northern direction. "The Cairngorm Tavern is not but a half hour's march up the road." He said this as if the angry wind did not threaten to snatch her up and toss her into the nearest snowdrift.

Swallowing a spurt of temper and no small amount of desperation, Vanessa squared her shoulders before offering, "What if *this* rank idiot can pay you double your room rate to sleep in the stables?" She pointed to the rickety livery next to the sturdy stone building. 'Twas the season and all that. If it was good enough for the baby Jesus, who was she to turn her nose up?

At this he paused, eyeing her with speculation. "Ye'll pay in advance?"

A knot of anxiety eased in her belly as she nodded dramatically, her neck stiff with the cold. "And triple for a warm bath."

He immediately shook his head, his jowls wobbling like a winter pudding. "Doona think I'll be spending me night hauling water for ye and yers."

"J-just me," Vanessa said, doing her best to clench her teeth against their chattering. "N-no m-mine."

"No husband? No chaperone?" For the first time, he looked past her as the storm finished swallowing the last of the early evening into a relentless chaos of white snow and dark skies.

"I'm—I'm alone." Vanessa told herself the gather of moisture at the corner of her eyes was the sole fault of the untenable weather. *Not* her untenable circumstances.

A banshee-pitched shriek sliced through the wail of

the storm. "Rory Seamus Galbreath Balthazar Pitagowan, ye useless tub of guts and grog!" The door was wrenched out of the innkeeper's hand and thrown open to reveal a woman half his height but twice his width.

She beat him about the head and shoulders with a kitchen towel, the blows punctuated by her verbal on-slaught. "Ye'd leave this child to freeze to death? And the night of the solstice? If no one were here to witness, I'd wake up a widow tomorrow, ye bloody heartless pil-lock! Now go make up Carrie's chamber, lay a fire, and heat water for this poor wee lass's bath."

Mr. Pitagowan's arms now covered his head to pro-tect it from the stinging abuse of his wife's damp towel. "Carrie's chamber? But...me love...it's haunted. And what if she—"

"I'm sure the bairn would rather sleep with a ghost than become one, wouldn't ye, dearie?"

At this point, she'd sleep next to the Loch Ness Monster if she could get warm. Besides, the very idea of a haunted bedroom in an ancient structure such as this one couldn't be more tempting. She would be warm *and* entertained. "Oh, I don't really mind if—"

"And tell young Dougal to put a kettle on!" Mrs. Pitagowan hollered as her husband plodded away, looking a great deal shorter now that his wife had cut him down.

Arms truly trembling now, as much from the weight of her burden as the cold, Vanessa took a step toward the door, which remained blocked by a large body. "Do you mind very much if I come insi—?"

"Are ye hungry, lass?" Mrs. Pitagowan's hand rested atop her ample belly, which was accentuated by the ruffles of an apron that might have struggled to cover a woman two stone lighter.

"I'm actually colder than any—"

"The wee mite is starving to death, just look at her!" she shouted after her husband, snatching the case from Vanessa before she could so much as protest. "So, make sure to set aside a bowl of stew and bread!"

Panicking about her case, Vanessa held her arms out. "Oh, do be careful, that's ever so fragi—"

"Well I doona ken why ye insist on standing out there in the cold, little 'un, come in before I can snap yer skinny wee arms off like icicles." The round woman carried her burden like it weighed a bit of nothing as she waddled into the common room.

Vanessa shivered inside and closed the door behind her, struggling with the ancient latch. She knew she was a rather short and painfully thin woman, but at eight and twenty, she'd not been addressed as *child, bairn, wee mite,* or *little one* for longer than a decade.

If ever.

Turning to the common room, Vanessa swallowed around a lump of anxiety as she noted that, indeed, the place was filled to the exceptionally low rafters with wayward travelers.

Most of them male. All of them staring at her.

A glow from the over-warm room rolled over her as a blush heated her stinging cheeks.

"G-good evening," she stammered, bobbing a slight curtsy before brushing quickly melting snow from her cloak.

The only other woman looked up from the table where she tended her husband and four unruly children to send her a pinched and sour glare. No doubt she made assumptions regarding Vanessa's vocation due to her lack of chaperone.

She was aware unfortunate women traveled to such taverns looking to pay for their lodgings with their company and favors. And after what Mr. Pitagowan had said in front of the entire assembly,

Vanessa couldn't exactly blame the woman for her speculation.

Besides, she was used to it.

Her attempt at a smile was rebuked, so she turned it on the handful of men clustered in overstuffed chairs around the hearth, nursing ale from tankards that might have been crafted during the Jacobite rebellion.

"Bess!" a kilted, large-boned man crowed, wiping foam from his greying, ill-kempt beard with the back of his hand. "Tell 'er if she's afraid to bed down with the ghost, I'll be happy to offer an alternative arrangement." His eyes traveled down Vanessa's frame with an uninvited intimacy that made her feel rather molested. "One that would keep the wee lass warm, but I canna promise ye'd be dry."

As she was wont to do, Vanessa covered her mortification with all the imperious British pomposity she could muster, lifting her nose in the air. "You needn't speak as if I were not standing right here. I am capable of understanding you exceptionally well, sir. Correct me if I'm wrong, but I highly doubt you've ever had a woman accept such a crass and ridiculous proposition. One you didn't have to offer recompense, that is."

The men gathered around the fireplace all blinked at her, dumbstruck.

"I thought not," she said. "Now I'll thank you not to make such ill-mannered and indecent suggestions in the presence of children." She gestured to a grubby lad of perhaps eight, who promptly tossed a piece of bread into her hair.

The boy's father boxed his son's ears, and the child let out an ear-splitting wail, setting her teeth on edge.

"English." A thin, pockmarked highlander harrumphed the word into his ale glass. "The night's too cold for a frigid, prickly wee bundle of bones, Graham," he said to her harasser.

"Aye, she's hardly worth the trouble." Another spat into the fire, and the resulting sizzle disgusted her.

"Ye barbarous Douglasses behave!" Mrs. Pitagowan thundered over her shoulder as she turned sideways to squeeze herself down the aisle created by the six or so tables in the common room. "Or ye'll find yerselves arseways to a snowdrift and make no mistake! Now follow me, lass, and let's get ye out of those wet clothes."

Vanessa turned to obey, cringing at the Douglasses' disgusting noises evoked by the innkeeper's gauche mention of her undressing. She passed a long bar, against which two well-dressed men in wool suits picked at a brown stew and another grizzled highlander wore a confounding fishing uniform in the middle of winter and leagues away from the ocean.

She'd heard tell the Scots around these parts were an odd lot, but she'd underestimated just how truly backward they might be.

Balthazar's Inn, at least, was charming. Though the pale stone walls were pitted with age, a lovely dark wood wainscoting rose from the floor to waist height, swallowing some of the light from the lanterns and the fireplace to create a rather cozy effect. In observation of Christmas, boughs of holly and other evergreens were strewn across the hearth and over the doorways, tied in place by red ribbons. Similar braided wreaths moated the lanterns on each table, filling the room with the rather pleasant scent of pine.

"Thank you for taking me in, Mrs. Pitagowan." Vanessa remembered her manners as she followed the woman through a chaotic scullery.

"Call me Bess, everyone else does," the lady sang.

Vanessa jumped out of the way when Bess's grumpy husband threw open an adjoining door and stomped past them carrying an empty cauldron and muttering in a language she'd never heard before.

"Bess, then. I appreciate your generosity—"

Turning in the doorway, Bess narrowly missed smashing the case against the frame, causing Vanessa to blanch. "Doona get the idea I'm being charitable, lass. I heard ye offer thrice the room rates. And I'll be needing payment afore I ready the room."

Right. Vanessa sighed, digging into the pocket of her cloak for her coin purse. "How much?"

"I'll take half a crown what with the bath and stew."

Vanessa counted out the coin, fully aware she'd pay half as much at any reputable establishment in London, but she was beyond caring, what with a bath and a hot meal so close at hand. "You called this *Carrie's room* before," she mentioned, more to make conversation than anything. "Is Carrie the name of the apparition who will be keeping me company?"

A dark, almost sympathetic expression softened Bess's moon-round face as she used a free hand to tuck a pale lock of hair back into her matronly cap. "Oh—well—that's just a bit of local superstition, isn't it? Nothing to worry about. A lady like ye'll be perfectly safe."

Local superstition was exactly what drew her to the Highlands for Christmas, but Vanessa thought it best not to disclose that to Bess just now.

What had the woman meant, *a lady like her*? Someone wealthy, perhaps? English? Or female?

Either way, fate had left her little choice but to find out.

CHAPTER 2

*J*ohnathan de Lohr was awoken from his blank torpor by the sound of a delicate sneeze.

It was time again. The solstice maybe, when the sun flared and tugged at the planet in such a way the tides became wilder. The storms became more violent. The creatures of the earth more feral.

Untamed.

And those dead like himself, cursed to still inhabit this plane, were called to be restless.

Reminded what it was to be human.

Only to have it ruthlessly taken from them again.

He materialized—for lack of a better word—by Carrie's old bed in time to have a dust sheet snatched right through his middle by a large, apple-cheeked woman in a matronly apron.

He didn't recognize her at all.

"We've a water heater but no piping to the rooms, far as we are from civilized Blighty," she said, snatching the last of the covers off a tall wardrobe as a portly man with wild tufts of greying hair dumped an empty metal basin on the floor with a derisive clang.

Ah, *there* was Balthazar, or at least one of his kin. John had known generations of them to come and go, but this iteration he'd seen when the man was younger. Much younger.

The innkeeper stomped out with nary a word and was replaced by a lad of maybe fifteen with longish unkempt dark hair and a cauldron of steaming water, which he poured into the tub.

Wait, they'd let the room? *His* room? This was not to be tolerated.

He could make himself visible, of course, on a night like tonight, could take to wailing and thundering and all manner of ghostly things. He might even be able to summon the energy to touch or move something. To breathe on or even grab at someone with icy fingers, terrorizing them away so he could regain his own tranquility.

It took so much from him, though, exerting his will in the realm of the living.

Waking always discombobulated John. For a moment, the chaos of the round woman's tidying, the noise of a full inn and the water crashing into the metallic basin, along with the press of three or more bodies in such a small chamber overwhelmed him. A storm screamed and battered at the ancient window, the snow knocking like the very fist of a demon in gusts and surges.

The blasted woman—whom he assumed was the current Balthazar's wife—had tossed the dust covers out the door and was now rushing toward where John stood in front of the bed, with a fresh pile of sheets and new pillows.

He didn't like the odd sensation of people walking through him; it rankled like that odd tickle one felt when bashing their elbow, but without the pain.

Unable to easily avoid the rotund woman in the cramped space, he retreated a few steps until he found himself standing inside the wardrobe, his vision hindered by the closed doors and the darkness inside them. Much better. Was this piece new? He tried to remember if he'd seen it the last time he'd lingered here. They'd no doubt procured it to cover the door that led to—

Another small sneeze interrupted his thoughts. "Forgive me," begged a British female voice before a delicate sniff. "Dust always makes me sneeze." She cleared her throat. "It *is* kind of Dougal and Mr. Pitagowan to draw a bath. I feel it is the only way I'll ever be warm again. And the room is really so charming, I'm certain I'll be comfortable here. I might not have survived a march to the Cairngorm Tavern."

John closed his eyes as a strange, incandescent vibration shimmered through him.

The new feminine voice was husky and smooth, like smoke exhaled over the most expensive brandy. It slid between his ribs like a smooth assassins' blade, nicking at a heart that hadn't ticked for at least a century. It both stirred and soothed him in equal measure.

"Like I said earlier, miss, this isna kindness, it's a service. One ye paid generously for, so enjoy it with our blessing and warm yer wee bones before ye shiver right out of them."

John had always been an appreciator of the Scottish brogue, but *this* woman's pitch could likely offend sensitive dogs. It was especially jarring after the crisp, clear notes of British gentility.

He poked his head back through the wardrobe doors to find who belonged to such a sound, and realized immediately why he'd missed her before.

Dressed in the most peculiar plain grey wool cloak

that'd been soaked through, the slip of a woman had flattened herself against the grey stone wall just inside the door, her skirts protecting an oddly shaped brown case on the floor beneath her. A plain, dark felt hat shadowed her features in the room only lit by two dim lanterns, but he could tell it had obviously not kept her ebony curls dry. The impression of a sharp jaw and shapely lips above a thick black scarf drew the rest of him from the wardrobe to investigate.

She'd been out in that bastard of a storm? This waifish girl? No wonder the Pitagowans had interrupted his peace to prepare the room for her. The laws of Highland hospitality—if there still was such a thing —would not have allowed them to deny anyone sanctuary.

"You have my gratitude all the same, Mrs. Pitagowan," the woman said.

God, how he had missed the dulcet pronunciations of the gently bred ladies of his homeland. It'd been so long. He wanted to bid her to speak, to never stop.

"I told ye, call us Bess and Balthazar, everyone else does." The innkeeper trundled over to the door and accepted a tray of tea, which she set on the small stand next to the bed. After, she squeezed around her husband, who'd returned with yet another cauldron of water, to the small brick fireplace on the far wall. Rolling up her sleeves, she squatted to arrange a fire.

"You must call me Vanessa, then."

Vanessa. John tested the name on his tongue, and he thought he saw the woman tense beneath her layers.

Could she hear him already? The sun hadn't gone down yet.

"Where are ye from, lass?" Bess asked, carrying on the conversation.

John found himself equally curious.

"My family resides in London, mostly," Vanessa answered. "Though I am compelled to spend most of the time at our country estate in Derbyshire."

John thought her reply rather curious, not only the phrase but the bleak note lurking beneath the false cheer she'd injected into her voice. Compelled. An interesting word.

If Bess thought it odd, she didn't mention. "Where were ye headed in such a storm, if ye doona mind me asking?"

"Not at all." Bending to drag the case with her, Vanessa rested it by the tea-laden table, out of the way of Balthazar's and Dougal's stomping feet. "I was on the road to Fort Augustus on Loch Ness when the blizzard overtook us." She poured herself a cup of the steaming brew as she answered.

"Is yer family there?" Bess turned to cast a queer look at her. "Will they be fretting after ye?"

The lady didn't bother to sweeten the tea; she simply lifted it to her soft mouth and puckered her lips to blow across the surface before taking a sip.

A strange, hollow longing overtook John as he watched her shiver with delight as she swallowed the warm liquid and let out an almost imperceptible sigh.

Christ he'd give his soul to taste tea again.

"My family is in Paris for Christmas this year," she answered vaguely after the silence had stretched for too long.

"And ye're not with them?" Bess prodded, catching flame to a bit of peat she'd laid beneath the kindling.

"No. No, I am not invited to—that is, I don't travel with them, generally. I am more often occupied by my own adventures."

An awkward silence fell over the room like the batting of a moist blanket. The lady sipped at her tea, retreating deeper into her cloak and her thoughts as the tub was filled.

Once Bess had built the fire to a crackling height, she added one more extra-large, dry log from the grate next to the fireplace, and stood with a grunt. She reached in to test the water and flicked it off, wiping her hand with her apron.

"A strange trunk, that." She nodded to the ungainly square case. "Not quite a trunk, I suppose, and not a satchel either."

"It's a camera." Vanessa abandoned her empty teacup to the tray to stand over it. "I was to be on a winter photography expedition at Loch Ness before the storm hit. I left my trunk with my belongings on the abandoned coach."

A camera? John squinted at the case. He'd never heard of such a thing.

Bess clapped her hands together in delight. "Och, aye? Now's the time to find Nessie, if there ever is one! No doubt ye caught wind of the Northern Lights this year. We could see them snapping across the sky afore the clouds covered them. 'Tis, no doubt, the reason this storm is so powerful. All things are intensified during the *Na Fir Chlis*. And during the solstice, and Christmas after that..." She let the words linger, winking conspiratorially. "All things are possible, are they not?"

"That was my hope." Vanessa smiled broadly, and John felt a catch in his throat, as if the very sight of that smile had stolen something from him.

"Well, here's ye a toweling and some soap. Though perhaps not as fragrant and fancy as ye're used to."

"It'll do perfectly," Vanessa assured her with a kind smile.

John had always appreciated a woman who was kind to those beneath her in rank, stature, or wealth. It had been one of his greatest irritations when a shrewish lady was demanding or unfeeling to the help.

"I'll leave ye, lass," Bess said with a smile. "I'll see if I canna find ye something to sleep in. Get warm and dry and then come to the common room for some supper."

The moment the door latched, the woman, *Vanessa*, locked it and immediately grappled with the knot on her scarf. Unraveling that, she hung it close to the fire, pulled the pin from her hat, and discarded it, also.

John was stunned into stillness at the unfettered sight of her face.

Lord, but she was lovely. The structure of her visage delicate enough to be elfin, pale and sharp, even in the golden firelight. Her eyes, he was pleasantly surprised to find, were as grey as a winter sky. On many women, such dramatically precise features appeared to be cold and fathomless. But not so in this case. She seemed to glow with this sort of...radiant luminescence that was initiated behind her eyes and spilled over the rest of her like a waterfall.

What was the genesis of such a phenomenon? he wondered. What would he call it?

Life, he realized. An abundance of it.

As someone who hadn't been alive in—well he couldn't remember how many years, precisely—he was drawn to the way it veritably burst from her. Like such a diminutive frame could barely contain it all.

Damned if he didn't find that alluring as hell.

After bending to unlace and remove her boots, she turned her back to him, facing the fire. She shucked her woolen cloak and hung it on a wall peg close to the heat to dry.

Then, she went to work on her blouse.

Bloody hell and holy damnation. This desirable creature was about to strip bare and bathe. *Here*. In the room that had been his prison for so damnably long.

Her movements were harried and jerky, as if made clumsy by exhaustion and the cold.

John had been bred a gentleman in his day. Over-educated and imbued with codes and creeds and ratified rules of behavior. That breeding tore at him now. He should turn away. He should leave her to wash and dress. This interloper upon his dark, abysmal existence —if one could even call it thus. This tiny creature of light and life.

He might have done the noble thing...

If he hadn't hesitated long enough to watch her peel her blouse down her arms, uncovering shoulders smooth as corn silk and white as rich cream.

Lord, but he was transfixed. Even though he technically levitated above the ground, his feet were as good as pegged to the floor.

He watched her unlace her own corset that knotted in the front and wondered when that had changed over the years. Her chin touched one shoulder to glance behind her, as if sensing the intensity of his regard. She looked straight through him, which was a blessing, because if he'd been visible, she'd immediately notice that he sported a cockstand large and vulgar enough to offend even a courtesan.

His conscience prickled. He *shouldn't* watch her... but in this bleak and lonely hell so far from home, she was an oasis of beauty. An English rose among Scottish thistle.

The firelight silhouetted the fullness of her slightly parted lips, the pert upturn of her nose, and the astounding length of her lashes in stark relief.

He was helpless to do anything but appreciate the vision.

Sighing and shaking her head slightly as if to ward off her own silliness, she fiddled with the buckle of a wide belt and pushed her skirt from her hips, drawing down a thin white cotton undergarment at the same time.

Had he knees, they would have buckled. Had he a fist, he would have bitten into it to stave off the hollow groan of longing fighting its way up his chest.

As she assumed she was alone, she was neither self-conscious nor was she self-aware. This was no slow, practiced uncovering of a mistress, meant to tease and titillate. And yet, the sight of her heart-shaped bare ass as she bent to step out of her clothing was enough to unravel whatever matter remained of him.

If she'd been facing the light and not away from it, he would have been granted a peek at the intimate cove between her thighs.

The gods were not so kind.

She straightened, peeling a simple white chemise from her body with a shivering stretch, and turned toward the bath in the center of the room.

Toward *him*.

A watering mouth was the first thing that alerted him to the fact that he would slowly, with infinite, infuriating increments, regain a semblance of corporality.

He would have welcomed the sensation, if he wasn't so utterly distracted by the sight of her in all her nude glory.

Christ. She was a masterpiece, someone crafted by a loving artisan from some other material than the minerals and mud that forged the rest of man. Every other woman now seemed a clumsy clay attempt at the marble-smooth perfection of her.

Though her form was diminutive, her shoulders were not; they were straight and proud, held so by an erect spine and practiced posture. Said posture displayed her tear-shaped breasts to perfect effect, their nipples, peaked and puckered with cold, the same peach hue as her cupid's bow mouth.

God but his hands ached to touch her. To explore every creamy inch of her. To find the places that made her gasp and tremble.

To discover where else she might be peach and perfect.

As if she was loath to leave the warmth of the fire, she took up the soap and her underthings, and tiptoed to the edge of the bath.

The crude basin only came up to about past her knees, so she barely had to lift her leg to test the water within. She dipped a toe, then engulfed the delightfully feminine arch of her foot before wading in to her shapely calf.

John had never been jealous of an inanimate object in his life, but as she hissed and sputtered whilst lowering her chilled body into the hot water, he would have changed places with the liquid in an instant.

It's not as if he was exactly solid.

Though, he was getting *hard*…

He crouched when she did, his eyes unable to leave her as she drew her legs into her chest and settled into the heat with a sibilant sigh of surrender.

He'd give what was left of his soul to coax a sound like that from her. Especially now that he knew what she looked like with naked pleasure parting her lips, and the dew of steam curling the tendrils of her hair that she had yet to take down from its braided knot.

Abandoning her soap and undergarments to the side, she did little but enjoy the heat of the water for a moment, cupping it in her hand and pouring it over what parts of her chest, breasts, and shoulders, she couldn't completely submerge.

God, he remembered what that felt like, sinking into a hot bath on a chilly night.

He'd give anything just to feel warmth.

John made himself dizzy trying to follow every bead

of water that caught the firelight along the tantalizing peaks and valleys of her body. Though she was a woman in a crude basin on a packed floor on the edge of the civilized world, she might as well have been a winter goddess bathing in a dark pool.

Would that he could attend her. That he could follow the little bejeweled droplets with his tongue and find the intriguing places they would land.

Would that *he* could make her wet.

She eventually gathered up her undergarments, which were still rather clean all things considered, and scrubbed at them with the soap.

He remembered that she'd mentioned she had no trunk with her, and would likely need to wear them again tomorrow until her things could be fetched.

That finished, she wrung them out and set them aside before taking up the soap once more.

John had been no saint as a young man. He'd frolicked and fornicated in the presence of his young and noble mates, sharing courtesans and the like. He'd enjoyed watching women. What they did to each other, to other men.

To themselves.

But he could truly never remember gleaning as much intimate enjoyment as he did watching her start at her foot, and lather a bit of coarse soap up her leg to her thigh and in between them before working her way back down the other side.

Had he not been dead, he might have expired from the length of time he held his breath.

Restless, aroused, John drifted in circles around the tub as she washed, humming an unfamiliar tune softly as the firelight danced across her skin.

He found himself behind her as she ran a lathered hand over her shoulders and did her best to reach her back. She was about to get suds on a dark velvet curl that had escaped her coiffure and reflexively, John's hand made to brush it aside.

Knowing he couldn't. Understanding that his hand would pass through her before it actually did.

Even so, his body was helpless but to reach for her.

Which was why her muffled shriek startled them both.

CHAPTER 3

As gracefully as a gazelle, the woman surged to her feet, snatched the towel, and leapt from the bath to retreat as far away from him as possible.

John was almost too shocked to much lament the fact that she wrapped her torso in the towel and clutched it to her clavicles, protecting most of her lovely figure from view.

He looked down at his hand, pleased to note that it had become visible, or at least the transparent shadow of it, a flesh-colored outline through which he could see the floor beneath, interrupted only by the cuff of his crimson regimental jacket.

"Holy Moses," she gasped, breathing as if she'd run apace. Enough of her skin was still visible to notice that she rippled with tiny goosebumps. "You're a—shade. A man. A…"

"A ghost?" he politely finished for her.

She blanched unbelievably whiter, pressing a hand to her forehead as if to check for a fever. Apparently not finding one, she lowered her palm, unveiling a wrinkle of bemusement.

"You're not Carrie," she accused, her diction slow and uncertain.

"An astute observation," he answered wryly.

"Did you know her?"

"Know her?" He found the question odd and out of place.

"You're in her bedroom. Did you haunt her?" Brows lifting impossibly higher, her gaze shifted to the cobalt coverlet on the bed, and the spider-web thin lace of the curtains, no doubt making certain scandalized assumptions.

He opened his mouth to dispel them, but what came out was, "What year is it?"

She blinked back at him in mute confusion. Her eyes all but crossed and uncrossed as she looked at him, and then through him, and then at him again. "You're English," she said rather distantly. "But here...haunting the Highlands. Why?"

John drifted around the basin toward her. "Pay attention, woman, what bloody year is it?"

She swallowed, retreating from the bed and inching around the basin to keep it between them. "It's eighteen ninety-one."

He froze as his calculations astonished him. "I've been asleep for thirty-five years this time."

"My," she breathed, bending down to retrieve her undergarments from the edge of the tub as she backed toward the fire. "You must have been awfully knackered."

He scowled at her, not understanding the word. "You're quite calm for a woman being haunted. Why are you not running out of here, screaming for help at the top of your lungs?"

She seemed to consider his question carefully, letting go of one side of the towel as she tapped her chin in a contemplative posture. The towel slipped down her chest a little, and John felt his composure slip right along with it.

"For one, I'm not dressed. And for another, Bess warned me I'd spend the night with a ghost. I suppose it was my erroneous assumption that apparition would be female."

He allowed her to keep the basin between them, even though he could have passed right through it and not even disturbed the water.

Not yet.

"I do apologize if I frightened you, miss," he felt compelled to say. "Let me assure you I am a mostly harmless ghost."

"That's a relief to hear. Though I'll admit I was more startled than frightened...almost."

His scowl suddenly felt more like a pout, which irked him in the extreme. "I'll have you know, the mention of my very name has struck terror in the hearts of entire regiments. And you expect me to believe you are so bold as to be fearless? I am a bloody apparition after all. You're not even having a mild crisis of nerves?"

"I'm sure you were *very* terrifying, sir," she obligingly rushed to soothe his ego, which helped not at all. "But I'll admit I'm rather too elated to be scared."

"Elated?" He couldn't believe what he was hearing. Was the woman mad?

She nodded, her lips breaking into a broad smile, her slim shoulder lifting in an attractive and apologetic shrug. "I've always believed in ghosts, and I've never been lucky enough to meet one. I have so many questions. I could cheerfully murder myself for leaving my notebook back at the carriage." She said this as a muttered afterthought before looking up at him with a winsome smile. "Do you mind, awfully, turning around so I can dress?"

"I don't see the point," he challenged, crossing his arms over his chest and lifting a suggestive brow. "You act as though I haven't been here the entire time... watching you."

"How *dare* you?" she gasped in outrage, her notice flying to the bathtub as if it'd just dawned on her that he could have been present without her knowledge. Her color heightened as a comely blush crept up her chest and neck from below the towel.

He was coming to hate that bloody towel.

John bristled, but only because guilt pricked at him. "I *dare* because I'm dead and have been imprisoned in this godforsaken structure since before your grandparents were born, no doubt. What have I to do but observe the goings-on here? Most people are none the wiser."

Her eyes widened as she, no doubt, imagined what he'd borne witness to in so long a time. "That isn't excuse for your ghastly behavior! You are—were—a Lieutenant Colonel?" She raked her eyes over his form, a few more colors of his crimson regimentals lit by the fire at her back. "This is conduct unbecoming an officer, I say."

"Take it up with my superiors, then," he snorted, leaning in her direction with eyes narrowed until he willed himself to disappear.

"Wait!" Her panicked quicksilver gaze scanned the emptiness, hopping right over him. "Come back," she pleaded. "I'm sorry. I won't scold you. I promise. I was just—"

He reappeared paces closer to her, standing on her side of the basin now.

She made a little squeak as he did, hopping back as close to the fire as she could get.

An inconvenient conscience needled him again. He was behaving badly, but a century of isolation tended to strip a man of his manners. "Tell me. Would you have behaved differently were our places reversed?

Would you have looked away? Maintained my modesty, my privacy?"

Her gaze traveled down the length of him, and a very masculine sense of victory burned through his veins when he spied the glimmer of appreciation as it dashed across her features. An acute awareness of their proximity. Of his proportions in contrast to hers.

She was a woman.

He was a man.

They were alone in a room together with very little clothing between them.

And if he were naked, the warmth in her gaze told him she would drink in the sight of his body.

Just as he had.

"I cannot say what I would do in your case," she admitted, her voice lower, huskier. "But if you asked nicely, I *would* turn around."

He could refuse. What would she do then? But even as the thought flickered through him, so did another indisputable fact. One hundred and fifty years later, he was still a nobleman, one tasked to uphold honor.

And she was a lady deserving of his respect and deference.

Goddammit.

He bloody turned around.

The rustles of her unseen actions intrigued and tempted him, but he clenched his fists and forced himself to stay right where he was.

"I'm Miss Vanessa Latimer."

He heard the towel hit the ground and this time was able to bite into his fist. Death, it seemed, did not diminish desire.

"Johnathan de Lohr," he finally gritted out. "Earl of Worchester and Hereford."

"I don't think so," she laughed over the sound of her belt buckling.

"Do you presume to tell me I don't know my own name?" he asked crossly.

"Not at all, but I've been introduced to Johnathan de Lohr, Earl of Worchester at the Countess of Bainbridge's ball a few years past, and have it on good authority that he's very much alive. Also, the de Lohrs lost the Hereford title sometime in the eighteenth century."

He frowned, bloody irked by the entire business. "And how would you know that?"

Her rueful sound vibrated through the dimness. "My mother always wanted me to marry a peer, so I've studied *Burke's* more than the Bible, the encyclopedia, and most literature combined. More's the pity. I find it tedious in the extreme."

Hope leapt into his chest. News of his kinsmen never traveled to this place, and he always wondered about the fate of his family. "Tell me about him? About the Earl."

"Well..." She drew the word out as if it helped her retrieve a memory. "He's attractive but not in that charming, handsome way of most gentlemen. More like brutally well-built. Tall and wide, golden haired like a lion. His hand was warm and strong when we were introduced. And his eyes...his eyes were..." She drifted off, though the little sounds of friction and fabric told him she still dressed herself.

"Blue?" he prompted after the silence had become untenable. De Lohr eyes were almost invariably blue.

"Yes. But I was going to say empty."

"Empty?" he echoed.

She made a melancholy little sound. "He stared at me for a long time, and I could sense no light behind the eyes. They were cold and hollow as a hellmouth, I'm afraid." She seemed to shake herself, her voice losing the dreamy huskiness and regaining some of the crisp starch his countrywomen were famous for. "But worry not, he's possessed of an impeccable reputation and an obscene fortune, so you should be proud of your legacy, all things considered... When were you the Earl, my lord?"

"Please, call me John," he requested. "I've technically no title now; I died during the Jacobite rebellion of seventeen forty-five. My brother, James, became the Earl after I perished at the battle of Culloden."

"You had no heir?"

A bleak and familiar ache opened in his chest. A void that existed whenever he thought of the life he didn't have the chance to live. "I had no wife."

She made that noise again, one that made him wonder what she was thinking. That made him want to turn around to search her beautiful face. Her remarkability was evidenced in the description she'd made of his kinsman. Most people, when asked, would recount reputation and accomplishments, not impressions of one's soul behind their eyes. Miss Vanessa Latimer observed the world in a different way than most.

"It remains strange to me," she was saying, "that you are here. Culloden is miles and miles away."

"Yes. Well. I've gathered from listening to locals that we English won. That Scotland is firmly beneath the rule of King and Crown."

"Queen," she corrected. "Queen Victoria."

"Still?" he marveled. "Surely she's dead by now."

"She's ruled for fifty-three years. Though, while we're on the subject, I don't know many Scotsmen who would deign to call themselves British, though we are technically united under one sovereign. It's no longer a blood-soaked subject, but it's still a complicated one, even after all this time."

Of that, he had no doubt. "I always respected the Scots. I fought because it was my obligation. I was no great supporter of the Stewarts or the bloody King. The de Lohrs prosper regardless of what idiot ass sits on the throne, but we do our duty by our birthright, and sometimes that means going to war."

"Why, then, do you think you're stuck here haunting a small village inn some seventy miles from Culloden?"

He shrugged. "It's been a mystery I've been grinding on for one hundred and fifty years."

"Maybe I could help you," she offered, her voice bright with optimism.

"How could you possibly?"

"I'm stuck here too now, aren't I? At least until the storm blows over, and I love a good mystery. You're obviously not going anywhere, so why not?" She emitted a short sigh one might after completing a task. "There. You can turn back around."

The first thing he noticed when he did was that her damp undergarments were pinned to the fireplace mantle, drying in the heat.

Which meant beneath her clothing she wore... nothing but her corset. Somehow that knowledge was just as arousing as the idea of her completely naked.

Well. Almost.

He locked his jaw, glaring at her strange garments as if he could see through them. As if he'd never seen them before. The skirts of this decade were odd but ultimately flattering, spread tight and flat over the hips and flaring like a tulip toward her knees. A wide belt with an ornate buckle accentuated her impossibly small waist, and the bodice was made of some fabric other than silk. Something lighter that bloused out at the shoulders and bust.

Suddenly he wanted to know everything there was to know about this strange and extraordinary woman.

She peered up at him rather owlishly. "Goodness, I can see more of you now."

And he could see less of her, he silently lamented.

"You have color," she noted, as if to herself. "Your hair is as gold as your namesake's. In fact, you rather look a great deal like him."

Did he? And she'd called him handsome.

Sort of.

He did his best not to preen. "The fault of the solstice, it seems, and the strangeness of the Northern Lights at such a time of year. There's maybe been five such occurrences in the past one hundred and fifty years, and if this is anything like those, I'll become more corporeal as the night goes on."

Her eyes flew wider. She opened her mouth, no doubt to ask a million questions, inquisitive minx that she was.

So, he headed her off at the pass. "What sort of weapon is a *camera*?" He said the word carefully, tasting the syllables, trying to dissect its root words as he drifted toward the case. "You said you were going to take a *photo* with it. Do you really think to battle the Loch Ness Monster in the middle of winter?"

She blinked, moving in front of the case as if to protect it from him. Her delicate features, once so open and intrigued, were now closed, defensive.

Perhaps a bit reproving.

"Photo is the abbreviation for photograph," she informed him stiffly.

He searched his education of the ancient languages. "Photo meaning light. And graph meaning…something written."

"Precisely."

"I couldn't be more perplexed," he admitted.

"I'll show you." She crouched down to open the case, undoing buckles and straps and throwing it open to unveil the strangest contraption he'd ever seen. She didn't touch it, however, but took a flat leather satchel from where it was tucked beside the machine. What she extracted after opening the flap stole the next words from him.

Perching on the bed, one knee bent and the other foot still stabilizing her on the floor, she placed a strange and shiny piece of paper on the coverlet. And then another. And another. And several more until they were all splayed out in wondrous disarray.

John could have been blown over by a feather.

With unsteady fingers, he reached out to the first photograph, a portrait of the Houses of Parliament in London, but this depicted it with a cracking huge clock tower built. The edifice glowed and reached into the sky taller than anything he could imagine. The rendering was nothing like a painting. Colorless and with only two dimensions. But it was *real*, as if the moment had been captured by some sort of magic and...

"Written by light," he breathed.

She nodded, watching him with a pleased sort of tenderness as he discovered a modern miracle that she probably considered quite pedestrian. The next photograph was of the Westminster Cathedral. Another a close-up of a tall lamp. The flame fed by nothing he could imagine, as there was no chamber for wood nor oil. It was as if the fire floated on its very own.

He was about to ask after it when something else caught his eye.

"What the bloody hell is this?" He smoothed his hands over a rather terrifying-looking automaton comprised of arms, levers, whistles, and wheels.

"A locomotive engine. We call it a train, as it can pull dozens of boxcars behind it endlessly at astonishing speeds. I left England on the seven o'clock train last night and arrived in Perth early this afternoon."

He shook his head in abject disbelief, aching to see the real thing. To discover how his empire and world had changed in so long. "How does it work, this locomotive?"

"I'm no engineer, but the engine is powered by steam created with coal fire." She put up a finger as if to tap an idea out of the sky. "You'll be interested to know, ships are powered by steam and steel, as well, rather than wind and wood. We can cross to America in a matter of six days."

"America?" He scratched his head. "Oh, you mean the colonies."

Her lips twisted wryly. "Well...that's a long and rather disappointing story. But the short of it is, they are their own sovereign nation now."

He narrowed his eyes at her. "You're having me on."

"I am not. Declared their independence in seventeen seventy-six. They've their own parliament and everything."

"And what royal family, I'd like to know?"

"A democratic republic, if you'd believe it. A society whose aristocracy is chosen from the best capitalists."

"Not landowners, then?"

She shrugged, gathering back a few of the portraits from the bed into a tidy pile. "Some. But mostly industry giants and war heroes. Machines, factories and the like have changed everything. England's like that too, now. The new century will belong to innovators rather than aristocrats, I'd wager."

"Good God, what I wouldn't give to see that." He couldn't decide what would be worse, dying before his time and missing what might have been. Or existing past his death and learning what he was still missing. What if the Empire rose and fell, and he was still sitting here in the bunghole of Blighty, watching generations of Balthazars raise, eat, and sometimes bugger sheep?

Her eyes brimmed with sympathy, as if she could read his thoughts. "I wish you could see it all. I plan to.

I haven't been to America yet, though I'm dying to visit New York. I think I'll go there next if my journey to Constantinople is delayed."

"You're traveling to Constantinople? With whom?" He looked pointedly at her ring finger, which he noted was bare.

Why that ignited a little glow of pleasure in his chest, he couldn't say. It wasn't as though he could speak for her. It wasn't as though he knew he would. They'd been acquainted for all of five minutes.

"Oh...haven't decided yet," she hedged, glancing away and plucking at a loose thread in the coverlet.

"You mentioned your family wanted an advantageous marriage for you, but you didn't introduce yourself as nobility."

His observation seemed to displease her. "No. But my father owns a shipping company, and the thing to do is marry off rich heiresses to impoverished lords."

He made a sound in the back of his throat that he wished didn't convey the depth of his derision on that score. It wasn't that he thought women shouldn't marry above their rank.

It was that he instantly and intensely hated the idea of *her* being married.

She was young, but old enough to have been made a mother many times over. Maybe twenty and five or so...So why wasn't she spoken for?

John allowed his notice to drift to another photograph, this one of a woman in a dark dress seated in a velvet chair. She posed like one would for any master of portraiture, looking off into the distance. Her features carefully still.

From her place at his elbow, Vanessa said, "This is my eldest sister, Veronica. The Dowager Countess of Weatherstoke."

"A Countess. How fortunate for her."

"I wouldn't have traded places with her for the entire world." The melancholy note in her voice made him glance up at her, but her faraway expression didn't brook further discussion.

He saw the resemblance between her and the woman in the portrait. Hair the color of midnight. Bright eyes, a heart-shaped face, and elegant, butter-soft skin.

"My family is visiting her in Paris, where she lives among the beau monde," she said, her voice injected with a false, syrupy insouciance. She picked up the photograph as if to hide it from him, examining it with a pinched sort of melancholy. "Veronica is the beauty of the family."

"No," he insisted more harshly than he meant to. "No, she is not."

She peered up at him oddly, her gaze had become wary and full of doubts he dared not define. "Yes, well…the photo doesn't do her justice."

"It doesn't have to. She doesn't hold a candle to you."

CHAPTER 4

$\mathcal{V}$anessa's focus had been arrested. Nay, seized and held captive.

The air thickened between them and the storm seemed closer now. The wild chaos of it slipping into the night. Invading the space between them. Prompting her instincts to prickle and her hair to stand on end.

She was a kitten who'd stumbled into the den of a lion. Nothing more than a light snack. Something he could pick his teeth with.

So why did she have the very feline urge to arch and glide toward and against the lithe strength of his form?

To search for warmth. For protection.

His body, as iridescent as it still was, radiated as much heat as the firelight. His shoulders were wide and his arms long and thick beneath the fitted lines of his crimson jacket.

His features were distinguished, compelling, the product of centuries of such ancestors breeding his sort of perfection. His eyes weren't just blue, they held a startling lapis brilliance, as if backlit by something electric, like lightning. His spun gold hair was caught behind him in a queue. It shone lambent, as did his gauzy specter, barely able to catch the light that pierced through him rather than reflected off him. The square chin above his high, white collar framed a wide, hard mouth that curled in such a way, she might have called it cruel.

His eyes were kind, but that mouth was most certainly anything but.

The word *depraved* came to mind.

A corner of his lip lifted as she stared at it rather rudely. Not quite a smile, but the whisper of one.

The ghost of one.

He cleared a gather from his throat and turned away, dispelling the tension as he drifted over to the camera.

"So, this device is what you use to capture these photographs? This...camera?"

She would never not smile at the way he said that word.

Shaking off whatever had held her mesmerized, she hopped to engage. "Yes. Would you like to see how it works?"

"Very much."

Vanessa had to stop herself short of clapping her hands like a delighted child. Photography was one of her passions, and while many people were curious about it, she'd never had the chance to show it to someone quite so captivated.

Or, rather, captive. But who was she to split hairs?

His feet levitated some six inches off the ground, and his hands locked behind his back in a posture befitting an officer of his class. He looked down at her from over his aristocratic nose and she had the sense he mentally *disassembled* her for examination whilst she *assembled* her tripod.

"I eavesdropped on you and Bess before," he admitted.

"Oh?" She wasn't quite certain how she felt about that, so she remained silent on the topic.

"I'm given to understand you didn't go to Paris with your family because you'd rather stand on the frigid shores of the deepest lake in the world and try to photograph a creature that only exists in folklore?"

She glanced up from where she screwed on the mounting bracket. "And?"

He gave a rather Gallic shrug. "It can't be astonishing to you that someone might remark upon the decision. It seems…rather out of the ordinary."

Vanessa tried not to let on that his assessment stung, as if she weren't aware that her behavior was remarkable. That she was doing what she could to make the most of her exile without advertising it. She didn't allow herself to look up at him as she pulled the accordion-style lens and box from her case with a huff. "I'm a woman who is only interested in extraordinary."

"Evidently."

She cast him a censuring look as she affixed the camera to the tripod. "So says the iridescent apparition levitating above me."

"Touché." He twisted his mouth into an appreciative sort of smile as he studied her. "So, you believe in ghosts and lake monsters. What else? Fairies? Vampires? Shapeshifters? Dragons?"

"And why not?" She crossed her arms, wishing he didn't make her feel itchy and defensive. "Did you know a woman, Mary Anning, found dinosaur bones the size and shape of the long-necked mythos of the Loch Ness Monster only decades ago? Which means creatures like Nessie *have* existed, and perhaps still do."

She held her hand up against his reply. "And if you go to church, they'll tell you about angels and demons. Saints and spirits. Like you, for example. I've done extensive readings on the supernatural, and the stories are eerily similar across all sorts of nations and civilizations. If the native peoples of Australia and also the Scandinavians have similar myths of flying serpents and dragons, doesn't it seem like their existence might be possible? Probable, even?"

His mouth pulled into a tight, grim hyphen, even as his eyes twinkled at her. "Historically, I'd have said no, but at the moment it does seem ridiculous to argue the point."

"'There are more things in heaven and Earth, Horatio, Than are dreamt of in your philosophy,'" she quoted, wagging a finger in the air like some mad scientist as she bustled around her camera, checking bits and bobs. "Truer words were never written."

When she looked back up at him, he'd drifted close. Too close. Close enough that the fine hairs on her body were tuned to him, to the inevitability of his touch.

A touch that never came.

"People still quote Shakespeare?" he murmured.

She swayed forward, and had he been real—or rather, alive—she'd have bumped into him. Instead, her shoulder sort of just...passed through his and she was fascinated with that same odd sort of sensation she'd had in the bath.

Not contact but—but what? An impression?

She swallowed around a dry tongue. "Always. People will *always* quote Shakespeare."

Ye gods, it had been a long time since she'd been alone with a handsome, virile man. One who looked at her like that. Who crowded her and invaded her space in a way she didn't find the least bit irritating.

Overwhelming, yes. But in the best of terms.

She'd forgotten the heady experience of it. The places in her body that would come alive, and demand attention.

Once again, he retreated, floating backward to give

her space to work. "What do you call yourself? A mystic investigator of some sort? You travel the world looking to make these realistic portraits, these…photographs of the unexplainable?"

"Not exactly. I travel the world searching for adventure. I just like to capture these adventures in effigy. Because it's sort of like capturing a memory, isn't it? Sometimes that means a Grecian ruin or a Galapagos tortoise, and sometimes…" She snatched the dark cover she had to put over her head in order to see through the lens. "It means a ghost or a relic of something supposedly extinct."

He made a deep, appreciative sound in his throat. It plucked a chord inside of her that vibrated deep. Deeper than church bells or bagpipes or the crescendo of the most tragic opera. Deeper into the recesses of her body and soul than she dared contemplate just now.

She retreated beneath the dark cloth, looking through the lens of the camera, turning the dial to focus it.

When she spied him, she let out a little sound of triumph. "Put your hand to your lapel," she directed. "And levitate perhaps…three more inches toward the ground."

He leveled an abashed look somewhere above the lens, then tried to peek around it as if looking for her. "You're not—trying to photograph *me*, are you?" He seemed as if the idea had curdled his cream.

"I've heard any number of mediums have photographed ghosts. They say you can capture ectoplasm in photographs, and that's supposed to be a gelatinous sort of goo left by spirits and ghosts. You're ever so much more than goo."

"Do try to contain your effusive admiration." His voice could have dried the Amazon into the Sahara.

"I'm endlessly flattered to be placed above ectoplasmic *goo* in your estimation."

She giggled, a mischievous part of her wanting to trap the pinched and offended look on his savage features for posterity. "Come now, don't be missish. You look so smart in your uniform. Handsome, I'd dare say."

He straightened a bit, blinking this way and that as if looking for somewhere to place her compliment for safekeeping. "You think so?"

She looked him over, from his chagrined expression to his shiny boots. He was so tall and broad, almost offensively so. No one would call him elegant; he was too ferocious for that. But no one could call him wild; he was too regal for that.

So, what was he? *Who* was he?

So many questions almost choked her mute until one was allowed to spill out.

"How did you die?"

He stalled.

She poked her head up from beneath the camera. "Oh, lands. I'm sorry. I didn't mean to be uncouth. I just... Well you don't look at all injured. I'd have assumed your coat would be riddled with bullets, or you'd have some ghostly axe sticking out of your head. I suppose I read too many penny dreadfuls."

He didn't move, except to tug at his collar before he returned his hand to rest on the lapel of his jacket. "It was a bayonet to the neck," he informed her with almost no inflection at all.

"Oh..." Vanessa was sorry she asked. But his neck didn't at all look—bayonetted. So that was lucky for them both, she supposed. He would have made for ghastly company. "Don't move," she directed before pointing the flash at him and shooting.

He flinched.

"I thought I said not to move," she admonished him.

"You didn't bloody warn me it would be as loud as a musket blast," he muttered. "Can I move now?"

"You might as well," she sighed.

She was going to have to get used to the silent way he sort of—floated around her. It just wasn't seemly for a man of his stature.

"When do I get to see the photograph?" he asked, a boyish sort of anticipation making him appear years younger as he peeked over her shoulder.

A frown tugged at her lips as a heavy stone of sadness landed in her belly. "Well, you won't. After a few minutes, a negative impression will appear on a pane of glass, and I can get that developed into a photograph when I go back to the city. But—you'll only see shadows and light on the glass. I'll bring the photo back here, though, if it actually captured you."

"Perhaps it did," he said blithely with a smile that didn't at all reach his bleak, sapphire eyes. "For I am just like your negative...shadows and light."

A knock at the door saved her from bursting into tears. Vanessa shooed at him as she hurried to unlock it and opened to an anxious Bess.

"I heard the blast!" she fretted. "I came to make sure the ghost hadna gotten to ye."

"The ghost and I are getting along just famously," Vanessa said with what she hoped was an encouraging smile. "I was merely testing the camera to make sure the storm hadn't damaged it."

"Aye, well." Bess itched at her cap. "Would ye like to come through to the common room for stew, so Balthazar and Dougal can haul your bathwater away?"

"Of course, thank you." She turned to the ghost. The Earl...

John.

"I'll be right back," she promised him.

Bess leaned into her room and eyed the device warily. "Ye're really attached to that contraption, aren't ye? Talking to it and the like."

"Oh, no, I was talking to—" Vanessa looked over to see that he'd disappeared. "Well, actually, yes. It's my most prized treasure."

Bess regarded her askance, but ultimately shrugged. "I talk to me oven sometimes," she admitted. "It's a mite smarter and more useful than me husband and less temperamental, too."

Vanessa laughed merrily as she followed the woman through the adjacent storeroom and toward the front. "You called your husband Balthazar, but I heard you refer to him as Rory not too long ago."

"Aye well, the keepers of this inn have had Balthazar in the name since back when this part of the world was Caledonia. Since it is the name of the place, they all seem to take it on."

"I see," she murmured, not seeing at all.

Because the Douglasses were getting even more drunk and sloppy by the fire, Vanessa eschewed the mostly empty tables for the bar, at the end of which the two gentlemen in fine suits were nursing drinks and playing cards.

Bess placed a steaming bowl of stew in front of her and hovered as Vanessa tucked into it immediately.

"How do ye like it?" the proprietress asked, pretending to shine a glass.

"Oh, this is..." *Delicious* wasn't the word. She luckily had some incredibly fibrous and gamey meat to chew as a stall tactic. "It's really filling and—erm—flavorful."

"Aye, it'll put some meat on yer bones." Bess winked. "I gave that driver of yers something extra in his stew. He'll be up all night heaving into a chamber pot for leaving ye in the storm like a blighter."

Vanessa suppressed both a giggle and a spurt of

sympathy for the man while she reminded herself never to get on Bess's bad side.

Even after only a moment away, Vanessa was antsy to get back to her room.

To Johnathan. However, she thought this an excellent time to do a little sleuthing for his sake. "So, Bess, you were saying, about the inn. It was here during the Jacobite rebellion? And the battle of Culloden?"

"Och, aye!" Bess said, obviously delighted to have someone to tell, as she was a natural raconteur. "Like many crofts and castles around here, it was a safe haven for the Jacobites, to be sure."

"But, not the English?"

Bess's features wobbled as she narrowed only one eye at her. "Well, no offense to yer countrymen, but after the battle at Culloden, the English were everywhere were they not? They stayed at the inn, to be sure, as it was sedition to deny them entry. But, they never found our secret spots, did they?" She tapped her head as if she'd thought of those secrets herself.

Vanessa perked up. "Secret spots?"

"Just so. Like Carrie Pitagowan's Chamber of Sorrows."

"Chamber of Sorrows?" Vanessa echoed. "Now that sounds deliciously ominous."

Bess leaned closer, her chins wobbling in agreement. "Aye, Carrie worked beneath these old rafters during the days of Culloden. A saucy minx she was. Curious, like you. Always looking for something more."

Vanessa winced. Was she that obvious?

Bess seemed not to notice, continuing with her story. "Carrie would go to Jacobite battlefields and strip the English soldiers of their treasure. It was about this time of year back then, another blizzard, another *Na Fir Chlis* when 'twas said she cursed that room. Warned all who would listen that a lion lived there and would devour any who stayed."

Chills spilled over every part of Vanessa, and she took another bite just to distract herself from them.

Oblivious to her discomfiture, Bess continued, "Of course each new generation doesna believe in Carrie's lion, but every time we try to let that room, the occupants are haunted right back out of it again."

At this, Vanessa frowned. "Why let it to me, then?"

Bess cast her eyes down as she drew her fingernail through the pit in the wood of the bar. "I doona ken, lass, if ye want the honest truth. I couldna leave you out in the storm and…something told me the Chamber of Sorrows would welcome ye, and the lion with it."

Vanessa swallowed the dry meat in a lump that made its uncomfortable way down her esophagus, and drank a long swallow of dark ale to force it down.

She could see Johnathan de Lohr as a lion. Fierce and golden haired. Not only a conqueror but commander, ruler of all he surveyed.

And well he knew it.

"Ye've known a bit of the longing that lives in that room, I wager." Bess lowered her voice to the decibel of confidants. "And yer fair share of sorrow, too. Else why would ye be here alone what with Christmas bearing down on ye? If ye doona mind me asking, why's yer family in Paris without ye?"

Her pitying look speared Vanessa through the ribs as she cast about for an answer. "Well I—"

"Tell me the young, cheap whisky isn't making me see things, Priestly," a nasally, masculine, *British* voice slurred with a bit of a lisp. "Tell me this isn't little Vanessa Latimer, wot?"

Vanessa turned to see that the men who had been playing cards at the edge of the bar now crowded close around her, effectively trapping her onto the tall stool upon which she perched. They each had an empty glass in their hands, and the one who'd addressed her swayed, dangerously.

"By Jove." His dark-haired friend—Priestly, she presumed—might have been passably handsome but for sporting a pathetic, thin mustache. He leered down at her from marble-dark eyes held way too close together. "I thought she looked familiar when she blew in, but she was in such a state of disarray I didn't care to look at her. She cleans up rather well, though. I could almost believe she was respectable."

"Yes," the first one intoned, combing his hands through fair hair made greasy with too much pomade. The scent of it was nearly overpowering. "Quite respectable. But we know better, don't we?"

The food turned to ashes in her mouth. Vanessa locked everything down just as she'd taught herself to when preparing for just one such encounter.

"Gentlemen," she greeted soberly. "I don't believe we've been introduced and, therefore, it is not polite to approach me thusly."

Priestly's eyebrows shot up. "My, aren't we all grown up and putting on airs? What do you say to that, Gordie?"

Gordie's watch chain gleamed as he leaned in obscenely close, his breath reeking of scotch. "We've heard tell you spend your time galivanting to exotic places. Learning, no doubt, *exotic* skills."

Priestly all but tossed his glass to Bess. "I'd take a whisky, but not the kind that tastes like we've licked a peat bog. The good stuff you're no doubt hiding back there. And I'll make a bloody ruckus if you water it down."

Vanessa let out an outraged breath, ashamed of her countrymen. "That's beneath you, gentleman, talking to a proprietress like that."

Gordie leaned even closer, forcing her to bend over backward to escape him, which caused her to bump into Priestly. "I'd rather *you* were beneath me."

"I beg your pardon!" she huffed. She'd been heckled before, but not so publicly. Nor so rudely.

"Really, Gordie, don't be vulgar; we're sharing a room in this shithole, there's not privacy at all."

Gordie's suggestive expression caused the gorge in Vanessa's stomach to rise into her throat. "We can share other things. We've done it before." He raked her with a glare miraculously overflowing with both disdain and desire. "Woman like her will let you put it anywhere you like."

Before he even finished his last word, her entire bowl of stew lurched from the table and was heaved into his face, the scalding gravy latching onto his skin.

A shrill scream erupted from him as he clawed at himself, trying to wipe it off.

Vanessa's hands were still clenched at her sides. She'd never even reached for the bowl.

She looked across the bar at Bess in time to see that the whisky bottle she'd retrieved was snatched from Bess's hands and smashed over Priestly's head. The jagged neck hung in the air as if brandished by an invisible hand, ready to plunge into the man's throat.

"Sweet Christ in heaven." Bess crossed herself and made a few other signs against evil as well.

It was her ghost. Even though she couldn't see him, there was no denying it.

"John," Vanessa gasped into the empty air next to the floating bottle. "Johnathan, don't."

The bottle dropped.

Priestly turned on her. "You putrid slag! You're worth no more than a—"

His entire body flew back as if it had crumpled. He landed on the table by the fireplace, splintering it and scattering half a dozen drunk and slightly dozing Douglasses.

The highlanders launched into action, leading with their fists, assuming, no doubt, they'd nearly missed a tavern brawl.

Gordie managed to wipe mutton out of his eyes in time to catch a fist to the jaw, dropping him to the floor immediately.

Vanessa whirled to Bess, who wiped her hands on her apron and reached beneath the bar. "Go back to yer room, dearie. I'll restore order here." When she extracted a plank the size of an oar, Vanessa quickly retreated. She passed Balthazar on her way, grinning and rolling up his sleeves as if eager to join the fray.

Picking up her skirts, she ran to her room, dove inside, then shut and locked the door behind her.

Her skin burning with humiliation, she went to the window and threw it open, letting the cold air steal her breath in a welcome blast.

Johnathan appeared, his color heightened and sharpened as his entire form slammed into the room like a mountain of muscle and wrath. "Those bog-faced sons of a whore! Were I myself, I'd wrench his arm from his socket and beat him to death with it, and then I'd decapitate his friend just so I could piss into the empty cavity where his spine used to be."

"Please, calm down." Vanessa let out a few shaken puffs into the blizzard, pressing her freezing hands to her burning cheeks as the storm pricked her with crystals of ice.

She could stand it no longer than a few seconds, so she wrestled the window closed and latched it.

John paced the length of the bed next to her, his fists white with unspent rage. "Are all gentlemen in this age such smarmy, weak-limbed dandies? Makes one wonder how many cousins had to fornicate to produce such a slithering strop of a rubbish heap and call it a man. I have a few regrets in my life, and my afterlife, but not slicing him open with that bottle is going straight to the top."

Even as she pressed her forehead to the cool windowpane, she fought a sad little smile at his vehemence. "Yes, well, none of that was necessary, but thank you all the same."

"He called you a slag!" John roared.

"It doesn't matter," she whispered, her breath spreading in an opaque circle in front of her.

Even though his motions made no noise, she could sense that he stopped pacing. "Doesn't. Matter?" he said with a great deal of emphasis on all the T's.

She closed her eyes. "I've been called that and worse. I'm used to it."

"How is that bloody possible?" he thundered. "You're...well you're—"

"I'm ruined," she said gently, finally gathering the strength to turn around.

She had expected to see him be incredulous, but not his head cocked to the side in doglike befuddlement. "What? Ruined?"

She breathed in a deep breath through her nose, preparing to lose his respect and regard. Mourning it already. "This is why I am not with my family at Christmas. Or any holiday, really. I'm *persona non grata* in the eyes of society. My reputation couldn't be lower if I actually sold myself on Whitechapel High Street."

At that, he became impossibly still.

"It happened long ago," she explained, already exhausted. "I fell in love with William Mosby, Viscount Woodhaven. He gave me a ring with the largest diamond I'd ever seen. We made love beneath the Paris sky..."

"And then?" he growled.

"And then he married Honoria Goode, the daughter of my father's shipping rival, for her dowry was ten thousand pounds more obscene than mine."

"He broke his word to you." The statement was murmured softly, almost without inflection. "Did he break your heart?"

Vanessa couldn't bring herself to look at him.

"Well…not irreparably at first. Not until he—until he published a pamphlet scoring the lovers he'd had. Prostitutes, mostly. But I was on the list, and my score wasn't very favorable. *Pathetically eager, but impossible to please*, he said. He called my… my um…" She looked down, wondering why it was so difficult to say. Why she'd stopped feeling ashamed so long ago, but was suddenly afraid of the opinion of a dead man. "Well he said I am broken."

The rickety chair at the bedside shattered against the far wall.

"Have you no brothers?" John thundered. "Your father didn't kill him in a duel?"

She stared at him in open-mouthed astonishment for a moment. He was magnificently angry. His muscles seemed to build upon themselves as he heaved in breaths to a chest she could still mostly see through to the fire on the other side.

The effect was rather apropos, as the flames licked at his chest, seeming to ignite the scarlet coat with the same inferno that blazed in his eyes.

"Well," she answered somewhat demurely. "Duels have been illegal for some time now."

He gaped at her. "You're joking."

"I'm afraid not."

"You mean to tell me, there is no recourse to besmirched honor?" He gestured broadly as if he couldn't comprehend the idiocy. "Any blighter can walk around and say whatever they might to defame an innocent, and others do what... *believe* them?"

It did sound rather ridiculous the way he said it. "If they're a man of influence, they are believed," she answered. "That seems to be the way of it. I mean, there are libel laws, but...that recourse is rarely taken."

He made a disgusted face and threw a gesture at the door toward the chaos on the other side of it. "This age isn't enlightened, it's barbaric."

"I don't know about that. Fewer people die in duels, so...I suppose you might call that progress."

"Not in my opinion. Not this bloody—" He whirled on her. "What was his name again?"

"William Mosby."

"William... I'd cheerfully murder the ponce myself. I'd strike his entire legacy from the annals of time until—"

"No need." Vanessa held her hand up against him. "Truly. He's...well, he's met his fate. What's done cannot be undone."

Suddenly. Miraculously. His features softened as he looked down at her, his arms dropping to his sides as he lingered close. Closer. His hand reached out as if to lift her chin, but he never quite managed. "I am sorry that you suffered."

She summoned that false-bright smile for him. The one she'd learned so well. "I am lucky, in many respects. I still have a generous stipend from my father, to assuage his guilt, I imagine, for keeping me away from them socially. And with it I plan to see the world. I go on adventures like this one. And, reputation-wise, I've nothing to lose, so I may do what I please."

His brow furrowed in consternation. "But you're alone. Why not have a companion to take on such adventures with you?"

She let out a very unladylike snort. "The idea of compelling someone to keep me company with coin never appealed to me. Besides, then I'd be responsible for them, wouldn't I? And, if I'm honest, very few would consider an association with one as besmirched as I a very desirable position. No one would consider my references a boon."

The look on his face caused her own to fall. She couldn't bear the tenderness. Or the pity.

"It is not so much suffering," she all but whispered. "When there are so many in the world who know such pain, my bit of shame and isolation seems rather small in comparison."

He dipped his head, his lips hovering above her forehead. "Suffering can be profound or prosaic, but it is suffering all the same. Yours is not inconsequential."

His words melted her like honey decrystalizing in the summer heat. His presence washed over her like silk flowing in a breeze. Insubstantial, sensual, and yet compelling.

"You're not broken," he said. "You're not ruined. Not to me."

"You're being kind," she choked out over a lump of emotion lodged in her throat.

"I mean it," he said fiercely.

She ducked away from him, turning to hide the burn of tears, pinching the bridge of her nose against their ache. She was too proud for this. She could not come apart in front of a veritable stranger.

"What?" he asked. "What's wrong?"

"You—have a ruthless side," she admitted breathlessly. "It—um—it makes my blood rush around a bit."

He was close again. Right behind her. His presence a relentless affectation. "I frightened you?"

"No! I mean. Not entirely. You're the only person who has ever stood up for me before," she admitted, moving toward the fire and smoothing her dress down her thighs in a nervous gesture.

"Then why retreat from me?" he persisted.

She could tell the flames nothing but the truth. "When you touch me I…Well, actually, you don't *touch* me. But you were able to hold on to inanimate objects. To do a man violence."

He let out a long breath. "I'm little better than an awareness most of the time. Something I could slip in and out of at will at first, but the longer I tarry, the more I spend in the void. But there are holy days—solstices and equinoxes where, if I concentrate very hard, I can become something like corporeal. At least, for a moment. I can will things to move, but it depletes me. On nights like *Na Fir Chlis* I am the most visible, but I cannot sustain contact for long."

"I see," she whispered.

His voice ventured closer, until she could almost feel his warm breath against her ear. "When I reached for you in the bath, my hand went through you… You felt that?"

"I feel—something. Not your skin, per se. Something else. It's like…" She cast about for the word. "A tingling. No, stronger than that. A vibration, perhaps."

He made an amused noise deep in his chest. "Really?"

"It's disquieting."

"Does it cause you pain?"

"No. No, quite the opposite."

"The opposite?" He drifted around her, standing so close to the flames a normal man would have caught. "The opposite of pain is pleasure."

She retreated a step. "So it is."

He advanced, his eyes liquid pools of carnal promise. "Does my touch pleasure you, Vanessa?"

"I don't—I don't know how to answer that."

"Why?" he pressed. "Why after being so fearless, is it pleasure that scares you? Do you fear your desire for it?"

She swallowed. "Yes. Maybe. I couldn't say." She feared the ruin it had already brought her. The derision of another lover. Another man she thought she might care for. Who might profess to care for her. She feared the strength of her feelings, her desires, after only knowing this man for the space of an hour.

His hand reached out, a tremor visible in the long, rough fingers. His palm caressed her face, but not in the way she wished it would. It was there, but it wasn't. The warmth of his touch lingered; a callus might have abraded her soft cheek. *There.* Right there. But also, just out of reach.

It was both bliss and torment. The vibrations of his energy, of the very striations etched into the palm of his hand, were tangible. But whatever touched her was not flesh. Not exactly.

It was enough to make her weep, the longing she sensed in the gesture. The cavernous pain she read etched into the grooves branching from his eyes, and in the tension of his skin stretched tight over his raw, beautiful bones. "I haven't touched a woman in a lifetime. In a handful of lifetimes."

"Do you want to?"

"Is that an invitation, Vanessa?" His voice was like liquid velvet, his eyes twin azure flames. "If I could, would you let me?"

"I—Um..." She was a quivering, boneless puddle of sensation. Of desire. Her loins ached, moistened, bloomed for him. Her lips plumped and her skin burned to be touched.

Her entire body was one thrumming chord of need.

Was she the only one undergoing this torture? "John?" she whispered, turning her head out of his palm, if only to spare them each more impotent long-ing. "Can you *feel* desire as you are?" she queried. "Can you—erm—manifest it? Physically?"

His lips actually stirred her hair as he growled against her ear. "I've been hard as a diamond since the moment I watched you undo your buttons."

CHAPTER 5

*J*ohn leaned back and let his admission crash into the space between them, overflowing it with heady, carnal, unspoken reveries. His. Hers. All amalgamating into one frustrated frequency of need.

All the chaos of the common room had gone quiet, no doubt Bess had kicked everyone to their beds. In this abandoned corner of the structure, he and the comely Miss Latimer might have believed they were the only two people in the whole of the Highlands.

John watched her intently as she stared—or rather —glared at him. Unblinking. Her chest rose and fell beneath the high-necked blouse as she very distinctly did not allow herself to look down.

She'd have found the answer to her question if she had, straining against the placket of his trousers.

However, after what he'd just discovered about her, he realized he might have been too forward. Might have overwhelmed a woman who'd only just been harangued by undesirables.

He closed his eyes and stepped back, allowing her space. "I shouldn't have said that."

Squirming with shame and regret, she instantly

buried her face in her hands. "No. That is—the fault is mine. I asked you the vulgar question. I don't know what's gotten into me."

"I order you to stop feeling shame," he said with a stern frown.

She looked up at him askance. "You can't command emotions, that's not how they work."

"I can and I will," he shot back, looking to goad her past her mortification. "I insist the blame for our—indelicate interaction be placed on my shoulders. I've forever been a man too plain of speech. Too blunt and coarse and forbidding. It made for a successful Lieutenant Colonel, a mediocre nobleman, and well... ripe shit at relationships."

The tremulous tilt at the corner of her mouth told him his candor was working. "Which relationships?" she queried, her relentless curiosity returning. "With women, you mean?"

"'Twas doubtless why I remained a bachelor at five and thirty. I assumed one took a wife like one took a hill in combat. It was all strategy and espionage, if not an all-out battle. I was built to win, not woo, and I frightened many a maidenly noble lady into the arms of some gentler, more civilized man."

She wrinkled her nose at that rather adorably. He wasn't certain how to interpret the expression, but that didn't stop him from continuing, if only to put conversational space between their previous fraught interaction.

He marched around her, exploring the space of his chamber with his hands clasped behind him. He did his best not to prowl like the predator he was. To draw his tense shoulders away from his ears. "My social ineptitude reached past the fairer sex to anyone, really. My parents. My brother, James. Even after everything, he came to claim my remains all those years ago. Or perhaps he only returned for the ring, and taking my benighted bones back to the de Lohr crypts was an afterthought, though I couldn't say I'd blame him."

"The ring?" She grasped onto the one subject he'd only mentioned as an afterthought.

"A de Lohr signet. Given to my templar ancestor—the Lion Claw, they'd called him—by his ladylove so many generations ago." A Scotswoman, if he remembered correctly.

John summoned a picture of the piece into his mind. The head of a lion had been etched into the precisely crafted purest gold; rubies set into the ocular cavities as if the blood spilled by the apex predator reflected in his eyes.

"Surely your brother came to collect *you*, and the ring was the afterthought."

"You underestimate the significance my family put on that ring," he said gruffly. "And you didn't know my brother. We did not part on the best of terms. I regretted that. I was a hard man to know, and I did not understand his impulsive passions. His depth of emotion. And, if I'm honest, I envied him his freedom as the second son, his shoulders unencumbered by the weight of the de Lohr name." Unbidden, John looked into the past, seeing the familiar face of his brother, the disappointment in his eyes the last time they spoke. "I am confident James made a better Earl than I might have. At least, I hope he did."

"The Earldom of Worchester is still one of the most wealthy and respected titles in the Empire," she explained gently. "If that is any condolence to you."

It was, actually. "You're kind to say so. I don't get word of such things up here. It's mostly clan gossip and peasant revelry."

Something about that elicited a giggle from her, and when he looked, her silver eyes were twinkling like the little diamond bobs in her ears. "We don't call them peasants anymore. Not that it should matter to you much, I suppose."

He chuffed out his own sound of mirth. "Yes. A more enlightened age, you've mentioned." He was about to ask her to tell him about it when she began to pace as if puzzling something out.

"So not even your remains are here in Scotland. I still find it extraordinarily peculiar that your bones should rest in the de Lohr crypts but your spirit should be *restless* here of all places. Did you visit this inn before you died?"

"Never."

"Perhaps you killed the previous proprietor in the war?"

"No, I'm certain it has something to do with Carrie Pitagowan and her blasted curse." He'd been over and over it in his mind, and he wasn't exactly excited to re-work it with her. "Do you happen to know any witches who might be able to break it?"

She ignored his dry sarcasm. "What about her Chamber of Sorrows?"

At the mention of the room, he went still.

She continued, pacing the length of the bed. "I asked Bess, and she told me that Carrie went to Jaco-bite battlefields and took things, especially from Eng-lish officers. I've noticed you have no saber nor hat nor medals upon your jacket." She whirled on him, ceasing her pacing as she held her hands up in a mo-tion that might stop the entire world so it might listen to her next sentence. "John! What if she took your ring?"

Christ but she impressed him. She'd been here all of five minutes and she'd discovered what it'd taken him decades of eavesdropping to find out.

"I have no doubt my body was looted after the battle, by starving, angry highlanders. But I've searched the Chamber of Sorrows. Nothing in it belongs to me."

John had done many distasteful things in his life as a soldier, and also in his short tenure as the heir to an Earldom, but smothering the enthusiastic light shining from Vanessa Latimer's open, upturned face had to be the worst.

Still, he could tell he'd not defeated her as the wheels and cogs of what he was coming to understand was a sharp and restless brain didn't cease their machinations. "Can you take me to this Chamber of Sorrows?"

"Certainly, though it's not far." He motioned to the wardrobe, a piece of furniture almost as tall as he was. "The Pitagowans have merely covered the door with this."

She circled the thing, tapping on her chin as she was wont to do. Testing its heft with a little push. "I don't know if I can move it."

John didn't know if she could either, which meant he'd have to. "I'll do what I can to help you."

Clearly heartened, she gifted him with a brilliant smile that sparked a little flicker of joy in his guts before she flattened her back against one side, bracing her feet on the ground to pit her entire weight against the thing. It scraped and budged, but only an inch or so.

John joined her, levering over her and bracketing her head with his arms. If someone walked in at this moment, that person would do well to assume they were about to kiss.

Or had just finished doing so.

As if she'd read his thoughts, her eyes dropped to his mouth. Her tongue snaking out to moisten her own lips.

John's lids slammed closed as lust roared through him. "Goddammit, Vanessa. *Push.*"

The wardrobe gave way beneath their combined efforts, and he all but leapt away from her and retreated to the opposite end of the room.

It'd been a long time since he'd asserted himself onto the world of the living so often in one night. It tired him. Weakened him in so many ways.

The chief among them his self-control. In one respect a heavenly thing, and in others, pure hell.

He willed his inflamed libido to cool and ordered the heart that'd begun beating again to stop. He commanded his soul to stop yearning. To cease aching for what should not—what could *never*—be.

"That took a lot from you, didn't it?" she observed.

He looked down at his own outline and noted it was thinner, more translucent, the features blurred.

"I'll be fine," he sighed. "Though I'll hope you forgive me for not opening the door."

Vanessa took one of the oil lamps from the sideboard and pushed open the doorway that was really no bigger than a cupboard. Even someone as petite as she had to duck to get inside.

John merely went through the wall.

He found himself watching her more than noting any of the treasures in the dusty old place. Pure, unadulterated awe slackened her jaw, parting her lips as she twirled in the center of the tiny antechamber as if trying to take in the entire glory of the Sistine Chapel.

She all but floated to the haphazard shelves and rickety cases lining the long chamber.

As one could never do in a museum, she reached out trembling, elegant fingers and tested the sharpness of a saber mounted on the wall or threaded them through the plume on a hat. It was as if she could see with her eyes, but never truly had a vision of anything until she'd experienced it through touch.

John found himself wanting to trade places with inanimate objects as she caressed them with the reverence of a lover. Buckles. Buttons. A rifle, a medal of valor, irons for captives, chains and whips and other implements of violence and war.

She didn't belong in this place, this so-called Chamber of Sorrows. She was a creature of light and joy. One to whom melancholy and sorrow did not attach itself for long.

What must it be like to move in the world in such a way?

Vanessa Latimer had transfixed him like nothing or no one had done before.

Everything she did, every gesture she made was attractive to him. From the way she blinked the fans of her eyelashes, to the swift, almost sparrow-like movements of her graceful neck as she tried to look at everything all at once. The sway of her skirts soothed him, drew him toward her as she ventured deeper into the long chamber, which was actually more a corridor that ran the length of the inn.

She paused at a small table upon which letters and miniature portraits of women or children were stacked neatly. As if understanding they might disintegrate if she touched them, her hands hovered like butterfly wings above the loops of writing often stained with blood.

He'd known her for such a short time, and yet he understood that she burned to stop and read every word, absorbing it into her memory.

Eventually, she glanced back at him, her gaze brimming with so many things. "Have you read these?" she asked hopefully.

Once again, he hated to disappoint her. "This is maybe the third time anyone has ever brought a light in here when I was awake. I've rarely been able to truly examine these things, and when I could I was searching for something that might belong to me."

"You need light to see?" The very idea seemed to surprise her.

He felt his features melt, quirking into an endlessly amused half-smile. "I'm a ghost, not a vampire."

She rolled her eyes at his teasing, swatting at him with no real heat. "How should I know the rules? I mean, you float above the floor and you can walk through walls."

"Sadly, I cannot see in the dark." Or through things. Like her clothing.

She made a noncommittal noise as she moved further along the chamber. Her ankle rolled beneath her skirts and she nearly lost her footing.

Reflexively, he reached for her, but she righted herself before he could do anything.

Clearing her embarrassment from her throat, she pointed beneath her and offered an abashed explanation. "The floor is uneven."

He nodded his head, his heart too much in his throat to reply.

She returned to examining every single treasure. "Are you *sure* none of this is familiar? These sabers, a hat, perhaps? Even a button?" She sounded almost desperate now.

He shook his head. "No, none of these are mine. Though I recognize a few of them as belonging to compatriots."

Ones he mourned for many years.

She ran her hands across a bayonet, testing its edge. "You said you sleep a great deal. Is that truly what it's like to be..." She made an uncomfortable gesture at his general personage.

"Dead?" he clipped.

"Well I didn't want to seem indelicate."

She was so delicate, she'd never seem anything but.

"It's just I have so many questions. And I am afraid to ask them, but when else will I get the chance? Is there a light anywhere like people have claimed, at the end of a tunnel perhaps? Have you met others like yourself? Or angels? Or—or anyone else out of the ordinary? Out of our limited mortal understanding, I mean."

He wished he could spin her a hypnotic yarn that would make death seem less depressing, but he was an honest ghost, and a boring one, evidently.

"I've met no other apparitions and my torpor, it's—not even like sleep, exactly. It's nothingness." He almost hated to admit it, because sometimes the void terrified him. "I want to say darkness, but it's not even that tangible. I am gone, and then I surface. I am here, but I have no part of myself. I have nothing but a vague sense of who I am. And each time I go under...I stay for longer. There are days I fear I'll become one with nothing, and every part of who I was will be lost."

What he didn't say was that each time he went under, he was always disappointed to be brought back. He would rail and stomp and use what little power he had to throw things. To rattle the bedposts and windows and make the stones of his cage tremble. He'd frighten people just to do it. Because now that he'd found himself again, he'd have to dread the next time he was lost.

She blinked watery eyes up at him, her sharp chin pitting and quivering with emotion. "How do you endure it?"

"How can I do anything but?" he replied, his finger aching to smooth an unruly tendril of hair away from her furrowed brow.

Her throat worked over a difficult swallow. "I wish I could save you, somehow."

A tenderness welled in him in that moment and

threatened to spill over into emotion he had no idea what to do with. What a Countess she'd have made. So small and yet regal. So soft-spoken and yet brave. Independent. Unbiased. Kind. Honest.

God. He'd have offered for her hand after one chaperoned meeting. He'd have claimed her and planted children inside of her, creating an undeniable legacy of which any man would be proud.

It was almost worth one hundred and fifty years of loneliness to have met her.

She'd brought him back to himself, somehow.

Whatever she saw in his eyes caused her to step in toward him. And, once again, she stumbled.

Catching herself this time, she lifted her skirt to examine the packed earth beneath her.

Whatever she found caused her to gasp.

"Hold on." Rushing past him—nearly rushing through him had he not moved out of the way in time —she retrieved the lantern from the entry and plucked a bayonet from the wall.

Returning, she shocked him by placing the lantern on the ground, kneeling down in a pool of her skirts, and using the bayonet to scratch and dig into the dirt.

"What the devil are you about?" He hovered over her, worried that she'd finally reached the edge of her sanity.

"This floor has a dip right here about the size of my shoe," she said around the labor of her digging. "After I tripped this last time, I thought, if Carrie was a clever girl, she might *bury* her most prized possessions to make certain they weren't discovered. Even if the Chamber of Sorrows was."

Something within him ignited. He wished he could grab something and rake at the earth next to her. That he could reach into it and pull whatever might be down there above ground. But the bland weight of weakness still tugged his limbs until they were heavy, and he began to admit to himself that the torpor was calling to him.

Every moment he spent with her cost him, dearly.

But the darkness would have to drag him away. He'd not go willingly. Not while he could bask in her presence for one more moment.

She worked until she was winded, and the helplessness he felt made him want to throw things. To shake his fist at whichever angry god cursed him to such an existence.

Until a hollow sound announced the bayonet had struck something.

Their eyes met for a breathless moment.

Then, she attacked the ground around it with renewed vigor, scraping out a small, square wooden box. She stood, and John could hear Vanessa's heart beating hard enough for the both of them as she opened the simple container.

Every jewel inside the box glittered gem-bright in the golden glow of the lantern.

But it was the twin rubies he found that suffused him with a lightning bolt of sensation.

"Vanessa. The ring."

With trembling fingers, she plucked it out and held it up so they could both gawk at its magnificence.

He could feel it pulsing with a magnetism no inanimate object should possess. The lion stared at him from hot ruby eyes.

Claiming him. Calling to him.

He thrust his hand between them, splaying his fingers. "Put it on."

Her forehead crimped. "What if it doesn't work?"

"Vanessa."

She nodded, lowering her hand to slide it onto his finger.

His boots hit the earth with a heavy thud. He had weight. He had mass. The air bit at his cheeks and filled his lungs with a cold incredible breath. His heart threw itself against wide ribs and his muscles corded with strength. Veins pulsed with blood.

With need.

His hand gripped hers. Slim, cold fingers trembled against his flesh. His skin.

Her eyes were wide and watery as she stared at him without blinking.

"John?" she whispered.

He was almost sorry.

Almost sorry that a strangled groan was all the warning she had before he crushed her to him and captured her already open mouth.

CHAPTER 6

*H*is kiss was a sweet violence. Both a conquest and a claiming.

Vanessa welcomed the assault on her senses as this *man*, this solid, starving, sexual man clamped her entire body to his and devoured her mouth as if her kiss could restore his very life.

The sensation of his lips—his skin—was more than a tingling suggestion now. He was tactile. Warm. Almost as if fed by lifeblood.

Almost.

She still detected that the feel of his flesh was imperfect. A vibration persisted where the smooth whorls of his fingerprints should be. It was at once more than an ordinary touch, and not enough.

It didn't matter. She'd take whatever she could get.

He had a scent now, cedar and leather and the faintest trace of gunpowder.

It tantalized her endlessly.

Her hands clutched the lapels of his crimson wool coat, reveling in the coarse fibers abrading her fingertips because it meant he was *real*. Tangible. She suddenly wanted to explore everything. Everywhere. Every hot, smooth and strong inch of him.

He kissed like a man denied a hundred and fifty years of pleasure. Of pain. Of desire and release. There was a savage wildness in it, an untamed urgency that sent little thrills of anxiety and anticipation pouring down her spine and spreading into the deep, empty recesses of her womb.

With a strong, hot lick, his tongue parted the seam of her mouth and dipped inside to sample her flavor.

He tasted like a wicked sin. Like every drink too masculine for her to sip and every dessert to decadent to be indulged.

His arms felt like iron shackles around her, and she became his willing prisoner there in the Chamber of Sorrows. Surrendering to the inevitability of what he was about to do to her. Of what demands he would make of her body.

The very thought made her legs puddle beneath her until she feared she couldn't remain standing.

When she went all but limp against him with a sibilant sigh into his mouth, his kiss unexpectedly gentled, his lips sweeping across hers in featherlight drags. The contrast was her undoing as she lifted onto her tiptoes to seek more.

His large, rough hands drew up her arms and shoulders until he bracketed her jaw in his palms and tilted her face up, pulling back to look down at her with agonizing tenderness.

"My God, you are so pure and perfect," he marveled in a harsh, breathless tone.

His words evoked a hot blush that spread up her chest and heated the cheeks he cradled so reverently in his hands.

Vanessa's lashes swept down over eyes pricked with tears, as a familiar shame swamped her, dousing the flames of her ardor a few degrees. "You know I am not so pure. Not in the sense of the word that seems to matter to most people. I'm no virgin. No *ingenue*. But neither am I a whore. Do you understand that?" She worried the knowledge he had made her seem more accessible to him, and another part of her fretted that he would think less of her.

"Woman," he growled, his breath coming in agonized pants, his azure eyes smoldering down at her like the core of a flame burning too hot to be contained. "I'm about to do things to you that would make a virgin faint. I'm going to worship you in ways that would offend a whore. So, I suppose we should both be grateful you are not either of those things."

She gaped up at him, astonished by his wicked candor. "What sort of thing—Oh!"

He snatched her off the ground with unsettling strength and swept her out of the chamber in a few strides. This time, he had to duck to get through the doorway and deposit her on the bed.

Vanessa was glad for the sturdy wood of the frame rather than creaking brass as he ripped his coat from his heavy shoulders and joined her there.

She had a feeling they would have woken the entire inn with what they were about to do.

He prowled up her prone body like a great cat until he settled fully upon her, his weight a delicious press as he took her mouth once again.

Ribbons of desire unspooled within her as she wound her hands around his neck, tugging the leather thong that caught his long hair into a queue. Releasing it, she twined her fingers into the silky mass at his nape, curling them into claws and nipping at his lip.

His lips tore from her with a ragged sound. "Fucking Christ, Vanessa, if you do that, this won't last long."

Vanessa tried to appear contrite, but she very much

doubted she mastered the look if his urgent response was anything to go by.

He broke away from the circle of her arms to unlace his shirt, reach back and pull it over his head and down his arms in one graceful move.

Had she been less mesmerized by the magnificence of his figure, she might have been curious about the odd workings of his historical trappings as he divested himself of them.

But he loomed like Apollo above her, his skin like gold and honey poured over solid sinew and steel. The cords and veins in his arms danced and flexed as he worked his belt and trousers free.

Vanessa's fingers lifted to the buttons at her throat, but he stopped her with a curt order as he bent to kick away his boots.

"The thought of your bare ass beneath that skirt has teased and tantalized me all night," he said in a low rumble. "Now you'll let *me* be the one to decide when to undress you."

Dominance from any man had always caused a tight ball of frigid defiance to form in her chest, immediately freezing any warm feelings she might harbor toward him.

But *his* command released a flood of hot, liquid desire from her loins as she veritably bloomed beneath the intensity of his regard.

Vanessa let her hands fall demurely to her sides as she lay back on the coverlet. It was an excruciating exercise in a discipline she'd never actually possessed.

Her eyes touched him everywhere she could not, drinking in the fantastic breadth of his shoulders and the vast mounds of muscle that comprised his torso. She counted the obdurate ripples of his ribs and the corrugated plane of his abdomen before boldly following the vee of his hips to where his arousal jutted from a corona of dark gold hair.

Vanessa realized belatedly that one measly lover could never have prepared her for a man like Johnathan de Lohr.

She swallowed hard.

He groaned low.

And then his hands were upon her, circling her ankles and prying her legs open so he could fit between them. Rough palms rasped up the smooth swell of her calves, lifting the hem of her skirts, tracing those otherworldly sparkles of sensation in their wake.

He bent to kiss her in strange places she'd never imagined so seductive. The delicate skin on the inside of her knee, for example, as his questing fingers inched up her thigh.

Aroused and overwhelmed, she reached for him, tugging at his shoulders, needing the safety of his weight again. Craving the comfort of his kiss.

He obliged with a silent look of tender understanding, his lips returning to hers, one arm bracing his weight as his other hand resumed its wicked discovery of her.

She clung to him, greedy for more of the sensation sweeping like wildfire from his lips. From his fingertips as they glided over the thin skin of her inner thigh.

How could she have thought she'd known desire before? Never had it been like this with William. He'd been all charm and coaxing, evoking a maidenly curiosity from her born of innocence and not a little insecurity. This encounter was nothing like the weightless little butterflies he'd set free with his artless caresses and quick fumbles in the dark.

This. *This* was a tempest as powerful and encompassing as the one raging outside. Her belly quivered, her limbs trembled, and her breath caught on little gasps of need that he took into his own lungs as if to lock parts of her inside of him.

His kiss was ferocious where his fingers were not. He dominated her mouth once more, his tongue flexing and exploring in decadent strokes reminiscent of the act itself.

Gentle fingers petted through the intimate hair at the apex of her parted thighs, finding abundant moisture there.

They gasped against each other's mouths when he split the silken center of her with one lithe stroke.

Reflexively, her thighs clamped together, imprisoning his hand there.

William had struggled with her pleasure, had become frustrated with how complicated sensation had been to evoke from her body. He'd written about it. Told the world she was impossible to please.

That the fault had been hers.

And she'd believed him.

She understood now it was because she never wanted him like this. She never felt anything close to this unleashed frenzy of mindless, animalian need.

Sparks already threatened to take her over the edge as she realized that whatever miracle of magic and energy that made John corporeal also produced that strange, indescribable vibration wherever his skin connected with hers.

Against the sensitized flesh of her sex, it was an ultimately unparalleled sensation.

His finger slid easily between the slick ruffles, testing the damp folds and swirling her liquid desire around the little bud that throbbed with such fervency it bordered on pain.

"John," she implored against his lips.

"So wet," he groaned, his eyes unfocused as if he didn't mark her plea.

"John, I'm already going to—"

"Yes," he agreed fiercely. "Yes, you are."

With a couple expert flicks of his finger, he blew her entire world apart.

Vanessa felt as if the storm outside now originated from somewhere within her. The climax whipped her this way and then that, pushing and pulling her in powerful gusts of pure extasy.

Hoarse cries were ripped away from her throat as she threw her head back into the mattress, whipping it from side to side as if to escape the overwhelming intensity of the pleasure.

He seemed to instinctively understand when it became too much, and he slowed his lithe ministrations, bringing her back to herself in slow increments.

She lay sprawled out for a moment as his hands remained beneath her skirts, soothing and petting her. Cupping her as he crooned soft encouragements into her ear, nuzzling her neck and exploring it in little nips before soothing them with a glide of his tongue.

Vanessa wasn't certain what she expected from him, then. Perhaps that he would rip her clothing from her, spread her wide and sink inside of her for a few barbaric thrusts. Lord knew he'd earned it.

But no. He reclined away from her, covering her with her skirts.

His eyes glittered with masculine mischief as that cruel mouth spread into a dangerous Cheshire grin.

"What?" she queried with an anxious little gasp.

He gave her one dark command that both startled and stymied her.

"Kneel."

It occurred to her to explain to him that she wasn't one to be ordered about...as she obediently scrambled to her knees.

Yes. Just as soon as they finished, she'd certainly tell him so.

Curious anticipation dispelled whatever languor had stolen into her blood after her initial release, and she found that excitement began to build at this new and unique encounter.

In a moment he was behind her, fiddling with her skirts.

She had the idea that she knew where this was going, and the thought rather disappointed her. Not that she *minded* being taken from behind, especially not by him. She just didn't think that their first time would be in such a position.

"Would you like—that is—should I bend down?" she ventured.

"Stay as you are until I move you."

She did. Kneeling straight like a penitent at prayer as he rustled and disturbed the bed a bit.

And then his hands were on the insides of her thighs, prying her knees wider to make room for...

His shoulders?

Her eyes peeled wide as he maneuvered himself on his back beneath her skirts, his hands splaying her thighs wider, charting her bare backside as his breath grazed the intimate flesh splayed open over his face.

Her knees nearly lost their starch.

Thoroughly scandalized, Vanessa leaned to one side, meaning to wriggle away, when his long, unyielding arms clamped around her thighs.

Oh dear God. She blindly grabbed for anything, her fingers grasping the headboard.

"I—I don't think we—"

"Don't think for once, Vanessa," is what she thought he muttered, though the words were a bit muffled by her skirts.

Clearly, he didn't know her well. Which meant they

should not be doing something so astoundingly intimate and immoral. "I just—"

He stole her words with one wicked kiss. One wicked, carnal, wet, and languorous kiss to lips that had never before known the mouth of a man.

Suddenly the entire world was very far away. Anything and anyone she'd ever known might never have existed. She was not herself. He was not a dead Earl. They were not in Scotland on a snowy winter night trapped by a gale and perhaps by fate.

There was only what *his* mouth did to *her* sex.

First, he supped and sampled in teasing little tucks and twirls, using only his lips, causing her body to respond with little flinching twitches as the pleasure ebbed and flowed beginning at her core and sparkling through her entire body. She'd have not been able to support herself in such a position if it weren't for his arms winched around her thighs, taking the crux of her weight.

His tongue joined the fray before too long, eliciting a sharp gasp of delight from her as her knuckles tightened on the headboard. His mouth was relentlessly skilled as he slipped and slid around and through the petals of her flesh with inquisitive delight.

It was an exquisite torture. An excruciating bliss.

She wondered dimly where the distant, pathetic, demanding little mewls and gasps were coming from. Surely not her. She'd never dream of making such sounds.

Then, *oh then*, merciless monster that he was, he cleaved her with the flat of his tongue. Tasting the entirety of her topography, he laved at the little bud at the aperture of her sex with a relentless pressure that catapulted her into the stars.

Her fingernails scored the wood of the bed frame as he centered all his attentions on her core, his muscles tightening around her thighs as she bucked and writhed, arched and contracted against the onslaught of pulsating pleasure. She rode his magnificent mouth as unadulterated bliss rolled over her like a tide this time, slamming into her with the strength of a rogue wave and drawing her under. Each time she threatened to surface, the wave in the distance was upon her and again she would be dragged beneath it, helpless against the fluid potency.

And yet he was her anchor, his unfailing strength gifting her with the precious knowledge that she would never be lost. Not while he held her.

He unlatched himself from her with a noisy sound before the storm of her climax had truly passed. She made a plaintive sound in her throat as his strong hands held her legs open and he maneuvered himself into a sitting position. Resting his back against the headboard, he split her legs over his lap while she still shuddered and twitched in the aftermath of an orgasm woefully interrupted.

He stared at her for a moment, and Vanessa scrambled to find her wits so she could fathom what she read in his eyes.

But she never had a chance, not when he lowered her to where the hot, blunt head of his cock rested against the flesh still quivering with release.

Before she could beg him to do so, he lowered her onto him, filling her with one long, slow impale.

CHAPTER 7

*I*f John wasn't already dead, joining with this woman would have killed him.

The wet velvet sheath of her was a heaven in its own right as it welcomed his cock, giving way only in incremental inches as her intimate flesh pulsed around him.

He set his jaw against the storm of a release already gathering at the base of his spine.

It was why he'd not undressed her.

Of course, he'd wanted to see her body again. To unwrap her like God's very own Christmas gift. But also, he found her prim, high collar stitched with simple lace unwaveringly erotic when her sex was currently pulling his straining shaft into her body somewhere beneath her skirts.

It would last longer like this. Without the added tantalization of watching her unbound breasts sway in front of his eyes.

It'd been longer than a century since he'd been with a woman, goddammit, and a man could only take so much.

But she took all of him. And she gave as well, holding nothing back as he made his erotic demands

318

of her.

God, she was magnificent. Her lips bee-stung from his punishing kisses and her silver eyes a gunmetal grey, dark and dilated with passion and the aftershocks of a pleasure he was about to resurrect.

There wasn't a man alive who deserved her.

And neither did he.

Lodging himself to the hilt, he held her there for a moment, flexing within her, kneading the soft globes of her ass with restless fingers.

When he could stand it no longer, he arched away, lifting her up to enjoy the soft pull of her channel as it clenched at him.

She was so fucking small. So tight. So perfect. He couldn't use the word enough. Vanessa Latimer was the perfect woman. His perfect match.

He'd only had to die and wait a century and a half to meet her.

It had been worth it.

His every muscle clenched and corded with tension as he released her hips to run his hands down her smooth thighs.

Trembling as they were, she took over, her knees gripping his hips as she lowered her body to meet his relentless upward thrusts.

Of course they found a perfect rhythm immediately. Of course they did. Of course they *would*.

Even as they gathered speed, he reached behind him to unlatch her fingers from the headboard and nudged them to grasp his shoulders.

He wanted to feel the bite of her nails as he made her come one more time.

Licking his thumb, he reached beneath her skirt and found slick places where they joined—his hardness, her softness—and he thrummed the little peak of her pleasure, knowing her climax still lingered there because he'd left it at the ideal crest to make it crash upon her once again.

Her mouth fell upon his, open and gasping. And the moment he felt her silken sheath clench around him, drenching his cock with yet another release, he threw open the gates and allowed the storm of his own pleasure to devour him.

It took him with more force than even he expected, locking every muscle into a paroxysm of bliss. His skin caught fire, his veins constricted then released, filling his blood with an inferno of pure, carnal power.

One word swept through him as he released an agonized groan into her mouth, clenching her to his arching, straining body.

Mine, he thought, a wave of melancholy following on the wings of the most powerful pleasure he'd ever taken with a woman.

His woman.

Mine.

It was a fact. She was his. He'd claimed her just now.

And it was also a lie, because they could never be.

They stayed locked like that for an eternity, or perhaps only a few moments, it was impossible to tell in the dark.

She collapsed against him, her ear to his chest. John took entirely too much delight in wrapping one of her ringlets around his finger, uncurling it, and starting again.

Finally, after the silence had stretched between them for too long, she said, "I can feel your heart beating."

"Really?" he murmured. Because he could only feel it breaking.

She sat up, miraculously still joined with him as she blinked languidly with her doe-bright eyes. "But you're not—returned. I can feel you fading. I can see that you're diminished."

She swallowed what he knew was a lump of tears and summoned a brave smile for him, even though anguish shined in her eyes.

"I know." He lifted his knuckles to run them against her downy cheek, realizing that he could almost see her skin through his hand. He was tied to the ring, and it had given him precious time...

But it wouldn't be enough to keep her.

Slowly, with infinite care, he finally got around to undressing her. His fingers appreciating every button, buckle, and clasp. Delighting in every slip of skin he uncovered.

She lifted off him and they found a fresh ewer and towel left by the innkeepers, and washed themselves before sliding into bed like a couple long used to each other's nearness.

Like it was the most natural thing in the world.

He tucked her against him, her back to his front, and he rested his head in his hand so he could gaze down at her. Commit her face to his memory.

For who knew if he would ever see her again after tonight?

She snuggled into him with unabashed relish, greedily drawing from his warmth.

"You should rest," he murmured. Pressing a kiss to her temple as she covered a yawn with the backs of her knuckles.

"I'm not going to sleep," she mumbled, her eyes opening a little less each time she blinked. "I'm not going to miss one moment with you."

"I know," he said against her hairline. Pressing little love kisses to her eyebrows. Her lids, feathering his lips across them, tasting the salt of the tears she refused to let fall. He didn't want to say goodbye, either.

"Will you do something for me, Vanessa?"

"Anything."

He slid the ring that belonged on his pinky onto her ring finger. "Return this ring to Lioncross Abbey for me. Perhaps it can put me to final rest."

She curled her fingers into a fist. "Perhaps, if I keep the ring with me, I'll keep you, too," she slurred, half asleep. "You could be my ghost. You could haunt me."

Somehow, he knew it wouldn't work, but he didn't have the heart to tell her so. His fingers worked over her face, as if learning her features like a blind man. Smoothing at her brows with featherlight touches until her jaw cracked on a yawn.

"Don't make me sleep." She fought it valiantly as a recalcitrant toddler. "I haven't shown you your photograph yet. The glass negative."

"Tomorrow." He said the word like a promise. A promise he already knew he would break. "I love you, Vanessa."

She mumbled something he thought might be the reply he hoped for. It didn't matter. As much as he desired her heart, he also wanted it free. Because she would live the most extraordinary life, and he was just lucky to be a part of it for one memorable solstice night.

CHAPTER 8

CHRISTMAS DAY—LIONCROSS ABBEY

*V*anessa let out a violent sneeze as she once more descended into the dust of the de Lohr crypts, her body and her heart recoiling from what she was about to do.

She'd infiltrated the de Lohr crypt, a monolithic cavern beneath the granite cliffs upon which the incomparable stones of Lioncross Abbey lorded over lush and verdant lands.

If the noble family had been in residence, there'd be signs of life, but as she circled the grounds on horseback, she'd spied none. No gas lamps lit the predawn light, nor did even so much as a drape twitch in the tower.

The castle itself was an impenetrable fortress, but sometime over the past hundred years or so, an enterprising Earl had added on a lavish manner home to the keep and landscaped it in such a way that the gardens at Versailles would weep with envy.

The crypts, fortunately for her, were situated on a dark corner of the grounds and were accessible enough if an enterprising body didn't mind clipping away vines of ivy and squeezing through the slats of an iron fence that would have kept out an invading army.

But not one enterprising slip of a woman.

She'd eschewed her skirt for the mission, donning a pair of lad's trousers and a coat that swallowed her to the knees. She'd pinned her hair high on her head and hid it beneath a cap.

Frost had crunched beneath her feet as she crept across the outer bailey to the mausoleum-like crypt entrance. She descended a few of the spiral stairs down below the frosted earth, before lighting her lantern. She tiptoed past the stone slabs covering many a de Lohr ancestor until she came to the one marked the year of Culloden, chiseled with the same name as was etched into her heart.

She pulled the chain upon which the ring rested from beneath her blouse, and wrapped her fingers lovingly around it, letting it burn against her palm. Could she do this? Could she uncover his bones and not fall to pieces at the sight of them?

She'd only known him one night. And that was all it took to fall.

Whatever shame and sadness she wore as a coronet before was no comparable tragedy to the past few days she'd spent waiting for him to appear.

Awaking in the sunshine after a Scottish storm, alone in the bed they'd shared, had just about broken her spirit.

He was lost to her, of that she had no doubt. Lost so soon, when she'd only just found the one man to whom she'd consider relinquishing both her name, her hand, and her heart. A man who'd transfixed and teased her. Who'd pleasured and protected her. A man to whom true honor meant more than reputation.

He'd only ever asked one thing of her.

But it was a cruel thing.

She closed her eyes and took a fortifying breath, filling her lungs with the loamy scent of earth and frost and a hint of decay. She released the ring, letting it settle between her breasts, a comforting weight around her neck.

One she'd have to give up.

She could do this. She'd done difficult things before.

She set the lantern onto the earth and discarded her gloves beside it before placing her hands on the stone slab above his coffin and pushing with all her strength. She groaned and strained, even let out a few curses, but it didn't budge.

Blast. She'd need leverage. Perhaps a—

Strong arms seized her from behind, drawing her back against a body as hard as iron. One arm locked beneath her breasts, the other around her throat.

"I'll give you two breaths to tell me what you are doing here, before I snap your neck." The growl was ferocious, arrogant, and alarming.

And no sound had ever been so dear.

"John?" she whispered around the tightness of her heart throbbing in her throat. She turned her face to the side, instinctively searching for his warmth. "John, is it really you?"

"A woman?" As quickly as she was seized, she was released. Cast away from the embrace she craved with the strength of an opium fiend.

She turned to see him, drinking in the sight of him with the thirst of someone finding an oasis in the desert.

Before her glowered a man of pure flesh and blood. Sinew and strength. His golden hair was cut in neat layers, even though it now spiked in wild disarray, as if he'd rolled out of bed only minutes prior. It suited him, the lord of Lioncross. The structure of his body was achingly familiar. The same long frame, the same wide shoulders and tapered waist accentuated by a dark wool coat thrown over a hastily buttoned shirt.

Aside from deeper brackets around his hard mouth and longer sideburns, he *was* John.

Except.

His eyes were perfectly dull and flat. So empty a blue as to almost be called grey as they assessed her with all the emotion one might attribute to a shark.

"You address me so informally, madam," he said over an imperious look.

Her heart gave one powerful, painful thump, before sputtering and dying. "I'm sorry," she gasped. "I can explain."

One golden brow arched over a look of recognition. "We've met before."

"Y-yes," she stammered. "At Lady Bainbridge's fete."

Recognition flared in the dim lantern light. "You're Veronica's sister."

Just when she thought her heart could sink no lower. "Yes. I am."

He made a rumbly, pensive sound, half between a purr and a snarl. "I still don't understand why they call her the pretty one."

"What?" Suddenly it was impossible to breathe.

He shook his head, blinking as if trying to clear it. "Sorry. Do you mind telling me what the bloody devil you're doing in my crypt on Christmas?"

"I um..." She itched at her hair beneath her cap, wondering just how to get herself out of this predicament without being thrown in an asylum. "You wouldn't believe me if I told you."

He leveled her a droll look, propping his shoulder against a stone wall. "Try me."

She gazed at him a long time, at the lantern light splashing deep hollows beneath his chiseled cheekbones. Something in the imperturbable stillness of his gaze told her she could say anything.

So, she attempted the truth.

"I took refuge at a place in the Highlands of Scotland called Balthazar's Inn on solstice night. While I stayed there I...met..." She sputtered and stalled out a bit. It was impossible to express her experience without choking up, so she reached behind her neck and unclasped the chain, letting the lion head ring slip from it into her palm. "I happened upon this, and was told it belonged to Johnathan de Lohr, the one who was lost at Culloden. I was...tasked to return it."

Those heartless, ruthless eyes affixed on the ring, and she thought she might have read a spark of life in them.

But only just.

"The Lion's Head." His voice had become deeper, like a monk's at prayer. "All this time. All these many generations have searched for it...and it just walks into Lioncross at Christmas." He reached for it. Paused. And flicked his eyes back to hers. "May I?"

"It's yours." She offered it to him reluctantly, loath to let go all she had left of her lover.

He handled it as if it were made of spun glass, tilting it to unveil an inscription on the inside, which she'd never noticed. "Ever faithful."

She leaned over to take a closer look, immediately aware that if either of them tilted their heads a fraction, their lips would meet.

"I've seen so many drawings. We've always assumed the ring was lost at the battle of Culloden. This was crafted in the Holy Land and gifted to the Lionclaw to always adorn the hand of the Earl of Worchester. In fact, a replica was never made because this one meant so much. They said there was a bit of magic crafted with it."

Swallowing a surge of grief, Vanessa looked longingly at the coffin behind her. "I suppose I should have given it to you. I just thought...Well I wanted to return it to its rightful owner."

The corner of his mouth tilted, and for a moment she thought she might burst into tears.

"That is good of you." He hesitated, drawing a hand through his mane in an attempt to tame it. "It's freezing out. Might I invite you in for some warm tea?"

She shook her head, needing to lick her wounds. Unwilling to have to look at him in the brilliant winter sun. "Oh. I don't want to take up any of your—"

"Please," he murmured, capturing her hand. "It's a rather large castle, and it's just me, now. The last de Lohr...well of my line, anyhow. You'd be doing a solitary man a kindness on Christmas."

She swallowed a spurt of pity and called it ridiculous. He was one of the most eligible bachelors in the Empire. If he wanted companionship, he'd only have to crook a finger.

"I'm no sort of company," she argued. "And not someone you'd want to be seen socializing with, besides."

The tiniest hint of an azure flame flared behind his eyes, causing them to glow like black sapphires in the dark. "I'm a de Lohr. I do as I fucking wish."

Worry crimped her forehead. "Perhaps you haven't heard about me."

"Oh, I heard," he said meaningfully. "I saw the pamphlet that blackguard, Woodhaven, passed around my club." His voice took on a savage bite to match the ferocity of his features. "I burned them all and got his bloody membership revoked."

She smiled at that. "Well...maybe one cup of tea."

He took up her lantern and turned away, so she followed his shoulders up the stone steps, blinking against the brightness of the morning.

Which was why she bumped into him.

It was like running into a boulder.

Jostled by her, he dropped the ring, and it rolled between his feet as he took a few steps before he realized.

Vanessa bent to pick it up, and a snowflake landed on the tip of her nose as she straightened. She blinked and looked around, mesmerized by the drifting crystals of frost dancing toward the earth. It was as if the sky had released little diamonds, and they'd chosen to land in the Lioncross gardens, adorning them with indescribable wealth.

"Odd," he remarked, tilting his neck up. "It wasn't snowing when I followed you down here. In fact, it was a clear morning."

Something gripped her at the sight of his throat arched to the sky. Something both foreign and familiar, and she cleared her throat to dislodge any gathers of emotion and the odd impulse to fall upon it like a vampire.

"Here," she offered, taking the ring between her thumb and fingers and reaching for his hand.

He looked down at her and relinquished his hand to her grip. It was so similar to the one she'd become acquainted with, she thought she might expire. A few different marks and calluses, but nothing remarkable enough.

She slid the ring over his knuckles.

A perfect fit.

She wanted to rip it off again. To claim it for her own. Because it didn't belong to him, this man with the empty eyes and kind, familiar smile. It belonged to John. *Her* John. The ghost who'd been somehow more full of life than even this magnificent specimen of a man.

She wanted to go back down into the crypt and sit with his bones. She wanted to go back to Scotland and sleep in the bed she'd shared with him. And mourn. Wail. Cry.

She knew it was pathetic, and she couldn't bring herself to care, because he was gone. She could feel not only his body but his soul missing the moment she'd awoken after the solstice.

Perhaps he was finally at rest.

"Vanessa."

She jumped at the sound of his voice. Looked up into his face.

His face.

The hollows had disappeared and...the eyes! The *eyes* were the same. No longer a grey/ blue but sharp with that familiar larkspur brilliance.

His name escaped her on a choked whisper.

John.

She jumped into his arms and he caught her against his chest, sweeping her around in the cheerful flurry before setting her back down.

"How is this—? What are—? Is he still—?" She couldn't seem to finish a sentence, she was too incandescently happy.

He put his hand to his temple and then threaded it through his hair, testing locks much shorter than his had been. "It isn't just him. That is, it's me. But also him."

"I don't understand," she croaked, fighting tears of hope and disbelief.

His smile could have eclipsed the sun. "I can't say I do, either. All I can tell you is...when we, you and I, met at the Bainbridge ball all those years ago, I wanted you then. But I'd already planned not to marry because I didn't have a heart nor a soul to give to a woman, and you deserved everything of that and more."

Johnathan de Lohr, the Earl of Worchester lifted his face to the sky once again, allowing snowflakes to gather on his eyelashes as if he enjoyed the sensation for the very first time.

"I was born empty," he told the clouds. "It would scare my mother to look into my eyes. She said she didn't think I had a soul. It was why she never had more children. And I felt it too..."

"And now?"

He captured her with his gaze. "Now, I think I was always a vessel. I *am* Johnathan de Lohr. Perhaps was *meant* to be him—me—whatever. I still have my memories." He gave her a hot look that threatened to scorch through her trousers. "I have his memories, as well."

She tried to believe it, though her mind couldn't seem to grasp just what was happening, and then she realized. "I never told you my first name."

"Vanessa. I *am* the man you spent solstice with. You showed me photographs of locomotives and of what I now understand to be gas lamps. You stood with me in the Chamber of Sorrows and made love to me while a tempest raged around us."

A tear slid down her cheek as the marvelous truth of it slammed into her with all the power of that locomotive at full tilt.

Vanessa's entire body stilled. Her lungs froze in her chest and her heart forgot to beat as one word settled into her soul, looking for a home.

Made love.

Love... Dare she hope?

His expression was so full of tenderness it threatened to melt her into a puddle of pure, blissful sentiment. "It's as if for one hundred and fifty years, one hollow note was playing in my ear, driving me mad, and then you blew in on a blizzard and brought with you every symphony I could hope to hear. You are my match, Vanessa. I never needed more than a moment to know it with unquestioned absolution. And I want to see the world with you, if you'd let me."

He captured her hand and held it to his lips, pressing a worshipful kiss into her palm before he continued. "Like I said, I am *that* Johnathan de Lohr, and *this* one, who also lived an entire lamentable life without you. Since the moment I met you, you haven't been far from my thoughts. I might not have the same body you became acquainted with, the same scars or history. I don't have the hands that touched you. The mouth that tasted you, not exactly. But I have the soul that adored you from the first moment I laid eyes on you."

Eyes. Ye gods what immaculate and incandescent light beamed at her from those eyes.

What life.

"I like *these* hands," she whispered, fondling the ring, then she lifted it to her own lips to return his kiss, before peeking up at him from beneath coy lashes. "I would not mind acquainting myself with the rest of you. It is not as if my reputation can't handle going into your castle unaccompanied."

"Wait." He stopped her, held her back from marching toward Lioncross. "I would invite you in only with the understanding that my intent is to carry you across the threshold as my Countess as soon as possible. I would defend your honor, Vanessa, and restore your good name."

A smile engulfed her entire being, even as snowflakes landed on her heated cheeks like chilly little blessings from heaven.

"Let's start with tea and see where that takes us," she teased, knowing that the moment he proposed properly, she'd have no other answer for him but yes.

Yes. Forever yes.

"Kiss me, Vanessa," he growled, dragging her against

his inflamed body. "Kiss me because it's Christmas and you're in my arms. Kiss me because I'm the luckiest soul to ever live and then live again."

Yes, she thought as she was swept away by the potency of his kiss. Entranced by the same magic she'd experienced that first time in the Highland storm.

It *was* Christmas.

And never would a gift mean so much as the soul of the man she loved.

MORE IN THIS SERIES

ABOUT THE AUTHOR

Kerrigan Byrne is the USA Today Bestselling and award winning author of THE DUKE WITH THE DRAGON TATTOO. She has authored a dozen novels in both the romance and mystery genre. Her newest mystery release THE BUSINESS OF BLOOD is available October 24th, 2019

She lives on the Olympic Peninsula in Washington with her dream boat husband. When she's not writing and researching, you'll find her on the water sailing and kayaking, or on land eating, drinking, shopping, and taking the dogs to play on the beach.

Kerrigan loves to hear from her readers! To contact her or learn more about her books, please visit her site: www.kerriganbyrne.com

A MARQUESS FOR CHRISTMAS

CHRISTI CALDWELL

CHAPTER 1

LONDON, WINTER 1818

*L*ady Patrina Tidemore had always prided herself on being the most logical and reasonable of the four Tidemore sisters. She'd never had a grand flourish for the dramatics as did her sweet sisters, Poppy and Penelope. Nor was she the great beauty that Prudence had grown into. But what she always had been, was logical, and reasonable.

Or rather, she *had* been, until she'd met one gentleman who'd filled her ear with pretty compliments and gently teased her into *forgetting* she was the logical and reasonable of the four.

Patrina stared out across the frozen Serpentine as the smallest, almost infinitesimal of snowflakes drifted down and landed upon the layer of ice. She pushed back her red velvet bonnet and sighed.

Last spring, she'd imagined a very different Christmastide season than this one. She would have been wed, tucked away in a modest home, with the quiet companionship of the gentleman who loved her. Instead, she could readily admit with Christmas nearly upon them, this would be by far the most grim, lonely holiday season—even surrounded by the noise of one's garrulous family.

Her lips twisted in an acrimonious smile. Alas, there was to be no modest home or quiet companionship. Rather, her Christmas would be spent just as she'd spent the past twenty, nearly twenty-one Christmases —with her proper mama and three loquacious sisters.

Oh, it had never been that she'd minded the frequent mayhem and excitement of the Tidemore home. Quite the opposite, really. It was just that she'd imagined she would be wedded, perhaps expecting a babe of her own soon.

She drew in a shuddery breath. When a young lady scandalized the *ton* as she'd done, dreams of weddings and families were nothing more than fanciful wishes.

"My lady, we should return soon," her maid, Mary, called from over her shoulder.

Patrina looked back distractedly and managed a wan smile. "You may go back and wait in the carriage, Mary. I'll be just a moment."

Mary opened her mouth as if to protest, but must have seen the firm resolve in Patrina's gaze, for she nodded once, and then started down the walking path, through the dusting of snow that blanketed the deadened grass, on toward the carriage.

Patrina returned her focus to the Serpentine. As she did in all her daily visits here, she wondered about the poor birds and fish that made this their home during the warmer months. Where did they go when the cold of life set in? On most days, she dreamed of joining them, because then she could be free of her sisters' pitying expressions, or the pained regret worn in her mother and brother's eyes, and the abject guilt in her sister-in-law, Juliet's expression every time Patrina entered a room.

A hiss split the quiet of the winter snowscape. She stiffened and turned, just as something cold, hard, and very wet hit her temple. "Oomph!" Patrina touched her fingers to her head and brushed the flakes of snow from the edge of her bonnet.

A flurry of giggles met her ears and she glanced around. Two splashes of color in the stark white landscape darted from behind a boulder and over to a larger rock. A scamp, mayhap ten years of age, with mischievous green eyes popped up from their hiding place.

Her eyes widened as he drew his arm back and... "Oomph." This snowball connected squarely with her nose. She dashed her hand over the cold moisture that dripped down her cheeks and into her mouth.

Furious giggles met her efforts.

Patrina narrowed her gaze upon that boulder and stomped toward the two scamps. The giggling ceased. Good, they should be frightened. Unfortunately for the two hellions, Patrina had a good deal of experience in handling mischievous children. She made her way to the end of the path and froze at the edge of the boulder.

"Hullo," she said. Her tone drew on years' worth of experience in Mother's response to the four Tidemore sisters. "I said..." she gasped and dropped to her knees as a little girl with flaxen curls darted from behind the rock and launched a snowball at her.

The missile sailed ineffectually past Patrina's shoulder. Of all the... "Has no one taught you manners?" she snapped. She rose to her feet and shook out her skirts. "You cannot simply go to a park and—" A snowball hit her shoulder.

Oh, this was quite enough!

Patrina bent down, scooped up the moist dusting of snow and made a compact ball, unheeding the frigidity of cool moisture seeping through her kidskin gloves. She waited. And unfortunately for them, she'd become rather adept at waiting.

Bothersome Boy didn't disappoint. He jumped up.

His eyes went wide as Patrina hurled her snowball. The force of the throw knocked his black cap from his head and covered his crop of golden locks in a film of white snow. "Hey!" he cried. "You can't simply go around throwing things at children."

Patrina replied by tossing another snowball. "I didn't throw a thing." This hit him square in the chest. "I threw a ball of snow."

His eyes widened. He splayed a hand over his chest as though he'd been hit with the ball of a pistol. Bothersome Boy thrust a finger toward her. "I say, I say... ladies do not throw snowballs. They don't. My mother didn't. And she was a lady and—"

Well, when a young woman eloped with a gentleman of dishonorable intentions and Society discovered the truth, one tended to lose their status as lady, amongst respectable peers. Patrina threw another snowball at his shoulder.

He cried out and disappeared behind the enormous rock.

Good, little wretch should learn to not... The little girl, his sister? Miss Minx snuck out and hurled a rather impressive-sized ball at Patrina's face.

Patrina cursed around a mouthful of snow and set to work making another snowball.

"I beg your pardon!" A deep, angry baritone split the quiet.

She paused mid-way through the production of her ball. She looked up. And swallowed hard.

A gentleman strode toward her. He doffed his hat, exposing the most luxuriant golden locks, unfashionably long, and blindingly bright. He had the look of an avenging angel. Even with the distance between them, she detected the flash of something volatile and charged in his emerald eyes. "You, there!"

Patrina rose unsteadily and glanced around for the

fortunate 'you there' to have attracted the gentleman's notice. She jumped when he stopped in front of her.

He glared down his aquiline nose at her. "What manner of lady goes about cursing at children?"

Her eyes flew wide. What was he on about? "I beg your pardon?"

The two little devils scampered out from behind the boulder. They hurried over to the handsome faced, now devil. She snorted. Angel, indeed!

"Do you have nothing to say?" he barked.

Miss Minx tugged at the gentleman's cloak and looked up at him through wide, tear-filled blue eyes. "Sh-she h-hit us with s-snow, Papa."

"Did she, Charlotte?" Thunderous fury underscored the menacing gentleman's question.

Patrina directed her gaze to the white-clouded skies above. Their father. Of course, with his golden locks and like green eyes, the man bore a striking resemblance to the two little devils. "Of all the nonsense," she muttered under her breath.

He narrowed his eyes on her. "What was that?" he said on a silken whisper. Odd that a tone could be cold and soft all at once. She supposed if she'd not braved the scandal with Albert Marshville and the subsequent public demise of her good name, then she would wager that emerald-eyed stare might make her uneasy. But she'd grown immune to disapproving stares. Any stares, really. The angry kinds. The mocking kinds. The disappointed kinds.

It would take a good deal more than this fiend to rankle her. She tossed her head back, damning the foot or so difference between his towering figure and her mere five feet three inches. "I gather these wretches are your children, sir?"

"My lord," he said.

She blinked at him. What was he on about?

"I am the Marquess of Beaufort and these are my children."

Oh, the insufferable, pompous lout. Did he think she'd be impressed or cowed by a title of marquess? "Well, then, *my lord*, your children are reprehensible mischief makers in need of lessons on proper deportment." Her sisters and brother would surely have laughed at any of the Tidemore siblings instructing another family on matters of proper deportment.

Bothersome Boy rushed to his father's side. "Did you hear what she s-said about us, P-papa?" he said in a wounded voice, tears in his eyes.

She snorted. No doubt the little fiend had spent the whole of his years on this earth perfecting those very tears.

The marquess glared at her and then rested a large, gloved hand upon the boy's shoulder. "It's all right, Daniel. Mustn't let yourself be hurt by cruel people, remember that."

Laughter bubbled past her lips. "Of all the nonsense."

The marquess' terse response came on the edge of a steely whisper. "What was that?"

Bothersome Boy, Daniel, it would seem, peeked from the side of his father's leg, a gloating expression in his eyes. He stuck out his tongue.

She narrowed her gaze, and then shifted her attention back to the ineffectual father. "What I said, *my lord*, is 'of all the nonsense'. You clearly have very little idea of what reprehensible children you have here." She ticked off a list on her fingers. "Throwing snowballs. Taunting. Hitting a lady with snowballs. Lying," she directed that pointed statement at the two children. They'd apparently been far too long without a proper scolding for they took that recrimination with unblinking calm.

346

"But then," the marquess said softly, "a proper young lady shouldn't be out alone in the park, unchaperoned, on a stormy day. Throwing snowballs at those...?" He quirked a golden eyebrow. "What did you call them? Rep—"

"Reprehensible children," she supplied for him. "I called them reprehensible children," she said, filled with a perverse pleasure at needling the arrogant lout. And yes, he had her there. Proper young ladies shouldn't be out alone as she presently was. However, she'd not been a proper young lady in many months now.

"Are you finished?" he snapped.

She chewed her lower lip and then nodded. "Yes, I believe I am."

He jerked his chin, and without a word turned on his heel. His two little hellions trotted after him.

She stitched her brows into a line. "No, that isn't all," she called out before she thought better of it. Her sharp voice carried through the winter still of the quiet air around them.

His long-legged strides drew to a slow halt, and he turned back around. His midnight black cloak whipped about his feet. The marquess folded his arms across his chest.

"You should have a speaking to with their mother," she said, lest her confidence desert her. "Their mother should know the manner of children that—"

"We don't have a mother," the golden curled, little girl blurted.

We don't have a mother. Patrina curled her toes into the soles of her serviceable black boots. A pang of hurt for the troublesome children tugged at her breast. They were motherless. Which of course explained their less than desirable behavior. After all, hadn't the Tidemore sisters behaved much the same way after the death of their father long ago? "I am so sorry," she said softly.

347

"I…" *feel like an unmitigated ass.* "I didn't mean…" *to be a big bully.* "Forgive me," she finished lamely.

The Marquess of Beaufort stormed toward her. Fury snapped in the green, nearly jade irises of his eyes. She took a stumbling step backward, and then remembered herself. She might feel regret for the harsh words she'd spoken about their motherless state, but she would not be cowed by this fiend. He stopped a hairsbreadth away. The tips of his gleaming black Hessians brushed the tips of her boots. "My children do not need your pity, miss."

By the fury etched in the harshly beautiful planes of his angular face, Patrina realized this wouldn't be the time to point out she was in fact a 'my lady'. Instead, she tipped her chin up a notch. "I was not pitying them. Or you." No, she'd experienced too much of that undesirable sentiment to ever turn it on to another.

The marquess lowered his head, so close she could see the flecks of gold in his eyes, and snarled, "Good. Because we do not want such sentiments from one such as you."

From one such as her? Humph! "Well, then," she said, wishing she didn't have on the silly red bonnet as it lessened the effect of flouncing one's curls.

He spun on his heel and marched back toward his children.

Patrina stood staring after him, and hated herself for being a weak ninnyhammer at her relief over his departure.

In fact, the more she stood there studying his broad back, the angrier she became. At him. At Albert Marshville. At herself. But mostly, herself for allowing a gentleman to make her feel so singularly unimportant. How dare he come and interrupt the peace and solitude she'd managed to steal for herself? Before she knew what she intended, she started after him. The snow crunched noisily under her boots. Somewhere along the way, she'd ceased to care about the absolute dunderhead's cool treatment and had shifted to the rage she'd carried over Albert Marshville's deception. "You," she called after him. "I said, you!"

The marquess drew to an elegant, deliberate halt, then turned to face her. He leaned down and murmured something to the boy. Bothersome Boy's mouth tipped downward in a frown, and he glared at Patrina a moment, then with obvious reluctance grabbed the little girl's hand and stood in wait for their father. "What?" he snapped when Patrina reached his side.

"I'm not a miss," she blurted, and immediately heat flooded her cheeks. His eyebrows lowered. "You called me a miss," she went on, when it became apparent the laconic marquess had little to say on the matter. "And I'm not a miss. I'm a lady." Polite Society would disagree. She jerked her chin up a notch. "I am Lady Patrina Tidemore."

He said nothing for a long while, and she scuffed the tip of her boot along the ground, wishing she'd perhaps spent just tad bit more time considering what she would say to the insufferable lout who'd doubled back to confront her. She waited for the flash of awareness, the dawning realization of the scandalous miss before him.

"Is that supposed to mean something, my lady?"

Patrina angled her head.

"You say your name as though I might have an idea of just who you are."

And she realized—he didn't have a dashed clue who she was. "You don't know who I am?" she blurted. An involuntary smile tugged the corners of her lips.

He scoffed. "What is so remarkable about you, my lady, that you think I should know you, prior sight unseen?"

She expected she should be offended. Nay, outraged. The kind of outrage that had young ladies slapping rude gents across smug faces. Except... Patrina's smile widened. This great, insufferable, overbearing, condescending gentleman had no idea who she, Lady Patrina Tidemore was. A giddy sensation trilled through her body, as the marquess suddenly became vastly preferable.

"Has something I said amused you, my lady?"

"Er...no...I..."

"And was there a reason you've called me back here? To perhaps condescend my children further and throw your snowballs?"

She pressed her lips into a tight line to keep from delivering a nasty set-down. His children were the ones who could certainly stand a lesson in proper behavior. "I called you back to apologize. I'm sorry for my callous statement regarding your children's mother. It wasn't my intention to be cruel. I'm sorry for your loss."

And she was. He might be a pompous gent, but she'd not wish this sadness on anyone. Well...mayhap the dastard who'd ruined her good name. But she'd draw the proverbial line there.

The marquess eyed her overlong, and she resisted the urge to keep from shifting on her feet like a small child caught slipping ink into her governess's tea. "Don't be," he said gruffly.

She wrinkled her brow. "Don't be what?"

"Sorry, my lady. I certainly am not." With a curt bow, he spun back on his heel and took his leave.

It took a moment for the marquess' words to register, and by that point, he'd made his way back to his waiting children. Her breath caught at the absolute viciousness of such a statement, and as the winter flakes snowed down upon her, she wondered what had caused such a gentleman to become so heartlessly cold.

CHAPTER 2

*W*eston Aldridge, the 4th Marquess of Beaufort, resisted the urge to steal a glance back at the spirited, if tart-mouthed young lady he'd left behind at the edge of the Serpentine. With her sinfully black curls hanging past her shoulders and the creamy white of her skin, she put him in mind of all manner of things improper.

Which made very little sense. With Lady Patrina Tidemore's diminutive frame and nondescript plainness, she was nothing like the lush beauty he'd always preferred in his late golden-haired, tall, graceful wife. His gut tightened. Then, after Cordelia's great many betrayals, mayhap he'd found himself attracted to a wholly different beauty.

Charlotte tugged at his hand, and he slowed his steps. "Pick me up, Papa."

"Pick me up, please," he corrected automatically.

Charlotte giggled. "I can't pick you up, Papa. You're too big."

Daniel scuffed snow at her skirts. "He means you're supposed to say, please, you ninny."

"Don't call me a ninny," she cried and kicked snow back at him.

They proceeded to speak over one another in a flurry of unkind words that made Weston wince. "Enough," he barked.

They immediately fell silent, and glowered at one another.

Weston bent down and scooped his golden-haired girl into his arms. As they three trudged through the snow-covered grounds of Hyde Park, he reflected upon his encounter with the Lady Patrina Tidemore.

He'd been gruff and blustery where the young lady was concerned. After all, he didn't tolerate unkindness toward his children. If he were being completely honest with himself, he could acknowledge some merits to Lady Patrina's charges about his children. They were ill-behaved and angry—with good cause. A treacherous mother tended to have that effect on children. And since he was being honest—even with just himself—he acknowledged it also made for an oft-times too lenient father.

What was the diminutive dark-haired lady doing out on a blustery, winter day un-chaperoned? On the heel of that question was a niggling of guilt at having left the young woman unattended. Weston cursed.

Charlotte's eyes went wide. "Papa cursed," she whispered.

"Ballocks isn't a curse," Daniel said with all the indignation of an eight-year-old boy who thought himself more adult than child.

Weston spun back around and scanned the area for sight of Lady Patrina Tidemore. Where had she gone off to? He supposed the gentlemanly thing to have done was to ensure the young lady had not been in need of assistance. After the ten years he'd been married to his now deceased, deceitful wife, Lady Cordelia, he'd lost most remnants of the gentleman he'd once been.

His daughter pulled at his earlobe. "Is ballocks a curse?"

"Hmm?" he murmured absently, and started heading back to the edge of the Serpentine.

"Where are we going now?" Daniel groused, and all but dragging his heels, fell into step alongside Weston.

Young ladies had no right being out on such a day, un-chaperoned, no less.

"Ballocks," Charlotte muttered.

Weston frowned. "What did you say?"

"I said—"

"I heard what you said." He scrubbed his hand over his face. *Reprehensible and ill-behaved.* "Why did you—?"

Charlotte took his face between her little gloved hands and forced him to look her in the eyes. "You said it's not a curse."

"I said no such thing, Char." *Reprehensible. Ill-behaved.* "It's a curse," he said curtly when she opened her mouth to speak further on it.

She promptly closed her lips. "Hmph."

Christ, he detested when other people were right, particularly tart-mouthed misses who called him back to inform him of the proper form of address. He paused and surveyed the distance through the increasing snowfall. It appeared she had already...

He cursed. She hovered at the edge of that blasted shorefront, her back presented to him, and something in the set of her shoulders, he recognized. Forlornness. An unspoken sadness that required no words. Sentiments he saw and recognized because he himself had felt those very same things. Back when he'd felt something. "Wait here," he ordered Daniel. He set Charlotte down and she immediately grabbed her brother's hand.

"But I want to leave," his son whined. "I..." He fell silent at the hard stare Weston fixed on him.

Weston trudged through the fresh-fallen snow, back

to the young lady. "You there," he barked, knowing he should at least attempt to feign gentlemanly politeness.

The woman spun so quickly, the heel of her boot slid in the patch of snow and she landed in a fluttering, red, muslin heap in the snow around her. She slapped a hand to her chest, and glared at him. "You terrified me. What are you about, my lord?"

"What are you doing here?"

Seated upon the fresh blanket of snow, Lady Patrina tilted her head back and looked at him. "I beg your pardon?"

"Without a chaperone." He supposed he should really help her up.

Her mouth set at a mutinous line, but she made no attempt to stand. "That is none of your affair, my lord."

Well, for the love of God, he couldn't simply leave her on her backside in the midst of Hyde Park. He took another step closer, and held out a hand. "Surely you have sense to realize the perils of a young lady being out alone without escort?"

She eyed his hand the way she might a slithering serpent, and for a moment he thought the prideful young lady intended to reject his offer of help. But then, she placed her fingers in his.

He tugged her to her feet.

"I come here every day, my lord, but thank you. I'm touched by your concern," she said drolly.

Weston narrowed his eyes at those insolently delivered words. On the heel of his immediate annoyance was an unexpected curiosity as to what had a young lady visiting Hyde Park in the cold of winter, alone, unchaperoned. "May I offer the assistance of my escort home?"

"No." Her response was instantaneous.

Odd, through the years, before he'd wed Cordelia, and even after their marriage, young ladies had clamored for his attention. He didn't think he'd ever been the recipient of such a curt, immediate 'no' in the course of his thirty-two years.

"Are we going, Papa? I'm ever so hungry," Charlotte called from beyond his shoulder.

He ignored her. "I came back to apologize." He normally didn't make apologies, largely because he was usually in the right.

Lady Patrina's mouth fell slightly ajar, as if she sought to process his unexpected statement.

"About my children. They shouldn't have been throwing snowballs at you."

She closed her mouth, but still said nothing.

He bristled. The lady really should say *something*. An acknowledgement. A 'thank you', an 'it's-entirely-fine-don't-worry-any-further'. None of this absolute silence.

"Papa, we want to go."

As did he, but not before the silent miss said *something*. He spun back to face Charlotte and Daniel. "In a moment," he snapped. His children fell immediately silent. He faced Lady Patrina and a dull heat climbed up his neck. With their every word, his recalcitrant children proved her earlier statements correct—yet again. Weston bowed. "If you'll excuse me?" He took his leave. What had possessed him to come trotting back in search of...what? Understanding? From this woman. She couldn't be more than twenty-years if she was a day. No, she couldn't know the ugliness in life that turned smiling gentlemen into bitter, angry heartless men, or made innocent children become—reprehensible misbehavers.

"It is fine." Her words echoed through the still of the park, drawing him to a stop.

"Not again," Daniel grumbled at his side.

Weston ignored him and looked yet again toward Lady Patrina.

"And I thank you for your offer to escort me, but my maid and carriage are waiting for me."

The oddest disappointment filled him, which made so very little sense. He should be grateful to be relieved of the gentlemanly sense of obligation to see that she made it home without a need of his assistance. He nodded.

Lady Patrina seemed to dismiss him from her thoughts, before the final words had left her mouth. She looked to the iced river and presented him her back.

Weston lingered a moment more, unable to resist the urge to know why a lady so young should carry such a remarkable sadness.

"Papa," Charlotte urged, tugging his hand. She snapped him from his reverie. "I'm cold."

He bent and scooped Charlotte up one more time. "Off we go then."

Regardless, Lady Patrina was a stranger and would remain one to him. After all, he had little intention of reentering polite Society. Not after Cordelia's deceit, and he *certainly* had sense enough to not be intrigued by a tart-mouthed miss who'd hurl snowballs at his children.

The memory of her standing there pulled at him. He shot a final look over his shoulder taking in the side of her, and then jerked his gaze forward.

Yes, he'd little interest in the spirited Lady Patrina Tidemore.

Except...why did it feel as though he lied to himself?

CHAPTER 3

"*W*here were you?"

Patrina handed her snow-dampened cloak over to the butler, Smith, and glanced up to where her youngest sister stood at the top of the stairs. "I was out, Poppy."

Her sister pointed her gaze to the ceiling and skipped her way down the stairs. "Obviously. Mother doesn't like you to go out alone."

Patrina wrinkled her nose. No, Mother did not entirely trust her after the whole scandal with Albert Marshville. "I'm a grown woman," she said instead.

Poppy skidded to a halt in front of her. She passed her gaze over Patrina's face and frowned.

"What is it?" Patrina asked before she could call the words back. She should have learned long ago to not feed her sister's curiosity.

"You look different," Poppy said.

Patrina managed a smile. "Oh, and how is that?"

Poppy tilted her head at a funny angle and proceeded to walk a small circle around Patrina. She stopped when they were face to face. "You don't have the look of one whose pup got tossed under a carriage wheels."

A startled laugh burst from her lips. She shook her head. "That's a completely awful thing to say."

Her sister snorted. "What would you have me say? That you look like one who's happy her pup got tossed under a carriage's wheels?"

A desperate laugh bubbled up her throat. "Oh, Poppy." God love their mother for having survived raising four hopelessly incorrigible daughters. Well, thus far. Patrina had certainly tested the poor woman more than any of the siblings combined with that dreadful mistake last spring.

"Well, you do." Poppy folded her arms across her chest. "You usually walk around with that hopelessly sad look on your face." She frowned, her lower lip quivered, and she slapped her hands over her cheeks in what Patrina gathered was her best attempt at 'wounded-sister-with-a-broken-heart-expression'.

"I do *not* look like that," she said tersely. She started down the hall.

"You do look like that. And you still refuse to tell me where you're off to. Every. Day." Poppy, as tenacious as the day was long, trotted fast on her heels.

Patrina turned quickly down the corridor, and Poppy hastened her step to keep up. "It's not your business."

Her sister carried on as though she'd not even spoken. "At first I believed you merely went shopping. Except, you never returned with any packages." She shook her head. "So, you most assuredly weren't shopping."

"Most assuredly," she murmured.

"You're not like Prudence."

"Who is not like me?"

The sisters shrieked as Prudence stepped out of the Ivory Parlor, into the hall.

Poppy frowned at her. "Must you sneak up on a body like that?"

Patrina continued on, welcoming Prudence's unexpected, and much timely, intervention. Alas, Prudence appeared as bored as Poppy for she hurried to keep pace with Patrina. Patrina stepped inside the music room and made to close the door behind her.

Prudence stuck the tip of her slipper in the doorway. "That's not well-done of you," she said on a huff and then shoved her way through. Poppy followed suit.

A sigh escaped Patrina, and she made her way over to her pianoforte. She settled onto her bench and proceeded to play in a desperate attempt to divert her sister's attention.

"Ugh, must you insist on playing, Trina," Prudence said on a wince. "You know you're quite deplorable. Surely you know that."

Patrina continued to play. A particularly discordant note echoed throughout the room. She frowned. "I like to play," she said, a touch defensively. Her sister was quite right. There was not a single thing remarkable about her playing, other than how absolutely horrendous she was. Her pace too slow, her fingers too clumsy, she'd been mocked for playing at more than one musical recital.

Of course, salacious gossips would never mention anything so mundane as Patrina Tidemore's poor pianoforte playing now, not when she'd gone and eloped with a shameless cad who'd had no intention of ever making her his wife.

She sighed and shoved thoughts of Albert from her mind. She forgot her sisters' prattling on about some such nonsense, and lost herself in her playing. For everyone's derision over her pianoforte skills, Patrina enjoyed it rather immensely. The instrument provided the singular pleasure she found in life, and the one pleasure not dictated by others, one that she was solely in control of. Her fingers stumbled over the keys.

"Oh dear, you have *the look* again. She has the look again," Poppy said, this time to Prudence.

I will not engage them. I will not engage them.

Prudence sighed. "She does."

"Nor will she tell me where she goes off to everyday."

"Because it is not your business." Three pairs of eyes swiveled to the door as Penelope, their second youngest sister sailed into the room.

Patrina played all the louder.

Poppy slapped her hands over her ears.

"Must you do that?" Penelope called out.

Patrina played louder still. "Yes." As much as her sisters wore on her patience, in those dark days following Albert's betrayal, they'd been steadfast, and loyal, and somber...and for that she could never repay them. If she were being truthful, she could admit she far preferred them to the loquacious bits of baggage before her now.

"We're trying to determine where she's been off to," Poppy said over Patrina's playing.

"But she'll not tell us," Prudence groused.

Patrina picked her gaze up from the keys long enough to detect the flash of hurt shot her direction by Prudence. She fought back a wave of guilt. In sacrificing her sisters' own future marital prospects with her own foolish decision, her sisters had been far more forgiving than she deserved. In this, Prudence was indeed correct. She owed them truths and yet...could not bring herself to share her meeting with the marquess.

Penelope frowned. "Mother's concerned this has something to do with *that...him.*"

*That...him...*had become the term used when referring to Albert Marshville.

Albert Marshville, cad, scoundrel, fiend, and every horrid word between happened to be the brother of their dearest sister-in-law, Juliet. As a result, the Tidemore sisters seemed hesitant to fully ascribe an appropriate charge for the man who'd ruined Patrina's good reputation.

Penelope began hesitantly, "Never tell me you're still harboring affection for—"

Her fingers slipped on the keys. "No."

Their youngest sister, Poppy chewed her lower lip. "You're certain. Because—"

"I'm certain," Patrina said, snapping the cover closed on her instrument. With a sigh she accepted the end of her dreams of peace this day.

The girls shared a look. "We hate seeing you this way," Penelope murmured. "You're ever so sad—"

"Except today," Poppy interjected. "Today she returned from...from...wherever she goes, with a smile."

Prudence and Penelope spoke in unison, with wide eyes. "She did?"

Patrina pointed her gaze to the ceiling and prayed for deliverance from these her vexing sisters. Their outrageous behaviors gave her a renewed appreciation for the great chore given Mother in rearing four troublesome daughters—her present self not excluded, of course.

Poppy nodded emphatically. "She did. And now she won't tell me, er, tell us, anything."

Three accusing stares swung back in her direction.

And because Patrina recognized she had little hope of peace and solitude if she didn't give her tenacious sisters something, she slipped them a niggling of the truth. "Two little troublemakers set upon me at Hyde Park today and hurled snowballs at me."

Poppy gasped and slapped her hand over her mouth. "That is hor...er, horrendous," she corrected.

The girls' former governess, turned sister-in-law, Juliet, after she'd gone and wed their brother, Jonathan, the 5th Earl of Sinclair, had striven to strike the oft-used word horrid from the girls' vernacular.

Prudence continued to frown. "That is not funny."

"It really isn't, Patrina." Penelope nodded in agreement.

She smiled and remembered the two little hellions so very much like the three girls before her now. Albeit vastly younger versions of the three, but similar nonetheless. "I returned the favor."

Poppy laughed. "Well done, Patrina. I didn't believe you knew how to do anything fun anymore."

She frowned. Whatever did her sister mean by such a statement?

As if following her unspoken thoughts, Poppy said, "Not because of *that...him*, but because you've never been the laughing sort."

"I *am* the laughing sort," she replied instantly. Her sisters exchanged a look, and she shook her head at their silent, blatant disagreement. "I am," she said and snapped her skirts. "The laughing sort," she expanded." She tossed her head and stepped a deliberate path around the troublesome misses. "And I know how to do...fun things," she muttered to herself as she sailed from the room.

"No, you don't." Poppy's sharp laughter followed her down the corridor.

Patrina's frown deepened. Not fun, indeed. How very insulting of her sisters to say such a thing. Just because she'd never descended into quite the same level of mischief as the three younger girls didn't mean she hadn't been fun or the laughing sort. As she made her way abovestairs, she thought of her exchange in Hyde Park with the Marquess of Beaufort. Somber, scowling, and unsmiling, he'd been.

Is that how her sisters saw her? Is that how the world saw her?

She turned down the corridor that led to her chambers. The steady tick-tock of the longcase clock punctuated her quiet steps. It hadn't been her fault that when she'd come out, there had been a remarkable dearth of suitors. Hence her pathetic grasping for the pretty compliments Albert Marshville had poured into her ear.

Or so she'd thought.

Patrina stopped in front of her room and pressed the door handle. She slipped inside then kicked the door closed with the sole of her boot. Only now, as she stood and stared at her rather cool, lonely chambers, she confronted the ugly possibility perhaps there was some defect in her character that had deterred suitors. Perhaps they'd seen her as Poppy had claimed—an un-laughing, un-fun sort.

Just as the severe Marquess of Beaufort.

Patrina crossed over to the floor-length window. She tugged back the ivory brocade curtains and peered down into the empty streets below. Snow fell, thick and heavy outside and blanketed the paved roads in a pure, white covering.

As she'd confronted the marquess, she'd done so with no small trace of condescension. How dare he and his unruly children shatter the small time she stole for herself, away from the pitying gazes of her family members? She'd judged him as a cold, unfeeling sort. After Poppy's recent charge, however, she was forced to wonder about his story, this man who'd spoken so coldly of the loss of his wife. Still, for all his blusteriness, he'd marched back over to inquire after her. He had offered her his assistance when she'd already judged him and found him wanting as a singularly pompous ass.

Patrina let the curtain go and it fluttered back into place. In actuality, mayhap she and the Marquess of Beaufort were more similar than she even cared to admit to herself. Much like Patrina, this man, who'd initially earned her scorn and disdain had a story. Some great pain was surely to blame for the marquess' seething coldness. And she, who'd not moved outside her own self-misery these past months was suddenly besieged by a desire to know more about the darkly aloof marquess.

Oh, dear.

CHAPTER 4

*P*atrina stole down North Old Bond Street, the blessed peace of her own presence her only company. In spite of her sisters' needling and attempts to wheedle more details about her morning forays into Hyde Park, she had snuck free.

Her expedition to the bustling shops had little to do with a desire for any fripperies for herself, but rather for her sisters. "Don't know how to do anything fun, do I?" she said softly to herself. Did un-fun sisters sneak off to Bond Street for a special shopping outing? Why, it seemed like just the *fun* sort of thing a young lady who laughed a lot would enjoy doing.

She paused beside a random shop front and stared into the window of what was a bakeshop. She eyed the confectioneries within. The door opened and set a tiny bell a-jingle. The sweet, syrupy scent of baked treats and mince pies wafted through the crisp air. Her mouth watered. She took a step toward the door when her gaze snagged upon the image of a small girl in the windowpane. Something seemed so very familiar about the slight girl's furtive movements. Only she didn't know any—

Patrina's eyes widened. Mince pies forgotten, she

365

turned to stare curiously out across the street to where the little girl—the same one who'd hurled snowballs at her only yesterday morn—moved with deliberate steps onward to the Bond Street Bazaar. The large one-room establishment that featured numerous shops and vendors within its walls, popular during inclement weather and the colder months. The little girl, Charlotte, entered the bazaar, otherwise known as the Western Exchange.

She glanced around in search of the golden-haired, somber marquess, or even the troublesome little boy. Only, no one followed on the girl's heels. Not a father. Or brother. Or nursemaid. Patrina had engaged in quite enough mischievous behavior as a young child, and witnessed a fair share of it from her sisters to recognize the makings of trouble.

She cast a longing glance back at the cherry tarts and mince pies. And then set out across the street. Her maid hurried to match the pace. As Patrina crossed the pavement, two passing ladies eyed her a moment. They jerked their attention forward, whispering to one another. Shame burned her skin, but she tilted her chin up a notch and stepped by them, having if not grown immune, at least accustomed to Society's obvious disdain. She paused outside the doors a moment, and looked about in one last hopeful attempt at locating the marquess.

With a sigh, she entered the bazaar. She searched the crowded room. The chatter of lords and ladies as they moved between the vendors echoed throughout the high-ceiling space. She wandered down, past a row of tables, and ignored the glances tossed in her direction. As she made her way through the hall, the impulsiveness of her actions occurred to her. Surely the little girl knew well where her father or nursemaid was, and Patrina was merely worrying needlessly. She gave her head a rueful shake. She expected she should have learned the perils of impulsiveness from her mistake with Albert Marshville.

Patrina made to turn on her heel and mind her own affairs, when she caught sight of the little girl at the edge of a too-high table. The back of her golden-curls was presented to Patrina, as she seemed to study the miniature theatres on the table in front of her.

Alone. Charlotte studied the miniature theatre alone. *Sans* father, brother, or nursemaid.

With a beleaguered sigh, Patrina abandoned her attempt at escape and walked over to the child. Charlotte had her palms resting on the edge of the table, and leaned up on tiptoe to better view the replica of the cutout characters in Hamlet, with a vividly painted red curtain framing the proscenium and scenery. Patrina waved off the approaching vendor and placed her hands alongside little Charlotte's. "Hullo," she greeted.

The girl shrieked and jumped. She slammed a hand over her heart, in a flourishing manner similar to Patrina's youngest sister, Poppy. "Goodness. You star—" Her green eyes narrowed. "You," she groaned.

Patrina smiled. "Me. And where is your father, Charlotte?"

"My father?" The girl scratched her brow.

A wave of mortified heat climbed up Patrina's neck at her specific inquiry into the marquess' whereabouts. "Hm, er, yes, that is, your *family*," she amended. She hadn't given the aloof bounder another thought after their unpleasant exchange in the park. Not a single thought. Outside of her inability to sleep from wondering as to a man who seemed so gentle with his children and so cold with everyone around him. Nay, not everyone, she couldn't speak to that. Perhaps, it had just been her who'd earned his stern disapproval.

The little girl blinked. "My family?" she blurted.

And it occurred to Patrina in that moment... "You don't know where they are, do you?" she asked gently.

Green eyes widened like full-moons. Charlotte frantically shook her head, even as she stepped around Patrina, who matched the little girl's quick movements. "I...I..." Charlotte looked back at the miniature theatres with tear-filled eyes. "I w-wanted to see the toys, but n-nurse s-said no...and..." She made another move to go around, but Patrina settled a hand on a slender shoulder.

"Do not worry," she said in the tone she'd adopted over the years in addressing heated arguments amongst her three spirited sisters. "We'll find her." She glanced over the crowded tables and bit the inside of her lower lip. "Er...did you leave the young woman in here?"

Charlotte shook her head. A golden curl fell over her eyes. She blew at it, but the blonde tress fell immediately back into place. "I was outside and she insisted on looking at a bonnet shop, but I know it was only because there was a man she was making eyes at because she wasn't paying attention and..." The girl continued rambling, her words running together.

Patrina gave her shoulders a light squeeze. "Whoa," she urged, feeling the faint tug of a smile at her lips. The girl fell silent. "I'll help you home," she assured her.

Charlotte's eyebrows lowered and leaning away from Patrina, she folded her arms over her chest. "Why would you do that? Are you going to lure me away and cook me and eat me like the witch?"

A burst of startled laughter escaped Patrina. "That is horrid. Whatever are you talking about?"

The little girl tossed her hands in the air. "The witch in *Hansel and Gretel*. She lures the children away and—"

"I have no intention of luring you away and eating you," Patrina said with deliberate somberness. She schooled her features into what she hoped was a serious mask.

The girl appeared to be weighing the validity of her assurance.

Goodness, someone really must speak to the marquess about the appropriateness of his children's reading material. With talks of vile witches and their plans to eat a child, little Charlotte was surely kept awake by night terrors.

At long last, Charlotte nodded. "Very well, then. I give you permission to help me." She extended a hand and stared pointedly back at her.

Patrina glanced at the tiny fingers encased in white gloves. She swallowed a pain of longing for the life she'd imagined for herself.

"Well, are you going to hold my hand or not," Charlotte said a touch impatiently.

"I am," Patrina said and placed her hand inside the girl's.

Charlotte closed her fingers about Patrina's, and that blasted lump in her throat threatened to drown her with regret. The girl stole a sideways glance up at her. "Are you all right?"

"Certainly," Patrina said quickly.

"Because you do not seem all right. You seem all quiet and sad like Papa in his office at night when he thinks I'm abed, but I'm really hiding behind his curtains."

At the girl's words, something tugged at Patrina's heart. She imagined the tall, powerful Marquess of Beaufort with the hard planes of his face set in grief, unguarded and hurting, so vastly different from the commanding lout who'd dared insult her for reprimanding his children.

Charlotte scratched her brow. "In thinking on it,

you seemed sad at the park as well. Do you go to the park often, miss?"

"Every day," Patrina confessed. Not even her sisters and mother knew of her morning jaunts. When the sun was just peeking over the horizon, ushering in the morning, she reveled in the stillness of the park, away from Society's prying eyes.

"Oh, dear, now you've gone all quiet. Just like Papa." Her little mouth quivered.

"I'm fine," Patrina hastened to assure her. "I'm merely trying to determine the best manner in which to return you home," she lied.

"And you do not intend to eat me?"

She shook her head. "I have no intention of eating you."

The girl nodded, as pleased as if Patrina had offered her the last cherry tart.

Patrina gave the fingers in her hand a gentle squeeze and started toward the exit of the bazaar. They continued in silence until they reached the last table at the front of the building. Charlotte dug her heels in and tugged her hand free. "Look!" she jabbed a finger over toward a table littered with ribbons. "Might I look, my lady? Might I? I imagine Papa will not allow me to look at ribbons for a very long time after this."

She nodded hesitantly, and watched Charlotte sprint over to the table of ribbons.

"Miss, is everything all right?"

Patrina started at the appearance of her maid, Mary. "Fine," she said, following Mary's gaze to little Charlotte lifting and studying each ribbon within her reach.

"You must do me a favor, Mary. She's become separated from the Marquess of Beaufort. You must make inquiries as to the gentleman's residence so we might return her to her family."

Mary gave a brusque nod, and with a determined step, set out to make her discreet inquiries.

Patrina returned her attention to Charlotte, just as the girl held up an emerald green ribbon. "Miss, have you ever seen a more beautiful ribbon?"

She walked over and accepted the small scrap of fabric from the girl, turned it over in her hands. The vibrant green hue put her in mind of the marquess' striking eyes. She murmured, "It is assuredly the most beautiful ribbon here."

Charlotte's smile widened and she nodded in agreement. She made to set it down, and her smile dipped.

"Just a minute," Patrina said, before she fully realized what she intended. The vendor hurried over.

"May I help you, miss?"

"Just the green ribbon," she said, and withdrew a coin from her reticule. After all, it was nearly Christmas.

The young man's eyes went wide at the gleaming sovereign handed over to him. "Thank you, my lady. Thank you," he repeated.

Patrina returned her attention to Charlotte. "It is yours."

Instead of girlish excitement or any hint of appreciation, a mistrust far more befitting a girl of more advanced years, returned to her eyes. "Why would you be nice to me? I threw snowballs at you."

"I threw snowballs back at you," Patrina felt inclined to remind the girl.

Three lines wrinkled the girl's brow. "You want me to buy you a ribbon, then?"

Patrina laughed. "No, I do not expect you to buy me a ribbon." From the end of the room, she detected her maid, Mary weaving in and out of lords and ladies shopping throughout the bazaar. They eyed her with curious annoyance, as she slowed to a halt in front of Patrina.

Mary's chest heaved up and down from her exertions. "I've determined the gentleman's residence," she said and then glanced around quickly, as if to ascertain whether her scandalous words had been overheard.

"Come along, then," Patrina said hurriedly. Not out of any attempt at concealing her efforts. After all, not much further damage could truly be done to her reputation. She held a hand out and Charlotte slipped her fingers back into Patrina's. On the heel of that, were the stirrings of guilt for the repercussions her actions would surely have for her sisters in future years.

Charlotte tugged at her hand. "Do you intend to tell my papa?"

Patrina tamped down a smile, knowing the prideful little girl would not welcome any amusement on her part. "I do not see how I can keep any of this from your papa," she said.

Charlotte worried the flesh of her lower lip. "I suppose that is true," she muttered. "Perhaps I can say nurse left me to—"

"No."

"But—"

"No," Patrina said a touch more firmly. "You should never hold others to blame for your own actions, Charlotte." The words intended for the girl, as much as they were for Patrina herself.

Charlotte sighed and fell silent.

As they walked out of the bazaar onto the bustling pavement, toward Patrina's waiting carriage, she reflected on the unspoken resentment she'd carried for her sister-in-law. Poor Juliet, whose only mistake in life was the blood she shared with Albert Marshville, which was certainly no fault of her own. Since Albert's deception, Juliet had moved around Patrina with silent guilt in her eyes.

The driver scrambled from the top of the box and hurried to open the door. He eyed the child a moment, and then averted his gaze. Patrina murmured her thanks and handed Charlotte inside. She accepted the driver's hand and allowed him to help her up. She settled onto the bench beside a now quiet Charlotte.

Only now, in speaking to the little girl, did she acknowledge the truth to her own gentle recrimination. Her actions that day, the decision to elope with Albert, no one had forced her into his carriage. No one had demanded she go along with his vile plans.

Mary gave the driver their directions and scrambled inside. The driver closed the door behind them, and a moment later, the carriage rocked forward.

Not even Albert could be wholly to blame. Not when Patrina had known the scandalous nature of her actions and had instead allowed the desperate need for love and affection to fuel her flight to Gretna Green.

Charlotte shifted on the bench, until her red cloak brushed alongside Patrina's. "You look sad again," she observed.

That would be because she was more often sad than not. "I'm sorry," Patrina said, instead.

The girl lifted her shoulders in a little shrug. "You needn't be sorry for feeling sad," she said with that far too-mature tone Patrina was coming to expect from the small girl. "Is it because those ladies were whispering about you?"

Patrina proceeded to choke. The Marquess of Beaufort's daughter seemed far more astute than most ladies of Patrina's acquaintance. A knot formed in her belly. Well, the former ladies of her acquaintance. All general friendships she'd known had died a swift death after news of her elopement had become information for public consumption. "No, that is not why," she lied. Though, there was merit to Charlotte's claims.

"Did your husband die like my mama?"

Her heart cracked at the unflinching directness of such words from a little girl. Goodness, the girl had a tenacity to rival all the Tidemore sisters combined. "No," she said gently. "I'm not married." Nor would she ever wed.

Charlotte's brow wrinkled again. "Why? You seem old."

From across the carriage, Mary buried a laugh in her hands.

Patrina gave Mary a pointed frown and then turned back to Charlotte. "I'm not old."

The little girl angled her head up. "No, not old like Mrs. Watson."

"Mrs. Watson?"

"Our housekeeper," Charlotte said as though there were never a sillier question uttered.

"Oh, er...yes, Mrs. Watson."

"But you should have a husband," Charlotte said with a nod.

"Should I?" Yes, of course she should. It would seem even a young child should know that very obvious fact. Patrina should have a respectable gentleman who'd if not love her, hold her in his affection and protect her. Alas, Patrina had given up the right to all those simple things she'd taken for granted until they'd been forever snatched from her grip by her recklessness those many months past.

"Oh, yes," Charlotte went on. "You should be married, and have babies, and go to grand balls, just as Mama did."

Patrina bit back the urge to ask the girl questions about her now departed mother, a woman who'd been wed to the cold, curt marquess. Had he been a different man before that loss?

The little girl studied her a moment, as if silently weighing her. "You're pretty enough. Not pretty as Mama, of course, but pretty enough to find a husband."

Patrina's lips twitched. "Er, why thank you. I think."

Mary, through all the child's exchange, remained with her gaze fixed out at the passing scenery. Her shoulders shook, no doubt from amusement.

"Is something wrong with her?" Charlotte asked, jerking her chin at Mary.

"I don't know," Patrina said. "Why don't you ask her?"

"You there, is there something wrong with you?" The question rang with authority, no doubt learned at the heel of her commanding father.

Mary waved hear hand. "No. Fine," she cleared her throat, and regained her composure. "Forgive me, I'm fine."

"That isn't how we speak to people, Charlotte," Patrina gently chided.

The girl's mouth settled in a mutinous line. "I merely asked her a question."

"Ah, yes, but it is how you asked the question. You must still be polite."

"Even to servants?" Skepticism laced the three-worded question.

Patrina registered Mary's intense interest in the current exchange. "Especially servants, Charlotte. Can you imagine how very difficult life would be without them?"

The widest smile turned Mary's lips, which she covered discreetly with her hand.

Charlotte folded her arms over her chest. "Mama didn't agree. She said servants are there to see to the pleasures of their betters."

Patrina winced. She supposed she should be more lenient with the departed woman's memory, but the late Marchioness of Beaufort sounded like a perfectly unpleasant creature. "That isn't true. Servants are there to work and help and even be confidantes to those in dire need." She caught Mary's eye, and the young maid gave an imperceptible nod, a silent acknowledgement to the close bond they'd forged after Patrina's fall from grace.

"Truly?" Charlotte asked questioningly.

"Truly."

The little girl seemed to dismiss the matter instantly and returned her attention to the least favorite of all Patrina's topics—her marital status. "Do you not want a husband?"

"My, you are full of questions."

The girl stared on expectantly.

Patrina sighed. "No." That was the far easier reply than, the truth—she would never have a husband. Nay, she could never have a husband.

Charlotte settled back in the squabs. "All women want a husband."

Nay, women didn't necessarily *want* husbands as much as they *needed* husbands. It was the sad way of their world. It allowed little place for error in a young lady's life. For when a mistake was made, as Patrina had committed, then the resulting consequence was the uncertain life of spinsterhood, dependent on the continued generosity of her family members.

"Not all women do," she said at last.

"Hmph," Charlotte said. She looked out the window and then swallowed audibly as the carriage drew to a slow stop in front of a white stucco townhouse.

The driver jumped down from the box and hastened to open the door. He reached inside the carriage to hand Charlotte down.

The girl hesitated a moment, and continued to worry the flesh of her lower lip. She turned to address Patrina. "Will you come with me?" she blurted suddenly, unexpectedly. "To see Papa. Will you tell him that I became lost and..."

Patrina leaned over and place her hands over Charlotte's fingers, and gave them a light squeeze.

"Lady Patrina," Mary gasped, with a pointed glance in her direction.

Patrina hesitated a moment, and then gave her head a slight shake. She could not abandon the girl without at least seeing her properly settled in her home. Nothing remained of Patrina's own reputation; though there were still her sisters' good names to consider, the Tidemore sisters would well-understand the need to see Charlotte safely returned to her father. She accepted the servant's offer of assistance. "Thank you, Farnsworth," she said quietly. She waved him off and helped Charlotte down.

As they made the march toward the expensive Mayfair District townhouse, Charlotte had a white-knuckled grip upon the green ribbon in her free hand. How many times had Patrina and her sisters worn the same guilty looks on their faces, and had that same panicked glimmer in their eyes?

She and Charlotte hadn't even climbed the fourth step when the door opened, and the butler, a wizened gentleman with serious-looking eyes, said, "By the good saints in heaven, Lady Charlotte."

"Hullo, Russell," Charlotte returned with a wide, and what Patrina suspected was her most winning smile. She loosened her hand free and sprinted inside. The butler hesitated, his gaze alternated between Charlotte and Patrina. Charlotte motioned her to enter. "This is Lady...?"

"Patrina Tidemore," she supplied. The handful of

lords and ladies passing by the fashionable area shot her rabidly curious glances and she stepped inside the Marquess of Beaufort's house, grateful when the butler closed the door behind her.

"My lady, please allow me, on behalf of the marquess to—" The servant's words of gratitude ended abruptly as a shout bounced off the white Italian marble and filled the foyer.

She glanced up to where the marquess stood at the top of the sweeping staircase. He bounded down the stairs, and she took a nervous step backward, never having borne witness to such volatile emotion in a person's eyes.

"Charlotte," he thundered.

Patrina opened her mouth prepared to launch a defense of the small girl but then the towering marquess swept his daughter into his arms. He crushed her to his chest; his large hands stroked small circles over her narrow back.

"Hullo, Papa," she said as sweetly as if she were requesting the last cherry tart at the bakeshop.

"Miss Airedale returned without you. Where have you been, Charlotte? What have you done?" Even as the questions tumbled unchecked from his lips, he glanced over his shoulder. His gaze caught and held Patrina's. "You." The one word utterance came harsh and gruff.

She should be chilled by the coldness underscoring his tone and yet some indefinable emotion radiated from the green irises of his eyes, warming her. "Me." Then all hint of gentleness faded so that she wondered if she'd merely imagined the crack in his icy veneer. She folded her arms to shield herself from the heated intensity of his fathomless gaze.

Little Charlotte prattled on, seeming oblivious to the undercurrents of tension. "Lady Patrina found me, Papa." She angled herself away from him and held up the green ribbon in her fingers. "And she bought me this."

"Did she?" All the while his gaze remained fixed on Patrina.

She attempted to read something, anything in that 'did she', but his aloof tone matched the hard glimmer in his emerald eyes. Patrina shifted back and forth on her feet. She had nothing to feel guilty of. She'd done nothing wrong. Mayhap everything right where his daughter was concerned. How dare he make her feel... like...like...the exact way the rest of the *ton* would treat her? Patrina dipped a stiff curtsy. "My lord, I'm pleased Charlotte has come to no harm. I trust," she looked at Charlotte and held the girl's gaze. "She will not do something as reckless as wandering off again"

A slight frown marred the corner of his hard, perfect lips. She braced for a lofty tirade directed her way, but instead, he shifted his focus to his daughter. "Did you wander away from Nurse?"

"I did. But only with the very best of reasons. You see Nurse..." Her gaze met Patrina's, and then she dropped it to her father's immaculately folded white cravat.

"Nurse what?" he prodded in a tone belonging to a man accustomed to having all his wishes met.

"Nothing," Charlotte finished on a whisper. "I wandered away. I wanted to see the miniature theatres and I thought to steal away a moment, and...I'm sorry, Papa." She turned wide, tear-filled eyes up to her father.

All hardness melted from his unyielding eyes like the snow under a too-warm sun. "It's fine, sweet."

Patrina snorted.

His frown swung back in her direction. "Is there something the matter, my lady?"

If he didn't gain a better control of his unruly children, then there would be a whole lot of somethings the matter for the marquess in the future. Patrina could name four specific examples for him. Or four specific *someones* to be exact, whose names began with the letter P. Instead, she said, "It is not my place."

"Not your place," he repeated back, a bite in his words.

Perhaps she should have said nothing. Now, as she considered her previous response, she could certainly see how the whole 'it is not my place' sounded a bit condescending and judgmental. Having been judged quite extensively these past months, she'd rather not be guilty of the same charges. "I'm sorry," she said. "I..." She dropped another curtsy. "Good day, Charlotte. My lord."

Patrina sent a silent thanks skyward for the astute butler who cleverly interpreted her need to escape, and opened the door. She sailed out, and gave another thanks for her faithful driver, who stood with the carriage door open in wait. She made it no further than the edge of the street.

"My lady?" A deep baritone drifted out to her.

She stiffened and remained with her gaze fixed on the carriage door, knowing passersby studied both her and the Marquess of Beaufort with great interest, knowing her name would surely be bandied about by those who still remained in London for the holiday season, and hating that she'd become something of a spectacle for the *haute ton*.

"Lady Patrina," the marquess said quietly in deep, serious tones, for her ears alone.

She'd braved Albert's deception, her subsequent ruination, and the pain of her family's disapproval. She could certainly face this frowning bear of a man. Patrina forced herself back around to face the marquess. "My lord?"

He tugged at his lapels, the first hint of the marquess' discomfort. "I wanted to thank you, for helping Charlotte today. I do not find myself often in one's gratitude—"

"I don't want your gratitude," she interrupted. She winced as soon as the waspish words left her lips. Is this what Albert had allowed her to become? A bitter, shrewish woman?

The marquess' eyes darkened to the shade of the green-nearly black of a jade stone she'd once seen at the Egyptian Museum. They were sinful and dark and yet, at the same time conjured memories of the lush rolling hills of her family's country estate when she'd run with wild abandon through the land.

The ghost of a smile played about his hard lips. He cleared his throat. "Nonetheless, you have it, my lady."

She dug her toes into the soles of her slippers at having been caught scrutinizing him.

Before the scandal, Patrina would have been capable of a witty rejoinder, or a prettily polite response. That young woman might as well have been dead and buried by Albert's cruel hands. More than ever, she wished to be the same innocent, carefree woman from before, instead of this defensive, fractious creature she didn't much like. Because then, perhaps she and the marquess might not be these two combative souls spewing bitterness at one another.

The marquess stood stoic, and in his elegant black coat sleeves, seemingly unaffected by the chill of the winter air, clearly awaiting a response.

"Forgive me," she said softly. It seemed they two did that often when in each other's company. "Charlotte is a wonderful little girl and I'm so very glad I was there to help her. She is spirited," she said, thinking how she herself hadn't been all that different when she'd been an eight-year-old girl. His eyebrows knitted into a single line. Patrina fisted the fabric of her cloak. "Protect her, my lord." *Protect her from her future flights of fancy, protect her from the cruel grasping of those around her.* She turned back to the carriage.

"Wait!" A child's voice broke the winter still.

Patrina spun around.

Little Charlotte came hurtling down the steps, sailed past her father, and skidded to halt in front of Patrina. "My lady," she said, slightly winded from her efforts.

She dropped to a knee and brushed a hand over the girl's cheek. "What is it, sweet?"

"Ices," she blurted.

Patrina angled her head.

The girl turned to her father. "We must repay Lady Patrina. She saved me, Father. She found me and brought me home. Such a deed must be repaid with ices."

Patrina rose awkwardly to her feet. Warmth filled her heart. Had she herself ever been so sweetly innocent? Even before her own father's death?

The marquess came over and settled a large palm on Charlotte's shoulder. "Char," he began.

The little girl interrupted him. "But when we do good deeds, you always take us for ices at Gunter's. Lady Patrina did a good deed."

He cleared his throat and glanced momentarily over at Patrina. "It is too cold for ices, Char." He returned his focus to his daughter.

Patrina had been dismissed. She bit down hard on her inner lip in abject humiliation. It shouldn't matter that Lord Beaufort did not want to escort her to Gunter's. After all, she took great pains to avoid Society's scrutiny any more than necessary. So why did this keen regret dig at her?

Charlotte folded her arms across her chest with a mutinous expression on her determined face. "It is never too cold for ices, Papa." She looked to Patrina. "Isn't that right, my lady?"

Heat blazed her cheeks. "Er—"

"See," Charlotte supplied for her. "It's never to cold for ices."

"I didn't say that," Patrina said with bemusement. She glanced over at Lord Beaufort and tilted her chin up. "I never said that."

Another smile played upon his lips. "I know, my lady."

She tipped her head. He really was quite magnificent when he smiled. Not the cold, emotionless beauty of a stone statue he'd put her in mind of at their first meeting, but someone very real, and very much full of life.

"But Papa," Charlotte pleaded, jerking Patrina back to the moment. The girl tugged at her father's hand. "How can you not show appreciation for—?"

"That is enough." His softly spoken words brooked little room for argument and managed to silent the loquacious child.

She hated the deep, innocent part of herself that still longed to be invited on an outing to Gunter's. Patrina turned around.

"My lady?" the marquess called out to her.

She froze.

"Surely you wouldn't allow me to be rude, my lady?" A gentle teasing threaded the marquess' question.

She spun back on her heel. "My lord?"

He held a hand to his chest. The somber gentleman she'd come to expect had a lighthearted glint in his eyes. "Would you reject my offer of gratitude by not joining me and the children for ices to reward your efforts?"

"I didn't...." Her cheeks warmed yet again. "Oh." She'd been about to assure him she'd not assisted Charlotte for the promise of ices or rewards and stopped with the sudden realization that he merely teased.

Charlotte reached for her fingers and Patrina forced her gaze from the marquess' riveting stare. "Oh, please say you'll come. Please."

The proper thing to do would be to politely decline. What would the scandal sheets say about Lady Patrina being escorted to Gunter's with the Marquess of Beaufort and his two, motherless children?

Only... She dropped to a knee yet again. "How could I ever refuse an offer of an ice?' She tweaked the girl's nose.

Charlotte giggled. "That is splendid, my lady! Isn't it, Papa?"

Patrina glanced up to find the marquess studying her and Charlotte with his usual solemnness. He held Patrina's gaze. "Splendid, indeed." His mellifluous baritone washed over her like warmed chocolate, so very different than the curt, gruff responses she'd come to expect of this man.

As she took her leave she realized the absolute folly in accepting the marquess' offer. Yet as she peeled back the curtain to stare out at the passing snow-covered streets, a smile played about her lips.

CHAPTER 5

*W*eston remained closeted in his office. He tapped the tip of his pen rhythmically upon the immaculate surface of his oak desk.

Protect her.

Lady Patrina had encouraged him to protect Charlotte, yet, something in the deep, aching hurt in her eyes and etched in the lines of her heart-shaped face suggested she spoke of something so much more than his daughter's antics earlier that day.

Not for the first time since he'd come upon Lady Patrina at the frozen waters of the Serpentine, did he wonder at what could make a young lady so melancholy. She couldn't be more than twenty or so years, and though it seemed an eternity since he himself had been that tender age, he remembered the carefreeness of youth. He'd been very nearly that age when he'd first lost his heart to Lady Cordelia.

She'd been just nineteen, vivacious, bright-eyed, flirtatious, a diamond of the first waters—in short everything Lady Patrina was not. The subtle differences in the two women most likely spoke volumes to Lady Patrina's character. After all, as long as he'd known Cordelia, she would never have done something as plebeian as tossing a snowball, nor for that matter, personally escorting a lost child home to her family.

The gold brocade curtains fluttered, and his pen froze mid-tap. He glanced up, and dropped his pen.

"I wonder what I should do with Charlotte for giving me quite the terror today," he said into the quiet. He tapped a finger along his chin. "Perhaps I should take away her desserts through the end of the Christmastide season."

A gasp met his ponderings, followed by boyish snickering.

Weston leaned back in his seat and rested his forearms on the sides of his chair. "Then Daniel must certainly be punished, too."

The little imp from behind the curtain giggled.

His son stomped out and glowered in Weston's direction. "Whyever would you punish me? She's the one who left her nursemaid." He jabbed his finger at the gold brocade.

Protect her, my lord.

Weston quirked an eyebrow in Daniel' direction. "But as her brother, it is your responsibility to protect your sister." Where he could. Though, Lord knew he charged the boy with a difficult task. Especially considering that Weston had done a rather deplorable job in protecting his children from hurt at their mother's hands.

Daniel scuffed the tip of his shoe along the ivory Aubusson carpet. "But she was looking at gowns, Papa. Gowns," he said with a more pointed emphasis.

Charlotte shoved aside the curtains and raced out. "I wasn't looking at gowns. I was looking at a toy theatre." She clapped her hands together and a wistful expression settled on her face. "Oh, Papa, you should have seen it. It was magnificent. It had—"

"Papa doesn't care about your toy theatre," Daniel snapped. Charlotte and Daniel proceeded to argue, their voices increased in volume.

"That is enough," Weston said quietly. They immediately went quiet. He stood. "Now, I gather there is a reason you two have hidden away behind my curtains?"

Brother and sister exchanged a look. "Ices," Charlotte said on a frown.

"Beg pardon, Char?"

She stuck a foot out and tapped it on the floor "You promised to take Lady Patrina and us for ices. You know, for saving me," she said, drawing out those last three words.

"Only ninnies eat ices in the winter," Daniel muttered.

His sister shot a glare at him. "Then *you* don't have to have one." She dusted an imaginary speck of dust from her white frock. "You may stay in the schoolroom with Nurse and we'll go for ices."

"Why do you get an ice anyway? You're the one who left Nurse." Brother and sister proceeded to shout over one another.

"Silence. Silence!" Weston repeated with more firmness when they continued to argue. They fell quiet with Daniel favoring his sister with a pointed glare. He perched his hip on the edge of the desk. "Charlotte," he began softly. "It's not appropriate to take Lady Patrina for ices."

She wrinkled her brow. "Whyever not?"

He scrubbed a hand over his face. Because, if he wasn't careful, the young lady with her kind spirit and regard for his children, posed a threat to the steely guard he'd erected about his heart. "Well, for one, it is the winter and a gentleman must not be in the company of a young lady in the confines of a carriage."

Charlotte scratched at her head. "Why?" Yes, his

spirited daughter would certainly require close attention in the years to come.

"Because improper things can occur," Daniel said on a drawn out sigh.

"What kind of improper things?"

Oh, for the love of all that is holy. He glowered Daniel into silence and then directed his focus to Charlotte. "A gentleman can't just go escorting any young lady for ices." Ices might as well constitute dances and afternoon calls and a real showing of interest. All of which he could not offer a lady.

"Why?" Charlotte persisted. If she'd been born a male, she could have out-argued all the barristers in England combined.

"Because you just don't do it," Daniel interjected. "You only take ladies for ices if they are your intended or wife. And she's not his wife or his intended."

The hard edge in his son's words gave Weston pause. When had his son become this cynical, angry young child? And how had he not realized it before now? Gone was the grinning, dimple-cheeked boy with a fun spirit. In the wake of his mother's betrayal he'd become this combative, older-than-his-own-years boy before him now.

"That's not necessarily true," Weston said.

"See," Charlotte said, that one word more gloating than had she run around the room and waved her arms, yelling 'victory'. "So, then we shall go for ices?"

Weston swiped a hand over his face. "Char—"

"But you said we would," she cried. "You promised Lady Patrina, and gentlemen do not go back on their promises." Her words rang damning and true in the space of his office.

He sighed. His seven-year-old daughter had the right of it. He walked over to his desk and pulled out the top drawer.

"What are you doing?" Charlotte asked suspiciously.

He was trying to figure out how in hell he was going to manage collecting three frozen ices from Gunter's and discreetly carrying them to a more appropriate place. He withdrew a sheet of velum. "I'm sending an invitation to Lady Patrina."

His daughter clapped her hands together in pleasure, the sound drowned out by Daniel's groan of annoyance.

A gentleman did not go back on his promises. That referred to offers of marriages or ices where honorable gentlemen were concerned. Weston sat down to pen his note. It would seem they were to have ices. That was of course assuming Lady Patrina still cared to join him and his troublesome children.

CHAPTER 6

*P*atrina sat at the windowseat. She stared down into the white-covered streets below. Perhaps it had been the rather snowy weather to account for it. Or perhaps he'd merely been indulging his small daughter. Or even yet, mayhap he'd merely been teasing Patrina. But the Marquess of Beaufort had never sent 'round his invitation.

She touched her fingers to the frost-stained window and trailed her nail over the frozen flake upon the cold windowpane. And if she were to be honest with herself in this moment, she could admit to an overwhelming sense of disappointment.

Not because she dearly loved muscadine ices, which she did. Rather, too much. But because after months of being withdrawn from polite Society, she'd embraced the opportunity to go out, if even just for a bit and pretend she was still a respectable young lady with an interested suitor.

She considered the marquess' usually frowning countenance and smiled wistfully. Granted, the marquess in no way could be mistaken for an interested suitor. Still… She'd enjoyed the dream of it.

Logic had driven home the very obvious fact. Young, respectable ladies did not join gentleman in closed carriages for ices at Gunter's and sensible people didn't ride in phaetons in the cold of winter.

A knock sounded at the door and she glanced over.

"May I come in?" Her sister-in-law hovered hesitantly at the entrance of the room.

Patrina swung her legs over the side. The rustle of her skirts filled the quiet. "Of course."

Juliet ambled into the room, at an uncharacteristically awkward gait due to her swollen belly. She walked over to the window seat and lowered herself carefully onto the floral cushion. She grimaced.

"Are you all right?" Patrina made to rise, prepared to fetch her brother.

Her sister-in-law waved her off. "I'm fine," she assured her. "Please, whatever you do, do *not* fetch, Jonathan."

Patrina grinned. "He's been unbearable?"

Juliet returned her smile. "He's been unbearable."

Yes, Jonathan seemed to be constantly hovering at his wife's side. Who would have imagined her rogue of a brother would have fallen in love so hopelessly and helplessly with his wife? But then, with her kind heart and resilience, it was rather hard not to love Juliet.

Her sister-in-law placed her hand on Patrina's, as if having sensed the direction her thoughts had traveled. "I don't think I shall ever live a day without guilt and pain for what my brother has done to you," Juliet said softly.

Patrina winced, hating any and every mention of Albert Marshville "It isn't your fault, Juliet." How many more times would she have to assure the other woman she didn't hold her to blame? Oh, she would trade her right hand for the restoration of her good name so she might make a respectable match. But she'd never trade away any of her sibling's happiness for that of her own.

"Your brother was so certain he could silence all hint of scandal," Juliet said wistfully.

"Then, that is Jonathan." He seemed to think he could assure each of his sisters' every happiness.

"That is Jonathan," Juliet murmured in reply.

Gentlemen possessed an arrogance far greater than the clear logic of a woman. Patrina had known with the same certainty Juliet surely had, that Patrina's actions that day nearly a year ago would be the ruin of her.

"You deserve more than this."

Patrina managed a smile.

Juliet gently squeezed her fingers. "Might I ask the question I've longed to, Patrina? You needn't answer."

She stared on expectantly and her sister-in-law continued on a rush. "You are so lovely, so vibrant and talented. Why, Albert?"

Her heart warmed at Juliet's faithfulness. This was why she could never begrudge Juliet her relationship with that fiend. "He paid me attention." She grimaced as she realized what an absolute ninny she'd been trading everything for someone who merely 'paid her attention'. She lifted her shoulders in a slight shrug. "I'd had two Seasons. In that time, do you know how many suitors I had?" She didn't wait for an answer. "None. Not a single gentleman brought me flowers or wrote me sonnets or…" She allowed her words to trail off and looked out the window a long while in silence.

Then Albert had come along. And he'd teased her and flirted shamelessly with her. He'd snipped a black curl and tucked it close to his heart—his black, empty heart. And for that alone, she'd lost her pride and good standing in Society.

"I believe there is a gentleman who will be brave enough to overlook a youthful mistake."

"Then you're a fool," Patrina said harshly. Her cheeks warmed. "Forgive me," she said, immediately contrite.

Juliet waved her off. "I'm not too proud to admit I've been a fool more than once in my life." She squeezed her fingers yet again. "This, however, is not one of those times."

She was saved from answering by the sudden appearance of the butler. He bore a silver tray. "Lady Patrina, you have a letter," he shouted into the room. Her heart paused and then resumed a hard, fast beat. She scrambled out of her seat.

"It was delivered..."

She all but sprinted across the room and accepted the missive. "Thank you, Smith! That will be all." She gave him a pointed look.

The astute butler might be deaf, but he was still savvy. He glanced over her shoulder to where Juliet sat, surely staring with curiosity, clearly wondering who'd sent 'round a note to Lady Patrina Tidemore.

Patrina's heartbeat sped up again. She could think of only one such gentleman.

Smith bowed and took his leave.

Unable to resist the almost painful curiosity, she looked down at the missive in her hands. She studied the black wax of an unfamiliar seal. Her fingers fairly twitched with a desire to unfold the note, but... She glanced up quickly. Juliet remained seated at the window, head angled, a question in her eyes. Patrina folded her hands behind her back and concealed the letter from her sister-in-law's worried eyes. "None of this is your fault, Juliet," she said, returning to the matter that had brought her sister-in-law here.

"I would see you happy," she murmured.

The note fairly burned in her hands. The closest to happy intrigue she'd felt in a long while. "I am happy."

Now. I'm happy right now. Happy because with the arrival of a note, something uniquely different had happened to her in a world where everything had become so entirely the same.

Juliet placed her hands on the small of her back and arched it as though in pain.

Patrina frowned. "You're certain you are well? I shouldn't—?"

"No! You should not get your brother," she said. She walked over and kissed Patrina on the cheek. She ran a searching gaze over her face. Concern radiated from the depths of her violet-blue eyes. "If you need anything, Patrina, if there is anything you require of me, you know you must simply ask."

This offer referred to the note she still held out of her sister-in-law's line of vision. It spoke volumes to the woman's character that she didn't flat out distrust Patrina following the incident with Albert... "Thank you," she said softly.

The other woman looked as though she wished to say more, but then gave a nod and took her leave.

Patrina waited several moments after she'd gone and then turned her attention to the letter in her hands. She slipped a finger under the wax seal and opened the note. Her heartbeat sped up.

Lady Patrina,

Forgive the delay in my sending round this note. Alas, after your departure, I placed a good deal of consideration into the difficulty in coordinating a respectable trip for ices in the heart of winter.

Her heart slipped with disappointment and she paused mid-way through the missive. Of course, the marquess had surely realized the scandal in being associated with one such as her, after she'd left. She forced herself to keep reading.

After I discussed the logistics of such an endeavor,

considering the rules of etiquette and weather, with my very insightful *children.*

Her lips twitched at the heavily emphasized word.

I ask that you brave the winter weather tomorrow afternoon at the edge of the Serpentine where we first met, so that I might repay your good deed (my dear Charlotte's words) with ices from Gunter's. If you, of course, do not wish to brave the cold, you just need send word. I'll have to brace Charlotte for the disappointment...

She sighed, foolishly and wished some of that disappointment had been held by the gentleman himself—

And of course, myself

Your humble servant.

W

And, of course, myself. Those four words, so very important.

Patrina folded the note, an unwitting smile played about her lips. There had been no need to add that last 'myself', and yet he had. Perhaps she was reading more into those four words and a comma, but—

"What is that?"

She shrieked and spun around. "You scared me."

Poppy stood, framed in the doorway, a suspicious glimmer in her eyes. "What is that?" she repeated.

"What is what?"

Her sister shoved away from the door and advanced on Patrina like she were Boney on his march through the frozen wilds of Russia. "Why did I scare you?" She screwed her mouth up. "The last time I scared you was when..." Patrina braced for the hesitantly spoken words about Albert Marshville. "You went and made a cake of yourself over *that...man.*"

A bubble of laughter escaped her lips.

Her sister started. She stared unblinking at Patrina. "Did you just laugh?"

"I did."

The girl folded her arms across her chest, the suspicion deepening in her gaze. "You've not laughed in..." She tossed her hands up. "I don't remember how long. And when you do laugh, well it's not this...this...loud," she said on a skeptical whisper. "It makes one wonder..."

Patrina stared at her expectantly.

Her sister let out a sigh of exasperation. "Must you and Jonathan always do that?" she mumbled. "You're supposed to ask me."

Patrina bit the inside of her cheek to keep from laughing at poor Poppy's indignant expression. "Ask you what, dear?"

Poppy pointed her gaze to the ceiling. "You're supposed to ask *what* it is that makes one wonder."

She took pity. "Very well," she said, schooling her features. "What does it make you wonder?"

"Why you're so happy. Not because I don't want to see you happy," she continued on a rush. "And not because you shouldn't be happy, that is to say." An uncharacteristically serious expression settled over the girl's face.

"What is it?" she asked gently.

"I just..." Poppy's gaze wandered to a point beyond Patrina's shoulder, and then she returned her focus to her older sister. "I just want to make sure you aren't a ninnyhammer again."

God love Poppy for being direct with her when the whole world still tiptoed around the mistakes of her past. She stood there a moment and thought about the marquess, with his gruff demeanor but obvious love for his children. "I promise not to be a ninnyhammer," she pledged.

Though, if she was being truthful with herself for the first time since Albert's betrayal, Patrina could admit she still believed in and longed for her own true love.

Perhaps she really was a *ninnyhammer*, after all.

CHAPTER 7

*A*s Weston's carriage rattled along the quiet streets of London, but for the winter still, there was little else quiet about the day.

"I don't want to go meet Lady Patrina for silly ices," Daniel grumbled from the opposite bench.

Charlotte shook her head with a worldly-wisdom better suited a matron than a mere girl. "Oh, do hush. You'll enjoy the ices immensely."

"I won't."

"You will," Charlotte shot back. "Papa, tell him—"

"Both of you, please, stop arguing." Perhaps even at their young age they detected the thread of desperation in his words because brother and sister exchanged a look and fell remarkably silent. With a sigh, Weston sat back in the comfortable squabs of his seat. Charlotte burrowed against his side, with a total lack of regard as to how her shifting figure threatened the very existence of the sugary ices from Gunter's.

He frowned. He'd never considered the mere three miles between Berkeley Square and Hyde Park an over-long carriage ride. However, with the precariousness of the ices in his and Daniel's hands, he began to doubt he'd arrive with Lady Patrina's ice fully frozen. A bit of cream dripped onto his hand.

Or even frozen. It seemed more likely melting was to occur.

His son frowned and appeared torn between tossing his ice to the carriage floor and licking it. In contrast, Charlotte's eyes danced with excitement. She bounced up and down on the seat, in this instance the light-hearted child he remembered.

She clapped her hands. "I'm ever so excited to see…" She blushed. "Er…the frozen river," she finished lamely.

Daniel glared in his younger sister's direction. The look in his eyes suggested his thoughts had traveled the same path as his father's.

Weston gave his head a slight shake. He'd not embarrass his daughter with the transparency in her plans for he and Patrina. Why, Charlotte could easily displace Lady Jersey and Lady Cowper with ease from their respected places as matchmaking Society hostesses.

The carriage slowed to a halt and he gave a silent sigh of thanks when his driver threw the door open.

The servant smiled at Charlotte. "My lady."

Charlotte placed her fingertips in his gloved hand. "Why, thank you ever so much, Alan."

Weston blinked. He'd been schooling his children on being kind and appreciative to the servants since they were old enough to speak. Cordelia, however, had been nasty and vile to the staff and had seemed to view their presence as if there to please her and not much more than that. She had left a nasty imprint on Charlotte and Daniel.

"Did you just say thank you?" Daniel called after his sister as he hopped out of the carriage.

Weston climbed out with a murmur of thanks for the servant.

"Of course, I did." Charlotte patted the side of her

bonnet in a manner better suited to a seven-and-twenty year old woman and not his seven-year-old mischief-maker. "One must be kind to the servants. After all, imagine how very difficult life would be without them." She spoke the words as though reciting them back from memory.

As Weston and his children made their way through the peacefully empty grounds of Hyde Park, their boot-steps disturbed the untouched soft blanket of snow. His breath stirred puffs of white in the cool air, a silent testament to the madness in visiting Hyde Park in this godforsaken cold. With frozen ice treats, no less.

He glanced down at his children. They trudged slowly, he lightened his stride so that his small children were better able to match his pace.

Charlotte wrinkled her nose. "It's cold."

"Well, this was your idea," Daniel groused, nudging her in the side with his elbow.

"Be careful, Daniel, or you'll drop them. Papa, tell him he'll drop them."

Weston eyed the two ices in his gloved hands and for the briefest moment, considered stuffing the ice cream into his ears to drown out the constant bickering between his children. It had become a good deal worse in the years since his wife's death. In his attempt to prevent them from further hurt after their mother's betrayal and death, he'd allowed them to become hoydens, running wild, their ill-behaviors unchecked. Guilt burned in his belly as he confronted the accuracy in Lady Patrina's earliest charges against them.

Yet...as they continued on through Hyde Park, off toward the Serpentine, he glanced down at Charlotte. She'd thanked his driver when she'd only just recently viewed Alan and all the other members of his staff as mere servants. What would have caused such a radical change in his...? They walked about a slight crest and a red-cloaked figure pulled into focus. The breath went out of him as Lady Patrina shoved back her hood. She smiled at his children and raised a hand in greeting. Then her gaze moved to his. Their stares locked and Weston froze, at the sheer beauty of her, warm and effervescent amidst a cold, iced-over world.

"Lady Patrina!" Charlotte squealed and hurtled the short distance over to the young lady's side.

Not something. Someone had wrought this change in Charlotte. He'd wager Lady Patrina's influence accounted for his daughter's kindness toward Alan. He stopped before her. She continued chatting with Charlotte.

His daughter gesticulated wildly, her words running together. "Muscadine, but I said you most certainly preferred…"

Patrina laughed and leaned closed, and lowered her voice to a not-so-conspiratorial whisper. "I don't think one can truly have just one favorite ice."

"We got you muscadine," Daniel blurted and then kicked the snow as if embarrassed to have been pleasant and agreeable to a young lady.

Patrina turned her attention to his son. "Well, muscadine is quite my favorite. It is ever so delightful." She winked at Charlotte and then raised her gaze to Weston. "Isn't that right, my lord?" Merriment danced in her eyes.

You are delightful.

He expected to be horrified by his almost moonsick fascination of the young lady, but he'd never before known a woman like her. Young ladies did not fawn over young children or escort said troublesome mites home when they became separated from their nurse. Most young ladies would have placed the child in a carriage, with a servant, and sent them on their way.

That is if they'd so much as noticed the misplaced child in the first place.

"Papa?" Daniel nudged him in the side.

"Hmm? Oh…er, yes." Weston cleared his throat and resisted the urge to tug his cravat. "Delightful. It is delightful," he finished lamely. Wordlessly, he handed Charlotte's burnt filbert ice over and his daughter took it with eager fingers, all the while he remained fixed on the faintest cleft just under Patrina's full-lower lip. The oddest desire to place his lips to that slight indentation filled him.

Patrina angled her head and studied him.

Weston held out a hand. She hesitated and then placed her fingertips in his. "Lady Patrina." He bowed his head and held out the glass he'd purchased from Gunter's. "Your muscadine ice."

She stared wistfully at the sugared treat and then wet her lips like the kitchen cat about to swallow the canary and accepted the glass with its small silver spoon tucked in the softening treat.

"Papa, can we play?" Charlotte pleaded.

He waved his hand. "Take care to avoid the river," he instructed. Though one of the coldest winters since the Thames had last frozen, one could never be certain of the ice's thickness.

Daniel and Charlotte sprinted off. They waved their spoons about the air, they way they might a vicious rapier, yelling playfully at one another between bites of their ices.

Weston and Patrina stood at the frozen water's edge in companionable silence. How very unlike Cordelia and most other Society misses who seemed to think it their responsibility to fill all voids with useless chatter. "She misses her mother," he finally said.

"I imagine she does." She fiddled with the glass in

her hands. "My father died when I was just a girl and even now, not a day passes that I do not think of him."

Weston captured his chin between his thumb and forefinger. He should not ask for intimate details about her life. Such prying posed a threat to his carefully maintained world where his children were not hurt by those outside the folds of their family.

"What do you think about?"

She lifted her shoulders in a little shrug. "I wonder about the foods he liked. Did he detest chocolate the way I do?"

He glanced at the ice treat in her hands. "It is fortunate then I didn't come bearing chocolate ice."

Patrina widened her eyes. "Oh, no!" she said hurriedly. "I would have still been appreciative. I..." The rose hue of her cheeks from the cold, darkened to the shade of holly berries. "Oh, you're teasing me." She didn't sound at all upset by the truth of that.

He gentled his expression. "Yes, I was."

Patrina toyed with her spoon. She dipped the tip into her grape-flavored treat and took a bite of her ice.

"You detest chocolate? I rather imagined no one disliked chocolate."

"I do," she said around her spoon. She took another bite of her ice. "It is too sweet. I prefer a bowl of raspberries and strawberries."

As she spoke of the delectable summer fruit, he dropped his gaze to her bow-shaped, bright red lips. Desire surged through him. A longing to explore the sweetness of her mouth. He fought back a groan.

Patrina continued, seeming wholly unaware of his inappropriate thoughts and continued speaking once more about her father. "I suspect my sisters would be better behaved had he lived." She grinned. "Then I quickly realized they would have surely found different reasons to misbehave."

He grinned, forgetting until this moment how much he'd missed being happy just for the sake of being happy. His smile slipped. "I imagine he was a good parent." Unlike Cordelia who'd complained about Charlotte and Daniel since the moment she'd learned she was in the family way.

A wistful look stole over her face. "I was merely a girl when he died. Sometimes I can't quite sort out who he really was in my mind and who he really was while he lived. Does that make sense, my lord?"

"It does." Having heard the memory Charlotte crafted of the heartless woman who'd given her life, he knew exactly what Patrina spoke of. "Thank you for joining me..." He coughed into his hand. "That is to say, thank you for accompanying my family." He glanced around for Patrina's maid.

Patrina cleared her throat. "My maid is at the carriage. It seemed unfair to drag her along through the snow and ice for my own enjoyments."

Ah, this regard for servants. "I believe you spoke to Charlotte about her treatment of my servants?"

She caught her lower lip between her teeth but then squared her shoulders. "I understand it was not my place to instruct your daughter on matters of your household. However—"

"I'm not displeased, my lady," he interjected. He'd not have her believe he was a stodgy, pompous lord who'd abuse his servants.

She blinked. "You're not?"

"I'm not."

Patrina appeared deflated as though she'd been braced to defend her stance. She'd but known his daughter for a handful of days and yet, had exacted more positive change than Cordelia had managed in the course of all Charlotte and Daniel's lives.

With Lady Patrina's contemplative solemnity, it occurred to him, yet again, how vastly different she was than his late, viperous wife. Still, for the seriousness to Patrina, she always managed a gentle smile and kind words for his children. He enjoyed how carefree Charlotte was in Patrina's presence. Just as he appreciated the fleeting smiles that occasionally wreathed the young lady's cheeks whenever she was with his imps.

When it became apparent Patrina didn't intend to break the quiet, he said, "Charlotte has clearly missed the presence of other females in her life and would benefit from the gentle influence of a proper, young lady." Both of his children would.

Patrina froze, as stiff as the iced over Barn Elm tree branches overhead. Her skin turned an ashen gray to match the sky. He searched his mind for what inadvertent insult he must have dealt. "They are good children," she defended quietly. "Are they close?" The question emerged almost haltingly from her lips.

From the corner of his eye he detected the tip of her pink tongue dart out and lick the smooth cream from the edge of her spoon. He bit back another groan, wishing he could trade places with that muscadine ice. "They fight often," he said at last.

She smiled around her treat and it transformed her from serious woman to bright-eyed young lady. "That is part of being a sibling."

Filled with a desire to know more about this woman who'd slipped past the defenses he'd constructed, he asked, "And what of you, my lady?" He didn't understand this sudden, insatiable need to know more about her. "Are you close with your siblings."

"Undoubtedly," she replied, her response instantaneous. She wrinkled her nose. "Please, just Patrina," she offered. "After all, considering our relationship these past five days, I imagine we've moved beyond the category of polite strangers, my lord."

"Weston," he corrected.

"Weston," she murmured as though tasting his name on her lips like she had the frozen ice moments ago.

He paused. The sweet lyrical quality of his name upon her lips gave him pause. Their whole refined, polite world knew him as a title and nothing more and hearing her gentle tone wrap about the two-syllables of his name filled him with longing to hear her utter it over and over.

"It suits you," she said, and smiled.

They seemed to have begun as cold, angry strangers, and now? Now, the warm glimmer in Patrina's eyes made him want to forget the pledge he'd taken to never trust another woman.

Patrina continued on about her family, allowing him entry into her private world. "I am the eldest of four sisters and I have a brother. The Earl of Sinclair."

Weston paused. Sinclair. The man known as Sin. He remembered the gentleman from their earlier days. The earl was touted as an infamous rogue who quite enjoyed the gaming tables.

Clearly perceptive, the young lady hurried to assure him. "Oh, he's quite reformed, now." She ran her spoon around the perimeter of her ice.

"Is he?" he said wryly.

She closed her lips over the dash of cream. "Oh, he is." Patrina licked her spoon clean. Again.

He groaned at the erotic sight wishing she'd get on with finishing it so he didn't have bear the torturous sight of her inadvertently sensual movements.

"My mother and I had despaired of him ever settling down, but he fell in love." Something sad and wistful stole over Patrina's face.

Desire fled, replaced by an overwhelming urge to drive back the pained regret reflected in her eyes. "It must have been interesting in such a crowded household."

She grinned, and the sadness lifted. "It was certainly eventful." She took another bite and the faintest bit of ice touched the corner of her mouth.

"You have ice here," he gestured to his lip.

She colored prettily. "Here?" she murmured and used the back of her gloved hand to brush it away. Another dash of cream smeared her cheek.

His lips twitched. "Here," he murmured and withdrew his handkerchief. "Allow me." He touched the crisp, white fabric to her cheek and then the corner of her lip.

His breath caught. Or was that hers? This was madness.

Her sooty black lashes fluttered and he lowered his head, as reality slipped away and only they two remained. He longed to know the taste of her.

Playful shouts in the distance snapped him from his reverie. He jerked back and took a hasty step away from the tempting beauty. He glanced around for his children and saw them disappear over the crest, hurling snowballs at one another and laughing. "Forgive me," he said quietly.

She blinked as if she'd been spun in too many circles. "There is nothing to forgive, Weston. You've done nothing improper."

But he'd wanted to. God, how he'd wanted to. He'd wanted to take her lips under his and kiss her until she moaned with a desperate hunger for more of him.

Her chest rose and fell in a heavy rhythm and he suspected she wanted his kiss as much as he wanted hers.

He was lost.

With a groan, Weston lowered his head and claimed her lips. He dimly registered the crystal glass in her hands falling soundlessly to the thick blanket of snow at their booted feet. He slanted his mouth over hers again and again. He nipped at that too-full lower lip and when she moaned, he explored the hot, moist cavern of her mouth.

Her tongue, cool from the ice, heated his blood. She tasted of grape ice and lemon and if he could drown in the sweetness of her, he'd be content to go forever thinking of her in this moment. She twined her hands about his neck and pressed herself to him. Their tongues met in an age-old dance.

He groaned again, encouraged by her boldness and pulled her close. More than a foot smaller than his own frame, she molded to him as perfectly as if she'd been made for him and only him. *Help me, I want more of her.* Knowing now the battle faced by Adam in that garden of sin, Weston drew back. He lowered his brow to hers. "Forgive me now, then," he repeated. He should step away. He should set her from him. But he could not do either of those things. Instead, he touched his lips to her forehead.

Patrina brushed her fingers over his cheek. "There is still nothing to forgive."

He clenched his jaw. Except there was. She was an innocent young lady. "There is everything to forgive." He dragged a hand through his hair. He was not one of those depraved lords who went about kissing marriage-minded misses, in the midst of Hyde Park, no less. Weston glanced around at the snowy scape. It mattered not that the *ton* didn't tend to come out in such inclement weather and the threat of discovery was unlikely. It mattered that he'd acted in a wholly dishonorable manner.

WESTON, the 4th Marquess of Beaufort, had of course

drawn the erroneous assumption she was in fact a proper, young lady.

Patrina folded her arms to her stomach. What would a gentleman such as him say if he were to know how truly dishonorable she was? Guilt knifed at her. She'd managed to delude herself into believing it was entirely respectable to have her maid join her in Hyde Park for her daily constitution. Mary allowed her the privacy of her own thoughts, which was so very appreciated. Only now, Patrina had betrayed that trust. Just as she'd betrayed her mother. And brother. And three sisters.

And now... She gazed off at the distant crest, Charlotte and Daniel had disappeared to. The peel of their laughter spilled out into the cool, winter air. And now, by being in their presence, she posed a risk to the reputation of Weston's children.

She drew in a shuddery breath. She could not be selfish. Not again. Not as she wanted to. Not when her own self-centeredness had cost her family so much. She'd stolen from her sisters the opportunity to make, advantageous matches with good, honorable gentlemen. Shame burned like acid in her throat. She could not force that misery upon Weston's children.

"You've gone quiet, Patrina. Have I said something to offend you? If I have—"

Patrina waved a hand. "No. No. Not at all." He'd not offended her. Rather he'd unknowingly wounded her with the memory of mistakes she'd gone and made. He'd merely reminded her of the need to be truthful. "I'm...I'm just a bit melancholy at the mention of my father. What of you, my...Weston? I imagine you think of your wife quite often."

His jaw tightened. A flinty glitter sparked in his eyes. "I think of her with no real fondness."

Charlotte's infectious laughter behind them mocked

the coldness of such an admission. They paused and turned as Charlotte and Daniel darted about the snow, tossing snowballs at one another.

Burning fury laced his curt words. Under her cloak, gooseflesh dotted the skin of her arms. Questions burned her lips, but she tamped them down. She'd learned after Albert's treachery the pained awkwardness of people posing their questions; questions they didn't deserve answers to.

In the absence of any suitable reply for Weston, she said, "I'm sorry you feel that way, my...Weston."

A muscle ticked at the corner of his eye. "I imagine you think me heartless."

Patrina shook her head. "No. Not at all." Not heartless. She suspected Weston was a man who'd surely been burned by the sentiments of love—much the way she had. "I wonder as to your response, is all. Of course, it is none of my affair," she said on a rush when he opened his mouth to speak.

He chuckled, the grating sound mirthless and devoid of any real humor, belied only by the warmth in his gaze as he stared at his playing children. "You wonder because you're young, Patrina. You can't be any more than eighteen, perhaps nineteen? A lady such as you is surely filled with hopes and dreams of a future that doesn't exist as anything more than the sonnets penned by silly romantic poets. You can't know the ugliness of a faithless mother such as my children's mother." Something hard and condescending laced his heated charge, more in line with the man who'd first berated her at Hyde Park nearly a week ago.

Patrina straightened her back. How dare he presume to know what she had and hadn't experienced in her now nearly twenty-one years of life? "You speak with such absolute certainty. You speak as though you know how I live and of my experiences based on nothing more than my age and your perception of what a young lady is." No, he didn't know she'd loved and lost in the cruelest kind of way.

He scoffed. "Would you disagree with my supposition?"

"I would," she shot back. "I don't presume to know anything about your life because I see you in the park with your two children and a serious expression on your face." He might have known pain at his wife's *cruel* hands, but ultimately he'd become a parent, and now had two precious, if precocious children—two impossibilities Patrina couldn't even hope to have.

Weston studied her with such intensity she shifted on her feet. He opened his mouth, as though he wished to ask the very same questions she herself had fought back a short while ago, but then pressed his lips into a single, tight line instead. "You are correct. I should not presume to know your life. Forgive me."

Patrina gave a brusque nod, unaccustomed to others making apologies to her. She'd grown up in a noisy household among siblings who believed they were each, always in the right. A gust of winter wind stirred the untouched snow around them, and sprinkled her skirts with tiny remnants of the flakes. A stray curl escaped from the brim of her bonnet, and she shoved the recalcitrant strand back, but it only fell over her brow yet again.

"Here," Weston murmured softly. He lifted her bonnet slightly and her breath caught as he tucked the strand behind her ear, and then lowered the velvet piece back into place.

Her heart pounded wildly as she studied the chiseled planes of his face. "Th-thank you," she whispered. He possessed a hard beauty, like a marbled Adonis, so very different from Albert's stocky, non-descript plainness. Only, Albert's appearance hadn't mattered. She'd been so blinded by his false adulation.

"I wish I could ask you what causes such sadness in your eyes," he said quietly. "But I suspect you'd not answer, nor do I deserve one." He captured her fingers and turned them over. Even through the fabric of their gloves, her palm warmed at his gentle touch.

She should pull away. She should be indignant at his bold touch. But then, she'd done a whole number of things in her life that she should have done altogether differently. But he was wrong. "You deserve an answer." Because she couldn't allow him to meet her here with his children and risk jeopardizing Charlotte's future opportunity of making a match.

He lowered his eyebrows, his expression somehow probing and menacing all at the same time.

She wasn't a coward, but the words froze on her lips. She fought to free them. He made to speak. "I eloped with a gentleman," she said on a rush. Humiliated shame set her body ablaze with heated color.

His body went taut. He said nothing.

She continued before her courage completely deserted her. "Last spring. It was a colossal mistake and it is therefore in the best interest of your children, and you to avoid being seen in my presence." A sob worked its way up her throat and she disguised it as a cough. Her vision blurred by tears, she glanced down at the hole in the snow left by her now empty glass of muscadine ice. She bent and retrieved the delicate piece. Before he could utter another word, she fled, all the while wishing she'd made very different decisions in life.

CHAPTER 8

*S*mith pulled the doors open and Patrina stepped inside. Her snow-drenched skirts left a trail of moisture upon the marble floor of the foyer. She shrugged out of her cloak, awkwardly moving the crystal glass she'd fled Hyde Park with to her other hand.

The butler took the garment. "My—"

Patrina held a finger to her lips and implored the old, faithful servant with her eyes.

"Where have you been?"

She winced. Too late. Through the years, Mother possessed an uncanny sense of knowing just when her children were up to something they shouldn't be. Such motherly intuitiveness seemed heightened after Patrina's grand folly. The countess hurried down the stairs, a glare fixed on the crystal glass in Patrina's hands.

Patrina swallowed hard and managed a forgiving smile for the regretful Smith. "Mother," she said with forced cheer.

Mother stopped at the base of the stairs. She jabbed a finger at her eldest daughter. "To your brother's office." After all, Patrina's scandalous act had reminded Mother that not all her servants were entirely loyal.

413

Patrina glanced down at her damp skirts. "Might I first...?"

"No you may not. Now, Patrina."

She bristled with insult at her mother's sharp command better suited for scolding a small child and not a woman grown. Of course, she'd lost all right to be truly indignant. With a reluctant step, she followed behind her mother feeling more like one of the queen's terriers. They climbed the stairs and walked briskly on to Jonathan's office.

Mother didn't even knock. She tossed the door open and pointed her finger inside the room. Patrina sighed and entered in front of her mother.

Her brother stood with a hip propped on the corner of his desk, arms folded across his chest. "Trina," he drawled.

She feigned a bright smile and tucked the crystal glass into the folds of her skirts in a futile attempt to keep it from his sight. "Jonathan. How are you—?"

"Enough of the pleasantries," their mother snapped. "Where were you?"

She wet her lips, resenting the lack of trust but certainty understanding it. "Where was I?" She searched for an appropriate response.

Mother continued her barrage. "And what is that glass in your hand?"

Patrina blinked, her mind racing. "What glass?" She angled the crystal in a way that her skirts buried the damning piece of evidence.

Jonathan coughed into his hand. "I believe Mother refers to that particular one." He gestured lazily. "The one you've hidden in your skirts."

Her cheeks burned. "Oh. This glass."

His lips twitched. "That is the one."

"Er..." The crystal warmed in her hand as she remembered her meeting a short while ago with the marquess. Except there was nothing to say. How could she explain the urge to see a gentleman who'd first been a frowning bear of a man to the man who'd carried a crystal glass of muscadine ice beside the frozen river?

"Say something, Jonathan," Mother snapped.

"Excuse us, Mother."

Mother's eyes widened. Her mouth opened and closed, giving her the look of a trout floundering outside of water.

Patrina pressed her lips into a firm line to bury a smile that wouldn't be at all appreciated. That had clearly not been the "something" Mother had been expecting. Nor Patrina for that matter.

With a glower for her son, their mother turned on her heel and stormed from the room.

Jonathan scrubbed a hand over his cheek. "You do know she's going to be a good deal less than pleased with me?"

She sidled over to the vacant seat in front of his desk and sank into the chair. "I'm certain her displeasure with me will far outweigh any annoyance she might feel toward you."

He didn't disagree. Instead, he tipped his chin toward the damning glass. "Who is he?"

If his tone was harsh and disapproving she thought she might not answer. As it was, she'd brought too much disappointment to her brother. She sighed and glanced down at her hands. "I know what I'm doing, Jonathan. Which is nothing," she said on a rush when he lowered his black eyebrows. "There was a little girl who'd become lost from her nursemaid and I helped deliver her home."

Perhaps it was because her brother had been something of a rogue through the years, before his wife had properly reformed him, but he eyed her warily—a man who recognized there was more to the story, information she withheld. He glanced beyond her shoulder. "You know I can never forgive myself for having failed you as I did, Patrina."

She closed her eyes. "Not you, too, Jonathan." Mother, Juliet, Jonathan. Everyone blamed themselves for her actions. It grew tiresome dwelling amongst people who existed in a perpetual state of guilt. After all, she had a sufficient amount of guilt for the whole Tidemore clan combined.

He went on as a though she'd not spoken. "I didn't pay enough attention to the gentlemen striving for your attention."

Probably because there'd not really been any gentlemen desiring her attention.

"And as a result, Marshville took advantage of... of..." he cleared his throat.

"My naiveté? My foolishness?" she said in a self-deprecating tone. *My desperation.*

"Your innocence." He squared his jaw. "And I'll not have you make the same mistake again."

"I can't really make the same mistake, though, can I Jonathan?" She gently reminded him. After all, once ruined, forever ruined. The risk she danced with every time she met Weston further jeopardized her sisters' future hopes of a respectable match. That in itself should compel her to stay well-clear of the marquess.

It appeared she was the same selfish ninny she'd been nine months ago. Logic should keep her from the marquess, yet a desire to know more of him kept drawing her back to him.

Jonathan drummed his fingers on his desk. "I'm going to ask you the question I should have asked you more than nine months ago. The question that would have saved you from yourself." *That* she appreciated. His assigning her responsibility for her own actions.

"Who is he?" he asked with a bluntness that made her wince.

"It doesn't matter. I'll not see him again." Sadness pulled at her heart. Foolishly, she wished to see him again. She enjoyed his company. Welcomed that he was the only one to speak freely with her and didn't look on her with pity or scorn as the rest of Society did, family included.

She curled her toes into the soles of her slippers. Then, that had been before he'd known the truth of her past. After she'd shared it with him, she could be assured he'd fall into the pitying category or the scandalized category. Odd, she couldn't seem to place a powerfully confident man like Weston in either category.

Jonathan groaned.

Patrina started. "What?" she said with a frown.

"You're wool-gathering."

Her frown deepened. "And?"

"And I recognize all the implications of wool-gathering," he muttered more to himself. "I wool-gathered when I fell in love with Juliet." How very odd to hear her once-scoundrel brother speak so freely of his love for his wife.

She crossed a hand over her heart and schooled her features. "You may be rest assured I've no intentions of falling in love." No, it would be the height of foolhardiness to go and do something so irresponsible. Patrina stood. She reached for her glass.

"Stop," Jonathan instructed, the tone belonging more to commanding earl than affable brother.

She froze mid-motion.

"Ices in winter?" Of course he'd recognize the patent glasses given out at Gunter's. The crystal pieces were usually carried back and forth from Gunter's to waiting carriages across the street during warmer weather. Weston, however, had purchased the glass for her. And for his children, of course. "Please, don't make me ask you again, Patrina. Who is he?"

It was the please that did it. She directed her gaze to the delicate glass in her hands. "The Marquess of Beaufort." Maybe Jonathan didn't know him. She'd not heard mention of Weston in any of her Seasons.

"Beaufort."

She nodded.

"Beaufort."

Well, this repeating business from her brother certainly didn't bode well.

"Beaufort."

She wet her lips nervously. "Er…do you know him?"

"I do."

She bit down hard on her tongue to keep the questions from tumbling forth. "How do you know him?" What was the harm in asking one question?

"We moved in the same social circles at one point," he said curtly.

"What happened?" *Why did you stop?* And more… what if he'd continued his friendship with Weston? Perhaps, just perhaps he might have then been properly introduced to Patrina and there would have never been an Albert Marshville or a scandal or a—

"He fell in love."

Patrina flinched. That she'd not been prepared for. "With who?"

Jonathan seemed to be searching his mind. "A Lady Cordelia Something-or-Another," he supplied. "It was a love match."

She considered Weston's harsh coldness when speaking of his now-deceased wife. What had happened to the loving couple? "Did—?"

"You do realize for a young lady who's not at all interested in the marquess beyond returning the gentleman's son—"

"Daughter," she amended.

"—to him, you have a good deal of questions."

She screwed her mouth up tight. Yes, she could certainly see how it would appear that way. "I just—"

"Be careful, Patrina. I just want you to be happy." A muscle ticked at the corner of his eye. "I couldn't forgive myself if I failed you." Again. The word danced in the air between them, unspoken yet somehow still real.

"And you don't believe Wes..." Her brother's eyes narrowed into thin slits. "Er, the marquess," she corrected, "could make me happy?"

"No," he said flatly. "He can't. He's a dark, serious, somber, withdrawn fellow—now. You deserve better than that."

Patrina gave a tight nod and stood. She dropped a curtsy. "You have nothing to worry over, Jonathan," she assured him.

"I certainly hope not," he said under his breath.

As she took her leave she considered Jonathan's words. He seemed so confident in saying she deserved better than Weston. She staggered to a slow stop. Her pulse drummed a steady beat inside her ears. Only, what if she didn't want anything more than the Marquess of Beaufort?

CHAPTER 9

*W*eston passed a brandy back and forth between his fingers and stared down into the hearth. A roaring fire blazed within the grates, and warmed him. He braced for the not unexpected question.

"Your children need a mother, Weston." Ah, there it was. His sister, Amanda Callaway, the Viscountess Merewether usually wasted little time with her needling. Her visits usually began with the same six-word utterance.

Not, how are you doing? Never, it is a delight seeing the children. Rather... *Your children need a mother, Weston.*

He turned and held his glass up in salute, and then raised it to his lips. He took a much needed sip, welcoming the warm trail the fine French liquor blazed down his throat. "I thought you and Oliver intended to leave for your country seat for the holiday."

She slipped neatly down his path of distraction. "Do you intend to join us? I've asked you for the past three years since...since..." she waved a hand. The words needn't even be spoken. "But you've never accepted and so, of course you'd be welcome."

"We'll remain in London," he politely declined.

His sister frowned. "Very well, then." Alas, his reprieve was short-lived. "Do not try and change the subject. Your children need a mother, Weston. They're growing more and more incorrigible every time I see them."

He said nothing. In large part because his sister was loquacious enough to carry on this whole discussion by herself. In larger part because she was right. Charlotte and Daniel were becoming more and more truculent each day.

"You overindulge them. And they—"

"Do you know a Lady Patrina Tidemore?"

Silence met his question. His sister sat at the edge of the leathered sofa, unblinking. "Lady Patrina Tidemore? Lady *Patrina* Tidemore?" The slight emphasis she placed on that last Patrina suggested there was certainly more here.

He said nothing, knowing Amanda enough to know she'd fill enough of the silence for the both of them, and with answers to the questions he'd had about Patrina since they'd first met.

"Quite the scandal. Quite the scandal, indeed," she said with a flounce of her blonde curls. He thought of Patrina's earlier admission and usually one who loathed gossip; he hung onto his sister's words. "Rumors were circulated by...by..." She wrinkled her brow and seemed to search her mind for the name of the circulator of those rumors. "Some servant or another," she said with a flick of her hand. "A maid or a footman or—"

"Amanda," he said impatiently.

"Er, right. Well, this servant, whoever it may have been, claimed Lady Patrina had run off to elope, but beyond that, the details escape me. All rather scandalous."

Weston considered Patrina as she'd been at their first meeting. Somber, alone, staring out at that frozen lake. Her brown eyes, a kind of window into her private thoughts had alluded to heartache. *You speak with such absolute certainty, Weston. You speak as though you know how I live and of my experiences based on nothing more than my age and your perception of what a young lady is.* She'd been hurt more than any young lady ever should. Weston tightened his fingers around his glass, filled with the sudden desire to bury his fist into the face of that nameless bounder who'd ruined her and the faithless servant who'd sullied her name.

What had Patrina been like before the bastard had ruined her good name? He imagined a smiling, teasing, effervescent young woman. Not this guarded creature who only smiled with any real sincerity at his children.

"Why do you ask about Lady Patrina?" Suspicion underlined his sister's question.

"Charlotte became separated from the nursemaid." Wandered off, but that detail didn't need pointing out considering all his sister's talk of a mother for his children. "Lady Patrina returned her home." He chose to leave out all the other fascinating pieces of their three exchanges thus far. His proper sister would look at snowball tossing as a grave offense equal to elopement.

"That was kind of her," Amanda said with obvious reluctance. "Though in truth, I feel rather sorry for the young woman." She made a clicking sound with her tongue. "No young woman deserves to have her affections played with and her reputation in tatters as Lady Patrina."

No, indeed.

"She's not fit company for anyone, Weston, certainly not for your children."

From across the room, he detected the faintest rustle of the curtains. Charlotte poked her head around the brocade fabric, a frown on her lips. He gave his head a slight shake. She disappeared once more. The splash of color on her plump cheeks indicated outrage at Amanda's charges against Patrina. He flexed his jaw. An outrage he shared.

"That isn't to say she isn't a pleasant woman," his sister went on. "If I remember correctly, she is no great beauty but possessed a warm smile."

Amanda's casual dismissal of Patrina gnawed at him. He found he far preferred the gentle, sincere beauty of Patrina's heart-shaped face to the more obvious beauty of his late wife. His curtains were clearly of like opinion for they growled in response to Amanda's unforgiving words about Patrina.

He cleared his throat to cover Charlotte's clear annoyance from over at her hiding place.

"It has been three years, Weston. Time enough for you to mourn Cordelia's passing, and find a mother for Charlotte and Daniel." His sister, just as all of polite Society noted his withdrawal and attributed it to some foolish broken heart. They'd seen the dashing Marquess of Beaufort's whirlwind courtship of the Incomparable Beauty and only seen a love match amidst the cold, emotionless entanglements of the ton.

They didn't know, or mayhap care, about Cordelia's devotion to her lover, her plans to abandon Daniel and Charlotte, and ultimately the fleeing couple's subsequent death as they'd made off to some far-flung corner of England. Odd, the *haute ton* knew so much and yet so little of a person's affairs.

He raised his glass to his lips for another sip.

After a long stretch of silence, his sister seemed to register that he intended to say nothing further on the matter, for she stood and crossed over to him. "I want you to be happy, Weston."

"And you imagine a wife will make me happy?" he

drawled with a sardonic twist to his question. In his experience, a wife represented nothing but a headache and heartbreak.

Amanda leaned up on tip-toe and kissed his cheek. "I believe a wife will make your children happy."

Again, Patrina's face flitted to mind. He shoved the thought aside.

"And by your silence, brother, you know I speak the truth."

The curtains rustled yet again, and Amanda angled her head. "What was that?"

Weston schooled his features. "What was what?" After all, if his sister discovered Charlotte and Daniel's tendency to eavesdrop, he'd not be spared her scathing diatribe on all the ways in which he was failing as a father.

"Nothing." Amanda gave her head a slight shake. "I'd imagined I heard...nothing. And remember we would dearly love for you to join us for the holiday."

He sketched a short bow, and waited several moments after his sister had taken her leave. "You can come out now."

Daniel and Charlotte spilled out from behind the curtain. Daniel nudged his elbow into his sister's side. "You were stepping on my toes."

"It was an accident," she cried. "It was an accident, Papa."

Weston's lips twitched. "I imagine if you were both abovestairs where you're supposed to be and not hiding in my office then neither of you would have suffered wounded toes or an injured side."

Charlotte settled her hands on her hips. "But then we'd not have heard all those horrible things Aunt Amanda had to say about Lady Patrina. I think she's pretty. Don't you, Daniel?"

Daniel snorted. "Girls aren't pretty."

"Yes, but Lady Patrina isn't a girl. She's a lady. Isn't that right, Papa?"

"She certainly is, Char." And by his sister's accounts, she was a young lady with a wounded heart. Having himself known the same wounding, empathy tugged at him.

Perhaps that had been what had first drawn him to the woman who'd dared to hurl snowballs at his children. He'd recognized something inherently sad about her, largely because he recognized it in himself.

Charlotte skipped over to his desk and scrambled onto his leather seat. Seated in her stark white skirts, with her tousled golden ringlets, she had more the look of a small doll than an actual child. She swung her legs back and forth. "I think Aunt Amanda is correct." She wrinkled her nose. "Not about those mean things she said about Lady Patrina."

Weston raised his glass to his mouth. "Oh?" He took a long swallow.

Daniel slapped a hand across his eyes and shook his head back and forth. "Bloody awful idea," he mumbled.

His daughter's lips turned up in a wide smile *sans* two front teeth. "We need a mother. Especially that one," she pointed in her brother's direction.

Weston choked on the mouthful of brandy.

"My reaction exactly," Daniel said with a firm nod.

Charlotte glared in his direction. "Don't be a ninny. Lady Patrina would make a perfectly fine mother. And I think she's lovely. And she throws snowballs. And she bought me a ribbon. And—"

"All the most essential characteristics of a good mother," Daniel groused with a heavy dose of sarcasm.

Her lower lip trembled. "And she's nice," she shot back.

Pain blossomed in Weston's chest. His son might make light of Charlotte's simple list, but those details ticked off on his daughter's tiny fingers mattered very much to the girl. She'd never known a mother's love, but neither had she known what it was to have the gentle influence of a mother. His mind raced with his sister's revelation about Patrina, and the young lady's interaction with his children.

"What is it, Papa?"

He'd sworn to never wed again. His heart had died long ago. Long before Cordelia's death. He ventured it had been somewhere between the moment she'd hurled words of loathing at him and confessed she'd been carrying on with her lover and the time she'd slapped little Daniel across the cheek.

"Papa?" Charlotte pressed.

However, what if he approached marriage with a logical, clear focus? Love, emotions, and affection removed from the whole alliance. What if he wed for the benefit of his children?

Daniel groaned. "You aren't listening to her, Papa, are you?"

He downed the contents of his brandy. "Do you know, Daniel, I just might be."

CHAPTER 10

*P*atrina pounded away at the keys of the pianoforte. Her discordant version of "While Shepherds Watched Their Flocks by Night" filled the room. Sweet Poppy, ever faithful, her sister struggled to keep pace with Patrina's playing and belted out the lyrics in her flat voice.

"Fear not said he…" Patrina glanced up from the keys.

"For mighty dread had seized their mind."

"Their troubled mind," Penelope called from her spot over on the windowseat that overlooked the grounds below. "Their troubled mind."

Poppy stopped singing. "That is what I said."

"No," Prudence pointed out. "You said their mind, not their troubled mind."

"I believe I'm the only one with a troubled mind just now," Jonathan muttered.

Juliet, shot him a reproachful glance. Her hands fell to her waist, and Patrina's gaze traveled down to the swollen belly that carried their first child. Where most families of the *haute ton* retreated to their country estates for the Christmastide season, Jonathan had insisted on remaining in London close to the best doctors for Juliet's period of confinement.

Patrina's fingers stumbled over the keys, and she returned her attention to playing. Better to focus on the chords, and the keys, and the clumsy playing instead of the bitter envy twisting in her heart for all she'd never have. "Glad tidings of great joy I bring," she sang softly. Her throat seized. There was no great joy. The beauty of the Christmastide season, the absolute peace was nothing more than a grand illusion that acted as temporary veneer of goodness in an otherwise ugly world.

She jumped up so quickly, her knees knocked the edge of the bench. The delicate mahogany seat scraped the hard wood floor. Patrina's breath came hard and fast, and she rocked forward on the balls of her feet, filled with a desperate desire to flee.

"Patrina?" Poppy whispered into the absolute stillness of the room.

All at once, Patrina registered the five sets of eyes trained on her. She forced her gaze up, and then wished she hadn't. Ah, yes. Of course. The *looks*. These were the pitying kind. She detested the pitying kind above all others.

A knock sounded at the door and a sigh escaped her at the blessed intervention. Smith cleared his throat. "There is a visitor for Lady Patrina."

A roomful of suspicious gazes swung to Patrina.

She cocked her head, imagining she appeared as bemused as the gape-mouthed Tidemore siblings scattered throughout the room. A towering, golden god of a man entered the room. Her heart thumped a funny rhythm, and she reached a hand up to slow the rapidly beating organ, but then remembered herself. She let her fingers fall back to her side. "W...My lord..."

"The Marquess of Beaufort to see Lady Patrina." Smith scratched his shock of white hair. "I believe I asked the gentleman to wait in the foyer until I ascertained whether the young lady was receiving visitors," the deaf butler thundered.

Jonathan surged to his feet. He cupped his hands around his mouth and yelled, "That will be all, Smith."

"I am ever so sorry for your fall, my lord," Smith shouted back. "Is there anything you—?"

Her brother scrubbed a hand over his eyes. "I didn't fall. I, oh never mind," Jonathan said more to himself and waved off the servant.

Through the whole absurd exchange Patrina remained rooted to her spot alongside the pianoforte, her gaze trained on the perfect lines of Weston's inscrutable face. He was more beautiful than any man had a right to be. And she'd never been a lady to pay any attention to a beautiful face. Then, she'd not had the sense to pay attention to the lack of a heart in a certain gentleman, either. "My lord," Patrina repeated, detesting the fairly breathless quality of her words.

Jonathan's eyebrows dipped. A frown darkened his face.

And because he could command the King's Army with his aura of power, the marquess advanced deeper into the room as comfortable as if he himself were the owner of the Ivory Parlor.

Juliet rose unsteadily to her feet. Even with the cumbersome weight of her belly, she managed to drop an elegant curtsy. "My lord," she greeted. She looked to the Tidemore sisters, who shook their heads as if clearing away their earlier shock, and they all dropped curtsies as well.

Weston issued another bow. Through it all, he never looked away from Patrina. He somehow possessed an unholy ability of making a lady feel like she was the only woman in the world. "My lady," the greeting was issued to Juliet, yet by the heated intensity in his eyes, she knew he spoke to her.

Juliet motioned the wide-eyed Tidemore sisters over to the door. "We'll leave you to your visit." She glowered at Jonathan. "Won't we?"

Her brother hesitated, a frown on his lips, issued a short bow for the marquess, and then walked toward the door. He paused at the entrance to the room and by the concern in his hard stare, she knew he feared leaving her alone with Weston.

When they were alone, Weston clasped his hands behind his back and strolled over to her. "Patrina."

She'd thought never to see him again. Had imagined after she revealed her scandalous past, he'd give her the cut-direct just like the rest of the *haute ton*. Her mouth went dry, and because she never had known what to say in the presence of a gentleman, she said, "My lord."

Mild amusement lit his eyes. "I thought you'd agreed to call me Weston."

She had. Foolishly. Imprudently. "Weston, then," she said, as foolish and imprudent as she'd ever been.

"I..."

"You..." Her cheeks warmed as their words tumbled over one another's. "Forgive me. You were saying?"

He closed the distance between them. "I've thought of you often since you took your leave yesterday."

She dug the toes of her slippers into the floor to keep from retreating. "Have you?" Gentlemen didn't think of her. Or, they hadn't in the two Seasons she'd had. Now whatever thoughts they might have of her were surely not the proper kind.

He brushed his knuckles along her jaw. "Did you expect I should avoid you after you shared your past?"

Her breath caught at the delicious shivers that radiated out from the point of his touch. Her past. A past in which she'd been fool enough to elope and give up all hope of a proper match. She turned her palms up. "I rather expected you might, my lord. Avoid me, that is."

"Because you have a low opinion of Society?"

She managed a tight nod. "Because I have a low opinion of Society." The *ton* had given her little reason to trust the sincerity, concern, or regard of any of its noble members.

"Who was he?" he commanded.

She took a step away from him and wandered back over to her pianoforte. She thought she should feel some level of outrage at his bold inquiry. She didn't speak of Albert. Not to her sisters. Her mother. Certainly not Jonathan. Not even to Albert's own sister, Juliet. It was as though her family expected if she buried thoughts and memories of Albert it could somehow miraculously undo everything that had been done. "His name was... *is* Albert. Sir Albert Marshville," she amended.

Stop talking, Patrina Tidemore. Stop talking. Except the words tumbled freely from her lips. "After two full Seasons, I'd not..." She warmed. "I'd not garnered many," *any*, "suitors." She shrugged. "He filled my ears with empty praise." Fool that she was, she'd believed him. Patrina depressed an ivory key. "He asked me to go off with him." Patrina cringed, even now unable to believe the height of her idiocy. She took a breath and forced herself to look at Weston. "He was so repulsed by me, he'd not even kiss me." Her lips twisted with wry embarrassment. "I convinced myself his actions..." Or lack of actions. "Were born of a gentlemanly sense of honor." A little, humorless laugh escaped her. "How very ironic, no? I should be ruined, considered sullied when he never did anything more than touch my hand at polite *ton* events." Patrina expected the sting of shame in confessing just how undesirable Albert had found her. Instead, there was something oddly freeing in sharing with Weston the truth unknown by Society—a truth they'd never believe nor accept.

Weston walked over and stopped beside her. He caught a black curl and tucked it behind her ear. "He was a bloody fool, Patrina." Hot desire sparked in his eyes. "If you were mine, nothing and no one could ever stop me from taking you in my arms."

Her heart fluttered. It really was rather impossible drumming up memories of Albert with Weston near, with his fleeting touch upon her cheek.

She continued on a rush. "It was all a matter of revenge. Albert had lost property and a fat purse in a game of faro to my brother. My brother, in turn, employed Juliet, the baronet's sister, as a governess for my three younger sisters."

His expression grew shuddered. "Juliet?"

She nodded, knowing he'd connected the presence of Juliet a short while ago to the Juliet of her story. "Juliet Marshville, Albert's sister, is now wed to my brother."

That hard, stone-like set to his features indicated his annoyance.

"They fell in love," she said, a touch defensively. "She is a good woman, Weston. I would not blame her for the crimes of her brother."

The tension around his mouth eased. He ran his gaze over her face. "You are a remarkable woman, Patrina Tidemore. Most women would be consumed with bitterness and resentment."

She touched another key. "What will that accomplish? I've come to accept my circumstances." Although, she knew she lied to herself. She detested her present circumstances and wanted more, and even with the imprudent decision she'd made regarding Albert—she *deserved* more. She managed a small smile. "I don't imagine you've come here to discuss my scandalous past."

Weston captured her hand and raised it to his lips. "No, Patrina."

She furrowed her brow. "Then what—?"

"I've come to offer you marriage."

PATRINA'S HEAD remained cocked at an odd angle. She'd said nothing for—Weston glanced across the room at the ormolu clock atop the mantle—for several minutes now. He acknowledged he should have spent some time preparing his words.

Or in the very least, something slightly less jarring.

She pulled her hand free of his. "Have you come to make light of me?" The lyrical, sweet quality of her voice was belied by the hard glint in her eyes. Patrina spun away from him. She placed the pianoforte between them and braced her hands on the back of the instrument. "Because I assure you, I've dealt with far meaner, and far more vile, creatures than you."

He clenched and unclenched his hands at his side. God, how he'd wanted to hunt down the reprobate before and take him apart limb by worthless limb. "I assure you—"

She pointed a finger at him. "A true gentleman wouldn't come here and mock—"

"I didn't—"

She jabbed her finger again. "—mock me for the mistakes I've made. Not that I have much faith there are any true gentlemen in all of England."

"Have you finished?" he drawled. It was the absolute wrong thing to say. Patrina stormed out from behind the pianoforte in a flurry of skirts. She stuck her finger at his chest. He winced.

She opened her mouth, and then promptly closed it.

"Yes." She wrinkled her brow. "No. I'm not finished? What vile, loathsome, reprehensible, abhorrent cad would come here and be so very, deliberately cruel?" Well, that was certainly quite the vernacular the lovely Lady Patrina possessed. "Don't look at me like that," she snapped. "Pityingly," she said. "I neither want, nor need, your pity."

He held his palms up, in an unspoken truce "Does anyone truly want to be pitied?"

She pointed her finger as if to stick it in his chest, and he caught her wrist. He raised it to his lips and buried a kiss in the satiny smooth skin of her wrist. Her fingers trembled in his. He welcomed her body's telltale awareness of him, for it indicated he'd shaken her world just as she'd upended his.

"I've told you once before, Patrina. I wouldn't dare pity you, and neither would I mock you. Might I be candid?"

"Please," she said, eying him the way she might a thief come to abscond with her family's fine silver. Curtly.

"My children need a mother. I'm asking you to be their mother."

She folded her arms across her chest. "So, I'm clear. You want to wed me. A woman you met a mere five days ago."

"Six days," he corrected.

"Six days," she amended.

Odd, he knew the exact moment he'd seen her, and the exact number of hours to pass since he'd come upon her hurling snowballs at his children. "Yes," he said with a curt nod.

Patrina proceeded to tap the tip of her slipper in a steady rhythm. "A woman who scandalized the *ton* with her elopement." She ran her gaze over his face, as though expecting him to demonstrate a suitable level of horror and shock at her admission. He schooled his features. After Cordelia's treachery, it would take a good deal more than this slip of a young lady to shock or horrify him. "Should I continue on?" she asked tartly.

"Please." The more she spoke, the more he found out about this bold, tart-mouthed lady who'd fascinated him since he'd first seen her. "I have no desire to wed again, yet if I do not, my children would remain motherless."

A humorless smile played about Patrina's lips. "So, you would wed me to provide your children with a mother?"

He nodded. Only, the truth his mind shied away from was that he wanted her for far more than just as a parent to Charlotte and Danielle—he wanted her... for *her*. "You'd want for nothing. My only request is that you care for my children." He finished, realizing how wholly inadequate such an offer was. Any woman would want more and Patrina certainly deserved more. A pressure tightened about his lungs as he awaited her response.

She stood in silence so long he suspected she didn't intend to address his offer. He imagined outside of security, a young lady dreamed of love and happiness and laughter from a future husband. His coldly calculated offer was more an arrangement in line with the *haute ton's* well-ordered world.

She sighed. "My reputation is ruined, Weston. There would be little benefit in marrying me for the sake of your children." She paused. "Especially Charlotte."

It did not, however, escape his notice that she didn't say no, so he was encouraged. It appeared the young lady at least considered his outlandish proposal. "I'm the Marquess of Beaufort."

"My how arrogant you are, my lord." The rebuke

was softened by the sparkle in her eyes. Her lips pulled at the corners in the first, real smile he'd seen on her heart-shaped face.

He froze. The smile transformed her from rather pretty young lady to stunningly beautiful woman. He trailed his gaze over the delicate planes of her face. How had he failed to appreciate the extent of her beauty before this moment? How—

Her grin slipped. "What?"

He gave his head a clearing shake. "Charlotte is just a child. When she makes her Come Out, Society will not even remember—"

Patrina burst into laughter. "You are delusional then, my lord. The *ton* remembers scandals such as the one I'm guilty of."

Weston balled his hands into fists. He'd wager the totality of his holdings that the sole blame rested with the cad who'd ruined her good reputation. No, the innocent Patrina's one crime was tossing her love away on an undeserving bounder. God, how he detested the fiend.

Patrina cleared her throat. "I thank you for your offer, my lord, but I could not in good conscience risk your children's reputations, even if they do need a mother." She averted her gaze. "It is quite enough I've ruined my sisters' reputations." She dipped a curtsy and turned as if to leave then started for the door.

Hell, she did intend to leave. With just that perfunctory no. Weston closed the distance between them in three long strides. He laid his hands upon her shoulders. She stiffened but did not pull away. He leaned down and brushed his lips against the elegant line of her neck. "What if I tell you I want more than a mother for my children? What if I tell you I want you?"

Her body trembled and he continued to make

436

tender love to her neck with his lips. "I-I would say you're mad, my lord."

He moved his attention to the other side of her neck. "Perhaps I am, Patrina. I want you. And though you do not love me, I will give you a family of your own, I will give you children, and I will show you the pleasure to be had in my arms." He lazily turned her back to face him.

The tendons in her throat moved with her swallow.

"Marry me."

She studied him a long moment. He could practically see the flurry of questions in her intelligent eyes. Patrina closed her eyes a moment. When she opened them, he stiffened and braced for her rejection.

She gave a tight nod. "Yes, my lord. I'll marry you."

CHAPTER 11

The winter wind battered against the frosted windowpanes of her brother's office.

Patrina stared at her brother's bent head. Just as she'd been staring at it for...Her gaze strayed over to the mantle clock. Seven minutes now.

With a sigh, she looked over at her sister-in-law. Juliet stood at the edge of Jonathan's desk. She frowned at her husband.

When Patrina had been a girl of six, she'd placed ink inside her nursemaid's tea. She'd been summoned to her father's office and stood before the very desk she now stood, shuffling back and forth upon her feet awaiting the inevitable scolding.

This moment felt remarkably similar.

In fact, the prolonged pall of awkward silence was so vast she wondered if she'd not spoken the thoughts a—

"No." Jonathan did not pick his gaze up from the ledgers in front of him.

No, she'd spoken and her brother had heard. He'd merely not enjoyed hearing what she'd had to say to him. She cast a silent appeal in Juliet's direction.

The other woman placed her palms on the edge of

his desk and leaned forward. "Put your pen down now, Jonathan, and do not be a curt beast."

He tossed his pen down and glared at Patrina. "Very well. You may not marry him. Thank you for asking."

This time. He might as well have thrown those last two words dancing about the air.

She took a step closer and borrowed strength from the back of the leather chair opposite his desk. "I wasn't asking, Jonathan," she said gently.

Her brother leaned back in his chair with a glower on his usually affable face. "I didn't intervene before when I should have, Trina," he said, using her girlhood moniker. "I'm intervening now. I'll not have you wed a man you've just met—"

"Six days ago," she supplied.

"Fine, a week then. To what purpose? So he can have a mother for his ill-behaved children?"

She bristled. Though she'd held similar thoughts to Weston's children from their first meeting, for some reason, Jonathan's ill-opinion of them grated. She came out from behind the seat. "They're lovely children." Of course there was the whole business of throwing snowballs, but hadn't her sisters exhibited far more lamentable behaviors?

He shook his head and picked up his pen. "I said no. I'll find you a gentleman who will love you and take care of you and—"

A bark of laughter escaped her. "You are so very high-handed."

He tossed his pen down. "I love you," he said simply. "I failed you before. I'll not fail you again. You deserve a husband who will love you." Heavy regret laced his pronouncement.

"I lost the right to love when I eloped with Albert," she said with a bluntness that made her sister-in-law wince.

Except...Patrina thought back to earlier in the day. Warmth unfurled in her belly until she fair burned with the sheer memory of Weston's hands upon her naked shoulders, his lips on her neck. *What if I tell you I want more than a mother for my children? What if I tell you I want you?*

Her brother shoved back his chair and jumped to his feet.

"Jonathan," Juliet murmured, with a pointed look.

He raked a hand through his tousled black locks and began to pace. "What manner of gentleman would ask you to give up all hope of happiness just to care for his children?"

"You did," Juliet said gently.

Jonathan jerked to a halt. Patrina bit the inside of her cheek to keep from smiling. He stood still, unblinking. Then a mottled flush stained his neck and cheeks. "That is—"

"True," Juliet said arching a red eyebrow.

He cursed. "This is different."

"How?" Patrina pressed.

Jonathan resumed pacing. "Because...because... damn it, you're my sister and I was a worthless scoundrel. Just as Beaufort is for even daring to ask."

Juliet made a sound of protest.

He waved a hand. "It is true. I wasn't deserving of Juliet, but she managed to overlook the wrongs I committed against her. But you..."

"I want to marry him, Jonathan. I want a family of my own. And a home of my own." And if she didn't want to spend the rest of her days the sad, sorry spinster to the Earl of Sinclair remembered by her family and Society as one who'd made a great mistake that robbed her of respectability, she'd accept Weston's generous offer.

A knock sounded at the door. Smith stepped inside.

"The Marquess of Beaufort to see you, my lord." He coughed loudly. "I took the liberty of asking him to wait in the drawing room."

Jonathan scrubbed a hand over his face. "Bloody hell," he muttered either forgetting or uncaring about the ladies present. "Show him in."

Juliet took her husband's hand and gave it a squeeze. A look passed between them and he nodded once. With a smile, she walked over to Patrina. "I want you to be happy," she said quietly, the words intended for her ears alone. "And I suspect, Patrina, that you'd not marry the marquess if there wasn't more there than a desire for a family and home of your own."

Heat flared in her cheeks. She stared after her retreating sister-in-law. Patrina cared for Weston. In just six days, she'd come to miss him in his absence, smile when he was near, and Juliet was indeed correct—she wanted to wed him because there was more there. At least on her part.

Then, that wasn't altogether true. *I will show you the pleasure to be had in my arms.* She suspected everyone thought she'd thrown away her virtue on Albert. When in actuality, she was as virginal as the day she was born. Albert hadn't even attempted to kiss her. Her lips twisted wryly. That in itself should have been the only indication she needed that he'd been wholly uninterested in her.

Jonathan spoke, calling her back to the moment. "You're certain, Trina. You're certain you'd wed him."

Smith reappeared. Weston's broad-shouldered frame filled the entrance. "The Marquess of Beaufort."

Her heart pounded wildly in her chest. She smiled at Weston. He appeared so serious, so unyielding. And then he grinned. A thrill of awareness coursed through her. The absolute rightness in this decision filled Patrina. "Yes, I'm certain," she said softly.

441

Jonathan gave a curt nod and motioned Beaufort inside.

He paused beside Patrina and captured her hand. He bowed over it. "My lady," he murmured, placing his lips along the inner portion of her wrist. Most gentlemen would have gone ashen at the growl that escaped the tall, foreboding figure of her brother. Weston continued to hold her hand. He gently squeezed her fingers.

"Release my damn sister," Jonathan snapped.

Her soon-to-be intended placed another kiss as if in blatant challenge to her brother's command and then released her.

Patrina dropped a curtsy and with a smile took her leave.

THE EARL OF SINCLAIR motioned to the seat across from his desk.

Weston sat. "I want to wed your sister," he said not mincing words with the glowering gentleman who'd soon be his brother-in-law.

The other man's brows dipped. "I'd tell you no and send you to hell if I didn't think my sister would hate me for the rest of her days." He spoke as nonchalantly as if he'd offered a brandy and refreshments.

Yes, from what Weston had come to know, Patrina possessed a strength and determination that would put most gentlemen to shame. Even her powerful brother couldn't quell the woman's spirit.

"I don't like you, Beaufort," the earl continued. He remained standing, his face black like a thundercloud. Outrage fairly seeped from the other man's tautly held frame.

Weston folded his arms across his chest. "You don't even know me."

"I knew you," Sinclair reminded him. "I used to like you," he muttered under his breath. "You'd seemed like a decent enough chap." His eyebrows lowered in a threatening fashion that would mayhap terrify most gentlemen. The earl was to be disappointed. Weston wasn't most gentlemen. "I don't like that you'd wed my sister to give your children a mother. She deserves more than that."

Yes, on that, Weston would agree. Patrina deserved a good deal more than a man like him. She deserved love and a union based on nothing but mutual affection and warmth. His hand burned with the remembrance of her fingers in his. Then, there would be plenty of warmth.

"Get that bloody look off your face, Beaufort," Sinclair snapped.

He grinned, taking a perverse pleasure in riling the imperious earl. "What—?"

"You know the damned look." The earl cursed roundly. He strode over to the sideboard against the far left corner of the room and poured two glasses of brandy. He carried one over to Weston. "What do you know of my sister?"

Weston accepted the drink. He rolled the glass back and forth between his hands. "I know about Marshville," he said quietly. He stared into the amber depths of his drink wanting to know more, *needing* to know more…and yet appreciating any further telling belonged to Patrina.

Sinclair's mouth tightened. "The bloody bastard ruined her. Hurt her. I'll not see her hurt again."

The earl's admission hit Weston with the same force of a punch being driven into his mid-section. "I have no intention of hurting her," he spoke with quiet conviction. He'd come to Patrina intending to offer her a marriage of convenience, but now, he could admit there

443

was more. He wanted to be the gentleman Patrina deserved. Wanted to restore her smile, fill her days with laughter. Make her forget there was ever a heartless cad by the name of Albert Marshville who'd disabused her of her gentle innocence.

The earl took a long swallow and grimaced. "But you will hurt her," he said. "Sooner or later you will. She'll grow to care for you and you'll not return those sentiments."

He clenched and unclenched his jaw. Sinclair was wrong. Weston cared for Patrina. He could admit that to himself. Though he didn't love her, he would do right by her in every other way. "I'm not Marshville."

"There is something to be said for that," his soon-to-be brother-in-law muttered.

He went on. "But I'll give her the protection of my name. She'll want for nothing."

The earl stared into the contents of his glass. He swirled the brandy in a small circle. His lips pulled in a grimace. "I wanted more for her than this." He finished the remainder of his drink in a single swallow. "As there are no other prospects, this will have to be enough," he said more to himself.

Weston remained silent as the protective brother grappled with letting go of his sister to an unworthy man.

At last, the earl looked up, a hard glint in his eyes. "If you hurt her, I'll kill you." He set his glass down hard and reclaimed his seat. "Shall we discuss the terms of the contract?"

CHAPTER 12

A short while later, Weston strode up the handful of steps to his townhouse. His butler pulled the door open, and cleared his throat.

"My lord, your sister, the Viscountess Merewether arrived a short while ago. I took the liberty of showing her to the drawing room."

He shrugged out of his cloak. "And the children?"

"Are abovestairs attending their lessons," the servant replied, accepting the cloak.

Weston gave a nod of thanks and continued down the corridor toward the drawing room. He hadn't known what he'd expected in terms of his meeting with Sinclair. He understood the earl's reservations. As a father, Weston would have snarled and sneered at any bounder who'd had the ill-sense to present such an offer to his daughter. All assurances Weston had given the other man had been met with wary silence.

He rounded the corner and continued down the long hall. Surprisingly, he found the whole and absolute truth to his promise. He'd told himself he'd sought Patrina out and offered her marriage following his children's deplorable behavior in the park and his sister's constant reminders of their need for a mother. In truth,

445

the lady's effervescent spirit had become a flash of light in his oftentimes dark, lonely world. Oh, he loved his children. Yet, every day he lived with reminders of his wife's faithlessness and the heartbreak he'd known after her treachery. He'd convinced himself all women were duplicitous, faithless creatures. Ah, God...he'd pledged to never love again. Only, with Patrina's good-ness, spirit, and convictions, she'd forced him to ac-knowledge just how very different she was than all others.

Weston paused beside the doorway of the drawing room. He braced his palms upon the walls and pressed his forehead against the cool, silk wallpaper. In this short span of time, she'd slipped past his defenses, shat-tered his ugliest perceptions of women.

He shoved himself from the wall and took a steadying breath. So, Sinclair and the world would see any union between Weston and Patrina as nothing more than a match of convenience. They'd not see a woman who'd shown him that not all women were ti-tle-grasping, indulgent creatures who'd place their own happiness before all else.

They'd not see how much she already meant to him. That thought in itself should terrify him...and yet...

He smiled and stepped inside the parlor. "Amanda," he greeted.

His sister sprung to her feet, a stiff smile on her lips. "Weston."

He strolled over to the sideboard and reached for a glass and decanter of brandy. "To what do I owe the honor of this visit?" He turned to face Amanda.

Her lips flattened into a tight line. "Oh, do hush. I'd identify your sarcasm from across a crowded ballroom at Almack's on the first event of the Season." He arched an eyebrow, studying her over the brim of his glass. She planted her arms akimbo. "Is there anything you'd care to mention?"

He silently cursed. She'd discovered his interest in Lady Patrina. There was no other accounting for the glare of disapproval in her eyes or the pinched set to her mouth. Weston took a sip and knowing it would infuriate her, he drawled, "Nothing immediately comes to mind."

"Your children were forthcoming." She folded her arms at her chest and drummed her fingertips upon her forearms. "*Very* forthcoming."

A little, curled head peeked in from the doorway. *Sorry, Papa*, Charlotte mouthed. Daniel yanked her backward.

Amanda ran her gaze over the room. "What was that?"

"What was what?" Couldn't his children remain abovestairs and attend to their lessons but once?

"Er, nothing. I'd thought I'd heard a..." she waved a hand. "It matters not. Charlotte mentioned that you took ices with *that woman*."

Rage thrummed through him at the icy disdain in his sister's tone. "I'll not defend my actions," he bit out.

"She is a scandalous creature who'll never be welcomed back into polite Society, Weston. A young lady does not simply elope and then return to the folds of the *haute ton*. Your reputation—"

A cold, mirthless chuckle cut into his sister's fiery diatribe. "Do you imagine I'm over-concerned with my image after...?" His gaze strayed to the doorway. Two heads quickly withdrew. He crossed over and closed the door with a soft click then strode back to his sister's side and dropped his voice to a near silent whisper, mindful of his children's presence. "Do you imagine I'm over-concerned considering the scandal of having a wife who took a lover and abandoned her children?"

Lady Patrina's only crime had been to give her heart to an undeserving cad. And yet, a woman of her strength, loyalty, and courage would be forever cast out by the *haute ton* when shameless mothers incapable of love were welcomed within the cold embrace of the glittering *ton*.

Amanda gave her head a pitying shake. "I understand you were hurt by your wife's...proclivities."

His jaw tightened reflexively. So, that is what they were to call disavowing one's marital vows and parting her thighs for lover after lover, and then forsaking all others for one bastard?

"But you must think of your children. The scandal in even being linked to *that woman*." Amanda shuddered as though repulsed by the very thought of his intended.

"Patrina," he said, gruffly.

Her mouth fell agape. "I b-beg your p-pardon?" she sputtered.

"Her name is Lady Patrina Tidemore and she does not owe Society any type of explanation." Patrina should be made an outcast while that bastard Marshville was free to move about, unscathed by his own ignoble deeds; the unfairness of it knifed at Weston's insides.

The color leeched from Amanda's cheeks. She touched a trembling hand to her throat. "Oh my goodness. You've come to care for *that wo*—" He glared. "Lady Patrina," she wisely amended. She pressed her fingertips along her temple. "Weston," she began slowly in the tone she reserved for his troublesome children. "I understand you are lonely but—"

"This isn't about loneliness. Lady Patrina has far more strength and courage than all of the Society's peers together."

"Oh, dear. Oh, dear. Oh, dear." The nervous mantra an indication of his sister's thinly held control.

He took pity. "Amanda," he said quietly. "I appreciate your concern and the love you've shown my children. But be assured, I'll not make any unwise decisions where Lady Patrina is concerned." He hadn't. "I've been rational and logical and carefully considered the implications of a relationship with the young woman." And ultimately arrived at the inevitable truth—she'd be a good wife. When most ladies would never be good wives. And what was more, he wanted her. Wanted her smile and her laughter and even her deplorable pianoforte playing—he wanted that endearing part of her, too. He swirled the contents of his glass, staring into the amber depths, the rich brown shade putting him in mind of her eyes. "She has been good to the children."

"She shouldn't be around your children," she said bluntly.

He took a steadying breath. Then, when he still felt like having her turned out, took a sip of his drink. Now that the lady had agreed, she'd be around his children every day. "Patrina saved your niece from certain harm."

"Patrina?"

"And such a woman should be treated with the utmost respect."

His sister's eyes slid closed. She mouthed what appeared to be a silent prayer and then gave a slow nod. "You know, my concern merely stems from—"

"I know," he assured her.

She leaned up on tiptoe and kissed him on the cheek.

"Is that all?" he said dryly, taking a sip of his brandy.

She drummed her fingers together, contemplatively. "Why, yes. I do believe it is. We leave for the country in two days and I didn't want to leave without ..." She blushed.

Meddling in his life. He arched a brow at her unfinished thought.

She gave a toss of her curls. "Er, Happy Christmas, then Weston," his sister said softly.

He inclined his head. "And a joyous holiday to you and yours, Amanda."

She smiled and made for the door...

"Amanda?" he called out as she pressed the door handle.

She turned back, a question in her eyes.

"I'd mention one more thing."

She tipped her head. "What is it, Weston?"

He drained the contents of his glass. "I paid a visit to the Earl of Sinclair earlier this morning. I'm to wed Lady Patrina." He bit back a grin. "Again, a Happy Christmas."

CHAPTER 13

a howling wind beat angrily against the frosted windowpane of the parlor. Patrina pulled her knees close to her chest. The roaring fire ablaze in the metal hearth bathed the late afternoon winter-darkened sky in shadows. She fanned the pages of *The Bride of Lammermoor* on her lap and stared out at the rapidly falling snowflakes.

She was to be wed. To a gentleman she'd met but six days ago. She expected the idea should terrify her, yet an absolute sense of rightness filled her at the decision. Oh, she'd told herself marriage to the marquess would fill her empty life. She'd have the children she'd given up hope of having after the scandal with Albert. She'd have a home of her own.

She set the book down on the windowseat. With his somberness and cool logic, Weston would never have been the gentleman she'd dreamed of with her girlish hopes. With a woman's eyes and a woman's heart, however, she appreciated that he didn't fill her ears with platitudes. Weston represented the logical choice of a woman staring down the life of a spinster. Yet, if marriage to him was based on little more than logic, why did marriage to Weston stir a rapid beating of her heart in ways Albert had never managed?

Patrina began to quietly sing *While Shepherds Quietly Watched Their Flocks at Night*. She trailed the tip of her finger over the cold glass and marked MofB in the frost, testing the letters of her soon to be title and then embarrassed by such a flight of fancy, hastily scratched out the slight carving.

Footsteps sounded in the hall. "What is it, Jonathan? If you've come to try and convince me not to wed him, I'm afraid you're wasting your time," she said drolly.

"The Marquess of Beaufort to see—"

Patrina's leg jerked reflexively and she knocked her book over. Heat blazed through her body as she made to rise. Except she forgot her legs were otherwise awkwardly covered by her skirts. She stumbled and pitched forward. Weston swept across the room in three long strides and caught her in his arms. The air left her lungs on a soft, whispery gasp. She swallowed hard as she took in the handful of inches between her head and the floor.

"Is there anything else you'll require, my lady?" Smith boomed, seeming wholly un-phased by one of the Tidemore girls nearly toppling onto her face before a powerful nobleman.

Weston grinned down at her. Words. She tipped her head, studying him in all his golden beauty. She really required a handful of proper words, at the moment.

"Thank you, perhaps?" he supplied on a quiet whisper.

She wrinkled her brow. Why in thunderation was he thanking her?

"The butler. I was suggesting you thank the butler." He winked.

"Er, right." Her cheeks warmed. "Thank you, Smith. That will be all."

As the old servant left, his mumbled words carried into the parlor. "Unfortunate the manner in which everyone seems to be falling."

Patrina stared up at the marquess. She really should insist he set her away, yet her body burned from the point at which he touched her, inspired all manner of fluttery sensations in her belly she could neither identify, nor care to. It was enough he still held her...and she wanted him to continue doing so.

HE REALLY SHOULD SET her back on her feet. He really should do all manner of things that were appropriate, but instead he was besieged with an unholy desire to take her in his arms and kiss her red, bow-shaped lips until she was moaning with need for him. Then the tip of her pink tongue darted out and touched her lips. He groaned.

Her brow furrowed. "Are you all right?"

"Quite," A lie. His reply came harsher than he intended. He battled his desire for this small slip of a young lady. Then, he recalled the words she'd uttered mere moments ago.

Her eyes formed wide circles in her face. "Oh. Dear." Her gaze skittered away from his. "I suppose you heard the words I inadvertently spoke aloud."

"Indeed," he drawled. It was hard to hate her brother for saying what Weston already knew to be truth. Lady Patrina deserved more than a cool, emotionless entanglement.

"He was merely..."

He quirked an eyebrow.

She sighed. "Trying to convince me not to wed you," she finished.

His heart thumped painfully in his chest. He straightened and set Patrina back on her feet. "Oh?" He affected an attitude of indifference. "And what have you decided, my lady?" He'd originally offered her marriage to provide his children a mother, and yet if that was all he wanted of Patrina, then why this cloying panic that she'd wisely changed her mind?

She touched his cheek. The delicate caress a blend of boldness and innocence. "I made my decision when I accepted your offer, Weston." Again his body thrummed with awareness of her. "I'll not change my mind."

At the resoluteness of her words, the vise-like pressure in his chest lessened. He raised her knuckles to his lips, this woman who with each meeting became increasingly important to him. He supposed the idea of it should terrify him. Oddly, it didn't. Oddly, this felt right. *They* felt right. He cleared his throat. "You sing," he said, the statement surprising the both of them.

She tipped her head at the abrupt shift in discussion.

He gestured lamely toward the pianoforte.

"Often." She waggled an eyebrow. "And poorly."

"Not at all," he insisted with the familiar ease he'd used before Cordelia had turned him bitter.

She snorted. "That is quite kind of you, but I've no delusions about my capabilities." She strolled over to her pianoforte and dusted her fingers along the keys. "I merely do it for the enjoyment it brings me. My one guilty pleasure, if you will."

He closed the distance between them and placed his palms on the top of the instrument. "And muscadine ices," he reminded her.

"Yes, of course. And muscadine ices."

They shared a smile. Something passed between them. A somberness settled in the delicate plains of Patrina's face. Her brown-eyed gaze searched his. He took a step toward her, truly appreciating for the first time the extent of her beauty. Had he ever truly considered her drab? Her eyes sparked with intelligence and her trim waist and thick black hair conjured all manner of forbidden thoughts, most of which involved Weston and Patrina in bed and her long tresses wrapped about them like a silken curtain.

"What is it?" She touched a hand to her head, displacing a black curl. "Is there something wrong?"

He swallowed hard. There was everything wrong. He desired her. Weston claimed the single strand and took it between his thumb and forefinger. He rubbed the silken strand, and then raised it to his nose, inhaling deep. Lavender filled his senses, a bright contrast to the dark, storming winter day.

"W-Weston?" The faint tremble to her words, the manner in which her lashes fluttered indicated her body's awareness to him.

He dropped his brow to hers. "You sing beautifully, Patrina."

A snorting, breathless laugh bubbled past her lips.

He stroked his thumb over her cheekbones. "You sing from your heart with joy and laughter and that passion passion is far greater than any soulless, perfectly sung melody."

Her laughter died.

Weston dropped his gaze to the tempting red flesh of her lips and with a groan, claimed her mouth. Gentle at first, and then his body registered the heat of her pressed to him; the sweet curve of her hips, the small, perfectly rounded breasts practically made for his hands and he was lost. He slanted his mouth over hers again and again. She moaned and he slid his tongue inside her mouth, tasting, exploring all of her. She twined her hands about his neck. Encouraged by her response, he began his search of her. He gripped her delicately flared hips, drawing her close to his manhood and then continued his quest. He palmed her breast. Patrina's head fell back on a desperate moan.

"Weston," she pleaded.

He weighed the flesh of first one breast, then the other in his palm. Through the fabric of her dress he devoted attention to the bud. She groaned in protest when he drew back, but he only continued his exploration of her graceful back, the curve of her buttocks. He drew her closer and angled his head down to shower her neck with kisses.

She arched into him, tightening the grip she had on his hair as though she never wanted him to stop, as though she wanted to meld their bodies as one, even as he wanted the same.

Weston wrenched away. Even as he ached to lay her down and lay claim to her body, he would not disrespect her. He imagined soldiers had waged far easier battles than this, setting Patrina from his arms.

Her smoky, dark lashes fluttered open. "Why...? What...?" The tendons of her throat worked up and down. "Did you not enjoy...?" Color flared in her cheeks, like the holly berries on mistletoe.

He pressed a kiss against her temple. "Do not be mistaken, Patrina. I want you." Her blush deepened. "I want to lay you down and make you mine, but I'll not disrespect you." She deserved more than that. He'd not fall into the ranks of the Albert Marshvilles of the world even as he wanted to trade his soul to know the pleasure to be found in her arms. Weston fished around the front of his pocket. He withdrew a small box, wrapped with a neat red ribbon.

She stared down at it and then looked to him questioningly. "What...?"

"Here," he said softly, pressing the box into her fingers. "It is for you." As his intended, he could present her with a small gift. As his future wife, he would shower her with anything and everything she could or would ever desire.

Patrina took it. She eyed the small package in her hands a moment and then worked the ribbon free with the tip of her finger. She removed the lid and gasped. Her fingers hovered hesitantly over the small snowflake pendant dusted with diamonds.

"Here," he murmured. "Allow me." He took the box from her hand and drew out the gold necklace. He turned her around and placed the chain about her neck, fastening the intricate clasp. "I thought it would serve as a reminder of our first meeting."

Patrina touched the pendant. "It is beautiful," she said softly. She turned back toward him. The ghost of a smile played about her lips. "I'll always remember that day."

He'd been an utter bastard to her in the park. He took her hands in his and raised them to his lips one at a time. "I was an arse that day." He pledged to spend their days together atoning for his callous disregard.

"You were a father defending his children," she said automatically. "It is hard to fault a man for being protective of a small boy and young girl."

"Even children who were unpardonably rude and throwing snowballs at polite young ladies?"

She snorted. "Polite young ladies wouldn't have hurled snowballs back at those children."

Weston dropped his brow to hers, imagining how very different this moment would be even now if she hadn't hurled a snowball at Charlotte and Daniel. "I'm so glad you did." Because if she hadn't, then he'd still be the harsh, angry man teeming with resentment, a man who'd never imagined he could smile again.

The door flew open so hard it knocked against the plaster wall. Their gazes swung to the entrance and they jumped apart at the unexpected appearance of a young girl.

"Penelope—" Patrina began.

The girl gulped, heavily out of breath. "Mother," she rasped.

Patrina angled her head. "I don't know where Mother—"

"Is on her way," Penelope said on another gasping breath. "I raced from abovestairs, down the servant's entrance, back up to the main floor to tell you." She looked pointedly at Weston. "She has heard from one of the servants you are currently with the marquess. Alone. With the marquess."

"Er, you said that part once before, Penny," Patrina said, a smile tugging at her lips.

Penelope rushed into the room. "It felt important enough to point it out. Twice."

Weston looped his arms behind his back and studied the younger girl with tight black ringlets, now eyeing him as though he'd come to make off with her family's silver. He sketched a bow. Her narrow gaze deepened and he was struck by the loyalty of Patrina's sisters.

"Even if you are to be married, it still isn't done." Penelope troubled her lip. "Or at least, that is what Mother has said, anyway. Therefore, you sit," she ordered Weston.

He blinked. "I beg your pardon."

Penelope jabbed her finger toward the ivory sofa. "Sit. As in you bend your legs and—"

"I gather the marquess knows the meaning of the word," Patrina said drolly.

Penelope's glare deepened and Weston knew enough to claim the suggested seat. He flashed forward another seven years and saw his own daughter in this feisty, spirited young miss. He groaned at the thought.

The two young women looked to him. He waved off their concern.

Penelope gave a short nod and looked to her sister. "Now, play." She guided her sister by the shoulders onto the pianoforte bench.

A protest sprung to Patrina's lips. "The marquess doesn't want to hear me play."

He and Penelope spoke in unison.

"He most certainly does."

"I do."

A flash of approval lit the girl's determined brown eyes.

And Patrina began to play and... sing... *God Rest Ye Marry Gentlemen?* Well, he imagined it was *God Rest Ye Marry Gentlemen*. He couldn't quite make out the particular words of the sharp verses. Her head tipped back and forth to the quick, lively, if disjointed tune. She caught his gaze and winked.

His smile widened and for the first time since Cordelia's betrayals, and the shame of her scandalous affairs, the last vestige of bitterness slipped away, replaced by the light, carefree enthusiasm he'd once had for life—restored by the spirited young lady banging away a discordant tune on the pianoforte.

"My lord, it is of course a pleasure to see you."

He moved his gaze, reluctantly away from the woman he'd make his wife to the beaming matron in the doorway. He rose and sketched a bow.

The older woman's smile deepened as she hurried forward. "Isn't my Patrina just splendid?" She glared over his shoulder at the loud snort emitted by Penelope.

Weston held Patrina's stare. "Yes. She is just splendid," he said quietly.

Her throat bobbed up and down.

"I insist you and your children join my family for Christmas."

"Oh, Mother. No, the marquess doesn't want to do that," Patrina implored.

His mother and father had died when he'd been just a boy away at Eton; but for a handful of childhood memories of he and his parents during the Christmastide season, there were very few times he could recall of a festive, happy holiday. As a husband and then father, too many years he'd spent with a smile pasted upon his face for the benefit of his children, stirring the Yule log and partaking in mince pie while Charlotte and Daniel's mother remained in London with her lover. He folded his arms across his chest. "Of course I do."

"I imagine his family has already…" Patrina paused, angling her head. The lone strand of hair fell over her eye. "You do?" She blew it back.

The countess clapped her hands. "It is settled, then!"

It was settled.

There was no place he'd rather be than with Patrina.

CHAPTER 14

he noisy chatter of the Tidemore sisters filled the cavernous space of the parlor. They sat snipping bright clips of paper and pieces of evergreen.

"I have heard the Viscountess Redbrooke has a yew tree in her house," Penelope said loudly, speaking of the young American woman recently wed to the Viscount Redbrooke, a friend of their brother. "Can you imagine a tree in one's house?"

"I should dearly love a tree in my house," Poppy said wistfully.

Penelope carried on with a wave of her hand. "She is an American, you know," she said to no one in particular. "All very exotic. A custom brought to America by the Germans." She wrinkled her nose. "That is what I've gathered from the papers."

Patrina held up the paper flowers she'd snipped and studied her work a moment, ignoring her sisters' prattling. A knock sounded at the door. She glanced over disinterestedly...and her heart kicked up a funny rhythm.

"The Marquess of Beaufort."

The chatter died as her two sisters looked toward the doorway. The girls jumped up and hurried to stack their items. Their maid rushed forward to help tidy the mess.

Weston wandered over. He waved off their efforts. "Please, carry on as you were. I wouldn't dare interrupt your pleasure."

"We're decorating for Christmas," Poppy explained. Penelope stuck her elbow out. It connected with Poppy's side. She winced. "Ow. Well, we were." With a very mature flounce of her dark curls she looked to Weston. "Would you care to help, my lord?"

On a wave of embarrassment, Patrina spoke. "Oh Poppy, the marquess doesn't..." her words trailed off as Weston slid into an empty seat and reached for a pair of scissors and a long red ribbon with gold trim. "What are you doing?" Patrina blurted.

He paused mid-snip and arched a golden brow. "I believed I was cutting ribbon for the..." He gestured to the array of items littering the table. "For the kissing bough, I presume?"

His mellifluous baritone washed over her as she recalled the taste of his lips, a blend of brandy and mint and she imagined she and Weston using that bough exactly as it was intended...

"Are you all right?" Poppy scratched at her brow.

"Fine." Heat flared in her cheeks. She fanned her burning face. "We had it sent from Jonathan, my brother's," she clarified, "country seat in Surrey. Merely for the Christmas season."

Poppy scratched her head. "Are you warm?"

"Of course not," Patrina said. Her gaze skittered toward the window that overlooked the snowy scene outside.

"Then why are you fanning yourself?" Penelope shot back.

Patrina widened her eyes and stopped at the ghost of a grin upon Weston's firm, knowing lips. She let her hand fall back to her side and smoothed her skirts. "I was merely...that is to say...it matters not." She returned her focus to Weston. "I feel inclined to point out we're not making a kissing bough, per se, but rather a mistletoe."

Weston grinned; his even, pearl white teeth gleamed bright.

"A mistletoe that is not for kissing..." *Hush, Patrina. Hush this instant.*

Poppy snorted. "Well, isn't that the point of the whole kissing bough, business?"

His smile deepened, revealing the hint of a dimple in his right cheek. Odd, she'd never noticed the faint indentation. It somehow made the hard, austere, handsome Lord Beaufort more...human. Human was good. She vastly preferred wedding someone who was human and not someone who was...well, far more beautiful than she ever could be.

Patrina cleared her throat, and striving for nonchalance, wandered over to claim the seat beside Weston. She picked up her forgotten scissors and the paper peonies.

"I have it!" Poppy exclaimed.

"What—?"

The youngest girl took Penelope by the arm and tugged her up. She proceeded to propel her toward the entrance of the room. "We shall search for my forgotten dolls." She folded her hands at her waist and inclined her head much the way their mother had done when imparting her very countess-like lessons through the years. "I'm ever too old for dolls."

"Undoubtedly," he concurred with such somberness that Patrina suspected he'd learned the proper tone rearing two recalcitrant children.

"We shall include them in the arrangement. Come along, Mary," she called to the maid. "You must help us."

The maid hesitated then hurried after the girls. Poppy stole a glance over her shoulder and winked. "We shall need the baby Jesus, his mother, Mary, and the shepherd..." The trio took their leave with determined steps.

"What of Joseph?" Penelope's voice carried from the corridor. "I imagine he played a pivotal role in the Nat..."

Blessed silence reigned. The raging fire hissed and cracked. She'd known Weston but a handful of days and suspected any proper lady would feel a modicum of nervousness in being alone with him. Perhaps she was wicked and all things improper, for she craved the intimacy of this solitary, stolen moment.

"That was rather well-done of your sister." He claimed her hand and raised it to his mouth. He placed his lips along the inner portion of her wrist.

She closed her eyes as shivers of awareness fanned out, her body responding to his gentle ministrations. "My m-mother would disagree," she said. Her lashes fluttered.

"They are lively," Weston murmured.

Those three words, an accurate testament to her sisters' personalities pulled her back to the moment, reminding her that at one time she too had been like Poppy, Penelope, and Prudence. "They certainly are." A wistful smile tugged at her lips. "I can hardly fathom I was ever so unrestrained."

THE HINT of melancholy in Patrina's tone gave Weston pause. His fingers tightened reflexively about his scissors as he carefully studied her. He tried to imagine her when she'd been Poppy and Penelope's ages, with an unadulterated laugh and an unguarded smile. And he, who'd imagined his heart deadened, and had pledged to never turn himself over to the feckless emotion called love—was filled with a sudden desire to be more, for this woman—a woman who *deserved* more. He wanted to make her laugh once again, the carefree, unfettered sound pure and joyous.

Weston gritted his teeth and damned Albert Marshville to the devil yet again for having altered her life. "My first marriage was a love match."

Patrina stiffened but remained silent.

"Oh, I'd imagined it was love." His lips twisted with wry amusement. "In considering Cordelia now, I realize I was in love with the idea of her. She was beautiful as a carved ice sculpture you might see on display, yet, to truly know her, I found out too late what was concealed underneath." Cordelia had never loved him. He'd allowed himself to believe she had, because his younger self had imagined to have something more than the cold, polite partnership evinced by his parents. But just as Cordelia hadn't loved him…he realized he'd never truly loved her. He'd loved the dream of her.

Patrina, however, was no dream. She was real amidst a world of glittering insincerity.

He continued. "I presented the best option. A marquess, when there is a dearth of dukes available to title-grasping ladies." He stared absently at the table littered with brightly colored scraps. He still recalled the precise moment when he'd come to the staggering, numbing realization that Cordelia not only hadn't loved him, but that she detested him. "The moment I learned she was pregnant with Daniel was the happiest day of my life." He shook his head ruefully. "Not very long after Daniel's birth, we learned she was carrying our next child. Do you know what my wife said to me, Patrina?"

"What did she say?" Her quiet whisper barely reached his ears.

"She said now that I had gotten two brats upon her, after her confinement, she would carry on as she pleased." And she had. After Charlotte's birth, Cordelia had gone off to London and began living her scandalous life. He expected the familiar pain-like pressure to tighten about his heart, and yet, it didn't come.

"Oh, Weston." She covered his hand with her own.

All the tension drained out of him at the satiny softness of her touch. Somehow, in the span of days since he'd met Patrina, he was oddly free. He continued his telling, removed from the pain of that night. "The night she died, she'd left me and the children. She was going off with her lover." He expected a gasp of shock. Horror. Pity. Instead, a kindred connection passed between them. Two people who'd given their love to wholly undeserving people. "Do you know why I'm telling you this, Patrina?"

She shook her head.

"After she left, I was filled with so much hostility. So much resentment and anger, it threatened to destroy me." And if his children hadn't hurled snowballs at Lady Patrina Tidemore in Hyde Park, then he imagined it inevitably would have. "Only in the last few days, since I've met you," he clarified. "I remembered how very important it is to smile and laugh." He touched a finger to her lips. "And do so as though you mean it."

Her lips parted and he continued to rub his thumb over her fuller lower lip. "You made a mistake, Patrina. You needn't spend the remainder of your days trying to atone for that one decision."

She said nothing for a long while. Then, she touched his cheek. "Thank you," she said softly.

Weston nodded and picked up the partially assembled kissing bough. He lifted the piece of evergreen with interwoven ribbons and paper flowers tied to its center. He held it above her head.

"What are you—?"

He kissed the question from her lips. Unlike the passionate explosion of their kisses before, this one was a gentle meeting of two people once broken who'd begun to put back the fragments of their life. And in this kiss, for the first time since Cordelia, he felt—free.

CHAPTER 15

$\mathcal{A}$s Patrina banged away upon the pianoforte at the chords of *Good Christian Men Rejoice*, she thought back to Weston's visit yesterday afternoon. But for her brother and Albert Marshville, she had limited understanding and experience with gentlemen. Yet, as she reflected upon the kissing bough he'd helped her assemble, she could say with a good deal of confidence she couldn't think of a single gentleman in the whole of the kingdom who'd have helped three young ladies with the fanciful Christmas décor.

The gold chain around her neck served as a warm reminder of Weston's kiss, of his gift—of him. He'd given her a necklace. Her voice raised in a discordant harmony with Poppy's. And it didn't matter that it contained diamonds and was made of the finest gold. It mattered that the fragile gift, a small snowflake, harkened back to their first meeting.

Prudence cupped her hands around her mouth and shouted into the cacophony. "You do know, I'm not certain who is more dreadful? Patrina with her high-pitched squeal or Poppy with her husky, gasping attempt for breath."

She ignored her sister's deliberate baiting. Her marriage to Weston was to be one of convenience. Such an arrangement didn't require the exchange of intimate gifts or passionate embraces. When he'd slipped the delicate piece about her neck, what was once convenient somehow signified more and her heart ached under the truth that she longed for more, craved it... but not to avoid the state of solitude she'd lived in. Weston represented her more...and all she wanted.

"I don't have a husky voice." Poppy paused mid-verse to glare at her sister, pulling Patrina back to the moment.

Her lips twitched with amusement mid-note and the key of E soared sharp.

Prudence winced.

Mother picked her gaze up from the embroidery frame upon her lap and frowned at her daughters. "Do behave, Prudence."

The girl bristled at the reprimand. "I'm merely being truthful, Mother."

"And you do remember Juliet's lesson on being truthful?" Penelope called from her seat alongside Mother. She pulled the needle through her own frame and then gave her sister a pointed look.

Properly chastised, Prudence settled back in her seat with a flourish. "I didn't intend to be mean," she said solemnly to Patrina and Poppy.

Patrina took one hand off the keyboard and waved it about. "Do not worry about it, dear."

The girls fell quiet as Patrina and Poppy resumed their song.

Give ye heed to what we say...

Prudence dropped her chin into her hand and propped her elbow onto the arm of her seat. "I merely thought if we weren't singing then we could, *should*," she corrected, "at least consider the very important, the essential *chore* of finding you a suitable wedding dress."

Four pairs of eyes swiveled to Patrina. Her fingers stumbled over the keys and she quickly dropped her stare to the pianoforte, continuing to play. Her sisters had fairly oozed girlish excitement at the prospect of purchasing a bridal trousseau. With their youthful innocence and naiveté, they didn't realize the terror in wedding a gentleman only to be thrust back into polite Society as the scandalous woman who'd had the poor judgment to elope.

"Yes. Though it does pain me to have to visit a modiste, I'd venture it is a sacrifice I must make," Penelope said and threw a hand over her brow in a flourishing manner. "Er, a sacrifice we *all* must make," she said. "That is, for the good of Patrina."

All three sisters nodded.

"I don't need a new gown." And she didn't. She only needed him. Until yesterday, when Weston had let her into the pain he'd known, she'd believed their marriage was merely a matter of convenience. Some subtle shift had occurred and she knew that just like the necklace signified more, so too did the sharing of his past. Silence met her somber pronouncement. She ceased playing and looked up at her family. "There is no need for fancy gowns and any kind of fanfare."

Poppy's eyebrows drew into a single line. "You make it sound so perfunctory." The words exploded from her lips. "Do you not care for him?" She began to pace. "What of affection? What of laughter?" She slammed her fist into her palm with each word. "What of *love*?"

Patrina blinked. She cocked her head, considering Poppy's words. What of love? "I've only just met the marquess a handful," *eight* "of days ago." And yet, the mere thought of him stirred excitement in her heart. He and his children had taught her to smile once again.

"Oh, time has nothing to do with matters of the heart," Penelope called from across the room. She shifted in her seat when everyone's gazes swung in her direction. "Well, it doesn't. Or it shouldn't."

Patrina folded her hands. She dropped her gaze to the interlocked digits. She'd fancied herself in love with Albert Marshville. After she discovered his perfidy she'd viewed her mistake with a woman's eyes; knowing with a maturity which could only come from betrayal, that she'd loved the idea of him. She, with her suitor-less Seasons, and longing for some element of romance, had been enamored with the idea of being in love. It had blinded her to Albert's true character and that would always be her pain to bear. In this way, she was more alike than different to Weston who'd loved the ideal of his late wife.

"You needn't marry him, Patrina," Poppy said with more seriousness than she'd come to expect of her youngest sister. "Jonathan would never require you to marry a gentleman just so you'll be wed."

"Of course she must marry him," Mother cried. At the uncharacteristic explosion of emotion, the daughters looked to her. She gave her head a shake. "That is, they are indeed correct, *Jonathan* would never require you to marry."

Mother, on the other hand would likely drag each one of the Tidemore sisters by their troublesome heels, to the proverbial altar if need be.

Patrina returned her attention to her sisters. "No. No, I know that," she hurried to assure Poppy. She drew in a breath. "I know Jonathan wants me to be happy." Not because he felt guilt over failing to note Marshville's vile intentions, but truly because he loved her. She didn't doubt that for a moment. "I want to marry Weston," she said simply. And she did.

"Why?" Penelope asked with a world-weary edge she'd never detected in her sister's words before.

Why, indeed?

Because he has a love for his children that filled her heart with warmth. Because he'd not peered down his nose at her with a look of scorn when she'd revealed her truth. Because he reminded her that she deserved to smile and laugh again.

Because I care for him.

The whisper of truth danced around her mind and her palms grew damp at the implication of such a revelation. She'd come to care for him. And all manner of dangerous things could come in caring for a man who'd never see her as anything more than a mother for his children. Especially a man whose embrace she burned for.

"It doesn't matter why," Mother cut into the silence. "It only matters that Patrina does want to wed the marquess."

Yes, to Mother, that much was true. To Patrina, however, the reasons she wanted to marry Weston mattered very much.

"Patrina?" Penelope prodded, gently, disregarding their mother's pronouncement.

A knock sounded at the door, saving Patrina from responding. Their gazes flew to the door in unison.

The butler coughed loudly. "My ladies, the Viscountess Merewether to see Lady Patrina."

Patrina stared blankly at the unfamiliar woman in the doorway, and then the name registered. Weston's sister.

The Viscountess Merewether peered about the room and then fixed her gaze on Patrina. The other woman's blue eyes did a momentary, up and down path over her, and from the slight sneer on her lips, Weston's sister had found her lacking.

Smith made his pronouncement again. "That is, the Viscountess Merewether to see—"

Mother jumped to her feet. She set the embroidery

down on the table beside her. A wide smile wreathed her face. "That will be all, Smith," Mother shouted to the butler. She rushed over to greet the woman.

He scratched his brow. "No, er I don't believe she fell, my lady."

"What? I didn't say..." her words trailed off and she waved a hand. "Thank you," she called after him.

The viscountess glanced back at the unconventional butler and then around at the wide-eyed girls scattered about the room. "It is an absolute...pleasure." That last word sounded dragged from the woman's lips.

Patrina's stomach flipped over at the underlying disapproval in the woman's pretty eyes. Something in the firm set to her shoulders and the hard, flat line of her lips indicated this visit was no mere social call. She slowly took her feet. "My lady." She sank into a deferential curtsy.

Her sisters, reminded of their proper deportment, fell into suit.

Mother spread her arms wide. "What an absolute pleasure to see you, my lady. May I ring for—?"

"I'd hoped I might speak with..." She glanced back to Patrina. Her lips tightened. "Your daughter."

Mother's eyes flew wide and she looked from the viscountess to Patrina and back to the viscountess. "Er, why, yes, of course," she said on a rush. "Of course!" She clapped her hands once and the other girls fell into a neat line. They shuffled from the room with more lady-like decorum than Patrina ever remembered. Mother walked over to the door. She hesitated at the entrance and then took her exit.

The viscountess glanced over her shoulder until the door clicked shut. Then she returned her attention to Patrina. She said nothing for a long while, just continued to study her with that reproachful, condescending glint in her pale, blue eyes. "You are Lady

Patrina Tidemore," she said at last. As though speaking of the infamous woman who'd eloped would forever ruin her own reputation.

Patrina bowed her head, battling back a frown. "I am," she said. "It is a pleasure to meet you, my—"

"May I speak plainly, Lady Patrina?"

She went still. "My lady?"

"Plainly?" the woman said with a wave of a hand. "I'd like to speak with you on a matter of the gravest importance. You see, mine is not a social call."

"Oh." Because really what more was there to say? Patrina wandered over to the ivory sofa. Praying the woman didn't detect the faint tremble to her hands, she motioned to the seat. "Would you care to sit?"

The woman hesitated and then took the seat directly across from Patrina. She folded her hands primly on her lap. "My brother means a good deal to me, as do his children. I'd not see them hurt."

She wet her lips. "Nor would I do anything to hurt them—"

"Ah, but you would. With your very decision to wed my brother, you've placed your own happiness, your own well-being, over the welfare of two innocent, wonderful children."

Patrina's heart skipped an odd beat. Her mouth went dry and she searched for appropriate words. Assurances that she'd be good to Weston and his children. But she could not force the words out. She fell quiet.

The woman carried on. "I'm sure you are a perfectly lovely lady." Her tone indicated anything but. "But my brother had his heart was broken by his wife. And you...well, he would be making another grave mistake if he were to wed you."

If he wed her. Not when.

For all the shame she'd visited upon her family, Patrina had felt the needles of shame thrust into her heart by the *ton*. Even as her world had crumpled around her feet, they'd looked at her as nothing more than the latest *on-dit*. Their ill-opinion, their rejection; however, was so very paltry when compared with the truthful words of Weston's sister. The woman who would be her sister-in-law.

"You can't marry him," the woman said with an almost achingly sweet scolding. "Surely you know that?"

"I..." She caught the flesh of her lower lip between her teeth. She *did* know that. Only, she'd convinced herself that if her past didn't matter to Weston, well then perhaps it didn't really matter at all. She'd convinced herself she could be happy in this formal arrangement.

"If you care for my brother. If even at all, then do not do this thing, Lady Patrina. I implore you."

That this lofty noblewoman should come here and do something as common as beg her to break off the arrangement with Weston, spoke to her ill-opinion of Patrina.

Fury stirred in Patrina's belly. She fed the simmering rage, embraced the indignation for it dulled her to this woman's scathing attack. "He asked to wed me." She firmed her shoulders. "And I intend to marry him."

The viscountess narrowed her gaze. The blue of her eyes lost to the thick, impenetrable slits. "Tsk, tsk. Never tell me you've gone and fallen in love with Weston?"

Heat burned Patrina's cheeks. She ticked her chin up a notch, refusing to be cowed by this vile woman. "I'll not discuss my feelings for Weston with you, my lady."

A muscle ticked at the right corner of Lady Merewether's lips and then she tossed her head back, a cool, mirthless laugh bubbled past her lips. "Oh, Lady

Patrina. You've fallen in love with a man who could never have real feelings for you."

Patrina curled her fists along the edge of her seat and gripped hard, filled with an insatiable urge to toss the other woman out on her ear. "I believe you are wrong, my lady." She prided herself on the steady deliverance of those handful of words.

Weston's sister shook her head, pityingly. Pity. That bloody awful emotion Patrina detested above all others. "You aren't very smart, are you, showing feelings for inappropriate men? First that Marshville fellow and now, my brother who could never love again after his Cordelia."

The truth of the woman's words sank into Patrina with an agonizing slowness, gripping her with the numbing truth. Agony tugged at her belly.

"No, Lady Patrina," she pressed, as relentless as Boney's forces marching through the barren wilderness of Russia. "We can't have you wedding Weston. You're wildly inappropriate for him and…" She paused. "You will damage his children's reputations." The hard glint faded from the viscountess' eyes, replaced by a hint of softness. She leaned over and touched her hand to Patrina's. "If you'll not think of Weston, then think of his children. Think of young Charlotte. The day will come when she makes her entrance into Society and all will remember the horrid tale of…" The viscountess' words trailed off and she cleared her throat. "I really needn't continue. I imagine you can very well supply the details."

Patrina could. She'd not for this woman. But she could. She knew the details so very well they haunted her waking and sleeping thoughts, robbed her of the ability to sleep.

Lady Merewether's visit had forced her to confront the selfishness in the decision to wed Weston. If only she and Weston were involved, then she'd jump to her feet and jab her finger toward the doorway, and order the viscountess gone.

But there was more to consider.

There was Charlotte and Daniel.

Her eyes slid closed a moment. She could not wed the marquess. Not because she didn't care about him. She couldn't marry him because she loved him and he didn't deserve to know any more misery than he'd already known at his first wife's hands. He deserved far more; he *and* his children.

She stared at her lap, swallowing past the blasted lump in her throat. With the lamentable mistake made, Patrina had already brought pain upon others. She could not so hurt Charlotte and Daniel. With their mother's infidelity, they'd already known too much of life's harsh cruelty.

"*You* must end it," the viscountess urged. "You know Weston would never rescind his offer."

Patrina glanced away, the meaning clear. She must release him from his obligation. Her lips pulled with bitterness. First a scandalous flirt who'd elope, and now a jilt. My, the papers would relish every last shameful bit of this great tale. She touched the snowflake at her neck.

"Thank you, Lady Patrina," the viscountess said, with the most warmth and sincerity she'd evinced this whole curt, perfunctory meeting. Perhaps because she saw the decision in Patrina's stare. *And knew.*

She gritted her teeth so hard pain radiated down her jawline. "I'm not doing this for you, my lady." Patrina's hand fell back to her side. The tension seeped down her body and to her toes as the fight went out of her. How could she give him up? How when he'd filled her life with such happiness these eight days, fleeting moments which, would never be enough? "I don't know what to say to him," she whispered more to herself.

"Oh, merely pen him a note," she said so breezily Patrina's head shot up with disbelief. "Thank him for his very generous offer, but tell him..." She tapped the tip of her finger to her lip. "Perhaps tell him you still love the gentleman who—"

"No," Patrina bit out. The fury and outrage laced in that one-word utterance seemed to penetrate the flighty woman's ramblings. She smoothed her palms over her skirts. When she'd manage to reign in her temper she began again. "No, my lady. I'll not tell a lie even to set your brother free. The gentleman who ruined my reputation isn't even deserving of false words of pretend love uttered even to protect your brother."

"Very well." The viscountess' lips tightened so that Patrina wondered if she'd merely imagined any earlier softness from the cold woman. "Allow me to be perfectly honest with you."

Patrina quirked an eyebrow, tired of the role of wounded woe-is-me-young-lady, pitied by young ladies throughout the *ton* and scorned by nobles across the whole blasted English isle. "You haven't already?"

The other woman pressed on. "I do not care if you profess to love another, claim tedium drove your acceptance of Weston's offer, or simply offer no explanation at all. My only concern is my niece and nephew's future happiness and that happiness cannot, will not, ever be tied to you." Her chest rose and full with the passionate fury of her deliverance. "Have I been clear?"

Patrina stood in a flurry of skirts. "Perfectly," she said coldly.

The viscountess gave a toss of her golden curls. "Thank you for speaking with me. I wish you a very Happy Christmas, my lady."

Patrina did what she'd been longing to do since the

harridan had stolen the small vestige of happiness she'd grabbed for herself in these nine months. She pointed to the door. "If you will. I'd like you gone."

The Viscountess Merewether stood. Her mouth opened and closed several times and then on a huff she swept across the floor and pulled the door open. Mother and the three Tidemore sisters spilled into the room. Weston's sister snapped her skirts and all but shoved past the array of black-haired girls.

"Well, I never!" Mother exclaimed, striding into the room. "Of all the outrageous, heinous, *impolite* things to do." By her heavy emphasis on impolite Mother clearly indicated what charge she found to be the most egregious.

"That shrew!" Prudence chimed in.

"She is horrid!" Poppy said on a cry. "Er, horrible," she amended when everyone looked to her. "This isn't a time to scold me on my use of horrid," she said quickly. "This is about—"

"*That woman*," Penelope seethed.

And just like that, the viscountess became *that woman*, joining the ranks of the Albert Marshvilles of the world.

Her sisters' loyalty tugged at her heart. Even Mother, who'd moved with an impersonal politeness around Patrina since the failed elopement, staunchly defended her eldest daughter. Her family's unwavering love made the pain of regret somewhat less aching.

Mother began to pace. "Well, it is no matter. She can demand whatever she wants a million times to Sunday. The decision is not hers. The decision is yours, Patrina."

Yes. And sadly, she'd already made it. She'd made her decision when she'd run off recklessly with Albert Marshville, and that act could never be undone. "I require paper and a pen."

Mother paused mid-stride. Her eyebrows shot to her hairline. "Never tell me…you do not intend to…"

"I cannot marry him, Mother," she said quietly.

"Of course you can!" Mother and the Tidemore sisters exclaimed.

She shook her head. "I can't. I'm ruined. And I'll not ruin his children." Even though he'd told her nothing else mattered—it did. He, Charlotte and Daniel, *they* all mattered.

"Bah, his children are young. They'll not be affected by the scandal."

Patrina would wager not even her own mother believed that effortless lie.

Poppy touched a hand to her shoulder. She started, not having realized her sister had made her way over to her. "What will you say, Patrina?"

Tears clogged her throat. She shook her head. She really didn't know.

CHAPTER 16

*W*eston picked up a roll and smeared butter upon the flaky, white, still-warm bread.

"Will Lady Patrina have a new gown?" Charlotte called from across the breakfast table.

He glanced over at his daughter and opened his mouth to speak.

"Who cares whether she has a new gown?" Daniel grumbled.

"Daniel," he scolded.

The nursemaid seated beside Daniel leaned over and whispered something in the boy's ear.

His son shoveled a heaping spoonful of eggs into his mouth. "Well, it's true," he said around the food.

"When will you two wed?" Charlotte continued. "Will she live here?"

"Surely you don't expect she'll live with her own mama," Daniel shot back.

Weston fixed a hard stare on him and his son dropped his gaze to his plate. "Yes. Lady Patrina will live here," he said to his daughter. "Will you," He hesitated. "mind having her share our home?"

Charlotte wildly shook her head. "Oh, no. Not at all,

481

Papa. It shall be good fun having a mother. Do you believe she will take me for ribbons?"

A footman entered bearing a silver tray. He carried the missive over to Weston.

"I imagine she will, Char." He absently picked the note up, studying the delicate scrawl upon the sheet. His daughter beamed and continued to prattle on. He unfolded the sheet and scanned the page. His heart thudded to a stop. And when it resumed beating, it beat a hard, painful rhythm inside his chest. He quickly reread the lines.

Dear Weston,

I wanted to thank you so much for the short, though beautiful gift of your children. Both you, as well as Charlotte and Daniel's presence, has brought me much joy in a recently dreary world.

Upon further consideration, however, with strictly the well-being of your children in mind, I must rescind my acceptance of your very generous offer of marriage.

I bid you and your family every happiness...

Signed...

Weston surged to his feet. "My horse," he thundered to a footman at the edge of the door. She'd simply sever the connection after having accepted his offer to protect his children? She did so with his family's happiness in mind? If that had been the case, she'd have realized Weston, the Marquess of Beaufort didn't do anything he didn't wish to do. And more, she'd filled his life with more happiness than he'd ever thought to know after his wife's treachery. A knot formed in his stomach. He'd allowed Patrina to believe he would enter into a union with her for the sole purpose of providing a mother for his children. He scrubbed a hand over his face. He should have told her earlier how much she'd come to mean to him. The day they'd sat piecing together the kissing bough, he should have taken her in his arms and assured her that he wanted her for her... wanted her because he loved her.

Such a revelation should riddle him with terror.

And yet, it didn't come. Instead, a semblance of calm and the absolute rightness in loving her filled Weston.

The liveried servant hurried out of the room.

"What is it?" Charlotte called. Lines of worry creased her small brow.

He forced himself to take several calming breaths. "Nothing, poppet," he assured her. "A matter of business." It had begun as merely a kind of business proposal "to see to." But at some point, it all changed. He needed her when he'd not allowed himself to depend on anyone for all these years now. He craved her smile and her laughter. He yearned for her gentle teasing. He longed to lay her down and lay claim to her lean, lithe body. And he'd be damned if he let some misguided sense of honor allow her to snuff the happiness she'd brought him.

"Is it about Lady Patrina?" Daniel, clever and world-wary for one of his tender years, asked. "She probably decided she didn't want us, too," he mumbled that last throwaway comment beneath his breath.

Weston's gut wrenched at the reminder of the pain wrought by Cordelia—a woman who had placed her happiness before that of even her own children. Unlike Patrina who would set them aside to keep them safe. He clenched his jaw. Like hell, she would. "Look at me, Daniel."

His son hesitated and then raised his stubborn, angry gaze to Weston. "Lady Patrina cares very much about you and Charlotte."

Daniel pushed the uneaten egg about his plate with his fork and gave a reluctant nod.

Now, it became a matter of convincing the young

lady that not only his children needed her...but he needed her, as well. And he'd never wanted anything or anyone more.

PATRINA SAT on the wrought iron bench and stared at the boxwoods, heavy with snow. She pulled her cloak close, burrowing into the thick woolen fabric to brace herself from the chill.

By now, Weston had surely received her note, read her wishes, and knew she no longer would wed him. She'd sent it round yesterday morning. Yesterday. She scuffed the tip of her foot into the thick snow, drawing a faint circle in the fluffy white substance.

She really didn't know what she'd expected of him. The illogical, foolishly naïve woman who still longed for love and hoped for happiness had imagined an extraordinary scenario in which he stormed from his home, ordered his horse, and charged after her. He'd declare his feelings...

Patrina shoved aside the pathetic yearnings. More likely, the marquess had realized how wholly unsuitable she was and had found a good measure of relief in being absolved of his—

Something landed hard at her back. She stiffened as the cool, wetness of snow seeped into the material of her cloak. She turned, just as another snowball found its mark at her shoulder. Outrage thrummed through her. "What—?" She leapt to her feet and froze. Her throat worked painfully at the sight of him in his towering golden glory, a shimmer of sun in the cold, wintry world.

Weston stood, some seven yards away, a snowball in his hand. He pointed an accusing finger at her. "I am displeased with you, madam."

She swallowed hard. "My lord?"

His next snowball found its mark at her opposite shoulder. She stared down at the white fragment left upon her cloak. "Did you just hit me with a snowball?"

"No," he barked. "I hit you with three snowballs."

Well. "How did you know I was here?"

"*That* is what you'd ask me?" His golden eyebrows dipped. "Your sisters were quite forthcoming."

Oh, she could just imagine. She imagined such forthcoming-ness also included mention of a certain viscountess to whom Weston shared blood. Her sisters' betrayal needled at her heart. "Why are you here?" Surely he knew she made this sacrifice for him.

"I don't want nor need you to make any sacrifice for me, Patrina Tidemore," he snapped, having clearly followed the unspoken direction of her thoughts.

If his tone wasn't so harshly angry, she would have been warmed by his—She gasped as he bent down and hastily put together another missile. "What are you doing?"

He stood. "You do not get to enter my life...the lives of my children...and then send around a letter politely refusing an offer."

"I—"

"An offer you already accepted."

She stiffened her spine at the biting fury in his clipped tones. "I'll have you know I've done this for you."

He glowered. "What have you done for me? Taken away all happiness you've brought into my life? Plunged me back into an icy, solitary world?"

His words tugged at her heart. "Oh, Wes—" He launched his snowball. It collided with her chest. She looked at the white splattered mark upon her breast. "You do know it is ungentlemanly to throw snowballs."

He took a step toward her. "Is that all you'd say to me?" Then another. His black cloak snapped angrily

485

about his ankles. Patrina glanced around at the small drifts and bushes preventing escape. Not that she feared him.

"Do you fear me?" he snapped.

Her head shot up, startled at his uncanny ability to know just what she was thinking. "Er, no." She paused. "Should I?"

The low-growl that rumbled from his chest provided very little reassurance. He reached into the front of his cloak and withdrew a familiar note. He tossed it toward her. A gust of wind caught the thick sheet and carried it several feet where it fluttered silently into the snow. "What the hell is the meaning of this?" His booming voice carried through the empty park, echoing in the stillness.

Even as her heart was breaking for all she'd never have with him, she tipped her chin up a notch. "That is a letter." His golden brows met in a single, furious line. Who did he think he was coming here and wreaking havoc on her already tumultuous mind? "I did not mean to wound your ego, my lord. Upon careful consideration—"

"By God, Patrina, if you say *upon consideration, however, with strictly the well-being of your children in mind, I must rescind my acceptance of your very generous offer of marriage.*"

She flattened her lips as he tossed her words back at her, as though they had no meaning, as though she'd not cried until she feared she'd break from penning those blasted words.

He claimed her gloved fingers in his. "Did nothing I say mean anything to you?" he demanded, his tone harsh and guttural. "I spoke to you about the happiness you've shown me. I spoke about how you've shown me how to laugh and smile again." He dropped his voice to an angry whisper. "And then you'd so effortlessly cut me from your life." Gold flecks glinted in his eyes. "Will you not say anything?" He released her suddenly and spun away. Walking away. Out of her life. And the glimmer of happiness he represented would be forever extinguished.

Patrina swallowed hard. "I-it mattered," she called after him, hating the break in her voice that signified weakness.

He froze, his back presented to her.

She fixed her gaze on the immaculate fabric of his cloak. "You must understand, with my decision, I sacrificed not only my own happiness but that of all of my sisters. Even as they don't fully realize the consequences of what I've done, the time will come when they enter Society and are spurned for their connection to me." She held her palms up, forgetting he could not see her silent entreaty. "Don't you see, if you were to wed me, the same will happen to Charlotte and the time would come when you resented me?" She sucked in a shuddery breath. "Maybe even hate me for a brash, girlish mistake I made seemingly a lifetime ago. And that I could not bear, Weston." That would destroy her in way Albert Marshville's betrayal never could have. "Please, don't leave." *Not you.*

He whirled around. "Is that what you believe? That I'm leaving you?" His long legs ate away the distance between them.

Patrina trailed the tip of her tongue over her bottom lip. "Well, I did assume... that is to say..." She sighed. "Yes." She paused, her breath coming in labored gasps. "Weren't you?"

A gust of wind whipped his unfashionably long golden strands about his eyes. "I was not."

"Oh." She studied the tips of her boots while waiting for him to say more. Wanting him to say more, *needing* him to say more. The winter wind gusted about them, dusting her cheeks with flakes of snow. The scent of him, honey and mint filled her senses, intoxicating in its sweetness. She ached for him.

He nudged her chin up with his knuckles. "I swear, Patrina Tidemore, you are the only woman I know who'd not ask me where I was off to."

"Where were you off to, Weston?"

He fished around the front of his cloak and withdrew a small packet. "Here." He held it out.

Her fingers, nearly numb with cold, shook as she fumbled through the pages. Her heartbeat paused and then sped up. Her gaze flew to his. "What does this mean?" Her words emerged as a breathless whisper.

"I went to gather the only people that matter."

Her gaze wandered past his shoulder. Her breath caught at the collection of individuals a short distance away. Her brother paced back and forth, rubbing his hands together, and occasionally breathing into his gloved fingers. Penelope, Prudence, and Poppy chatted excitedly beside Weston's children and a beleaguered, official-looking gray-haired gentleman. Then Patrina looked to her mother, smiling for the first time in nine months. And Juliet, who, in her delicate condition, really shouldn't be out, yet was here anyway. Her sister-in-law gave a slight shake of her head, as though interpreting Patrina's thoughts. A wide smile wreathed the woman's cold-reddened cheeks. Patrina swallowed and managed a nod, assuring her that at last everything was all right.

Weston took her gloved hands. She returned her attention to him. He dropped to a knee. "Marry me, Patrina. Marry me not because my children need a mother or because I'm your only option. I ask that you marry me before the only people who matter, in this place where we met. The rest of the world, the *ton*, polite Society, my sister," he said pointedly. "They can all go hang. Marry me because I love you and though you don't—"

She flung her arms around his neck. He grunted and toppled backward into the snow. Her mother's shocked cry sounded as he tumbled onto his back, catching her to him. "I love you," she whispered. In spite of the frigid winter chill, the heat of his body warmed her through the thick fabric of her cloak, a contrast to the cold snow.

"Patrina," her brother's sharp bark of disapproval carried in the wind.

Weston touched a hand to her cheek. She closed her eyes a moment and leaned into his touch, feeling for the first time in her life—cherished. "And I love you, Lady Patrina Tidemore."

In the distance Poppy cupped her hands around her mouth. "Is there to be a wedding?"

For nearly nine months she'd resigned herself to the inevitable fate of spinsterhood. Had recognized she'd bartered away her happiness, and given up on the dream of a husband. Only now she realized everything that had occurred before this moment had occurred to bring her *to* this moment. For if there had never been an Albert Marshville, then there never would have been a lonely walk along the Serpentine River, and a chance encounter with a devoted father and once-stern nobleman.

And with Weston before her, she knew she'd not wanted simply any gentleman. She'd wanted no one else but him.

A smile turned her lips upwards at the corner. "There's to be a wedding," Patrina whispered.

EPILOGUE

*P*atrina looked around the noisy table. Cook had prepared a wedding feast that reflected the Christmastide season. From plum pudding to the marchpane and roast turkey, it was a wholly festive meal, which from the laughter and exclamations was enjoyed by the children of varying ages clustered about the table. She nibbled at the edge of gingerbread.

Prudence buttered a flaky roll. "I wanted to help select a new gown," she muttered.

Mother glared her into silence.

"What? I did," Prudence persisted. "All brides should have a new gown for their wedding day."

Poppy nodded. "It's true," she said around a mouthful of bacon. "She at least—"

"Do not speak with your mouth full, Poppy," Juliet, said gently to the youngest Tidemore sister.

The girl swallowed and then patted her lips with a napkin. "She really..." She glanced to Patrina. "You should have at least had a new gown." Her gaze swung over to Weston who sat beside Patrina. "You really should have waited so she might have a new gown made." She winced. "Ouch."

Penelope frowned at her.

"Don't kick me, Penny," Poppy complained.

"My foot slipped."

She started when under the cover of the table, Weston placed his hand over hers and gave a faint squeeze.

From his other side Charlotte cleared her throat. "Why didn't you allow her a new gown, Papa?"

Weston leaned close and whispered against her ear. "We really should take care to keep this lot apart."

Patrina's shoulders shook with laughter. She took another bite of her sugared treat.

He touched his free hand to his chest and looked solemnly at her frowning sisters. "I promise to have an entire new wardrobe fashioned by the finest modiste and invite you ladies to assist your sister."

She groaned, the sound lost to her three younger sisters excited squeals and chatter. "You've done me no favors, my lord," she whispered.

He raised her knuckles to his lips and pressed a kiss there. "It seemed like the safest response for me to make."

She snorted. "Perhaps the most cowardly one."

His lips twitched.

"I don't know what all the fuss over a silly gown is anyway," Daniel mumbled. He shoved his fork around his plate.

Patrina finished her gingerbread and dusted her hands together. She eyed the untouched treat on Weston's plate and sighed with longing for the last piece of his sugared treat.

"Why don't you share with everyone again how you met my sister, my lord?" Prudence called from across the table.

Mother and Jonathan shot matching glares in her direction.

Her sister shifted in her seat. "I imagined that was a safe topic of discussion."

"It wasn't," Jonathan snapped.

Weston picked up his glass of sherry and smiled around the rim. "It's entirely fine," he assured Prudence.

Her sister jerked her chin up and looked pointedly at Jonathan. "See, he said there is nothing wrong with..." She fell silent at her brother's darkening glower.

"We met at Hyde Park," Charlotte blurted. The table went silent and looked to the little girl. Her young years likely made her immune to the intensity of the questioning stares. She dipped her spoon into her plum pudding. "Daniel hit her with a snowball," she said after she'd swallowed.

Daniel sank back in his seat. "She did it, too."

Charlotte nodded. "It was a rather impressive hit. Wasn't it, Lady Patrina?"

Patrina inclined her head. "A splendid one," she agreed. "She hit me here." She touched her lip. "And here," she touched the corner of her eye. "Fortunately, Lord Beaufort handled the situation as any gentleman would." She winked up at her new husband. Then froze. *Husband.* She rolled the words around her mind. *Husband.* He was her husband. A giddy sensation filled her heart at the idea of him belonging to her just as she belonged to him.

Penelope propped her elbows on the table and sighed, pulling Patrina from her musings. "He defended you."

"He scolded her," Daniel said with his first grin of the day.

Weston frowned, but Daniel was encouraged by the interested stares from the table around him. "Papa of course defended us. He reminded her that a lady shouldn't throw snowballs at children."

Mother sat forward in her seat. "You threw snowballs, Patrina?"

She winced at the high-pitched squawk of her mother's voice. Her mother spoke with the same shock as when she'd scolded her for eloping with Albert. "Er…" Well, she'd rather suspected being wed to the marquess she'd be spared Mother's mothering. Apparently not.

Charlotte and Daniel nodded in unison. "She did."

"She is ever so good at it, my lady," Charlotte said with only a seven-year-old girl's appreciation.

A flurry of discussion ensued, led by Daniel and Jonathan, as to the best snow to be used for making snowballs.

Weston leaned over and said something to Charlotte. She nodded once and then her small fingers closed around the fork. She speared a piece of cold ham and proceeded to eat. He picked up his gingerbread. "I should be grateful you didn't realize the extent of their mischievous ways until after you'd agreed to marry me," he said wryly, waving the confectionery treat close to her lips.

"Are you bribing me, Weston?"

Gold flecks danced in his eyes. "It is a bit past a bribe now that you've wed the father of the troublesome pair. I would shower you with jewels and trinkets instead to show my appreciation for your wedding this marquess at Christmas."

"I don't require jewels and fripperies." With a smile she plucked the gingerbread from his fingers. "Surely you have realized the truth by now."

He lowered his head, his lips so close they nearly brushed her ear. "The truth?" Warmth spiraled through her being at his nearness, heated her blood, and set her ablaze from the inside out just thinking of becoming his marchioness in every sense of the word.

She turned and touched a finger to his lips. "I would marry this marquess any day of the year."

The End

Coming October 25, 2016 by Montlake Publishing:
"The Rogue's Wager", Book One in Christi Caldwell's
brand new Sinful Brides series!
The Sinful Brides features ravishing tales of London's
gaming hell rogues—and the women who love them.

MORE IN THIS SERIES

ABOUT THE AUTHOR

BIOGRAPHY

Christi Caldwell is the bestselling author of historical romance novels set in the Regency era. Christi blames Judith McNaught's "Whitney, My Love," for luring her into the world of historical romance. While sitting in her graduate school apartment at the University of Connecticut, Christi decided to set aside her notes and try her hand at writing romance. She believes the most perfect heroes and heroines have imperfections and rather enjoys tormenting them before crafting a well-deserved happily ever after!

When Christi isn't writing the stories of flawed heroes and heroines, she can be found in her Southern Connecticut home chasing around her feisty five-year-old son, and caring for twin princesses-in-training!

For first glimpse at covers, excerpts, and free bonus material, be sure to sign up for my monthly newsletter! Each month one subscriber will win a $35 Amazon Gift Card!

THE ART OF KISSING
BENEATH THE MISTLETOE

TANYA ANNE CROSBY

PROLOGUE

SHROPSHIRE, DECEMBER 1823

"*B*en!"

The single word was, indeed, a rebuke, but rather than hold in its timbre any true censure, it was gentle, forbearing, and filled with good humor.

"You simply cannot go about dangling mistletoe from your greasy fingertips," she said. "'Tis... unseemly."

"Why not?"

"No respectable lady will ever accept such a rude proposition—most certainly *not* your precious Amanda."

Alexandra Huntington had known Benjamin Wentworth for most of his life, and despite that he looked like a man, at sixteen, he was hardly more mature than a five-year-old—mischievous and easily bored, endlessly seeking the mysteries of life in a bowl of Plum Pudding. In response, he turned his top hat over, careful not to allow the contents to spill onto her mother's carpet.

"This," he said, "is a hat—H.A.T." He assumed the tone of a staunch professor. "Fingers..." He wiggled his digits in front of her. "...have an entirely dissimilar sort of form, like this," he said. "You must really learn this if you intend to depict them." He tried to peek at her sketch, and she shielded it from him, rolling her eyes.

"Really, Ben. I am *not* drawing *any* part of the human anatomy." She lowered her nose to her sketch book, trying desperately not to notice that impish twinkle in his eyes. "I am attempting to represent something else entirely."

"What's that?" he asked with a note of disdain. "Flowers?"

Alexandra twisted her lips into a grimace, and her delicate brows pinched in disapproval. "Perhaps," she said.

A lifetime of watching Ben tease his sister for her bluestocking tendencies had taught Alexandra to keep her own predilections well hidden. And it wasn't merely Ben she had to worry about. She daren't ever flaunt her passions for fear that her mother and father would empty their bookshelves. According to her father, it was not within a woman's purview to trouble her pretty head with matters of academia. And, according to her mother, there were more important matters to be concerned over—namely, the full and tireless pursuit of making certain one was not left upon a shelf. Although Alexandra did know a few fortunate young ladies whose fathers had agreed to allow them tutors or private schooling, she was not one of them, and the closest she might ever come to any particular scholarship was through her friendship with Claire. However, despite that Claire's father and mother had been quick to allow their offspring to do whatsoever their hearts desired, Ben was not quite so merciful with his sister.

Yes, indeed, she was drawing flowers, but it was *not* for the reason Ben might suppose. She had a keen interest in botany and horticulture, and someday, she desperately hoped to convince her father to build a proper conservatory.

But really, it wasn't that she didn't find such great delight in the thought of kissing Ben Wentworth, it was this: There was only one reason he was harassing Alexandra for a kiss, and it wasn't at all because he loved her. And here was the hopeless dilemma: Lexie *did* love him.

Desperately, incontrovertibly, and without reason.

Silly though it might seem, she often dreamt about having Ben's babies—all the while she sat listening to him prattle on and on and on about Amanda Butterfield's soft, golden hair and her all-too-kissable lips.

"Flowers are *boring*," he said in complaint.

"Go bother Claire."

"She is reading."

"So?"

"She will box my ears."

Alexandra began shading a leaf. "And so will I."

"No, you won't."

"I will," Alexandra said, trying very hard to ignore his diablerie, but it wasn't easy. She returned to her sketch, reinforcing the serrated edges of her rose leaf. Sadly, this was supposed to be the Red Rose of Lancaster she was depicting, but you couldn't tell its color shaded only with pencil. However, it didn't matter, because unlike the White Rose of York, which was quite distinctly white, the *Rosa Gallica Officinalis*, the Red Rose of Lancaster, was really quite pink—as pink as her cheeks must be this instant, with Ben staring at her so intently. "Go away," she demanded.

"Only one," he reasoned. "Please!"

"No."

"Please, Turtle Dove! I should very much like to kiss you."

Alexandra stopped drawing, leveling him a look. "Why?"

"Why what?"

"Why do you wish to kiss me?"

For a very, very long moment, the cat seemed to have caught Ben's tongue. He thought about it at length, then drew out a sprig of mistletoe to inspect it. "Why not?" he argued, and he shrugged. "Really, if you never wish to do it again, you might simply go wash your lips, and never think of it again."

That was hardly true at all. One kiss might ruin her for years to come. "It's not *me* you wish to kiss," she told him smartly. "And, at any rate, there must be rules for kissing beneath the mistletoe and you are disregarding every single one." She tilted her head, studying the Viscum album, elsewise known as common mistletoe. The transparent little drupes weren't truly berries at all. The plant was entirely hemiparasitic in nature—like more than half of London—depending on a host to survive. Although... she tilted her head to better examine it... she did wonder why they were so transparent, and what medicinal qualities they possessed. In another life, she would have dearly loved to have been an apothecary, although, alas, women were not afforded such opportunities.

Ben's look was utterly defiant. "What rules?"

"Just rules," she said, hitching her chin.

"Bloody Norah! There are no rules," he argued, plucking up the sprig of mistletoe and wiggling it about so that all the berries jiggled. He grinned. "*We* shall make the rules!"

Alexandra couldn't help herself. She giggled— mostly because Ben was delightfully enthusiastic over the prospect of kissing her. And, at this point, he had already leapt out at her behind a plant, hung his mistletoe over her head under his father's top hat, ushered her into a corner where he'd pinned a sorry sprig to a lamp, and she could plainly see that he wasn't going to give up.

Really, what harm would there be in a simple kiss?

Much harm, according to her mother. It could be her ruin. She was very nearly a woman now, with a woman's form. And Ben, too, was changing, his body firming, his shoulders widening, his whiskers sprouting, and his eyes so full of yearning that it spoke to Alexandra in very, very private places... places she dared not even allow her thoughts to linger.

And yet... this was Ben.

What, after all, was her greatest desire?

"Come on, Turtle Dove... it's only a kiss," he argued. "One wee kiss. No one need ever know, and truly, don't you want to know what it feels like to kiss a man?"

Alexandra gave him a little smirk. "*You* are not a man yet, my Lord Wentworth. You are still only a very annoying *boy*."

The youthful mischief in Ben's stark green eyes transformed mysteriously, filling with dark promises that gave lie to her words. "Think so, do you?"

Dangling his mistletoe, he dared her, and for an instant, Alexandra wasn't sure...

Benjamin Wentworth certainly didn't behave like any grown man she'd ever met—not at all like her ill-tempered father. He was eternally curious, waggish, and if she pretended to be so blithe as he, it was only because she very desperately craved a lasting connection with him. And nevertheless, to date, he wasn't all that different from the young boy she'd come to know and love—quite unlike his sister Claire, who'd gone directly from being a baby to a very sober adult, leaving Alexandra and Ben to be silly together.

"Very well," she said, with a feigned sigh, and she put her sketchbook down on the settee, then laid her pencil atop it. "Only one," she declared. "And then you'll leave me be?"

Ben's brows lifted waggishly, but he nodded, very clearly delighted. His eyes shone with a devilish joy that made her heart skip two beats and flail like a turtle on its back.

Abandoning her drawing altogether, Alexandra stood, smoothing her hands down over her skirts, suddenly feeling very timid, when in fact she had never been so at odds in Ben's presence, ever. Her palms grew damp, her tongue suddenly felt too thick for her mouth, and it stuck like fish glue to the roof of her mouth. And then, despite Ben's insistence over this kiss, he stood looking like a bump on a log, and for the longest time, they stood together, staring... neither breaching the distance between them.

BEN DAREN'T LOOK AWAY.

Swallowing convulsively, he stood drinking her in— the delicate freckles atop the bridge of her nose, the sparkle in her whiskey-colored eyes. If he spoke incessantly about Amanda Butterfield, it wasn't because he liked her. In truth, he thought she was a witless chit. And though Alexandra often had her head in the clouds, speaking to him about the silliest of things, he very much liked the way her mouth moved, no matter what she was saying, and he could watch her talk for hours.

In fact, he liked *everything* about her... the way those flecks in her eyes seemed to twinkle like fairy dust whenever she was happy, the way her nose scrunched whenever he revealed things that were only meant to shock her, the way—he swallowed—her breasts rose and fell when she was even the tiniest bit breathless... precisely as they were doing... right now...

It was all Ben could do to keep his eyes on her face.

"Well?" she said, and he dropped the hat in his hand, never bothering to hang the mistletoe over her head. She'd said yes, and the last thing he intended to do was lose the chance to kiss her over some stupid ritual. Rules, or no rules, when it came right down to it, this was Ben's first kiss as well, and he didn't know what to do. He liked Alexandra. He liked her so much, and he'd liked her ever since he'd come aware that she was not a tiny little boy. Whilst Lexie and Claire might be the dearest of friends, he and Lexie had far, far more in common, and there were times he liked to believe that she was only his sister's friend so in fact she could be his as well.

He swallowed hard, afraid to move, thinking that the instant he turned eighteen he intended to speak to her father. If Lexie would have him, he would marry her tomorrow.

Pretending a fearlessness he didn't quite feel, he reached for Alexandra, swallowing convulsively as he slid an arm about her waist, pulling her close as he'd watched his father do with his mother. Only then, once he had her fully in his arms, he didn't know how to proceed. It hardly seemed masculine to get up on his tippy toes to kiss her, and he could feel her body trembling against his palm.

THE MOMENT WAS MAGICAL, *sensational, surreal.*

ALEXANDRA'S BREATH left her in a rush as Benjamin's firm, warm fingers settled upon the small of her back, pressing her close, until, in the space of a heartbeat, the two stood nearly shoulder to shoulder.

He sighed then, and the sound of it filled Alexandra's ears, like a beguiling song. Standing far, far too close, she could feel every single contour of his body —oh, my!

Ben tilted his face up, and she instinctively tilted hers as well. Their lips hovered, never quite touching, and she marveled over the minty taste and scent of his breath. They were standing so close now that she could taste it like salt mist in the air. Had he been nibbling on genus Mentha from her mother's kitchen garden? Whatever the case, this was the most enthralling, scintillating, wonderful moment of her life... every nerve in her body coming aware. Every breath she took came labored. And then there was that strange, but exciting tingling in her breasts. And that naughty appendage— that very thing a proper lady mustn't ever consider— hardened like steel between them.

At long last, his lips found hers, pressing softly, only awkwardly at first, but then warm and velvety, sliding gently over her tremulous lips... wet, hot and sweet...

Alexandra lifted a trembling hand, perhaps thinking to push Ben away, but it landed squarely upon his chest and her fingers splayed against his shirt. The feel of his heart beating beneath her palm sent her pulses skittering and blood singing through her veins. Looking perfectly drunk, he lifted his gaze, fingers pressing her close, as he whispered, "Lexie... I—"

"What for the love of God are the two of you doing?" Came her mother's shrill voice.

Alexandra and Ben parted at once—like oil and water—but not before her mother leapt at Ben, seizing him by the ear. Alexandra gasped aloud as Lady Eveline pinched Benjamin's ear, jerking him away. Without a care that she might be hurting him, she bent to pick up the mistletoe he'd dropped on her carpet, and said, "The devil's own instrument in my own house—never again, young man!"

Once again Ben howled over the pain she inflicted upon his ear, but nevertheless, he didn't fight her. Red-faced, he allowed Alexandra's mother to lead him away, all the while railing. "We'll be sending you and your sister home at once—this very day!" she said. "And when your mother asks why, you must say it is because I said she raised a goatish little boy!"

Stunned over having been discovered in such a ruinous predicament, Alexandra could only watch as Ben was dragged away. He gave her a sad backward glance before disappearing through the doorway, and long after Benjamin was gone, Alexandra remained standing precisely where they'd parted, lifting a hand to her breast...

Only then, once there was no one about to see it, and even despite that she knew the holiday was over, her lips curved into a secret grin. Someday, indeed, there would be another opportunity. And when that opportunity arose, she wouldn't say no again. In fact, when that day arrived, Alexandra was certain to teach Benjamin Wentworth the subtle art of kissing beneath the mistletoe, and then he mightn't ever think of Amanda Butterfield again.

CHAPTER 1

19 DECEMBER, 1831

RULE NO. 1:

ON THE PROPER HANGING & EXECUTION OF MISTLETOE.

Your mistletoe *must* be fresh. It must also include drupes. Only so long as there are drupes remaining to be plucked, kisses may be commanded. Pluck one for every kiss request, and once all the drupes have been plundered, there will be no more kisses to be commanded.

The London house was running amok. Proof was plain to see—right there—a ravaged sprig of Viscum album hanging near the kitchen.

Mistletoe.

Hands upon her hips, Alexandra Grace Huntington eyed the well-plundered sprig with keen disapproval. With her father gone (*yes*, indeed, *gone*; this was a euphemism), the servants were well out of hand. With little more than a week remaining till Christmas, the drupes were all plucked. *All. Of. Them.* And nevertheless, despite that there were no more kisses left to be commanded, she knew that wouldn't stop the servants from canoodling in closets. So, it seemed, everybody had somebody to kiss... *everybody except Alexandra.*

Really, though, it wasn't so much that she was resentful. That wasn't the thing at all. It was more the fact that she felt as though she could be losing control—not only over the household she'd been left alone to manage, but over her entire life. Like that confounded little sprig of mistletoe, she, too, was hanging by a thread.

Unbidden, a bittersweet memory accosted her, bringing a telltale sting to her eyes and a burn to her cheeks—why, she hadn't any clue, because, in truth, she had so little left to be scandalized over. After all, how did one forget one's own father was a villain?

After everything that transpired this past year, her mother was in high dudgeon, her best friend had forsaken her, and her father was in *gaol.*

There was nothing left to celebrate.

Nothing left at all.

Moreover, her best friend's wedding plans were proceeding entirely without her. All of London was atwitter over the news, and everything Lexie had learned about the exalted occasion, she'd gleaned from the paper, not from Claire.

Supposedly, confronted by his long-lost son, the King of Meridian was now abdicating his throne, leaving his entire kingdom to a penurious lord from Scotland. From rags to riches, that was the story. Brought together by extraordinary circumstance, a London bluestocking was now a society darling, and a penniless Earl would soon be a celebrated king. And to make matters worse—or better, depending upon the perspective—the two had overcome ill-fortune at the hands of Lexie's own father, only to rise above it all and shine.

Astounding.

Incredible.

Unthinkable.

And nevertheless, Alexandra had half a mind to tear down that bloody sprig, although she couldn't quite allow herself to indulge in such a fit of temper.

Really, if she was angry over the turn of her own fate, it wasn't Claire's fault, nor was it the servants' faults.

Claire was brave, smart and beautiful, never afraid to speak her mind. Nor was she one to sit idly by, leaving the men in her life to save her. When hardship presented itself, Claire took her brother's trials to heart, putting on her walking boots and scouring the streets—quite literally—for an answer to save him. In doing so, she'd stumbled upon her own providence. During the course of saving Ben, she'd met her fiancé— or rather, he ran her down, again very literally, as she was crossing High Street. The thought turned Alexandra's lips ever so slightly, and really, if it weren't due to the troubles her own father heaped upon that poor family, she might have laughed over the sweet turn of fate.

Let the servants have turns in the closet, she decided, and feeling lonelier than she had in her *entire* life —and that was saying quite a lot—she turned her back on the offending sprig and walked away, any desire for peaches and cream for breakfast entirely quashed.

Tears pricked at her eyes.

Sadness enveloped her.

Somewhere out there, folks were ringing in the holidays. House parties were being planned, Christmas geese were prepared for roasting, pianofortes being tuned and shined, and all about good cheer was being had. But not here at Huntington Manor, and not for a long time.

If Alexandra must speak true, this misery had been a

long, long time coming. Her mother had retreated to the country years ago, and her father had never bothered to see himself home for the holidays. Most often, he'd spent his Christmases abroad. Her parents were adversaries in every respect, and so it had seemed to Alexandra that her mother was too quick to find fault and too easy to rile, not merely with her father, but with Lexie as well—and particularly after that "incident" in Shropshire. Don't think for a moment she didn't recall all the arguments ringing through their halls, only now that she understood so much about her father, she felt chagrined over ever having taken his side. Sadly, her mother now refused to forgive her "betrayal," considering it a disloyalty of royal proportions that her only daughter had chosen to remain in London with her "tosspot" father.

Siblings had never been in question for Alexandra, and she had so oft wondered how she was ever conceived at all. And now, here she was, with her father incarcerated, her mother disaffected, no siblings to consider, no friends... and so it was that, here again, she was pathetically alone for the holidays.

"Fa la la la la," she groused.

And really, who cared if the servants were all cavorting! She had spent too many years being overly concerned about propriety. What had it gotten her?

Nothing.

Nothing at all.

Conversely, Claire had flouted nearly every rule, and here she was, soon to be a queen! How very extraordinary! How titillating! Or, at least it might be if Alexandra were allowed to share in her good friend's fortune. Instead, she was left alone to oversee a household of delinquent servants.

Missing Claire so very desperately, she made her way toward the stairwell, fully intending to go upstairs and read... or sketch... or perhaps both. After all this time, sketching was still her greatest joy. It helped to pass the time and kept her mind off other matters she ought not to be dwelling upon. She no longer cared what anybody thought about her passions, and Claire would marvel most of all over the changes that had come over her—but this was the saddest part of all: Claire might never know it.

And Ben...

Well, she'd rather not think about him at all.

Ben, with those startling green eyes. Ben, with his silky, sun-kissed hair. Ben, with his ever-so-patrician nose. And, no, don't dare think about his lips!

No, no, no, no.

Determined to forget the Wentworths entirely, Alexandra had one foot on the steps, ready to ascend when there came a very unexpected knock on the front door.

A bell rang in the servant's quarters, and a distant door opened and closed. Before Alexandra could turn, she heard the butler's footsteps rushing down the hall. Hair mussed and red-faced, Mr. Robinson appeared, straightening his collar. "I'll get it, Miss Huntington," he said, hurrying past.

"Certainly," Alexandra said, curious to see who it might be. No one ever called upon their residence anymore. Huntington Manor was nothing more than a curiosity now, a thing to point the finger at whilst passing in a hansom.

"It's for Lady Alexandra," the courier said—a man with a foreign accent. Alexandra lingered, eavesdropping.

"Thank you," said Mr. Robinson, "I will deliver it."

Lexie frowned. Turning on the step, curling her toes in her slippers, waiting eagerly for Mr. Robinson to close the door, and when he did, she tilted him a questioning glance.

"For you," the butler said, the color still high in his cheeks—no doubt flushed over his exertions in the closet.

"Thank you," Alexandra said, and though she would have also liked to give him her blessing for whatever he was about in that closet, she hadn't very much good will left to squander. Even so, she wouldn't scold him, either.

Sighing wearily, she accepted the envelope... a letter addressed to her—perhaps from her father in Newgate. He'd been placed in a convict's prison—no mere debtor's gaol, like Fleet or Marshalsea. And now that his fate was sealed, he was doling out their private, financial information and instructions in measures. But the letter wasn't from her father. It smelled of... lavender. She turned it over... and sucked in a breath.

Claire.

Like a child with a present, she thrust a finger eagerly beneath the seal in order to break it and tore open the envelope. Alexandra was still holding her breath when she drew out the folded invitation and began to read...

His Royal Highness, the Prince of Meridian and his esteemed wife cordially invite you to spend the holiday in celebration with friends and family. Wednesday, 19 December through Sunday, 1 January.

Surrey. There was an unfamiliar address attached, with instructions for the driver.

Was it true? Was Claire inviting her to share the holiday?

A glimmer of joy ignited in Alexandra's breast. Months and months and months had passed without word from Claire, but no matter. Here was an invitation to share the holiday!

"Thank you so much!" she exclaimed to Mr. Robinson. "Thank you!" And she pressed the note to her bosom and rushed up the stairs, her stomach flip-flopping with glee—a feeling not so unlike the one she used to get when she thought about seeing Ben. Joy soared through her.

Let the servants have their way with the house.

Surrey, here I come!

* * *

It was high time to set things right.

Claire and Alexandra had been estranged for far too long now, and, really, it wasn't so much that Claire was avoiding the confrontation, she simply had too much to do. It didn't matter how sensible one could be; when one was marrying a prince, all thought of austerity flew out the window. There was a certain standard that must be kept, regardless of one's personal sensibilities. After all, a prince was a future king, and a future king must have a wedding in accordance with his station. But at least she had a kindred spirit in the daily struggle, because her fiancé had not been raised to take his seat upon a throne. If indeed it could be possible, Ian MacEwen was even less concerned with proprieties than she was. Unfortunately, they hadn't only themselves to think of anymore. Until now, there had been *so* much to do that Claire hadn't had a moment to stop and think how the scandal with Alexandra's father must have affected her dearest friend.

No doubt Lexie was still brooding. She was so much like Ben, and now more than ever, she believed those two were meant for each other.

For months now, Claire had hoped Lexie would come of her own accord. She had been more than prepared to allow her the time she needed to come to terms with the entire sordid affair, but it was becoming very apparent that she would not do so, and time was growing short.

To begin with, some tiny part of Claire had insisted that Alexandra be the one to come and offer support. But really, beyond apologies for something Alexandra had had no control over, she was bound to be feeling ashamed, guilty and perhaps even unwelcome in Claire's home. It was only natural. And, having realized as much, she had resolved to put her good friend's mind and heart at ease. Alas, one week turned into two, and two into six, and six into months—all the while Claire had far too many people tugging at her skirts. Do this, do that, see to this, see to that—and all "right now."

Now, after all this time, Alexandra couldn't possibly understand that Claire didn't blame her, because she couldn't read minds, and sadly, Claire hadn't had the wherewithal to see past her own whirlwind affairs to help make it easier for the poor dear to bear.

To be sure, some small part of her also dreaded seeing Alexandra. How could she face Lexie knowing full well that Lexie would know exactly what her odious father intended?

Even now, the memory of the ordeal—the offensive place Lord Huntington had taken her—was enough to put a tremble on her lips. If she never saw that man again so long as she lived, that would be too soon. But as far as Lexie was concerned, it was now or never. In less than two months' time Claire would be departing London, perhaps forever, and she might never forgive herself if she didn't find some way to make things right with her oldest and dearest friend.

What was more, she couldn't abandon Lexie to spend another holiday alone in that terrible house.

Long, long before the scandal with her father, something had transpired between mother and daughter to damage their relationship. Lady Eveline might never return to London, but neither would she invite her daughter to Shropshire, and Alexandra was clearly not the sort to press herself upon others. And meanwhile, until his recent incarceration, Lexie's odious father had spent nearly every holiday abroad, leaving his only daughter to manage his estate—such as it was, because Lexie never had much say over what transpired in that house. Essentially, she had been a tenant herself, achingly alone in the absence of her embittered parents.

But there it was... someone *must* rise above these circumstances, and so it, seemed, that person must be Claire. Love was the catalyst for her own happiness, and she felt that if only she could put Ben and Alexandra together, they would find a way to work it out. Those two had always been flirtatious, even when neither would admit it. As different as they were, Claire had even wondered if Alexandra befriended her only to be close to Ben. And Ben, well... for all that he was a fanciable bachelor, he didn't seem to have eyes for anyone but Lexie. Oh, but he liked to talk a good game —so did Lexie—but the proof of the plum pudding was in the eating. Claire adored Lexie. She loved Ben. Two more deserving people she had never known. If only she had her druthers, she would leave both with a hopeful future. But so, it seemed, this schedule would be the death of her; she was rushing toward yet another appointment when Ryo returned from his errand, giving Claire a nod as he walked in the door.

"You delivered it?"

"Hai," he said.

"And she accepted?"

Her fiancé's newly acquired manservant shrugged. "I cannot presume to say, *okusama*."

He gave her a reverent nod, placing his hands behind his back, the slight gesture a heartfelt bow. Claire liked him. Though ofttimes he was a walking riddle, and sometimes his deference was odd, she enjoyed his wit. And, besides, she recognized a loyal servant when she met one. He might have served Ian's brother loyally, but his new assignment didn't appear to be the least bit of a conflict. His duty was to the family he served, and to the royal house of Meridian, to which Claire would soon be attached. He was ever present, and yet invisible besides.

"Of course," said Claire, her shoulders drooping, only belatedly realizing that, yes, of course, he would have given her invitation to a butler. Alexandra would never, ever presume to answer her own door, and she would be less inclined now since she could never be entirely sure it wasn't a correspondent from the *Times*. Hopefully, that scandal with her father would soon die down, and in the meantime, Claire had an urgent appointment to keep with her dressmaker. She'd kept the woman from Courtauld's waiting too long already, only to be certain her special "holiday decorations" were off and away. However, if she didn't hurry back upstairs, the lady would lose patience and depart, and, according to the Duchess of Kent, there was simply no one else available to deliver a wedding gown befitting a royal bride, not to mention the bridesmaids dresses she required.

"Thank you," she said. "Please tell my brother I will join him directly."

"Yes, *okusama*," he said, but she turned once more when she was halfway up the stairs. "Oh!" she said. "And Ryo... please, please don't tell anyone where I sent you—particularly not my brother."

"Yes, *okusama*," he said, once again, only this time with the barest hint of a smile... as though he knew what she was up to, and nevertheless, Claire knew he would keep her confidence. The man was a godsend. Already once he'd saved her life, and knowing how much she'd come to count on him, Ian had lent him to her service until after the wedding. She simply didn't know what she would do without him. "Thank you," she said, and flew up the stairs.

CHAPTER 2

*B*enjamin Alexander Wentworth, the seventh
Earl of Highbury, sat fiddling with his pancakes, pushing them about his plate.

It was perfectly inconceivable how lonely a busy
household could feel. It had been years since their
breakfast table was so well laden, and now Claire
hadn't two seconds to spare to stop and fill her belly.
She woke in a tizzy, ran about like a maelstrom, and so
much as Ben loved how happy Claire was, he was beginning to dread the indubitable fact that she would
very soon be departing London. If, indeed, he thought
the house felt lonely now, he knew it would feel lone-

lier then, though at least their fortunes were much improved.

Months ago, mired in the gaming hells, he might not have imagined things going so well. Now, his house was in order, his sister was marrying royalty, and, no thanks to his own poor choices, his debts were fully paid. Not since his youth had he had so much hope for their futures, and, for the first time since their father's untimely death, he wasn't at all concerned over Claire's future or welfare. Moreover, it would be a cold day in hell before he endangered their prosperity again. And nevertheless, despite the rosy color of their futures, there was a certain melancholy plaguing him of late— nothing he could put a finger to, not precisely, though it was *there* just the same.

Something was missing; what it was, he daren't say.

On the surface, there could be nothing at all to inform his mood. He was, in truth, the man of his own household now. The future was his alone to shape.

Pancakes. Juice. Bacon. Biscuits...

What could he possibly find to complain about?

For Chrissakes, his future brother by law was a finer man than any man he could have ever hoped for. And to boot, Ben had made himself a new associate besides. Wes Cameron was an interesting bloke, with stories enough to entertain him for a lifetime, so then... why did he feel so... utterly...

Bored?

Glum?

Restless?

Perhaps it wasn't possible to endure what he'd endured and come out of the ordeal unscathed. But there it was, he supposed. He wasn't the same bloke he was this time last year, and no matter that he was pleased enough for Claire, he could not abide the glitter and gold—nor the influx of servants, or the eternal and cloying scent of flowers wafting in and out from every corner of the house.

Highbury's halls were brightly lit, with Chocolate Limes, Brandy Balls, Clove Rocks and Wine Gums filling nearly every porcelain dish on every table in every common room, and there was enough sweetness and light to curdle the buttermilk cakes settling in his belly.

Bloody Norah!

A servant brought in a bit of rich plum pudding to set it on the buffet—not so much a breakfast choice, but since it was made weeks ago, and they would be gone for Christmas, it must be eaten. He detected the tangy scent of citron, orange and lemon peel, and it triggered a memory he preferred not to remember. Frowning, he pushed back his chair, rising up from the table, his appetite effectively quashed.

He no longer had *any* stomach for extravagances— and perhaps this, too, was natural, considering that he spent so many weeks in debtor's prison, wallowing like a pig in his own filth. After worrying so long about keeping his neck out of a gibbet, or whether he'd ever again feel the warmth of the sun on his shoulders, he couldn't care one whit about bon bons, or company, or idle chatter—though he did enjoy the scent of pine drifting through the air.

Christmas.

Bah, humbug!

It gave him visions, though not of sugar plums, but of fresh country air, and made him long for simpler days when he and his sister had spent holidays in Shropshire.

Unfortunately, Ben could no longer think of that particular estate, without thinking of the man who'd tried so hard—and very nearly succeeded—in destroying everything he ever held dear.

And Lexie... sweet though she might be, she was only a bitter reminder of her father's treachery.

It wasn't Alexandra he missed, he told himself. And neither was Lexie the sort of lady he enjoyed—not any longer. While he'd once found her whimsy endearing, she was too done up. Already, his sister had made several intimations that he should call upon her, but no, indeed. There was no way in damnation he would saddle himself with an empty-headed miss, who cared more about ballgowns than she did her own best friend. It had been months now since Claire had been wrenched from the clutches of that fiend, and Alexandra had yet to so much as inquire.

No, the Huntingtons could rot in hell for all he cared—that included Alexandra.

Sighing wearily, he made his way back up the stairs, passing a seamstress as she rushed down, avoiding his gaze.

Today, his sister was being fitted for her royal wedding gown. Her fiancé was due to arrive soon, and minute by minute the house was filling to the rafters. Thanks to bloody hell, the servants had all returned, or the management of this estate would drive him to distraction. And moreover, they would be leaving later for a nice, quiet retreat in Surrey before the insanity of the wedding celebration. That thought put a new skip in his step as he ascended the stairs, but the joy didn't quite soften his glower.

"Good day," said another woman as he passed.

"G'day," said Ben, scarcely aware that it sounded more like a growl, and the young woman hurried by, flying fast for the door.

* * *

Fresh from an appointment with his father and associates, Ian discovered Claire seated in the dining room, wolfing down a bite of breakfast.

"There you are," he said, and her answering smile brightened the room more efficiently than did her chandelier filled with a hundred twinkling candles. She never failed to steal his breath away.

"Oh, yes! Here I am," she declared happily as he came to sit beside her, pecking her gently upon the lips, but not so briefly that he didn't glean the taste of bacon upon her lips. He smiled then, for who didn't love the taste of bacon, and particularly when served upon lips that were so delectably sweet.

"How is your father?" she asked.

"Off again to Glen Abbey, I suppose."

"Oh?" She tilted him a curious look. "Did Fiona invite him for the holidays?"

"No," said Ian, mulling it over. "I don't believe she did. Rather, I believe he has taken it upon himself to make certain a certain constable has no opportunity to come between them."

Claire laughed, the sound entirely musical, warming Ian's heart and stirring the greedy beast living in his trousers. After their glorious lovemaking, before their engagement became official, the abstinence was murdering him.

"It's amazing what motivation jealousy holds."

"Yes, indeed," he said. "Though I hope 'tis more than jealousy that drives him. Rather, I hope my father comports himself as he should, because my mother will have none of his shenanigans any longer."

"I dare say."

Ian took the seat right beside his lovely bride, preferring it to the one across the table. It wasn't entirely polite to sit directly beside her, but he'd rather sniff the lavender infusion in her tresses than smell eggs and bacon any day of the year.

"And Merrick?"

"He and Chloe are already there. My brother didn't wish to travel so near to the babe's birthing."

"First of January?"

"Thereabouts."

"And the house has been prepared?"

A special bed had to be installed in the couple's private quarters. Additionally, there was to be a midwife in residence—a sister to one of the kitchen maids.

"Oh, yes," he said. "Thankfully, Victoria has also made arrangements for an attending physician. But since Chloe's not due until the New Year, he won't be in residence—not precisely, though he'll be just a stone's throw away."

Most people preferred to travel to London for deliveries, but since there were no better doctors anywhere than at Hampton Court Palace, this was yet another reason the Duchess had facilitated the use of her late husband's former estate.

As it so happened, Glen Abbey's only doctor also happened to be the lady presently in expecting.

"It will be easier after the child arrives not to have to travel so far for the wedding," suggested Ian.

Naturally, though Prince Merrick had repudiated the crown, he was still expected to be present for the nuptials and coronation. His presence would go far to reassure the people of Meridian that his wishes were being met. After all, it wasn't as though his father disowned him.

"It's such a complicated matter."

"Indeed," said Ian. "But then again, even had they wished to remain in Scotland, that wasn't an option— damn Edward to hell."

"Well," said Claire, wincing. "I do believe that poor man may be accommodating your wishes."

"Poor?" Ian argued, with a lifted brow. "That *poor man*

burned down my house—very nearly with my invalid mother inside it." The very fact that Fiona wasn't precisely the invalid they had believed her to be didn't matter. After so long in that chair, his mother's limbs had been weak, and she could never have gotten out on her own. Were it not for his brother's quick response, she might be naught more than ash and bone. So then, if indeed, Edward was so very accommodating as to be occupying Hell this very instant, it was precisely what he deserved. Not only had Glen Abbey's steward endangered the lives of many, but he'd embezzled enough money to put Glen Abbey and its denizens in peril for years, and Ian had been forced to resort to a somewhat less than legitimate means to support them. Thankfully, that entire ordeal was over, though in the absence of a proper home in Scotland, they were now forced to lease an estate from one of his father's associates—one General James Moore, equerry of the late Duke of Kent. But, in fact, the man wouldn't accept a penny for the rental. He'd donated the use of his estate as a wedding gift, and that was fine with Ian. He'd take every bloody penny his father allowed them and donate it to the residents of Glen Abbey so they too might have a bounteous Christmas.

The thought of Rusty Broun and his brood dining on ham and venison made his heart gleeful. And really, the only reason Ian had accepted the crown in his brother's stead was so he could make dead certain Glen Abbey's coffers remained full enough to care for the people who depended upon it most. "Hawk" was dead and gone. And that, too, was well and good.

"So, it's official, then. Fiona will not join us?"

"She will not," said Ian. "She didn't wish to travel, though that seems odd—quite, in fact, considering the circumstances."

The circumstances being that Fiona had one son preparing to depart England for the foreseeable future, and another whose firstborn child was imminent—regardless of the date given, a Christmas babe was entirely possible.

Thoughtfully, Claire tore a bite from her biscuit. "I would think Fiona would wish to come spend the holidays with her son before he quit London?"

Ian sighed as he plucked up a bit of her bacon. "As would I," he said, "but I believe it's making her glum... else she's gotten close to Tolly and doesn't wish to leave him. But I don't know. In either case, my father has his job cut out for him."

Claire sighed as well. "Alas... that makes two glum folks amidst our loved ones. What shall we do?"

"About Ben?" he asked.

Claire peeked out of the dining room door to be certain her brother wasn't loitering, and then she nodded, but then tilted her fiancé a beautiful green-eyed glance, betraying a twinkle of mischief. "But I have a plan," she confessed.

"Claire," Ian protested. "Really, love. Don't you believe you've enough to deal with already? It's not as though you don't have enough to contend with."

Claire shrugged, unfazed. "It's only a bit of nothing," she declared, and waved away the notion with a hand.

"Nothing?" he asked. But then, he too cast up a hand.

His bride-to-be was a wise little bird; he knew better than to assert himself against her. He had more than enough experience with strong-headed ladies to know he daren't get in their way. It was enough to keep up with his own affairs—a mountain of changes that would put an entire nation under his care. "Never mind," he said. "I don't want to know. Please, pass the butter."

With a lovely curl to her beautiful lips, his fiancée reached over to take a small plate of creamy butter and handed it to him, smiling with the light of love in her eyes.

"We should be away after breakfast," she said giddily. "There's so much to do, and I'd dearly love to arrive before our *guests* do." She grinned. "I have holiday decorations to hang."

"As you wish, love."

She laughed quickly. "Will you always be so accommodating, Majesty?"

He grinned. "*Always* for you, Majesty."

Her blush crept down from her cheeks into her décolletage—a lovely, delectable flush that tempted Ian's lips, because he knew her sweet skin would be warm to the touch. Ever since her brother's return, they'd been forced to sleep apart, if only for the sake of propriety. Only the two of them knew the secret they shared— that he had already tasted her in the most shocking of places.

"You will ever be my queen," he said, "with or without a crown." And he couldn't help himself. Far hungrier for the taste of his beautiful wife than he was for the spread on the table, he bent to kiss the sweet temptation of her bosom.

"Ian!" she exclaimed. "What would my brother say?"

"Damn, that miserable fool," he muttered, but without any rancor, because, in truth, he liked Ben, and he hoped to Hell that whatever his bride had planned, it would drag the fool out of his doldrums once and for all.

CHAPTER 3

20 DECEMBER

RULE NO. 3:

ON THE MISUSE OF MISTLETOE.

There is *no* obligation for anyone to ever kiss beneath mistletoe hanging from a hat or hand. Please understand: Mistletoe is *not* a portable kissing booth. Please do not harass ladies with mistletoe. It is very bad form!

*S*hivering beneath her light pelisse, Alexandra watched as the landscape scuttled by—clear, blue skies, green, green grass.

Weather-wise, the Parklands were not so different from London proper, and yet, unlike the hustle and bustle of Grosvenor Square, the sight of those dew-dusted fields, glittering like tinsel, made her yearn to apricate.

Bits and bobs of memories teased and tormented her, but Alexandra blew them away with the cold vapor of a mournful sigh and took pleasure in the scenery.

Fallow deer grazed in small, familial herds—bucks and does, with their awkward-limbed kids.

Even animals had families, and Alexandra wondered idly upon whose home were they descending for the holidays. So far as she knew, Claire's family hadn't any connections South of the City, and neither did Alexandra. It must a friend of Ian's family, she surmised.

No matter. She was pleased over the turn of events, and even the thought of seeing Ben shouldn't dampen her spirits. It was Christmas, she told herself. Melancholy be damned!

Pinching her coat together once more, she reconsidered her wardrobe. Even despite the apricity, the air held an unusual sharpness that stung the tender bits of Lexie's nostrils, and now she worried about inclement weather.

It was only natural to worry when traveling, because one could never be certain what to expect.

And, regardless, she was perfectly thrilled to be spending yet another holiday with her oldest, dearest friend. After months and months apart, she couldn't wait to hear all about Claire's plans—and more to the point, to put the unpleasantness of her father's treachery in their past. If she was nervous at all, this was why. And yet, she should have had *no* doubt Claire would forgive her. She should have had more aplomb than to sit alone in her big, empty house, brooding all the while, when, in fact, she might have easily gone to Claire.

Naturally, she had been unsettled by the entire ordeal but now she was doubly embarrassed after having waited so long, and she didn't know what to say when she faced Claire.

Thankfully, they had never minced words; hopefully they wouldn't begin now. And, in retrospect, the time apart hadn't been all for naught. For one thing, Lexie now understood herself better. She knew who she was and why it was she was drawn to Claire in the first place, and it wasn't at all because Claire Wentworth loved a good Season.

No, indeed, Claire was the last person to be fond of such drivel, and all the while Lexie had been pretending to be a gadabout, she had secretly longed to be doing precisely what Claire had the gumption to do all along: stay at home and read a good book. What a silly chit Alexandra had been.

Really, who cared what her father or mother thought of her predilections. Who cared if they wouldn't approve of her drawings. Who cared if her passions left too little time to allow her to present herself to the *ton* appropriately, and really, most of all, who cared about marriage.

Did she truly want a husband to tell her what to do?

Did she want a man to pinch her purse strings?

No.

From here forth, she determined to be a changed woman, and the one true blessing of this entire ordeal was that her father had left her quite flush. She now had the means to choose her own destiny.

Indeed, the *distinguished* Lord Huntington might never again see the light of day, but he had been quick to deny her mother any legal tender. He'd left Lady Eveline nothing but her dowager estate, and everything else he'd assigned to Lexie. She needn't worry ever again about being left upon a shelf, or how to get along. If, in fact, she desired, she could sell the London apartment and travel abroad... and yet something about both of those choices left her feeling bereft.

Perhaps it would be lovely to keep the house and build the conservatory she'd always dreamed of?

The carriage slowed, the deer vanished and, the landscaping looked a bit more manicured.

Alexandra peered out the window, trying to glimpse ahead—where were they going?

They rounded a bend, and when at last she spied the Lion Gate, it finally dawned on her. It wasn't any old estate they were descending upon; it was Hampton Court Palace! But, of course, she should have realized sooner, particularly considering their affiliation with the Duchess of Kent. Where else would the Royal Family of Meridian stay?

The carriage veered onto a small service road, careening toward Home Park and the Bowling Green. On the grounds of the Palace, surrounded by lush green hedges, the Garden Pavilions included a quartet of residences and a *parterre*—a formal garden connected by paths. She had only heard about these mentioned in whispers. They'd served as gaming hells under the protection of the Duke of Kent. The Duchess never embraced the home—or perhaps was never invited, since rumor would also have it that the Duke had often kept his lovers here. After his death, the entire estate was assigned to his loyal equerry—a gift from the Duke's brother, the late King George.

Gobsmacked, Alexandra stared as they approached, thinking of all the scandals that were born here...

How ironic it must be that at a time when she couldn't care less about tittle-tattle, she would find herself *here*.

Only for the briefest instant, she wondered what Ben must think of it all. And then she frowned, pushing the thought of Ben right back out of her head.

Who cares what Ben thinks!

She was not here to see Ben.

She was here to see Claire.

Whatever rapport she'd once had with Claire's elder brother, it was over now, and good riddance!

Long before the carriage came to a halt before the largest of the red-brown brick buildings, Claire was already standing outside waiting, clapping her hands, surrounded by servants all prepared to help Lexie disembark.

Oh, Claire! she thought, tears stinging her eyes at the sight of her beloved friend. Dressed in a pale green chiffon morning gown, Claire was even more beautiful than Alexandra remembered. She glowed like an emerald flame! Standing with shoulders back, her head tall and back straight, she looked every bit the part of a queen.

The instant the carriage came to a halt, Alexandra was up from her seat, tears brimming in her eyes. She threw open the door and fell out of the carriage, straight into Claire's waiting arms.

For the longest bittersweet moment, it was as though they'd never parted—friends forever, with nary a care between them. But, oh, what Alexandra would give for a return to simpler days.

"Lexie!" said Claire. "Oh, Lexie!"

But Alexandra couldn't speak. Tears clogged her throat. The only sound that emerged from the constriction was more like a piteous gurgle. Blessedly, Claire seemed to understand—as only friends ever could—and she squeezed Lexie tighter, which only brought forth another cascade of tears.

Really, for all that she'd considered it endlessly, Alexandra hadn't any notion at all what she'd meant to say at this moment, but it all came out in a rush in five little heartfelt words. "I am so sorry, Claire."

"Think nothing of it," said Claire easily, smiling and patting the long strands of Alexandra's hair that fell loose at her back—what a sight she must present, fresh from travel, eyes red-rimmed and stinging. Her voice softer now, barely a whisper at Lexie's ear, Claire said, "All's well that ends well, my dear friend. I never blamed you even once."

And then she wrenched herself free of their

maudlin embrace, somehow understanding how it could end if she didn't take matters in hand. Smiling, she turned Lexie about, linking their arms, and said brightly, "Let me show you where we'll be sleeping. Isn't this grand?" And she patted Lexie's hand, and gave her the state of affairs.

Some of the guests had already arrived, including her fiancé's twin brother and his wife, who was apparently very, very pregnant. Alexandra and Claire would be sharing one suite, Merrick and his wife another, Ian and Ben another. Mr. Cameron, perhaps inspired by the accommodations, was bringing a "guest."

"Chloe is a doctor," Claire explained. "Can you imagine?"

Alexandra blinked in surprise. "A true doctor?"

Claire nodded. "True as they come. As I understand it, she's the physician for all of Glen Abbey as her father was before her."

"How incredible!"

Claire smiled artfully. "I suppose no one ever told her she couldn't do it."

"Good for her," Alexandra said, and meant it.

"She's delightful," Claire said. "I know you'll be fast friends. And Ben will be so pleased to see you."

Ben.

Alexandra wrinkled her nose.

Unfortunately, Benjamin Wentworth, the man who'd once held her heart without ever realizing it, was the very last person Alexandra wished to see.

Certainly, she blamed her father most of all for the majority of Claire's troubles, but Benjamin had had a part to play as well. It was his gaming, after all, that had brought his family to ruin, and if he'd never gambled a penny, her damnable father would never have had the chance to abuse him—and all for what? Really, it *had* to be Ben's fault. Alexandra couldn't imagine Claire's father leaving them in too deep.

But she didn't wish to think about those travails any longer. She was determined to make the most of the weekend, and judging by the size of the house, she need not ever see Benjamin Wentworth if she didn't wish to. "So, have we the entire Pavilion?" she asked.

"Oh, no. Only this one was restored by the Duke before he died. The others are still in disrepair. Mr. Moore and his wife are both currently abroad, so the Duchess impressed upon them to lend it for the holiday. Of course, how could they refuse, when it was originally her husband's?"

"Lovely," said Alexandra, though it struck her yet again how fickle the *haute ton* could be. Less than a year ago, the Duchess had barely tolerated Claire. Now, she was arranging holiday accommodations?

"I know what you're thinking," said Claire, with a hint of a smile, because, despite their recent estrangement, Claire knew her only too well. "She's family now."

Alexandra lifted a brow. "Victoria?"

"Be nice. She may be joining us and she's bringing Drina along with her."

"Lovely," said Alexandra, torn. She did enjoy little Drina— infinitely more than she did her meddling mother. But where that child got her good cheer, no one could say, because, by all accounts, her father had been utterly loathed by his peers and her mother was a dour-faced matron.

A flutter of movement caught her eye, and she peered up, spying an all-too familiar face in the upstairs window. Against her will, her heart did a flip and a flop. But that wasn't joy, she apprised herself. Those days were done. It was merely that she hadn't seen *him* in nearly a year, and she didn't know how they would get along.

It's all well and good, she reassured herself.

Chin up, do it for Claire.

* * *

ALEXANDRA HUNTINGTON.

But, of course.

His sister had a heart of gold, and there was no wonder why Claire would invite her. Those two had been friends since the cradle. Their mothers had met with prams in the park, and Ben himself had scarcely been old enough to pull himself up to peer inside at the round-faced babes within.

She was not a child any longer.

From the upstairs window, he watched as she descended from her coach—or, more like spilled from it, into a billowing cloud of sapphire skirts—quite sedate for her. She was usually aglitter, with gems in her tresses and jewels at her throat. From his vantage it seemed that she hurled herself into Claire's arms, clutching his sister in a veritable death grip. Frowning, Ben watched the pair embrace, releasing the curtain as they started for the house.

It wasn't that he was unhappy to see her. Quite to the contrary. Claire and Lexie *should* make amends.

But.

And that was the word of the moment...

But.

Seeing Alexandra left him feeling bedeviled on so many fronts; the worst of it being the guilt he felt over what her father did to Claire—held her at pistol point, fully intending to defile her. He took Claire to that house of ill-repute—the one where he'd swindled Ben.

And some believed Huntington intended to do his worst.

But there was this as well: He didn't wish to feel pity for the daughter of the man who'd brought him to his knees.

Lord Huntington was an abomination.

Ben had gone to the man for help, and Huntington had not only swindled him, but then had him thrashed and tossed into debtors' prison with no one the wiser. He still bore a small scar where the pipe had caught him on the chin.

Naturally, he was still furious over it all, but no more furious than he was that Huntington had set his sights on Ben's sweet sister, preying upon her in much the same fashion he would hunt some beast of prey. In the end, he'd not gotten what he'd deserved. Gaol was too good for the man, and Ben hoped to God that Huntington found himself buggered every day of his miserable life.

Unfortunately, seeing Alexandra only roused his darkest emotions, and he didn't relish thinking about his time in Fleet.

So what if Alexandra was alone for the holidays. He'd come dangerously close to spending every day of his life alone in a cell, with only her father to account for it.

Moreover, he had a feeling in his gut that his sister was up to no good and he really didn't appreciate Claire's meddling. No matter that he was, in fact, still attracted to Alexandra—who wouldn't be; she had grown into a fine young lady—she stood for everything he could no longer bear.

Point in fact: He couldn't remember the last time— or even the first time—they'd had some meaningful discourse that lasted more than three minutes that didn't revolve around some juicy bit of gossip. How pleased she must be to be spending the holidays in this bastion of inequity, where, no doubt, her father would have felt right at home. No matter that the place was changed now, altered by bits of velvet and lace, Ben could still smell its taint in the walls themselves.

Gambling, whoring, drinking.

All that gibberish was behind him now. Consequently, he wasn't remotely interested in spending time with Alexandra Huntington.

"Claire," he whispered. "What are you up to, sister?" Whatever it was, she wouldn't get away with it.

CHAPTER 4

*H*olly. Ivy. Mistletoe.

No expense had been spared to illicit good cheer, every room in the manor festooned with boughs of holly and sprigs of mistletoe as well—a small, but annoying detail Alexandra might have happily overlooked had she not encountered the frippery in her own home. Only to make matters worse, unlike in her own home where there was a single sprig hidden along the back hall, here the mistletoe was everywhere, and full of drupes, besides. One must be vigilant to avoid them, but the sight of them bedeviled her all the more because she and Benjamin were presently the only ones in attendance without sweethearts. Never in her life would she have believed she would say such a thing— or even think such a thing—but she desperately hoped the Duchess and her daughter would be arriving soon, because, at the instant, she felt as though she were attending a party for twains.

Merrick, Chloe.

Ian, Claire.

Mr. Cameron and his flamboyant paramour...

Waiting for the dinner bell to chime, Alexandra chose a spot at the back of the parlor, next to the pianoforte—as far as possible from mistletoe—and there she remained, awkwardly alone... certain of only one thing: *Nothing* was as it used to be. *Nothing.*

Bittersweet memories of her youth accosted her— holidays in Shropshire, wassails with Ben and Claire, plum pudding at midnight in the kitchen...

Like a comfortable old friend, the pianoforte's hood was left ajar, the ebony and ivory keys winking brilliantly beneath the light of a glittering chandelier. The urge to tap a key was nearly irresistible, but Alexandra daren't call attention to herself. Placing her hands firmly behind her back, she managed a smile, only considering the changes in their roles. For so many years, Alexandra had pushed and cajoled Claire into the spotlight, but for all her wallflower tendencies, Claire was now a model hostess, seeing to her guests with all the ease of a seasoned socialite—something her dear friend had always claimed she would never be. And yet... here they were... and there she was...

A trickle of laughter drifted over as Claire delighted over something Chloe Welbourne said, and Alexandra felt an immediate and unmistakable tweak of envy— although, really, why shouldn't Claire and Chloe be friends? On the surface they had more in common than Alexandra and Claire. Against all persuasion, both had remained true to themselves, flouting convention at every turn. And really, were Alexandra Claire, she might prefer Chloe as a best friend too. Not only was Chloe a notable physician in a day and age when women were not afforded such choices, she was effervescently lovely besides.

And look at her—only look at her. Despite her left-handed marriage and increasing belly, she moved about the parlor with a grace born of confidence, something Alexandra was sorely lacking. Under different circumstances they might have all been good friends, but it was far more likely that they would part ways after the holidays, and Alexandra would never see any of these people again, including Claire.

Feeling the loss acutely, her gaze moved to Ben, who was now speaking with Mr. Cameron—the detective Claire employed some months past to investigate her brother's disappearance. Only watching them together, she frowned. Because if, indeed, Ben was ignoring Lexie—and he was—he didn't seem the least bit inclined to ignore Mr. Cameron's guest, one Lady Morrissey, whose husband was not entirely deceased, and yet here she was, cozy in public with Mr. Cameron, and flirting with Ben besides.

She wasn't jealous. That wasn't the thing at all. It was just that Ben had only spoken two words to her.

"Lady Alexandra," he'd said, with a polite bow.

But he didn't take her by the hand, nor did he embrace her. Instead, he'd wandered into the gallery to study portraits, only returning at the lure of Lady Morrissey's laughter.

And there they were, laughing gaily, whilst Alexandra had never felt so out of sorts, or completely at sea.

So, yes, indeed, she was feeling sorry for herself, and fighting the most incredible impulse to pound most vigorously upon the piano keys, if for no other reason than to remind certain persons in attendance that the occasion was *supposed* to be gay... and yet, really, there was only one person lacking in joy here, and it wasn't Lady Morrissey.

Nor was it Ben.

Nor Claire.

Nor Chloe.

Nor Merrick, or Ian.

Certainly not Mr. Cameron, whose ears were now blushing as fiercely as his cheeks.

Fa la la la la, Alexandra groused silently, feeling like a crosspatch to the nth degree, and looking everywhere but at lovers or at the mistletoe—one hanging from the chandelier, another from the arched entry—all the while trying desperately not to remember the minty scent of Ben's mouth... or the way his long, lean fingers had splayed over her back... all so chaste considering the way Lady Morrissey and Mr. Cameron were canoodling in public.

Where, indeed, was Lady Morrissey's husband?

Wasn't she concerned over her reputation? Particularly with the Duchess expected. Victoria would no doubt report every *faux pas* to the gossip-mongering *ton*—and if Lady Morrissey was not concerned, who was she to be spared the Duchess's cutting tongue? Alexandra stood wondering about that when Claire approached to whisper in her ear, in precisely the manner she used to do. "Penny for your thoughts?" she said.

Alexandra's answering smile was quick as she turned to her friend, answering the way Claire would expect her to, "Give me two and I'll tell *all*."

"*All?*" Claire teased.

"Yes, indeed." She lifted her chin. "Three will get you a song about it as well."

Claire laughed, and reached out to embrace Alexandra, leaving an arm about her waist. "Enjoying yourself?"

"Quite," she lied, and, truly, she might have had the opportunity to do so if only she could temper the demons raging on her shoulder—an entire host of them now: one to needle her about Ben, one to harangue her about Claire, one to pester her about the mysterious Lady Morrissey, and yet another to bedevil her endlessly about the mistletoe hanging throughout the manor. Glancing up again at the sprig of mistletoe hanging from the crystal chandelier, she said, "It's a lovely home."

"Indeed," said Claire, whispering now. "Although I do wonder how many scandals were born here..."

"Truly. How can Victoria bear to spend the holiday?"

"Well... my guess is she will not," said Claire. "She advised close proximity to Hampton Court for Chloe's sake, but I'm quite certain she pressed General Moore as much for her own designs as she did for Chloe." It was not Victoria's way to lose an opportunity to see to her daughter's welfare, and now that King William was aging, without legitimate heirs, and Drina was the heir apparent, there was hardly any chance the Duchess would bypass Hampton Court only to reside in the Pavilions, especially since Ian's royal father wasn't in attendance.

"Lawd," said Alexandra, "when I think about my own wretched family... I should remember poor Drina."

Claire's brows lifted. "Poor Drina?" she exclaimed. "That child will be Queen some day!"

Alexandra smiled. "So will you."

Claire shrugged, dismissing the notion with a hand. "Hardly apropos. I shall be Queen Consort of a small province—smaller even than Leiningen."

"And regardless…"

"Well, you know it doesn't matter to me, Alexandra, but if it affords us the opportunity to make better someone's lot, I will welcome my crown whole-heartedly."

Alexandra smiled genuinely at the familiar glimpse of her old friend. "You shall be splendid," she said, returning Claire's embrace as Lady Morrissey chirped with laughter. Like a lodestone, Alexandra's gaze lifted to the trio across the room, and following Lexie's gaze, Claire smiled knowingly. "If you must know, the holiday decor was *her* idea."

"Lady Morrissey?"

Claire nodded.

"And the mistletoe, as well?"

"Oh, yes," said Claire. "She's been helping with wedding plans, and she's quite amazing, although I presume, like Victoria, she must have had her own designs when suggesting the mistletoe." Her lips curved impishly. "What do you think?"

"Indeed," said Lexie, lifting her brows. "And where did you meet her? She's rather… *bold.*"

Claire lifted a hand to her lips and bent closer. "Believe it or not, she's a very close acquaintance of Victoria's. In fact, I'm told she's some relation to the Saxon Duchy."

"Interesting," said Alexandra. Claire shrugged.

There were whispers of a distant marriage arrangement in the works between royal cousins Alexandrina Victoria and Prince Albert of Saxe-Coburg and Gotha, but Drina was still far too young. However, if Lady Morrissey was present with Victoria's blessing, perhaps she was here to protect the interests of the Saxe-Coburg-Saalfeld house.

Claire shrugged yet again, and Alexandra startled as Prince Merrick suddenly barked with laughter, then leaned to clap his brother on the shoulder—the twin he'd not met until they were both well past their salad days. How must it feel to discover so late in life that one had a sibling... and more, that he shared the same face? In fact, they shared the same hair, the same coloring, the same broad shoulders, the same blue eyes. They were identical in every respect, except for the mode of dress: While Prince Merrick was inclined to more formal garb, Claire's fiancé wore a simple frock coat that was far more relaxed, even down to the grade of wool and lack of cravat. Truly, Prince Ian looked more like a commoner than he did any sort of prince.

"It's hardly any wonder their father couldn't tell them apart," said Claire, perhaps reading her mind.

"Can you?"

"Well," Claire confessed. "It mightn't be so easy if they were dressed alike... but, really, there's a certain quality to each of their voices. *And...*"

"*And?*"

Claire flushed brightly, and Alexandra gasped. "Oh, Claire! You haven't!"

Claire nodded very slowly and deliberately, her blush heightening. "Oh, yes, I'm afraid I have!" And she giggled.

Like old times, they put their heads together conspiratorially. "Will you do it again?"

"Of course!"

"But here? Now?"

"Heavens, no! Ben would call him out. Nor would I dare give Victoria yet another reason to wag her tongue."

"*If* she comes," reminded Lexie.

"*If* she comes" agreed Claire, and once again her gaze was drawn to the brothers, sighing contentedly.

It was more than apparent to Alexandra that Claire was besotted—and why not? Ian was a charming prince, to be sure. And really, it was fascinating to observe the brothers together. Even their mannerisms were uncannily similar. One was raised a prince, groomed to rule a nation; the other was raised in exile, none the wiser that he, too, was a prince. And yet somehow, even their taste in partners was the same as well. Both Chloe and Claire had rich auburn hair, both were slight of build. And while Chloe's eyes were bright blue and Claire's were a vivid green, both ladies' gazes were marked with intelligence.

"Excuse me just a moment," said Claire, and she wandered away to whisper into Ian's ear. After a moment, the two of them quit the parlor, and Alexandra sighed wistfully, her gaze automatically seeking Ben.

He was gone.

It shouldn't be like this, but the room felt entirely depleted in his absence, the mood entirely deflated.

Where was he? Out wandering the halls? Was he too plagued by that Christmas kiss so long ago?

No matter how she tried, Alexandra couldn't seem to forget, and it was becoming increasingly difficult to keep romantic thoughts out of her head. Fortunately, it was only a moment before Claire and Ian returned, and behind them came a manservant carrying a tray, urging everyone to take a goblet of champagne. After everyone was served, Claire awarded them each with a nod and a smile. And then, performing like a seasoned toastmistress, she said, "Welcome, friends! Welcome! Welcome!" Casting a loving glance at her fiancé, her eyes sparkling brighter than the polished marble floors, she said, "As you must know... we will soon be swept away by a joyous occasion. However, before then, we hoped to spend a quiet holiday amidst those we love best— that's you. And to show our appreciation for all you have done for us through the ages, we have a small token of our affection."

She urged another manservant to enter; this man was holding a golden, velvet sack.

Everyone raised their goblets when Claire did, but Claire wasn't through. "Ben," she said, singling out her brother, standing on tiptoes, searching for Ben and frowning when she didn't spy him. But then she waved him away, dismissing him for the instant, and turned to Alexandra. "Lexie," she said. "My dearest, most beloved friend."

She gave Alexandra the sweetest smile as the manservant lifted his golden sack, and Claire reached inside, rummaging about, lifting up a small package and putting it back. At last, she found the precise gift she was searching for, and handed it out to Alexandra. "Please don't open it yet," she said.

And then, she turned to Prince Merrick and his lovely wife. "Chloe, Merrick," she said. And she repeated the effort with the golden sack, handing each in turn a small golden gift.

Smiling still, she turned to Wes Cameron and to his lovely, but mysterious companion. "Mr. Cameron, Lady Morrissey, thank you so much for all you have done for us. We will ever be in your debt." And then she handed both guests small packages as well. "Thank you, Ryo," she said, hugging the manservant before he left, then she turned to lift her glass for a toast. "Thank you *all* so much for sharing our holiday!"

"Hear, hear!" said Ian, and barely suppressing his grin, he tossed his entire glass of champagne down his gullet.

When Claire drank as well, Alexandra lifted her goblet to her lips, wishing she had the gumption to drink as Ian drank and then ask for a dozen more.

Try as she might, she couldn't shake the feeling of distress. She was grateful to be with Claire, and she was very glad to know Claire's new friends, but something wasn't right at all, and she could hardly bear the fact that Ben was so aloof.

But then again, how could she blame him?

Unlike Chloe, Alexandra was no diamond in the rough. She was the daughter of a fiend, and very, very clearly, neither Claire nor Chloe nor Lady Morrissey were pretending to be other than they were. Meanwhile, for all these past years, Alexandra had tried so desperately to mold herself to please her mother and father, and she'd tried no less to mold Claire as well—all to no avail. Thank God, or else where would Claire be?

Alone, like Alexandra.

Certainly not marrying her charming prince.

Prince Merrick was the next to speak. He toasted his twin, and clearly emotional, the brothers embraced, clapping each other fiercely upon their backs. It was difficult not to catch a sting to the eye when they broke free of their embrace and Merrick took his brother by the face, kissing his cheek.

(At least Alexandra presumed it was Prince Merrick, since he was not the one giving googly eyes to Claire.)

"You may now open your gifts," announced Claire, and Alexandra set down her goblet, lifting up the gilded gift, so beautifully wrapped.

Upon closer inspection, she realized the golden wrapping was patterned differently for each guest. Hers displayed an explosion of silver-leaf butterflies— a shared love for both Lexie and Claire, though for very different reasons. Ever since she was a child, Claire had imagined herself a butterfly cocooned, and Alexandra had dearly loved discovering chrysalises in her garden.

Excited, she made short work of the wrapping and tucked inside a small velvet box she found a necklace, with a lovely clasp in the shape of a butterfly. On the chain itself was an engraved locket, and inside the locket she found a portrait of Claire...

Beautiful, beautiful Claire, whom she'd known most of her life.

Sweet, wonderful Claire... who would be gone all too soon.

Alexandra swallowed with some difficulty, hard-pressed to note what anyone else had received. Her own gift shattered her heart to small bits. It was beautiful, certainly, though it was a bittersweet reminder that very soon this golden locket was all she would have remaining of oldest, dearest friend... and... Claire was no longer a butterfly cocooned... she was a lovely winged butterfly preparing to fly away soon.

Her very first instinct—her only instinct—was indubitably the one thing she could never again do... seek solace against Ben's shoulder.

CHAPTER 5

RULE NO. 5:

ON KEEPING ONE'S BREATH FRESH.

Fresh breath is festal breath! Keep peppermints in your reticule, or, if your reticule is not handy, opt for a sip of brandy or port. Also, please remember you are not required to kiss any animal, no matter how adorable, although you may sometimes find it preferable.

*A*lready well in his cups, Ben reappeared shortly before dinner, still avoiding Alexandra's gaze.

It didn't matter, she told herself. She didn't need Ben's approval, nor his attention, but then, to make matters worse, she was assigned the worst possible seat at the table. To her right sat Ben—of course—his body rigid and his demeanor inhospitable.

Directly across from her sat Prince Merrick, and flouting all convention, he sat beside his cheery wife.

Naturally, Ian and Claire took seats of honor, and after everyone was settled there were still a few empty seats remaining for the Duchess and her brood. It was all Lexie could do not to rise up and take one of those, because Ben's proximity was making her feel... *confined.*

Tipping her goblet, she drained what little remained of her champagne then smiled amenably at Prince Merrick, hoping against hope that he wouldn't remember the horrible night at Almacks. To her relief, he smiled back, and said conversationally, "As I understand it, you and Claire have been friends for quite some years?"

Very gently, as though the glass might break, Alexandra put down her now empty goblet. "Yes, Your Highness," she said very politely.

"Call me Merrick," he insisted. "Amidst friends, I am neither prince nor regent." He lifted his glass, knocking it toward his brothers and said, "In any case, the honor now belongs to my brother."

"Merrick," she relented. "Thank you."

But she couldn't help it; tears stung her eyes as she cast Claire a discomfited glance. It seemed inevitable that every person in attendance must know her history with Claire... and her father's, as well.

"Oh, but Merrick," said Ben, lifting his gaze—like a viper. "Perhaps you don't recall, but you two have already had the pleasure of an introduction..."

Judas!

Alexandra blinked, refraining from casting Ben a baleful glance. Forcing a smile, she tried hard not to fling out an elbow and "accidentally" poke him in the eye. That night at Almacks was easily the most embarrassing evening of Alexandra's life. She'd gushed incessantly over Prince Merrick, only to share a very brief dance with him—completely orchestrated by her mother—and then, after suffering his unyielding silence and countering it with endless chatter, he'd discarded her wordlessly by her mother's side, his boredom and disdain perfectly equitable in his expression.

Far from that now, Prince Merrick smiled very warmly, casting yet another loving glance at his wife. "Actually, I do recall," he said good-naturedly. "One of Victoria's soirees, is that correct?"

"Yes," said Alexandra, her cheeks burning hot. "I believe it must have been the first time you visited London."

More to the point, it was the first time he was invited by the Duchess of Kent to shop for a bride amidst her protégées. Her mother had gotten it into her head that Alexandra should be the one, and despite that she hadn't had any romantic notions over becoming a queen, she'd felt beautiful that night, dressed in blue-pink shot silk taffeta—until.

She slid Ben a thankless glance, only to discover he was watching her now, one brow raised. So then, was he trying to embarrass her on purpose?

"If memory serves," continued Merrick. "I recall you to be quite the cheerful young lady. I'm afraid, for personal reasons, that was not my finest moment." He gave her an apologetic tilt of his head. "At any rate, it is, indeed, a pleasure to see you again, Lady Alexandra—and this time under far more pleasant circumstances. I very much look forward to your good cheer."

"As do I," said his wife. "I'm so pleased to meet you, Lady Alexandra."

Alexandra swallowed. "Yes... well... I, too am thankful for the opportunity."

And she was.

Truly, she was.

But heaven knew, she hadn't felt "cheerful" in months and months, and she was beginning to fear she might never again—certainly not with stabs in the back such as the one perpetrated by Ben. Why in the name of love would he say such a thing? Only to needle her?

Lady Morrissey added, "If you're anything at all like my dearest Claire, something tells me we shall *all* be fast friends!"

"Claire is wonderful," agreed Lexie, and she lifted up her fork—not because she was hungry, but imagining herself thrusting it at Ben, and wishing vehemently the evening were already over. With her left hand, she fingered the locket at her breast, taking comfort in Claire's thoughtful gift.

Except for Ben, everybody was treating her so kindly, their joy over being together more than apparent—so why did she feel so inexorably glum?

Because Ben mattered, she realized. And it seemed to Lexie that he must despise her. The entire evening was proving to be almost as much a disaster as Almacks and it was all she could do to hold back tears as she sat listening to the remainder of the discourse.

Only perhaps to make her feel more comfortable, Claire went on and on about hers and Alexandra's childhood together—to utter exhaustion, because despite her bright and colorful description of Alexandra, Alexandra didn't like the way it made her sound: vacuous, insipid, puerile, silly, frivolous and completely irresponsible. Really, how could anyone have any adulation for the girl Claire described?

Oh, yes, she understood Claire meant her account with the kindest of regards, but Lexie was no longer that same foolish chit. And neither did she care to remember how very close she had been with Ben—not when he seemed so perfectly content to toss her beneath a carriage!

Gracious as ever, Claire thanked Alexandra for dragging her out of the house on the night of Prince Merrick's London reception, mainly because, had she not, Claire might never have married the man of her dreams. Despite that she and Ian met previously, it wasn't until that reception that she suddenly, unexpectedly found herself engaged to a Prince—or so everyone believed.

(As it turned out, Merrick was not Merrick at all. Prince Merrick was really Ian. And Prince Ian was really Merrick. It was all so confusing!)

Thankfully, Claire left out the one reason they'd gone to the silly ball in the first place—because she had dearly hoped to make Ben jealous.

Sadly, it was true. She had only ever longed for Ben to realize that if he didn't make some move forthwith, she might be lost to him evermore.

And then, when she was proven to be less than desirable, he was a witness to the entire disaster.

That was the only reason she'd cried—not because Prince Merrick discarded her. There was simply nothing about the Prince that appealed to her, and it was only now, in the comfort of this holiday-inspired home, that she realized he must be more than she'd once supposed. It was quite evident that he loved his wife, and he wasn't as cold as she'd feared. In fact, he was far, far kinder to her throughout the evening than Ben seemed inclined to be.

She was grateful when the conversation ventured elsewhere, but all the while she quietly drank whilst she listened to Benjamin and Wes discuss their recent collaboration—what it could be Alexandra daren't ask because it sounded suspiciously as though it were born of the troubles Ben endured with her father—not a topic that would endear her to anyone. So, then, every time her champagne glass was refilled, Alexandra lifted the bubbly to her lips, quaffing the contents.

During the course of the evening she also learned that the abdication of Meridian's throne was not yet official, that Prince Ian would accept his crown in a ceremony to be held in the province of Meridian one month following his and Claire's nuptials. As a compromise to the bride and her family, the wedding itself would be held in London, witnessed and blessed by King William.

Alexandra herself might have been wounded over the fact that not only did she not know anything about the extraordinary event, but now she wondered who would be Claire's maiden of honor... Chloe... Lady Morrissey... God forbid, please not Victoria?

And yet, so much as she would like to take offense over it all, it was really impossible to feel any enmity toward anyone but Ben, because amidst all the things Alexandra learned this evening, she was also discovering how very rude Ben could be—utterly and hopelessly.

Rude.

Indeed, she was only beginning to realize how very fine that line was between love and hate—and, yes, indeed, she had loved Ben... truly, madly and passionately. As passionately as she was beginning to loathe him right now.

Blackguard.

Cad.

Rude, insufferable bore.

She took yet another sip of champagne, her melancholy turning to unmitigated fury.

"Alexandra," said Chloe, lowering a hand to her belly—a gesture not entirely encouraged in polite society, though it gave a very nice sense that she was caressing her unborn child. "Will you be joining us in Meridian for the coronation?"

"I..."

"Oh, we haven't discussed that yet," interrupted Claire. "But I suppose now is as good a time as any." She turned to address Alexandra, smiling genuinely. "Alexandra, since we are rushing away directly after the ceremony… I dearly hoped you would allow—" She turned her brilliant gaze upon Ben— "My brother to escort you to Meridian."

Blinking in surprise, both Alexandra and Ben turned to look at each another, their gazes mirroring the same sense of horror. Ben smiled tightly. And then suddenly, their gazes skittered away—Alexandra's to her plate, and Ben's to meet his sister's hopeful gaze. He sighed then, and it sounded as though his entire chest deflated before answering, but he said, "Yes, yes, of course. It would be my pleasure."

And then he glanced at Alexandra—or at least she *felt* his regard, and realizing all eyes must be upon them, Alexandra lifted her gaze to meet Ben's glinting green eyes. She forced a smile. "Yes," she said. "I, too, would be delighted." Though her heart beat so ferociously over that lie that she feared the entire company must hear it.

"Wonderful," said Ben.

"Wonderful," said Alexandra.

"Wonderful," said Claire. "Now that that's settled, would anybody like to try a bit of plum pudding?"

When nobody reached for it, she said, "Funny. The General and his wife made us promise to try it. They made it weeks and weeks ago, only to learn they would be traveling. Alas, we did the same, never dreaming we would eat so much plum pudding!"

Like a small brown hill, the lump of pudding sat unclaimed, pitifully ignored—like Alexandra. All eyes traveled elsewhere—the ceiling, the walls, the buffet, and Alexandra's gaze traveled to the door, feeling as lamentable as the lump of pudding. Why, oh why had she come?

* * *

ESCAPING the very instant she could, Lexie found a quiet place to hide in the *parterre*. What a change—Claire holding court, whilst she hid from the revelry. Only tonight Alexandra felt quite certain Claire wouldn't be searching high and low for her, because Claire herself was at the center of attention and in rare form.

The entire lot of them were now ensconced in the parlor, drinking arrack punch and playing charades.

Alexandra didn't need any punch. She'd had more than enough sparkling champagne over dinner—nervous drinking, she supposed. A little time out in the fresh, crisp air would do her good.

Except... now she wished she'd brought herself a heavier coat, especially if she was going to be sequestering herself out in the garden. And nevertheless, at the moment she was far too furious with Ben to be the least bit sad, or even cold. Anger kept her warm as surely as would a hearth fire. And still there was *nothing* cozy about this holiday—*nothing* at all to remind her of those days in Shropshire. Those days were done!

You must not grieve them, she told herself.

He's not worth it!

Peering up at the night sky, she noted that the stars appeared to be completely obscured, not a single one remaining to be wished upon—not that she had wishes to make, mind you.

None beyond the simple fact that she wished her father wasn't such a scoundrel and that her life wasn't such a mess. But, really, where to begin?

If there were but one thing she could have undone... what would that be?

Shivering under her pelisse, she wandered through the garden, distracting herself with the flower beds.

Most of the beds were filled with roses and *heliotropium*—fine, fine choices, particularly during the heat of summer because the scent was bound to conceal even the worst from the Thames. In full bloom, the *heliotropium* would give off a nice vanilla-almond-scent that attracted butterflies en masse. Smiling, she fingered the necklace, taking pleasure in the thoughtful gift.

This time of the year the flowers were already spent —looking as brittle as she felt. And yet, like dabs of hope against a mantle of gloom, some of the roses were still blooming, peppering the garden with a smattering of pink and white blooms. Drawn instead to one of the *heliotropium* plants, she wondered if it had any medicinal properties. Most plants did, and she wished she had her notepad with her so she could sketch this particular leaf. That's what she enjoyed best: sketching flowers, putting notations on the pages. Someday, she might like to bind them, and maybe publish her efforts. Brushing her thumb across the edge of the serrated leaf, considering an appropriate *nom de plume*, she wondered how many women published in secret...

If not that, what was she supposed to do with her life from here forth? Certainly, she would visit Meridian, but she didn't wish to move there, nor had Claire even proposed such a thing. In fact, Alexandra had never felt more disconnected from Claire in her entire life.

At some point, she could descend upon her mother in Shropshire. But wouldn't that be cozy?

She snorted inelegantly over the very notion, although, at some point, she really must make amends. Only considering that her mother hadn't been very forthcoming, Alexandra supposed she must be the one to make concessions. Lady Eveline was her only remaining blood relation, aside from a few distant cousins she didn't know well, but, Lady Eveline wasn't the most forgiving woman. Nor was she very warm.

It might help if Alexandra were already wed by the time they came face to face. But, in truth, no one was good enough for her mother—neither titled nor monied. A gentleman must have both money and title, and it was no wonder that Lady Eveline had pressed her to meet Prince Merrick, only to fume so miserably when he'd dismissed her out of hand. Only a royal prince had ever piqued her mother's interest—and, if Alexandra could be honest with herself, that, too, had been yet another reason she'd wept so bitterly over Merrick's unintended insult. She was left stung by her mother's unvarnished disappointment, and entirely hopeless to make amends for something she'd had no means to change.

Really, she loathed to think what her mother would say if, like Prince Merrick, she chose to marry a commoner. But there again, he was a man, as well as a Prince, and no doubt empowered to do whatsoever he pleased.

Sadly, she'd suffered her father's scrutiny no less. Unlike her mother, Lord Huntington hadn't cared overmuch about the financial wellbeing of any particular suitor, but he was incessantly concerned over titles —not that he *ever* had a chance to obtain a shred of nobility in his wife's estimation. And now... there wasn't a soul in London who would raise Lord Huntington above the villain he was.

Really, for all practical purposes, Alexandra had been alone for much of her life. The only bright spots had ever been Claire... and Ben...

Don't think about him!

Cursing beneath her breath, she plucked a frostbitten leaf, dreaming about a design for her *new* conservatory. She should get rid of that stupid ballroom once and for all. She hadn't a taste for balls anymore. There was more than enough room for a conservatory, and what was more, that particular room overlooked the garden. It would be perfect... and then she could design a *parterre* like...

Alexandra never heard the footfalls approach. "*You,*" said Ben, and the single word felt like the pointy end of a dagger.

Alexandra spun to face him, the look on his face openly contemptuous, as though someone were holding a stinker beneath his nose. "Yes, it's me," she said flatly. "What do you want, Ben?"

"Not a bloody damned thing," he said. "Gad! Don't you have some gown to press, or something?"

Alexandra tilted him an affronted glance, lifting a hand to her breast, crushing the *heliotropium* leaf. "*I* was here first," she pointed out. "Really, Ben, don't *you* have some other poor soul to delude?"

In answer, he lifted his brow, drawing forth a cheroot from his coat pocket and putting it between his lips, though he didn't light it. Alexandra eyed the cigar with open distaste. Before Ben's sweep through the Gaming Hells, he had never smoked a day in his life— not so far as Lexie knew. And regardless, the Benji she had grown to admire would never have dared smoke in front of a lady, nor would he speak to her so rudely.

"When did you become such an ash mouth?"

His dark brow lifted higher, and he offered Lexie a wintry smirk. "What concern is it of yours, Alexandra?" —Alexandra, not Lexie!— "Despite all the bloody mistletoe hanging about, you'll never be troubled by my ash mouth... *never again.*"

His green eyes glinted, and she knew... oh, yes, she knew... he was as tormented by that kiss as she was. Something about that gave her immense satisfaction. And, furthermore, if he thought for one second that she was going handle his effrontery the way she had Prince Merrick's—with tears—he was sorely mistaken. She was *not* that sweet, little innocent girl any longer. It might not be a butterfly that had emerged from her chrysalis—only a common, ugly moth—but she was still ready to fly away.

He searched for and found his striker, ferreting it out of his pocket, offering Alexandra a thin smile, as though to spite her. He struck it once, putting the flame to his cheroot, inhaling deeply as he lit the foul-smelling cigar. The tip glowed bright red against the darkness, lighting his face red, and he drew it away from his sinfully beautiful lips, exhaling a stink that lingered like a frost cloud in the air. Alexandra waved it away before it could venture near, and said, "I hope you won't be indulging during our travels, or at least in my presence."

His stark green eyes, so like Claire's, glittered fiercely. "Ah, yes... your presence... something I intend to suffer as little as possible, I assure you."

Suffer?

Alexandra had had enough. She tossed away her leaf very indignantly. "Really, Ben, if you didn't wish to escort me to Meridian, why would you agree to it?"

In answer, he shrugged, taking yet another puff and once again pulling the cheroot from his lips, ever so slowly. There was something not quite civil about the way he blew out the smoke in the shape of an O. "Because Claire asked," he said, "And, as you must realize by now, I am quite fond of my little sister."

"Yes, well. So am I," Alexandra reminded him.

"Naturally. So there you have it. I agreed for the very same reason you agreed, *Lexie*." He eyed her coolly. "And yet... this is why you came running to Highbury with apologies... because you care?"

His accusation stung because it was true... she had been so overcome with grief and so self-involved after her father's arrest that she hadn't dared go to Claire...

"For Claire," he said. "I would walk through flames... especially since she did so for me... thanks to your father."

And there it was.

He blamed her. He blamed her very, very much. But for all his blame, did he ever bother to take any for himself?

Injured by his words, nearly as much as she was by his animosity, Alexandra stamped her foot, and spun on her heels, bolting away before he could spy the angry tears forming in her eyes, even against her will. She hurried into the house, past the parlor, past the laughter, past Claire and her new friends—

"Lexie!" shouted Claire. "There you are! Alexandra!"

Alexandra didn't stop. She hurried toward the paneled stairwell, but Claire rushed into the hall to catch her before she could flee.

"We're singing," she said brightly. "Please, please, please... come join us. You're the best!"

Alexandra shook her head. "I really shouldn't..."

"Please," begged Claire, smiling such an irresistible smile that Alexandra couldn't possibly say no.

Like Ben, there wasn't very much in this entire world she wouldn't do for Claire.

"For me," she begged, and what could Alexandra do but surrender. Pasting on a brave smile, she cast one last glance toward the door from whence she'd come and then followed Claire into the parlor.

* * *

HE WATCHED HER GO, utterly disgusted with himself.

The truth was that he hadn't the first clue why he was driven to bedevil her.

He knew that none of his travails were Lexie's fault.

But her father was such a shiftless, heartless bastard—a wastrel, a blackguard.

And nevertheless... so was he. *He* had put himself into a position to be done up by impost takers. He, himself, had given Huntington the means to beggar him, and that was neither Alexandra's father's fault, nor was it hers. It was his. The problem was... he couldn't look at Lexie without remembering that bit of truth.

Nor did he wish to fall back into his old ways, enabling a child, consoling her tears.

He was no longer quite so glib as he one was, no longer so beetle-headed, nor... respectable.

Ash mouth.

He plucked the cheroot from his lips, lifting it to his nostrils for a sniff.

Bloody vixen.

Ash mouth.

As he stood contemplating Alexandra and his sister's meddling, snow began to fall, and that too was an oddity for these parts.

A cold day in Hell.

That's what this was.

It was a cold day in Hell and Ben rather suspected he understood why he was so vexed by Alexandra's company. She made him recall things he didn't wish to recall... lost youth, lost opportunity, lost repute.

Some part of him desperately longed for simpler days when he could be lost in her sweet laughter, those sweet, amber-flecked eyes. But she wasn't the same anymore either. In fact, there was something about Alexandra that was distinctly different, something he couldn't put his finger to...

Counting all the weeks he'd spent in Fleet, it had been nearly a year since he'd last seen her, much less spent any time in her company. And, in truth, he hadn't seen her much before that terrible night—not since before his father died. As soon as he'd discovered the state of their finances, he'd set himself the task of restoring their good fortunes—a lot of good he'd done. He'd gambled away the last of their legal tender, and then he'd made himself a fool...

He stared a long, hard moment at the doorway through which Alexandra had fled. He had, indeed, spied her out here, in the garden, and damned if he wasn't drawn to her like a moth to a flame. No matter that his anger was simmering too near the surface, he had longed for her company, and yet he'd approached her with enmity—why?

In fact, he had always suspected there was more to Lexie than what she allowed people to see... a certain something that called to his spirit. And really, there must be some reason she was drawn to Claire.

More to the point, there must be a reason he was drawn to her...

Only now he feared what he saw in the depths of Alexandra's eyes... sadness—a sadness she generally hid with good humor and frivolity. Only now that he understood its root cause, he wasn't entirely certain she would ever heal.

And worse, perhaps Ben was a cause for it.

Or perhaps he still feared she was too much like her father—and yet no... that wasn't it at all.

It was this: He loved her. He still loved her madly; he just didn't *like* her anymore—no more than he liked himself. And that was the rub, he supposed. Alexandra was too much like him, and he hadn't recognized that before because there was no shade put upon his life. His parents had loved both their children deeply, and if their father had left them without funds or options, it wasn't because he was a bounder. He'd spent every penny caring for his family and tending to their ailing mother. His father had had only noble intentions... but... Ben had not.

For a while, he must confess, here and now... he had enjoyed that life for a moment... smoke curling in the air, bosoms heaving near his face... glasses clinking on the table...

Now... well... he was changed... and not for the better... and all because of Alexandra's father.

Snow fell harder, leaving white specks on his dark frock coat, and nevertheless, he didn't stir himself to go back inside... there was nowhere to walk in there without standing within five feet of damnable mistletoe —and if Lexie so happened to be standing anywhere near a sprig, he might be tempted beyond reason to find out if she still tasted the way he remembered.... sweet and fresh, with just a hint of spice.

Gods bones. Even now... he was hard as stone over the memory... and what was worse, he knew she was plagued by those memories as well, and the blush in her cheeks... it made him yearn to give her another reason to burn.

Damn it, Claire.

The sound of music reverberated from within, and he tossed down his cheroot, stamping it out, realizing he couldn't hide forever. It was bloody cold, and already, the snow was growing thick enough to cover the stone path. Blast and damn! It was going to be a long, long week, and if they ended up being housebound, he was going to go mad.

CHAPTER 6

RULE NO. 6:
ON OBLIGATION.

Whatever you do, do NOT run away if you are asked for a kiss. Although you may, indeed, take strategic action to avoid it, once caught beneath a sprig, and a kiss has been requested, you simply *must* comply, or you will risk never receiving a marriage proposal for the duration of the year— worse yet, you might risk the fate of becoming a spinster! Remember, ladies: Every Season counts!

In fields where they lay keeping their sheep,
On a cold winter's night that was so deep...

*I*t was true: Alexandra might still be impaired by the spirits she'd drunk, though it didn't help matters very much that it had been so long since she'd practiced her piano—really, what was the point in practicing when there was no one about to entertain?

And regardless, no one seemed fazed by her blundering, and the more joyous everyone sang, the testier she became.

This was *all* Ben's fault.

How dare he speak to her so rudely!

How dare he make her feel as though she were the one to blame for *all* his ills!

He was the one who'd courted ruin. Ben did—not her! He was the one who'd put himself at her father's disposal.

Blast and damn. Alexandra didn't feel like singing nor making merry, not even when Mr. Cameron and the brothers joined the chorus, belting out the words with voices that were perfectly in harmony. Their joy should have been infectious, but Alexandra felt only like shouting, bah, humbug!

Nowell, Nowell, Nowell, Nowell
Born is the King of Israel!

Her emotions simmering just beneath the surface, she tapped out the keys, when, really, what she longed to do was give in to a rare fit of temper and pound angrily upon the keyboard. *Bloody damnation!* Ben had done this to her. *He* had made her feel like an undesirable—once again! Precisely the way she'd felt that night when Prince Merrick discarded her so rudely at her mother's side. The disgrace of it all nearly choked away her breath and it didn't help matters at all that she was still jug-bitten besides.

Together, they all sang...

...drawing nigh to the northwest,
O'er Bethlehem town took its rest;

But in Alexandra's livid mind, she heard:

...drawing that nasty cheroot with his
    fingers.
Why, oh, why did I linger...

Nowell, Nowell, Nowell, Nowell
Born is the King of Israel!

"Huzzah!" said Chloe.

"Beautiful," said Claire.

And then the entire lot clapped generously despite all the many ways Alexandra's piano playing must have sorely offended their ears.

One man clapped louder than the rest: Ben.

Rosy-cheeked from the weather, he'd come in from the garden, and was now standing beneath the arched entry, beneath a miserable sprig of mistletoe. Eyeing Alexandra very purposefully, he reached up, popped a drupe from the sprig, inspected it with disgust, then lifted a brow and tossed it away.

In that instant something mad came over Alexandra. Everyone faded from the room, and there was only her and Ben—miserable rotten cad that he was—and she longed so desperately to tell him exactly how she felt.

She hardly knew what possessed her, but whatever it was, it was a long, long time coming—every time she'd said yes when she'd rather say no, every smile she ever gave when she preferred to weep, every heartbreak she ever knew came rushing to the moment.

"I know a song!" she said sweetly. "An oldie but goodie—Welsh, I believe. Taught to me by my mother. Nos Galan. Here it is..." And before she could stop herself, she tapped out the keys, playing the pianoforte as loudly as you please, and then, tipsy though she was, she began to sing...

Cold is the man who cannot love
Fa la la la la, la la la la.

"I don't believe I know that one," said the entirely too delightful Lady Morrissey.

"Oh, Lexie," said Claire, perhaps recognizing the New Year's carol from their youth, warning of bills that followed the holidays and spending more than what was earned—a cautionary tale for wastrels, a jab from her mother to her father. And what better manner of delivery than to employ one's own daughter to deliver it! Alexandra ignored everyone, desperate to sing the next verse.

Chilling are the bills
Fa la la la la, la la la la.

Alexandra peered directly at Ben as she sang one final verse, not caring that she sang completely out of tune and her fingers were missing the keys.

Never spend more than you earn,
Fa. La. La. La. La! La. La! La! La!

She ended the song on a discordant note, realizing only belatedly how much sentiment she'd put into the last fa, la, las.

"My goodness. That certainly isn't very cheerful,"

said Lady Morrissey. "Someone should rewrite those atrocious lyrics."

Surprised by her outburst, even Ben looked appalled. His brow furrowed, and he looked at her as though she were a viper that had slid out from beneath the settee and she suddenly felt like one too.

It was all too much!

Alexandra was suddenly ashamed.

"I... I... am sorry," she said. "I don't know what came over me." She put a hand to her belly, and said, "I... I don't feel very well." And without another word, she rose up, pushing away from the pianoforte, nearly tripping over the bench in her hasty escape.

In all her life she had never dared succumb to such vociferousness, and in doing so now, she didn't feel any better. To the contrary, she felt far worse than before, and so much as she'd tried to stay strong, she needed desperately to cry.

* * *

"THERE, THERE," said Claire, patting Alexandra on the back.

How many times had they comforted each other just so? Ofttimes, it was Alexandra comforting Claire through some bit of outrage, most notably over the world's many injustices. Claire was precisely the sort to hand out pamphlets in the park or scold a man for shouting at his wife. And really, Lexie had understood that inclination only too well, so she'd often told Claire all the same things she told herself in order to tamp down her own sense of outrage: Not everything in life was fair —this wasn't: the simple fact that her father had effectively destroyed her two most cherished relationships, not to mention her relationship with her mother as well.

And yet, though Claire had so often taken the weight of the world upon her shoulders, she had never once been spiteful. Alexandra could *never* again claim such a thing.

Laying atop the strange bed she was meant to share with her dearest friend—perhaps for the last time ever—she sobbed inconsolably into a fat, fluffy pillow.

Claire sat beside her, patting her tangled hair, and for the briefest instant—so fleeting an instant—it *felt* as though nothing really had changed, that they were still young women, fresh-faced and ignorant of all the ills life held in store. Except... that was no longer the case... they were *not* in familiar surroundings. These bedrooms with their oak-paneled walls and shuttered windows were not at all brightly lit or cheery. Never mind all the scandals they had seen; Alexandra herself had never behaved so poorly!

Claire's life was taking a beautiful, magical turn—she was marrying a prince, quite literally. And meanwhile, Lexie was left to choke on her grief. And here, again, she lay sobbing on account of Ben—that terrible, heartless cad!

How many tears had she shed over him by now?

And mostly over these past six months.

"I am so, so sorry," said Claire. "I didn't realize... I should never have asked you to play for us."

"No! Please! Don't be sorry," Alexandra wailed. "We are celebrating, after all!"

"Yes, well," said Claire, tilting her head. "Still, I didn't realize you were feeling so... melancholy. And I really should have remembered... this time of year has always been so difficult for you."

Alexandra swallowed convulsively, rolling over onto her back, swiping tears from her eyes as she faced her best friend.

Who else in her life would know such a thing—that she cried despondently nearly every single Christmas?

"Please, Claire... don't feel badly," she said. "You had every right to ask."

"Oh, Lexie... I do hope you will come to spend holidays with me in Meridian. I promise you; I will see to it you are pampered and adored."

Alexandra wiped her eyes yet again and then hiccoughed, realizing that, no matter how many tears Claire had watched her shed, Claire could never truly understand.

It had never been easy with her parents so at odds, but it was downright miserable after her mother refused to allow Ben and Claire to join them in Shropshire. In retrospect, Alexandra had only ever been despondent when not in their company, and only ever aware of her misery because of the stark comparisons of their households. In so many, many ways, their relationship was a double-edged sword, and even so, Alexandra couldn't bear the thought of losing her dearest friends—and, yes, this included Ben.

Somehow that was the worst of it all. "I'm only sad to be losing you," she confessed.

Claire's expression softened. She tilted Lexie a questioning glance. "Losing me? Why ever would you think so?"

Alexandra swallowed yet again, only this time with great difficulty, because the knob in her throat seemed to have grown large enough to choke her.

"You are *not* losing me," insisted Claire, and she reached out to take Alexandra by the hand, squeezing very gently. "You will *never* lose me, Lexie! You're my oldest, dearest friend, and this you will *always* be, no matter where I live. And really, I have so much to thank you for..."

Alexandra grimaced, only thinking about all her father had done to Claire. "Equally as much to spite me for as well."

"This is *not* true," said Claire, shaking her head. "I already told you, Lexie. I do *not* blame you for what your father did. He was a despicable man, but you, his only daughter, are no less his victim. And if you do not mind me saying so, your mother is a selfish prig!" She lifted Alexandra's hand and pressed it to her breast, hugging it fiercely.

Lexie swallowed yet again. "Your brother blames me."

"He does not!"

"Oh, but he does, Claire! I see it in his face whenever he looks at me."

Despondent over the thought, Alexandra began to sob again, tears spilling from her eyes as she remembered the bitterness in Ben's words and that horrid look in his eyes as he'd tossed away that drupe. Bittersweet though it might have been, that kiss was a memory Alexandra cherished, and he was willing to throw it away so easily!

"Ben..." Claire paused for a long moment to better consider her words. "I must admit, he's still quite troubled by his time in Fleet. I cannot imagine what atrocities he endured there. But I promise you, Lexie, he will get over it, and I must confess, I did hope that in close proximity you two might find a way to come together."

Lexie remained silent, fervently wishing the same. It was bad enough that Claire would be leaving London... only with Ben she might bear it...

"It would please me immensely to know you were... *close*. Supporting each other in my absence." She squeezed Lexie's hand yet again, then let go, and then she, too, laid down on the bed to gaze up at the ceiling.

"When will you leave?"

Claire sighed. "The end of February."

"How wonderful," said Alexandra, and then... really... she didn't know what else to say.

She had always dreamt Claire would stand for her at her own wedding, and she would stand for Claire...

"I've asked Chloe and Lady Morrissey to stand as my bridesmaids," Claire said finally, as though reading Alexandra's mind.

"How nice."

"Very," said Claire, reaching out and taking her again by the hand, lacing her fingers through Alexandra's. "And you... I rather hoped you would stand as my first bridesmaid... will you?"

"Me?"

Claire nodded.

Bleary eyed, Alexandra tightened her throat so she wouldn't sob like a baby, and then they laid together without speaking, holding hands.

"I don't have a dress," Alexandra said after a while, but that wasn't a refusal... to the contrary, nothing would give her more pleasure.

"Oh, but you do," said Claire, with a smile in her voice. "I was going to give it you when I asked... not here, but at home. The dressmaker from Courtauld's made it in your favorite color."

"Blue," said Alexandra with a hitch to her voice. It wasn't a question.

"Blue," said Claire.

"Nothing would give me more pleasure than to stand at your wedding."

"Good," said Claire. And then there was nothing more to say. They were two old friends lying side by side, staring at the ceiling, and nothing would ever change that—not even marriage.

"Shouldn't you go down and tend to your guests?"

"Oh, no," said, Claire, with a smile in her tone. "They'll fare well enough without us. It's time to retire anyway, and…" She placed a hand to her belly. "I'm afraid you're not the only one who overindulged."

Alexandra giggled drunkenly, thinking of the first time Claire ever tried arrack punch—that night of her party at Vauxhall Gardens, at some gala planned by the Duchess of Kent. "I did warn you," Alexandra said.

Claire giggled softly. "But you didn't heed your own warning."

Both girls fell into sudden fits of giggles, squeezing each other's hands. They laughed until they couldn't any longer, then sighed contentedly.

"Say Claire… do you remember that night of Merrick's reception?"

"How could I *ever* forget?"

"That look on your face when Merrick put the ring on your finger!"

"Ian," Claire corrected.

"Ian," said Alexandra. "He's nice," she relented.

"He is, and so is Prince Merrick… if you'll give him a chance."

Alexandra tried to reconcile that man belowstairs with the man she'd met at Almacks—the one who'd made googly eyes at his wife and tried so hard to put a stranger at ease at the dinner table. "I suppose there's more to everyone than meets the eye," she said.

"Yes, which brings me to Ben," she said. "Really, Alexandra, you must know he blames himself." Claire squeezed her hand. "He'll never speak an ill word of my father, but you must know that my father left us in too deep, and Ben… well, he tried to save us."

"Really?" said Alexandra, turning to look at Claire in surprise, and Claire nodded very soberly. "But I thought—"

Claire shook her head, knowing only too well what Alexandra must have thought… that Ben was the one responsible for all their woes.

"I see," said Lexie, and suddenly she did. She understood something she didn't before... Ben didn't so much blame Lexie... he blamed himself... no less than she blamed him as well. It was no wonder he'd responded so coldly to her... he knew her well enough to see it all in her eyes... so then... if she wanted that to change, she must look at him another way...

"Feel better?" asked Claire.

Alexandra smiled. "I do," she said. "I really do."

CHAPTER 7

21 DECEMBER

RULE No. 7:
  ON KEEPING IT QUICK.
  A kiss beneath the mistletoe *must* be quick and close-lipped. Only a peck upon the cheek or the lips will do. If a napkin is required after, then you have done it all wrong!

*T*he very next morning, Alexandra encountered Ben in the gallery, with his hat in hand, studying a portrait. Embarrassed by her outburst in the parlor last evening, she longed to slip away unnoticed, but he peered up the stairwell to catch her eye, and she was forced to put on a brave face.

"Morning," she said, but not so coolly as she'd spoken to him yesterday evening.

"Morning," he replied.

It was only belatedly that she realized he had a hat-full of mistletoe and she tilted him a questioning look.

"This," he said, tilting the hat so she could see that it was already full to the brim. "I thought I'd spare us both," he said with a sheepish smile.

. . .

He couldn't help himself.

Ben swallowed as Alexandra approached. She was a vision this morning with that bright red ribbon tied about her ivory dress, looking like a Christmas present he'd like to unwrap... lovely as ever, though something seemed entirely different this morning... different, but inherently familiar... and seeing the Lexie he recognized only made him all the more determined to spare her the grief of having to endure all this mistletoe.

Damn Claire and her meddling.

He reached up, meaning to pluck down a sprig that was hanging from the chandelier in the foyer, but Alexandra approached him and reached up to stay his hand... "Don't," she whispered.

Ben swallowed convulsively. The scent of her was entirely too intoxicating... painfully familiar and he winced. She touched his hand very gently and withdrew as though burned.

"It's not for us," she said, and Ben stared miserably into his hat... remembering another time he'd stood before Alexandra with his hat in his hand, only begging... alas, he wouldn't do that ever again...

Beg.

Already, he'd swept through the house, and managed to remove every last sprig downstairs, except this one...

Alexandra smiled conspiratorially. "How will Lady Morrissey entertain herself if you take them all away," she asked, and he peered up to find a familiar glint in her eyes.

"Right," he said, with a bit of a smirk. "I'll put them back."

"I'll help," she said, and without another word spoken between them, they rehung the mistletoe, then parted ways. This time, when Ben watched her go, he didn't find her quite so vexing… nor himself quite so tormented.

* * *

IN RARE WINTER FORM, the snow continued to fall—more than six heavy inches over the course of two short days.

It was barely cold enough to keep the snow from melting, but not quite cold enough to keep it light and fluffy. The air itself was permeated with a dampness that sank straight into the bones, and there it remained. And therefore, the building of snowmen, or truly, any outdoor enterprise was less than desirable, particularly for those who did not plan for inclement weather—namely Alexandra.

All the fireplaces throughout the residence were lit and kept tended. Activities of preferences were any such endeavor that kept them near to the hearths. All except for singing by the pianoforte. No one else could play well enough to accompany, and Alexandra was too abashed to give it another go.

Using the drift-covered roads as an excuse, the Duchess and her brood did, indeed, end their journey at Hampton Court Palace (even despite the fact that only a mere seven hundred meters separated the Pavilion from the Palace). But that was well and good. Victoria was closer to Merrick's father than she was to Ian or Merrick, and perhaps knowing their father wasn't planning to attend the holiday, she was far less inclined to be present.

And really, although poor Drina was more than accustomed to adult company, it would seem a tad gauche to involve her in a holiday with so many twains. Alexandra herself might have considered it perfectly gauche to be invited, though she was beginning to catch a notion of what Claire had intended. And, it seemed to Lexie that God himself must be conspiring with Claire, because in these parts, they rarely experienced snow days, and when they did arrive, it was already melted by eventide. Quite to the contrary, it was piling upon windowsills, frosting panes, and generally turning everything white, white, white.

So, it seemed, Claire had some less than angelic help as well...

Chloe might be perfectly innocent of their schemes, but Lady Morrissey was conspiring even unto the finer details. Her attention was ever on the sprigs of mistletoe, which she appeared to be moving suspiciously, hither and thither. Either she was placing them strategically for her own designs... else she was plotting... with Claire.

And whatever her true intent, it didn't stop her from teasing Mr. Cameron every chance she got, greedily collecting mistletoe kisses.

In fact, their behavior was scandalous, locking lips, and suckling faces at every juncture in the house.

Regrettably, however, Alexandra no longer had any taste for gossip, and far more than stir her sense of scandalmongering, it fortified her resolve to avoid it at every cost—equally so much as she was resigned to avoiding Ben, as well as the mistletoe.

Ben, too, had made himself scarce after their meeting in the foyer. He and Alexandra formed an unspoken truce, avoiding each other whenever possible, and so it was that when everyone retired to the drawing room for another game of charades, and Ben decided to join them, Alexandra declined the invitation. Instead, she set out to find herself a safe location to sketch—not in the foyer, nor the ballroom, nor the gallery, nor the music room, nor the dining room, nor

the study. All of these rooms were infested with
mistletoe.

"Alexandra!" she heard Claire call as she passed by
the parlor, but this time Lexie daren't be caught. Unfortunately, it was beginning to feel as though her only recourse was to trespass into someone's bedroom, or
hide away in the servant's quarters... or...

She found the library only by chance, hidden away
behind another gallery. One glance about the room revealed it to be entirely free of mistletoe. No doubt
Claire believed it would be the one place in the house
she would have no interest in, which only proved how
clandestine Alexandra had been about her studies. And
meanwhile, Claire was rarely without a tome in hand,
and never much cared one way or another whether she
might be called a bluestocking. Her own father had lovingly called her a solitudinarian—a thing Alexandra
was learning to appreciate, if not entirely by choice.

Once she was safely ensconced in the library, and
blissfully sheltered from any possibility of bumping
into Ben, she perused the shelves, homing in on the
horticulture and botany sections. There, she ran a
finger across the leather-bound volumes, delighting in
all the titles...

*The Rambling Botanist, Trees and Ferns, ABC and XYZ
of Bee Culture, Culpeper's Complete Herbal, Hortus Cantab-
rigiensis: A Catalogue of Plants, British Botany,* and *Harold
Glover's Book of Botany...*

That one, she decided, because it was Glover's work
that most inspired her, along with Nicholas Culpeper's.
Someday, Alexandra hoped a proper woman would
join their ranks. And meanwhile, she discovered precisely what she was searching for within the pages of
Harold Glover's tome. Satisfied, she settled in to read...

The common name for *heliotropium was* Indian he-
liotrope. Species: H. indicum; family *boraginales.*

And yes, indeed, it did have medicinal properties, although it did appear to have a cumulative toxic effect upon the liver.

Occasionally, the leaves were used as a vegetable, but with disastrous results. However, the proper uses were many—in the treatment of warts, inflammation, tumors. It also served as an analgesic to ease rheumatic pain, and then, too, as a diuretic. A decoction of the entire plant could be used to treat thrush, control menses and dyspepsia.

Additionally, mixed with a bit of coconut oil and a very minute amount of salt, the leaves might be administered to children as a remedy for grippe and cough.

Moreover, a poultice made from the leaves could be applied to wounds and to insect bites.

Fascinating.

She only wished she had her sketchpad.

Itching to draw, she got up to search the escritoire, discovering an amazing mechanical pencil and a single sheet of paper. With both in hand, she sat again, placing the sheet atop the book, and putting her pencil to paper, trying to remember the precise form and texture of the leaf from the garden.

If she dared to brave the weather without her pelisse, or the chance of bumping into Ben, she might have gone back to pluck another, but, really, no need... the pencil moved of its own accord... outlining and shading. And yet, much to her surprise, once she lifted the pencil to examine the rendering, she gasped to find it wasn't a leaf she was sketching at all. It was...

Speak of the devil, who should appear... certainly *not* a chubby and plump, jolly old elf...

Benjamin Wentworth opened the library door, peering within. "Oh!" Alexandra exclaimed, and immediately concealed the evidence of her reverie. "Ben! What are you doing here?"

He lifted a brow, only this time, it hadn't a trace of contempt, only perhaps surprise. "I could ask the same of you."

Wholly embarrassed, she folded the drawing and slid it into the book, then hid the book between her hip and the arm of the chair. "I was... well... hiding," she confessed.

"From?"

You, she longed to say.

"The mistletoe. It's everywhere."

"I see," he said, and rather than leave her be, he sauntered into the room, closing the door behind him.

Alexandra's heartbeat quickened painfully. "What are you doing?"

"The same as you," he said. "Hiding."

Alexandra found herself entirely flummoxed. "But really, in here?" She asked desperately. "Why? Can't you find your own hiding place... elsewhere?"

"Actually," he said. "I'm here for the same reason you chose this room."

Alexandra tilted him a suspicious glance. "Why?"

He grinned. "Because there's no mistletoe in here, why else?"

Alexandra blew out a sigh, only grateful that he didn't ask about the book. Only now she wholly regretted having convinced him to leave the mistletoe up.

Seemingly without a care in the world, he slid into one of two red, leather wingback chairs, and then stretched his legs, reclining comfortably. Alexandra couldn't help but note the sinew of his thighs—so apparent even through the fabric of his too-tight trews.

Now what?

"Do you plan to stay... there?"

"Yes," he said.

"Why?" It was all she could do not to come off

sounding as though she were whining, because indeed she was.

Ben tilted her a curious look. "I've already said."

Alexandra pleaded again. "Ben, please! Can't you find another room?"

"Where?"

"I don't know... perhaps the garden?"

"It's snowing in case you haven't noticed."

Alexandra gave him a huff of frustration and began to tap her fingers restlessly atop the arm of the chair.

"Am I making you nervous?"

"No."

"Then *why* are you tapping? Or is that a new habit?"

Alexandra tilted him a long-suffering glance. "Like smoking?"

He smiled again and slid a hand into his jacket, then said, "Speaking of which..."

Alexandra put up a hand. "Please... do not!"

He gave her a half-hearted smile, and said, "Anything for you... Turtle Dove."

Alexandra's cheeks flushed at hearing his nearly forgotten term of endearment—but it also upset her, because she couldn't tell if he were being facetious. "Please don't call me that," she said.

"As you wish."

The two fell silent, though while Alexandra had the good grace to look away—at literally anything else in the room except for Ben—Ben seemed to be staring at her, and every time her gaze returned to his face, he was still watching her.

"You've been hiding quite a lot," he said.

"Yes." It was a simple word, devoid of any defensiveness. She was, indeed, avoiding him, and so she believed he must be avoiding her as well. It was a very keen arrangement, and she only wished he would go back to it forthwith, instead of sitting there, watching her with that ever-so-slight devil of a smirk on those sinfully beautiful lips.

"Because of me?"

"Only partly."

"Then, I must apologize, Lexie. I wasn't myself."

"Who were you then?"

He sighed. "Some angry bloke who mistook a lady for her father."

"And now you are?"

"Myself?"

Alexandra nodded very warily.

Ben lifted one shoulder in a half-hearted shrug, the look on his face oh, so glum. Of late, she felt that way rather often as well, so perhaps they were not so far apart, after all.

They fell into silence, only this time something about Ben's demeanor drew Alexandra out. The words came out in a rush. "I feel as though I don't belong here," she confessed.

"So much has changed," he said.

"Indeed."

"But you don't sound as though you like the changes?"

"Some, I do," Alexandra confessed.

"Same," he disclosed. "Our dearest Claire is off to be Queen, and we are left... alone... to communicate by letters, and perhaps to see her only on occasion."

Alexandra swallowed hard, flattening her hand atop the arm of the chair, a bit of a haze clouding her vision. She didn't want to weep anymore. She wanted to be sober and mature, but everything Ben was saying was perfectly true, and it called to the child within her. Once upon a time... she and Claire... and Ben... they had been a team. Alexandra would be hard-pressed to say which Wentworth was her closest confidante... sometimes Claire... sometimes Ben.

"Alexandra," he said, and his tone sounded entirely too sober.

Suddenly, Alexandra was wholly afraid of what he would say. "Please," she begged.

"I really don't blame you," he said, sitting upright and crossing his legs, wiggling his foot a bit nervously. This was the old Ben, she realized... and though it warmed her heart to see him, it terrified her as well. "Lexie... I don't suppose you will forgive my rudeness?"

"I do," she said. "Can you forgive mine?"

"There's nothing to forgive," he said gently, and Alexandra nodded dumbly.

"And nevertheless," she said, "I am so sorry for all that my father did to you, and what he tried to do to Claire. I only wish I had come to say it sooner." She looked away. "I was... embarrassed."

"I understand," he said. "I think I would have been as well." And there was no censure in his words, only candor. They sat a while, discussing the ordeal, why Alexandra believed her father had done all the things he had done—a sense of just desserts, perhaps, or anger over her mother's judgment. In the end, none of it was any sort of comfort or excuse. And yet, it was a good conversation, perhaps the most sober discourse she and Ben had had in years and years.

"Do you like him?" she asked.

"Ian?" He nodded. "I do. He seems to love Claire very much."

"I can hardly believe he and Merrick are twins, or, for that matter, that their father never had the first inkling when Ian arrived in London after all those years!"

"My father would have noticed at once," said Ben.

"Oh, yes, he would have," Alexandra agreed. "My mother might have, as well. She lives to scrutinize me. But perhaps *not* my father," she confessed. "He scarce paid me any mind at all, even after I took his side in his bitter feud against my mother."

Alexandra sighed ruefully. "In retrospect, I believe I did it to spite her for—"

"The kiss?"

Alexandra nodded, her cheeks blooming as she peered up at Benjamin. It was the first time since the kiss that they were addressing it so frankly, and it was long, long overdue.

"Well... Bloody Norah! I suppose I should say sorry for that, as well... but in truth... I am not."

Alexandra's heart skipped a beat.

Unwittingly, her fingers lifted to her lips, where she could, inexplicably, still taste him.

"Has she called you home?"

"No, and she will not. But she does write, though her letters are still quite full of censure: I should have done this, I should have done that."

"Really, Lexie... I cannot imagine your mother without complaints. And therefore, so as long as you are on speaking terms... there must be hope."

Alexandra smiled, taking heart in his advice. "Yes, well... I do suppose one day I shall have to pay her a visit."

Benjamin smiled. "Perhaps I will join you," he said, and Alexandra's eyes stung again.

"For moral support," he explained. "Though she would be apoplectic," he said, still smiling.

"Incandescently furious," Alexandra agreed, and the two of them laughed... like old times.

And then Ben said, "So... is that a yes... or a no?"

Alexandra's brows lifted in surprise. "You mean go with me... to visit my mother?"

He nodded, and her cheeks burned hotter. "I—" She felt suddenly tongue-tied. Her eyes swam. Uncertain whether he was serious, and heartily afraid he might not be, she bounded up from the chair, and said, "Oh, dear! I almost forgot! I promised Claire I would come play charades!" And then she quickly made apologies and ran away... abandoning Ben ... *and* her book.

BEN WATCHED HER GO... yet again... only this time entirely bemused.

So much for olive branches, he thought, and then his gaze fell upon the book where it fell on the seat... and he spied the bit of paper peeking out from the top... along with the pencil.

Curious, he reached out to lift up the book, opening it and plucking out the piece of paper, unfolding it...

His eyes widened at the sight that greeted him... a caricature... though very well done.

The subject sported not horns nor fangs. But there was, indeed, a bit of youthful mischief in the very familiar eyes. And in his hand he held a top hat, and inside the top hat was a single sprig of mistletoe...

It was Ben.

It was his hat...

Not from the other day, but from a long-ago Christmas in Shropshire.

That morning, bored and full of piss and vinegar, he'd bedeviled Alexandra with a sprig of mistletoe, following her about the house whilst his sister sat reading in the library. He'd worn that top hat all morning long, pulling it off and on and hanging that mistletoe over their heads every chance he got, until finally Alexandra agreed to kiss him...

He sat back, staring at the rendering... and then picked up the book from his lap, turning it to read the spine: Harold Glover's Book of Botany.

Really?

What a mystery she was turning out to be... botany books, caricatures... what next?

Not in all the time he'd ever known her had she ever cracked the spine of a book in his presence, and yet this was not the sort of tome of particular interest to an empty-headed miss whose greatest desires were ballgowns or a well-planned season. He flipped through the pages... drawings of every conceivable verdure... with notations that bent toward medicinal speculation.

Well, well, well...

So, it seemed, there was more to Alexandra Grace Huntington than met the eye, and perhaps it was high time to unravel that mystery for himself...

CHAPTER 8

23 DECEMBER

> **RULE NO. 8:**
> **ON TOUCHING.**
> All the while kissing, keep your hands firmly by your sides, or behind your back. Unless invited to do so, you are *not* to reach out and touch the person or the mistletoe. Wandering hands are bad form, and fodder for gossip. Respect your lady friend and keep your hands to yourself!

*A*lexandra stood eyeing the folded paper in her hand.

Like a frightened schoolgirl, Alexandra fled the library, but she didn't return to the parlor as she'd claimed. Instead, she escaped to her room, where she'd hidden a small book beneath the bed—André & François Michaux's Flora Boreali-Americana. And there, she remained, until Claire returned, arriving with a look on her face that, in retrospect, seemed entirely suspicious—only perhaps Lexie didn't realize because she herself had been behaving rather dubiously, thrusting her pirated book beneath the bed the instant she heard footfalls approaching.

However, only Claire could have slid this piece of paper beneath her pillow. And nevertheless, she had risen and dressed this morn, hurrying away without a word—and, really, since when was she ever so eager to break her fast?

Recognizing the nature of the fold, as well as the texture of the paper, Alexandra very carefully unfolded the parchment, grimacing over the artwork. It was her depiction of Ben—with his hat in hand and a sprig of mistletoe peeking out from within. Drawn from memory, he was younger in the drawing, with his best features in good show—the devilishly arched brow, the twinkle in his eyes, the sensuous lips...

Good Lord! She had forgotten about it in her rush to quit the library... and now, her cheeks burned again.

Had he discovered this and given it to Claire to return to her? And if so, why didn't Claire say anything about it?

Clearly, Claire was aiding and abetting her dear brother, and, so, it seemed, Alexandra encountered yet another plot once she descended to breakfast...

The instant she stepped into the dining room, everyone except Ben exited the room—clearing their plates at once, stuffing their mouths and abandoning their seats, making excuses one after another, until no one remained... except Alexandra and Ben.

Well... she wasn't going to let it bother her. She was quite famished, and, unlike Claire, she was a great fan of breakfast, and there was a little of everything on the buffet—eggs, toast, jam, bacon, bangers, mash, and even a bit of that leftover plum pudding.

"Did you sleep well?" Asked Ben, while she filled her plate.

The last to leave the dining room, Lady Morrissey gave them a giddy backward glance, and then made a good show of pulling Mr. Cameron beneath a sprig of mistletoe in the entryway. Alexandra frowned, hard-pressed not to toss the lady a napkin so she could wipe her chin.

"Splendid," she said, ignoring the pair, as she brought her plate to the table and sat as far as possible from Ben. "And you?"

"Excellent," said Ben. "Most excellent," he said. "I had a fascinating dream…"

"About?"

"Hats."

Filled with mistletoe, Alexandra supposed. Her brows collided, though she refused to rise to the bait. If in fact he meant to poke fun, she was having none of it. "Oh?" She said.

"Indeed."

"Oh," she said again. And then, for all their ease together in the library yesterday afternoon, she felt awkward. "I wonder where everyone has gone off to," she said, forcing conversation only to chase away the silence.

"Perhaps to find a closet," he said, with a grin, and really, it was precisely like him to jest about something so bawdy. It only seemed out of character because of their interactions over this past year. Still, Alexandra tilted him a reproving glance, and then occupied herself with inspecting the eggs on her plate—with an audience in the hall, unbeknownst to Ben, unless he had eyes at the back of his head.

Consequently, conversation was excruciating, but Alexandra did her best to ignore the wretches as Ben discussed the merits of bacon at length.

And then they talked about snow… lots and lots about snow: Apparently, the roads were impassable—it was no wonder the Duchess had remained at Hampton Court Palace. The last time they'd had such a heavy snowfall was back in '14, when Lexie was only six.

Mad King George was still on the throne when the Thames froze over and the city held a Frost Fair, where elephants marched across the river at Blackfriars Bridge and folks stood by eating gingerbread and sipping gin. Ben chattered incessantly, far more chipper than he'd been in ages—at least so far as Lexie knew—although the one subject he did not broach was the caricature Alexandra drew—talk about elephants in the room.

She had half a mind to bring it up now, but some cat got her tongue, and after a while, the silence on her part seemed to be a challenge for Ben.

"So... you enjoy botany?" he asked.

In the distance, Lady Morrissey's head bobbed behind a plant. Then Claire's did as well. "Hmmm?"

"That book you were reading."

"Oh, yes," she said. "I do."

"And what is it about botany that interests you, precisely?"

Annoyed, even though she didn't wish to be, Alexandra dropped her toast onto her plate. "Really, Ben. Do you truly wish to know?"

He nodded emphatically, and suddenly, inexplicably, her mood lifted, and she forgot about breakfast, forgot about time, and even forgot about the Peeping Tom's in the foyer.

"Well... of late, I have been following the works of Charles Darwin. Perhaps you recall him? He spent one summer a few years ago helping his father in Shropshire before attending University."

"You mean the bloke who was on about eating beetles and owls?"

Alexandra pursed her lips and nodded.

"I believe that was the same year—"

"Yes!" Alexandra said quickly, nodding again. "He came to dinner again after you and Claire left. I believe my mother had romantic designs, until he went on and on about bombardier beetles discharging in his hand."

Ben laughed. "Did she show him the door?"

Alexandra giggled, and nodded. "She couldn't see him leave quickly enough, though he did give me a book before he went away, and I've been enthralled ever since."

"Really," said Ben, nodding, his brow furrowing, and he seemed genuinely surprised. "I never even knew."

Alexandra smiled contentedly. "Most recently he wrote a paper about divine design in nature, and, so I understand, that on the twenty-seventh of this month —three days hence—he is to embark upon a journey to investigate geology."

"Where to?"

Alexandra shrugged. "Who knows. My mother didn't say. I suppose she's only pleased he won't be returning to Shropshire any day soon. And yet I shall, indeed, await his discoveries with bated breath."

"So… this is your interest as well—divine design in nature?"

"Oh, no!" said Alexandra. "It is not. I am, of course, fascinated with natural philosophy and zoological speculation, but I much prefer learning about the medicinal properties of plants more than their evolution."

"Medicine," he said, surprising Alexandra with an approving nod. "That's quite a profession. Your mother will be…"

"Don't worry," she said, lifting a hand. "I don't actually intend to practice," she said. "I only wish to—"

Suddenly, from somewhere in the manor came a peal of laughter and then an ungodly squeal, and everyone emerged from their hiding places to go see what the matter was.

Ben himself was up in a flash, and Alexandra was directly behind him. Altogether they rushed into the hall, only to discover that Merrick's wife was suddenly in labor.

Everyone stood staring at the puddle on the floor, as every last occupant of the house came scurrying out of the woodwork.

What was more, everyone, including Chloe's husband, stood staring at poor Chloe, who now stood in the middle of the foyer, looking terrified. No one seemed to have their wits about them to do anything at all— until Chloe bent over and gave another ungodly yowl, and Alexandra realized that, for better or worse, she might be the only one with the knowledge to help. "Is there a midwife?" she asked one of the servants.

The woman looked terrified. "She's late, mum, waylaid by the weather. Her boy took ill, she's—"

"Don't worry! I am a doctor," howled Chloe.

"A lot of good you'll do for yourself in that condition," said Alexandra. "Please," she said to the kitchen maid, "Send someone to Hampton Court at once to inquire about a doctor." And then she turned to yet another servant and demanded, "Boil rags, bring them upstairs." And then to Chloe's husband and to Ben, "Dear God, don't just stand there! Carry her upstairs!"

CHAPTER 9

24 DECEMBER

> **Rule No. 9:**
> **On Keeping It Private.**
> You are *not* required to kiss under a
> mistletoe hanging in any public place. Gen-
> tlemen, please! Be mindful! Ladies, please!
> Consider your reputation!

*B*en didn't recognize the woman possessing
Lexie's body; it certainly wasn't the retiring
young lady he'd known since early years. Proper
though she might still be, she was comporting herself
with all the confidence of a matron—only perhaps to
be expected, considering that she'd fended for herself
most of her life. And still, it surprised Ben. This was
not a face she'd ever allowed him to see.

Like nobody's business, she took charge of the situation, despite that he would have expected his dutiful
sister to fulfill the role. Caught off guard, Claire was as
dumbstruck as the rest of them.

"Well!" said Alexandra, clapping her hands, and
Chloe gave another hapless yelp of pain.

Afterward, all four men scrambled to do Alexandra's bidding, all at once attempting to lift Chloe, but

her husband impatiently shoved everyone aside and swept his wife into his arms to carry her upstairs. Only Alexandra followed, leaving the rest of them to stare, openmouthed, at their ascending forms, and long, long after they had departed, Ben stood staring up the stairwell as Claire wrung her hands with worry. "Well," she said. "We all knew a Christmas baby was entirely possible. But I really didn't believe it would happen."

"I shouldn't have made the poor dear laugh," lamented Lady Morrissey. "I—"

"Stop," said Ian. "We are *all* to blame for not minding our own affairs, but this was *nobody's* fault. That child was due to arrive sooner or later."

"And nevertheless, do you think she overexerted?" worried Lady Morrissey, and Mr. Cameron snapped, "What I believe, my dear, is that Chloe is very, very pregnant."

The servants all dispersed, while Claire, Ian, Cameron and Lady Morrissey all remained to pace the hall and to wait for the physician's arrival. Ben left them to do their worst to the marble floors and ascended to look for Alexandra.

He wasn't particularly worried. In truth, they weren't far from the Palace—only a few hundred meters. Snow or no snow, the doctor would arrive in due time. There was no way they would allow a member of the Royal House of Meridian—a guest of the Crown— to suffer through childbirth unattended. Whether the physician had to travel by horse or by foot, he had no doubt the man would arrive within the hour. And in the meantime, Chloe herself was a doctor, and he found that he was perfectly fascinated—and eager—to learn what more Alexandra knew—Alexandra, the woman he'd so long believed hadn't the head for anything more sober than ballgowns or jewels.

Waiting for her to emerge from Chloe's bedchamber, he stood on the upstairs landing, still watching for the physician's arrival from his vantage of the upstairs window.

His expectations proved entirely correct. A fine thoroughbred appeared in less than thirty minutes time, and once the man arrived and entered the birthing suite, Alexandra herself emerged, wiping her hands on her satin skirts, with hardly a care for stains. With a very shy smile, she came to stand by Ben at the window, and said, "Well... wasn't that exciting?"

Ben found himself grinning at her, seeing her through entirely new eyes—eyes that had never truly seen her before. "Indeed, it was," he said. "You were quite the champ." And he watched as her cheeks bloomed rose.

"I'm sorry if I was rude earlier," she said, looking chagrined.

He lifted a hand. "No need, Lexie. You did as you should have done faced with a lot of bumbling idiots."

"Not quite bumbling," she demurred, and peered down at her hands, then held them primly before her as she glanced out the window. "But sadly," she said. "I was rather enjoying our conversation..."

For once, she'd refrained from saying, but Ben knew very well that's what she was thinking, as was he. And yet, so it seemed, *he* was the one with the mistake in thought. Alexandra couldn't have changed so much overnight. *No, indeed.* She was entirely other than he'd ever supposed—more like Claire than even Claire was. She had a brain, and she wasn't afraid to use it.

"So was I," he admitted, and when Alexandra met his gaze, he could see that she had gleaned some of what he was thinking. Her blush deepened, and she peered down at her joined hands, looking for a moment as she had that day he'd wrangled the promise of a kiss from her...

He had been so callow then... and she so artless—all her feelings discernible in her eyes... as they were right now.

Ben had known then that he'd loved her. Something about that lovely, starry-eyed look she used to give him had always made him feel like a king in her presence—and wasn't that the thing about love? The way one *felt* in a loved one's presence?

Until recently, Alexandra had always made him *feel* as though he was more than he was.

She'd made him long to be the man she wanted him to be...

And then, after the ordeal with her father, he'd found he loathed himself, both in and out of her company.

"She's too good for you," he heard the echo of a voice from years past—a grim-faced ghost he should like to forget.

The one thing nobody ever knew—no one but he and Lord Huntington—was that, indeed, once upon a time, Ben had asked for Lexie's hand in marriage.

Fresh faced, with more balls than brains, and thinking there was no one in this entire world he'd prefer to spend his life with, he'd put himself in front of a monster. And, of course, her father had refused him.

Then later, after his financial burdens were made known, the man had made it a point to remind Ben of their conversation, and the denigrations he'd made. And so, it seemed to Ben that he had managed to live up to every disparaging word.

Not only had he despised himself for what he'd become, he'd feared what he would spy in Alexandra's eyes... so he'd avoided her entirely. And then, when he saw her again, and she looked at him with such disdain... he simply couldn't bear it.

Discomfited perhaps, Alexandra peered over his

shoulder, out the window, and then up over their heads, and her breath caught, drawing Ben's attention to a small sprig of mistletoe hanging over their heads.

He grinned then, hardly inclined to let this pass without pressing his advantage... and yet, before doing so, he intended to give her one last chance to walk away...

"It's everywhere," she said apologetically, as though its presence were entirely her fault, and yet she didn't leave. She stood, glancing again out the window.

Ben waited... but for what, he didn't precisely know —perhaps to savor the moment, to remember the way she looked this very moment, with her lovely green morning dress and her curls haphazardly escaping her coif.

She did, indeed, look a bit worse for the wear, but it didn't matter to him one bit.

He and Lexie stood together so long that after a time, Alexandra spied travelers traipsing through the snow and she tipped her chin so Ben would look as well.

Slowly but surely, a company of carolers took form —traveling from the direction of the Palace. They came laden with gifts, their voices carrying along the sun-warmed winter air, and in that moment, Ben couldn't explain the swell of emotion that compelled him, but he reached out to take Alexandra's hand, his heart hammering fiercely. Much to his relief, she accepted it without question, and still he waited... only wanting her to be certain.

After everything they'd endured, he didn't want to marry Alexandra to spite her father—that was the furthest thing from his mind. But, in that moment, he knew beyond a shadow of doubt that he still wished to marry her, and he didn't intend to kiss her until he knew she wanted the same.

Downstairs, the carolers came near enough that they could hear them, singing...

Silent night, holy night
All is calm, all is bright
Round yon Virgin, Mother, Mother and
    Child
Holy infant so tender and mild
Sleep in heavenly peace...

And when they were close enough to serenade from the stoop, Ben turned, releasing her hand only to clasp Alexandra by the arms, turning her to face him. "Lexie," he began, and the world faded away.

THERE WAS a certain something in Ben's eyes... something Alexandra remembered and realized she missed so desperately.

Was this happening, truly?

She held her breath, hardly able to speak, much less breathe.

In the space of a few days, something had changed between them—something she couldn't put a finger on, but it was evident nonetheless—in Benji's eyes, in the way he was looking at her right now...

"Are you in love?" asked a child's voice.

Alexandra gasped aloud, turning to spy the bearer of the voice. "Drina!"

The future Queen of England stood peeking about the bannister, grinning. Tiny as she was at twelve, she was already shedding the bearing of a child, acquiring the command of a queen, and curiosity danced in her clear blue eyes.

Ben gave the child a reverent nod, and said, "Yes, I do believe we are, Your Highness." And then he turned to Lexie, and asked, "Are we?"

Tears swam in Alexandra's eyes. "Yes," she said. "I do believe we are."

"Well," said Drina excitedly, clapping her hands with all the enthusiasm of a child on her birthday. "My mother says I shall wed my cousin one day, and I think the two of you should be wed as well!"

There was nothing that could have prepared Alexandra for the majesty of the moment. Benjamin gave the royal child a dutiful bow, then a nod and a smile. "Your wish is my command," he said to Drina, then he fell to his knees before Alexandra.

"Alexandra Grace," he said, once again taking Lexie by the hand. "Would you do me the honor of agreeing to become my lawful, wedded wife?"

"Wait!" said Drina. "You'll need a promise ring!" And she removed a small emerald ring from her thumb and rushed forward to give it to Ben.

Outside, the carolers came closer, sang louder, and if either Alexandra or Ben had any inclination to look, they might have glimpsed the Duchess of Kent amidst other royal guests—King William, too. Having been apprised of the impending birth of a royal child, they'd arrived bearing gifts and singing a song for the child to be born this eve.

"Will you marry me?" asked Ben, as he held up the gifted ring for her inspection.

Alexandra swallowed her emotion. "I will," she said, and Benjamin slid the ring onto her small finger. Peering up then, over her head, he grinned. And perhaps he shouldn't have needed to pluck a drupe for this kiss, but very, very slowly, and very purposely, he rose up to snap a drupe, showing it first to Alexandra, and when she nodded, he took her into his arms and drew her close. And this time there was no hesitation at all as he wrapped his arms about her to collect his long-overdue mistletoe kiss.

From her vantage upon the stairs, Drina clapped very exuberantly and squealed with delight. "Huzzah!" she shouted. "Huzzah!"

Inside the birthing chamber, Chloe howled, and her husband yowled.

Downstairs, in the foyer, the front door opened to admit the royal carolers amidst swirls of snow... but Benjamin Dylan Wentworth wasn't the least bit interested in what was happening anywhere but here... in his arms.

"I love you," he said.

"I love you," she said.

And then, truly, there were no more words. Benjamin's fingers splayed on her back, pulling her close... his lips descended upon Alexandra's, molding themselves against the soft-warm, supple flesh of her lips. And he kissed her thoroughly and tenderly... a smoldering, but gentle kiss hot enough to warm Lexie to the very depths of her soul.

Below stairs the carolers sang a brand-new song.

"Deck the halls with boughs of holly
Fa la la la la la la la la

This is not the end... keep turning the pages
until you reach the epilogue—but only if
you dare...

EPILOGUE

DECEMBER 20, 1834

"*B*en!"

The single word was, indeed, a rebuke, but rather than hold in its timbre any true censure, it was gentle, forbearing, and filled with good humor. Alexandra experienced an acute sense of *deja vu* as she worked very desperately to finish one last sketch before the household turned into a veritable circus.

"My love, I am trying to work," she admonished.

This year, they were hosting the annual Christmas party, and Claire and Merrick were soon to arrive. Tomorrow, Chloe and Ian were due, and this year they were bringing Ian and Merrick's parents, as well as their three-year-old son. There was so much to be done that she daren't take a moment, not even for kisses, sweet as they were.

"Yes, I can see that," he said. "It's quite lovely. What is it?"

"Epipogium aphyllum," she replied. "It has no leaves, and therefore remains devoid of the green pigmentation which allows plants to produce energy from sunlight. Furthermore, it is entirely dependent upon its relationship with the soil for survival and spends most of its time underground and seldom flowers. Some have taken up to ten years to bloom, but I have one blooming right now in the conservatory!"

"It looks like a common hummingbird—three, in fact, upside down and mounted on sticks."

Alexandra peered up at him, amused. "Hardly common, my love. This is a very, very rare species. Once my rendering is complete, I am sending it to our dear friend Mr. Darwin, along with my notes for cultivation."

"And where is *our dear friend* now?"

No matter that there was *never* any flirtation between them, the very mention of Charles still made Ben jealous. Alexandra beamed. "The Falklands, I believe."

"You know, I should be jealous that you know his itinerary better than you do mine." He paused for effect. "However, I am not," he said, laying a hand possessively upon her shoulder. "I am only pleased you two have remained penpals, and if living vicariously through his letters keeps you by my side, I shall ever be grateful to him."

Alexandra grinned mischievously. "And what if I should wish to travel myself?"

"Alas, I will follow you like a good little pup, my love. And, in the meantime, I will endeavor to keep you at home by plying you with gifts such as the one I have waiting for you now."

Alexandra's head popped up. "Gift?" she said, her interest piqued enough that she laid down her pencil.

"Indeed," said Ben, and he sought her hand, pulling her up from her seat at the escritoire.

Last year, he'd gifted Alexandra the conservatory. They sold her father's house, and put the funds into revamping Highbury Hall. Not only did she have a beautiful new conservatory, but an office as well, complete with expansive bookshelves filled with volumes on horticulture and botany. She didn't miss Huntington Manor anyway, and she had never truly felt at home there. Home, she'd come to realize was anywhere there were loved ones, and she'd brought her loyal servants along with her—her only true family to speak of before her marriage to Ben.

"Come," he said, and he led her out of her office, into the brightly lit conservatory, down the main center aisle, and there, she spied a large golden package perched atop the potting table.

"What is it?"

He gave her a conspiratorial wink. "You'll find out soon enough."

Alexandra sniffed. "You know I loathe surprises."

"You don't," he argued, as he bent to adjust the package and Alexandra stayed his hand and shouted for help.

"You'll give yourself a hernia," she said. "Arthur!"

"Hush," Ben said. "I gave the poor man the day off."

"You did?"

"I did. In fact, I gave *everyone* the day off. I want you *all* to myself today, before the house fills with guests."

"Not for long," Alexandra protested. "Claire and Ian are due to arrive soon, and they'll need—"

He put a finger to her lips to shush her. "They'll survive one single day without a bevy of servants at their heels, and I warrant both will be relieved to have the time for themselves—as will you and I until they arrive. Now, open your gift, Alexandra."

Alexandra smiled and turned to examine the box—a gilded contraption of enormous proportions.

How in the bloody blue blazes had he managed to get the monstrosity inside without any help?

Only when she reached out to touch it and it moved so easily, Alexandra realized the box must be empty, and she turned to tilt her husband a questioning glance and a bit of a pout. "Is this a jest?"

He shook his head, smiling very deviously.

"Very well, she said, inhaling deeply the scent of roses—an exciting new breed she was cultivating for spring. Uncertain how to proceed, she lifted up her hand and pulled at the paper, finding purchase in a fold and then, laying a hand aside the box to anchor it, she pulled at the wrapping, exposing what was inside, and her breath caught on a gasp. "It's not empty!" She said.

"No it is not."

"Oh, my!" she said, and tore at the wrapping with a fervor born of excitement. When the gift was fully revealed, she could see that it was a delicate cage filled with butterflies of every sort! "Oh, my!" She said again.

Benjamin reached over her shoulder to undo the latch, and opened up the cage to free the butterflies en masse.

At first, only a few found the exit and then, all at once, they billowed out the entrance and flew away in a beautiful, multicolored cloud... purple emperors, peacocks, red admirals, painted ladies, white admirals and silver-spotted skippers. They numbered in the hundreds!

For a moment, bewildered, Alexandra watched them fly about, their brightly colored forms vivid against the backdrop of the conservatory's glasswork ceiling. Tears brimmed in her eyes as she clapped her hands together, enchanted. "It's beautiful," she said, and then she lifted her tear-filled eyes to Ben, and said, "Thank you."

. . .

Satisfied with her reaction, Benjamin grinned broadly over the look of wonder on his wife's face. If he grew to be a thousand, he would never take her smile for granted.

"To help with pollination," he explained—not that he needed to explain anything at all to Alexandra. She knew. His wife was as brilliant as she was kind and gentle.

"How can I ever thank you?" she said, her hands still joined prayerfully. "You always seem to know what I want before I even have the chance to ask."

He reached out to take Alexandra by the hand, pulling her close, eager for the scent of his woman instead of the pungent scent of flowers. And he lifted up her chin, though she looked past him at a painted lady flittering by.

"I cannot wait to see Claire's face when she sees this," she said, and Ben lifted her up and sat her upon the potting table.

"I could care less what Claire thinks, in truth. I only care what *you* think, and I find myself suddenly eager to explore my favorite flower."

"Ben," she said, with a secret smile, as he circled his fingers about her ankles, then slid them up her calves, reveling in the tiny shivers it evoked.

"Ben," she said, again, as he ventured higher, caressing the soft flesh of her inner thighs.

"Shall I stop?" he asked, as one finger teased the silky petals of her woman's flower.

"Oh!" she exclaimed, as he pressed a thumb gently against her sweet bud, and then he too moaned deep in his throat upon finding her wet...

Whatever protest Alexandra had been about to utter died in her throat. Instinctively, she lifted her legs about his torso, pulling her dress to her hips, eager for everything she knew her husband would give her. Her gaze flicked down, then up to meet Ben's eager green eyes, and she said with an academic tone, "Pollination is so critical for the health of a species."

"Indeed," he said, and then, "Dear, God," as she turned the tables on him, reaching down to cup the hardening lump in his breeches.

"One must employ every means to assure reproduction."

"Christ!" he exclaimed, his head falling backward as she quickly unbuttoned his trousers, then pushed them down, and once again, he groaned deep in his throat, the sound feral and famished, as her hands found and closed about his manhood.

And still she didn't stop. "You wouldn't wish to be solely responsible for the extinction of a species?"

"Never" he said, swallowing, cupping her bottom and jerking her forward to the edge of the table, where he covered her mouth with his lips, kissing her hungrily.

Alexandra melted into his embrace, all coyness dismissed at the feel of his manhood begging entrance against her mons. Slick and insistent, he pushed himself inside.

And then, all words were lost as butterflies flittered about, a kaleidoscope of colors ebbing and flowing as man and wife danced a mating dance as old as time. Clinging to each other, kissing, feeling, undulating, culmination came swiftly and violently, wracking each of their bodies with delicious spasms that left them both reeling. And once they were done, and her husband's cock lay pulsing inside her—beating in time with the click of his heart, she whispered, "Merry Christmas, my love."

It was a long, long moment before Ben could speak again, but when he could, he could only say, with an emotional rasp at the back of his throat, "Fa la la la la la la."

It's a Prince!

His Royal Highness,
The Prince of Meridian
I Merrick Welbourne III
& His Esteemed Wife, Chloe.

Joyously Announce
The Birth of a Boy
I Merrick Welbourne IV

Born 2 a.m. Dec. 25, 1831
8 lbs, 3 oz.

My dearest beloveds

Please forgive
us for not attending your house party.
Your father and I have a Christmas surprise!
We are once and for all man and wife!
Officiated by our pastor, it was a
quiet, but lovely ceremony.

We will arrive in London Jan 5 to help
prepare for your nuptials and I will be
joining you in Meridian.

Yours Truly

Fiona

Best wishes

to you in this season

of merriment

MORE IN THIS SERIES

Seduced by a Prince
A Crown for a Lady
The Art of Kissing Beneath the Mistletoe

ABOUT THE AUTHOR

Tanya Anne Crosby is the New York Times and USA Today bestselling author of thirty novels. She has been featured in magazines, such as People, Romantic Times and Publisher's Weekly, and her books have been translated into eight languages. Her first novel was published in 1992 by Avon Books, where Tanya was hailed as "one of Avon's fastest rising stars." Her fourth book was chosen to launch the company's Avon Romantic Treasure imprint.

Known for stories charged with emotion and humor and filled with flawed characters Tanya is an award-winning author, journalist, and editor, and her novels have garnered reader praise and glowing critical reviews. She and her writer husband split their time between Charleston, SC, where she was raised, and northern Michigan, where the couple make their home.

For more information
Website
Newsletter